Damn the

Let's Take This Nice and Slow

B.I. Crosse

Copyright © 2023 B. I. Crosse All rights reserved

The characters and events portrayed in this book are fictitious. Any similarity to real persons, living or dead, is coincidental and not intended by the author.

No part of this book may be reproduced, or stored in a retrieval system, or transmitted in any form or by any means, electronic, mechanical, photocopying, recording, or otherwise, without express written permission of the publisher.

Revision 1
ISBN-13: 9798391638773

To Diane

June 23rd 2123

Emma rolled onto her back. Silence filled the room, both unexpected and unwelcome. Her shoulder pressed against a smooth surface. It felt cool, unlike the air around her, which was warm and laden with moisture. With effort, she opened an eye; the other did not respond. Nothing above her was familiar.

She shifted, and the sheet below followed her motion, unwilling to separate from her body. A gray tank top clung to her skin, damp on the front and wet down the back. Red hair was plastered to a cheek, covering the uncooperative eye. She sat up quickly, bringing the content of her stomach to the back of her throat. Lifting a hand to her mouth, she remembered.

"You suck, Coriolis."

With the one eye half open, she looked through the door of her darkened cube into the bright light of the passage.

"Stewart's up," Abby Webb shouted from around the corner.

Emma's roommate, Niko Sasaki, stepped into the rounded door frame, her tall silhouette pleasantly blocking out much of the light. She stared at Emma with sympathy building in the shadows of her face.

"You're a mess."

Niko, as usual, looked perfect: short dark hair, a smooth complexion, and an impeccable uniform.

"Headache?" She flicked on the light switch.

Emma closed her eye. "No, I just sat up too quickly, and … I need coffee."

"We have an hour before the shuttle leaves; you should get ready."

Emma gave a short nod and a weak smile and then swiveled her feet off the bottom bunk and onto the deck. As she stood, another wave of nausea surged through her.

"Gravity is overrated … and what's wrong with the chillers?" she asked, peeling the hair from her face.

"They're secured until the ship docks. You slept through that announcement, but stop worrying. In a few hours, you'll be on solid ground, breathing fresh air."

"Shifting from rotational to inertial gravity" sounded over the intercom.

A familiar clunk resonated overhead, telling them that braking was being applied to the ring, their home for the last three weeks and on and off for the last year. Emma grabbed the upper bunk as her momentum carried her toward one wall of the cube. Niko held steady to the door frame. Slowly, the acceleration that kept their feet on the deck dropped from a half gee toward zero.

Naomi Medina squeezed her head into the doorway next to Niko's, her blue eyes bright with excitement, and her olive skin faded after a year without natural sunlight. She kissed Niko on the cheek and declared with an exuberant smile, "Final burn coming." She then launched into a free-floating cart-wheel as the force holding them to the deck disappeared.

Niko rolled her eyes toward Emma and then turned to watch Naomi bounce against a wall and sail into her cube using a sharp kick. Her dark curls bounced chaotically with each maneuver.

"Graceful," she called out.

A light rattle started in the open door and spread throughout the cube. "Final burn," she repeated to Emma.

They both swiveled to point their feet at the back wall of their room about to become the deck. Niko shifted her left foot between two rungs of the ladder that would give access to the passage.

"Oh, thank God," Emma said as she landed softly between the two beds. Out of habit, she kicked the two supports holding Niko's bed vertical and allowed it to settle until horizontal. She then reached over her bed to do the same.

Niko looked down from the ladder. "We're all meeting on the observation deck."

Emma pulled at the side of her top in disgust.

"I'm going to shower off — I'll see you there."

With her last bag handed over to the shuttle's crew, Emma descended three additional levels and stepped onto the observation deck with her coffee mug firmly in hand. The space had the shape of a doughnut, a round transparent tube circling the narrowest section of the ship, aft of the shuttle docks and forward of the auxiliary engineering space. Just inside, a stanchion-mounted case displayed the ship's badge. Across the top, 'RFA Fort Rosalie.' At the bottom, 'Commissioned 8 May 2113.' Deck plates provided a flat walking surface about two meters wide. Forward of the deck, the lower lip of a radiation shield blocked the sunlight as well as the view.

No one was in sight, but the sound of an animated crowd came from both directions. Emma hesitated before the badge, reluctant to move until an eruption of laughter from the far side of the tube broke her reverie. She looked left and then right and then outward. Sunlight reflected from the cables of the Jarvis Island Elevator. The narrow line stretched away, disappearing into a field of stars. She approached the outer wall but failed to identify the counterweight among the points of light. Walking to the left around the tube, she followed the cable until it met the geosynchronous station that the ship was approaching. It was one of the largest structures built on Earth or in orbit but only a tiny part of the elevator. Non-rotating docking rings circled the primary port structure, some with attached ships.

The size of those ships varied, but all shared a basic design. The hemispherical shield at the forward end provided collision protection and held most of the fuel and reaction mass. The lead stages of the main drive were centered just aft of the shield: the separation chambers, optical accelerators, and cyclotrons. These fed the final stage of the drive, a linear accelerator that ran the length of the hull. The highly ionized reaction mass was accelerated to a speed that approached that of light before exiting as a nearly invisible beam.

Around the lead drive components were four independent fusion plants. Behind these sat the bridge, primary computing spaces, sensor spaces, and ship controls. All were deemed critical to the operation of the ship. On the larger ships, a habitation ring rotated about the protected spaces just behind the shield. The ring was safe from most small collisions when moving forward, but not when the aft end led the way, as it was now with Rosalie. The larger ships also had shuttle ports just aft of the protected spaces. All ships had a narrow hull reaching back toward the secondary systems.

On the elevator, below the port structure and docked ships, she could see a large, one-gee habitation ring slowly turning. From there, the cable continued down to the low orbit station, the high atmosphere landing, and finally, the floating island that acted as an anchor. None of the lower structures were visible, but Earth was coming into view as she rounded the deck. Departing passengers and well-wishers had gathered just ahead.

"No, stretch your arm straight out and open your hand as if you were holding the planet up."

Seaman Garcia demonstrated as he spoke.

Petty Officer Davies imitated the action and shook his head. "I'm not sure what you're getting at, mate."

Exasperated, Garcia cupped the imaginary ball in front of Davies. "It's the exact size of a soccer ball."

"I'm still not following."

Davies' growing smile and chuckles from the small audience told Garcia he was missing something obvious.

Emma slipped behind Garcia without saying a word and then maneuvered around several other knotted groups to find Abby Webb. Like Emma, she was thin. Like all others in their immediate surroundings, she was taller. Straight brown hair grazed her shoulders as she turned her dark eyes to meet Emma; their usual intensity softened in the moment.

"Ready to go home, Ensign Webb?"

"I sure am. How about you, Ensign Stewart?"

Nine newly graduated officers and 45 enlisted were given one-year tours to assist with a final set of experiments designed to test theories, methods, and technologies associated with planetary terraforming. Within the ranks of the nine officers, Ensign Naomi Medina had turned the prospect of a promotion into a competition. Since the start of that competition, the four friends had rarely overlooked the opportunity to emphasize the failings of one another. By the end of the tour, only Niko Sasaki had succeeded. Her specialization in life sciences proved useful to planet-side researchers. The other eight had spent the year evacuating teams and equipment before the final experiment made the planet's surface unsafe for all.

The largest of the icy rocks pushed from the outer belt had hit the surface as Rosalie left orbit with the final group of researchers. Another four, similar in size, would strike over the next year. Smaller ones had dropped for the last 15 years and would continue for the year. Science teams had hopes of returning three years after the last strike. Settlers, at least some, were planning to arrive ten years later, but realistic expectations were closer to twenty, and they would still require shielded habitats.

Most aboard Rosalie were military, but a few civilian researchers did stay until the end. Those researchers would take the shuttle to the lower station to avoid the three-day elevator ride from geosynchronous orbit to the surface. A small group of officers and enlisted were joining them. The remainder would accompany the last of the equipment considered too valuable to leave in a high Martian orbit.

"Don't turn around, but Anderson has noticed you," Abby warned.

Emma took a long sip from her mug. "Is he coming over?"

"No, not anymore." She didn't hide her sadistic smile. "He's noticed that I'm staring at him and turned away."

"He is the nervous sort," Emma said.

"At least around you." Abby poked her in the shoulder. "You have that effect."

Emma narrowed her eyes. "No, I don't."

"Oh, please. Ignoring those hazel eyes for the moment — Look at it this way; 16 nations and one company are responsible for the Mars project, sixteen nations and Stewart Life Sciences."

Abby crossed her arms as Naomi joined them.

"It's like a curse," Emma said into her coffee.

"It looks like he's found his courage," Abby warned. "Should I mention that you have a boyfriend waiting below?"

"It might help … as a reminder."

Emma started to turn when the booming voice of Chief Walker caught everyone's attention.

"Davies." He came around from the same direction that Emma had arrived.

"Get up to docking control; you two also."

The three turned and made a quick exit. The chief focused on one last group from Rosalie's crew.

"The rest of you find something useful to do."

In stature, he was very much average. She was always surprised by the volume he could reach when addressing members of Rosalie's crew. He glanced over the passengers that remained with his eyes settling on Emma.

"How is my favorite shuttle pilot today?" he asked, using a much softer tone.

Emma smiled broadly. "Retired, I'm afraid. My qualifications lapsed when we left the orbit of Mars."

"Oh, come on," Naomi said as she looked straight up at the shuttle they were about to board.

"You could easily qualify for one of these orbit runners."

"Sure could," the chief added. "After seventy trips between the surface and those damned cargo pods, you're ready to fly anything."

"Seventy-three," Naomi whispered in Emma's ear.

Emma returned a smile and then shrugged. "Something to keep a linguist busy."

"You certainly were busy the last three months," the chief said.

"I enjoyed it, but I don't think I'll be piloting again, not anytime soon. I received orders for Galileo yesterday. Three days at home, and then I'm shipping out."

"One of the new research vessels. Congratulations."

"Chief, are you joining us on the ride down?" Seaman Garcia asked.

"No, no, I'm with Rosalie until she docks, and then I'll be making Beagle my new home."

He pointed toward the station and a ship that stretched across two ports. She was smaller than Rosalie but larger than most that were in view. The teardrop hull was standard for all military vessels and was seeing increased use with commercial craft.

"That is sleek. What's hiding behind the hull?"

The chief looked up at Garcia, considering his words.

"Nothing you haven't seen already, just encased in a protective shell of carbon and polymers to keep us safe from our greatest enemies … and by enemies, I mean rays and rocks."

All aboard Rosalie knew the dangers posed by a loose piece of debris or a random cosmic ray.

"I'm growing more confident by the year that those two will be the only threats we'll ever face."

"I can just read it now," Petty Office Lee said as he squinted toward the station. "HMS Beagle UNSF."

"That's right, one big happy family," the chief said.

"HMS," Emma proclaimed. "You're transferring from the Auxiliary?"

"Sure am. Now that the United Kingdom is building warships, experienced crews are in demand. Well, two warships to date. We have about five minutes before we lose gravity. Anyone heading down to Leo Jarvis should load up."

All present followed the chief around the observation deck and up the ladder toward the shuttle. At the entrance, he pulled Emma aside, allowing others to pass.

"Your father would be very proud of you, Emma."

She nodded, feeling tears well in her eyes. "Thanks, chief. You take care."

She stepped forward and gave him a warm embrace.

"You too, Emma."

The descent to Leo Jarvis lasted three short, uneventful hours. Upon landing, all passengers were happy to feel the pull of Earth for the first time in over a year, but even at 90 percent of surface gravity, the strain was evident. Thankfully, all luggage was transferred to a waiting elevator car. All they had to do was descend a short flight of steps and find a seat in the car before continuing the trip down.

The level of chatter grew as they approached Jarvis Field, the elevator's seldom-used atmospheric platform. Emma sat quietly, looking out a window. Jarvis Island was off to the south. Aside from that tiny dot, all she could see was open ocean.

She felt tired. The added weight contributed, as did the last year of activity, but she knew those effects were transitory. In another hour, she would be making farewells to the closest friends she had ever had. She knew some of those farewells would be permanent. Waiting ahead was a family she desperately wanted to see, but fear invaded her thoughts as that reunion approached. She wanted the visit to go smoothly, with no awkward pauses when words failed and no moments of isolation when conversations turned to local events for which she had no part. She had much to tell but worried that her adventures would only belittle those who had lived quiet lives for the last year. Analytically, she knew her concerns were unfounded. Returns from extended stays at the academy had proved that, but now, in a small way, she looked forward to her first day aboard Galileo; only then would she know that all had gone well at home.

Her thoughts of Anay Mason were far different. When she left for Mars, she had worried that a year apart would be too long, their feelings for each other would diminish, and they would drift into a distant friendship. None of that had come true. Those feelings were stronger than ever, and his appeared the same from the letters they had exchanged.

The Mason family came to Montana from England along with many others, drawn to the research facilities that had built up around the shuttered launch complex. He was eleven at the time. She had just turned twelve. When Emma's father passed, Anay's mother reached out to her mother, and the families grew close. Anay and Emma were inseparable as children and more so when they became romantic. His interest in all things off-world led her to the Navy. She went off to Annapolis. A year later, he failed to get into the academy but followed her into service, attending a local university. Now, he had graduated and should have his first duty assignment.

In three days, they would be apart once again.

Jarvis Field passed in the blink of an eye, and the car started to slow as it approached the surface station.

Niko crossed the aisle and placed a hand on her shoulder. "This is new ... you look worried."

Emma took a deep breath and nodded. "I know. I'm going to miss you ... all of you ... and I want this visit to go perfectly."

Niko rotated Emma until they faced one another. "Are you ... Oh my god; you are actually worried about a visit with your family ... your family."

Emma met Niko's eyes with surprise and a little fear.

"No."

Niko narrowed her eyes. "You've been sitting here planning the conversations ... haven't you?"

"Not planning," Emma said with a small defiant smile.

"Good ... that's the Emma I know, the one who threw caution to the wind for an entire year on another planet. Stay with that; it's served you well."

Emma looked back defensively. "That doesn't sound like the advice of a perfectionist, and I gave up making plans because they never work out ... but this is important."

"Important but not within your control. Chaos is part of life."

Emma's smile grew. "Oh, give me a break ... Now, you sound like my grandfather."

Niko matched Emma's smile. "I'm three months younger than you, but I'll take that as a compliment — Hey, we're all meeting at The Figure Eight when we get to the surface. If you have time, join us. My flight arrives in five hours. I'm not sure about the others."

Emma shook her head. "No, I wish I could, but I'm sure mine is already waiting on the platform for me to arrive."

"Rich bitch."

Emma laughed aloud.

June 24th 2123

"Em," her mother screamed.

Emma stood in the kitchen doorway, her knees about to buckle under the weight of two small bags. A lock of red hair covered one eye, and strain was obvious on her face and arms. Only her bright white uniform appeared to have survived the journey intact.

Two older generations of her family filled the large rustic room; at a small table, around an island, and spread over the worn oaken floor. All were bathed in the morning light that streamed through a wall of windows. Outside of those windows, seated around a table on the upper level of the deck, her generation had taken notice. Her younger brother, Ian, was coming through the glass door, followed by a cool breeze that kicked up the valances and agitated the plants hanging to the side.

A woman stepped quickly to Emma's side. "Let me take those, Emma."

"Aunt Lucy?" Emma released the handles as her aunt pulled the bags away.

"Hi, Mom." She returned her mother's strong embrace. Her face pressed into the shoulder of a colorful, floral dress. She then looked up to receive a kiss on the forehead.

"Beth, let her sit before she collapses," her grandfather, Alexander Stewart, said from his seat.

With a firm grip, her mother led her to a chair one of her uncles had pulled out for her benefit.

She sat heavily and bent her head back.

"Thanks, Uncle Rob," and then louder, speaking to the room, "I'm not that bad off."

"Seriously?" her older cousin, Chloe, asked.

"Hi, Cthulhu," Emma said, using a childhood nickname.

Chloe wiggled her fingers at Emma. "Hey, Beanstalk."

Emma winced and then shifted to ease the pain in her lower back.

"Did you stick to your regimen?" her grandfather asked.

"Of course, but exercise and supplements can only help so much."

"Why are you all here?" she asked, knowing the answer.

"We've never seen a Martian," Ian answered. "Did you watch the impact?"

he was referring to the widely publicized strike on Mars.

Emma shrugged. "On a display, we had already left orbit. It was probably from the same feeds that you were watching."

"There was no shortage of choices," Uncle Jon said. "Dad's been streaming images from every satellite in orbit."

He lifted his eyes to her left at a large display in the family room. She recognized the dark body of water barely visible below the swirling clouds.

"Hellas Planitia? I'm surprised it's visible."

"Actually, this is a recording from yesterday," Uncle Jon said. "We've been granted an eighth of the surrounding shoreline. We'll need to see where that shoreline is in another three years."

"It's more like a cauldron now," her grandfather said. "It will take time."

"Coffee, Emma?"

Aunt Lucy was holding a mug over her shoulder.

"Oh, thank you. I'm running on empty."

"What then?" Aunt Lucy asked her grandfather. "Sell them off like the other parcels?"

"I'm not complaining," she added quickly as Robert, her husband, gave a questioning look.

"Likely. As long as people are willing to pay more for Martian real estate than Terran, I'd say, keep selling, make what money we can. That will always be a cold, minimally productive planet. If we don't manage to break out of our little Solar System, this portion of our business will come to a quick end."

"Not to mention some of our greater aspirations," Emma's Mother added.

"Thanks, Beth … for keeping my priorities straight."

Emma slid down in her chair, cupping her coffee in both hands, happy to be surrounded by conversations, even if her participation was small.

"What's next for you, Emma?" Chloe asked.

She sat upright and scanned across the windows, where those around her were not obscuring her view.

"Don't worry. He's on his way," her brother said.

"Thanks, Ian," she said, not hiding her sarcasm.

She twisted her head toward Chloe. "Relax for three days, report to medical in the Springs, and then up to Galileo as the Sensor Officer. After that, I have no idea."

"Sensor Officer? Not exactly your field of interest," Ian said.

"No, but I'll learn."

"No doubt," her mother said. "Emma has always understood the value of study."

Ian smirked at her.

"Hello."

Emma's head snapped toward the voice at the backdoor. She set her coffee down and quickly stood to see past her family.

Anay stepped into view with a look of concern on his face.

Her heart started racing as she pushed back her chair and walked purposefully toward him. Those between stood aside, expectant smiles on their faces.

Just out of reach, she stopped and looked around the crowded room.

"Come," she said, grabbing his hand and pushing through the door.

"Breakfast is ready, Em," her mother called.

"Toast, Emma, burnt toast," Ian shouted as she and Anay crossed the deck.

"We'll be right back," Emma said with a wave and smile, and then she stepped off the deck and onto a garden path. She continued with Anay in tow until they were out of sight.

Without a word, Emma threw her arms over Anay's shoulders as he bent to meet her lips, his hands gently holding the small of her back. Only a need to breathe finally broke their kiss. She leaned back against his hands and looked into his eyes.

"I'm so —"

Her knee finally buckled, honoring the threat they had been repeating since she put her feet on the planet's surface. Anay easily supported the soft grip she had around his neck.

"Are you okay?" he asked with a laugh.

"Great."

She leaned back further, her head brushing the soft green leaves from a sagebrush encroaching on the grass plot where they spent much of their childhood.

"I missed this." She released her hold and stretched her arms back into the brush.

He shifted his hands up her back and pulled her into another passionate kiss.

"Good idea, coming out here," he said as they separated.

Emma straightened with a hand on his shoulder, testing her weight.

"Yeah, one thing I learned up there was just how awkward public displays of affection could be."

Hand in hand, they started walking back to the family.

"Niko?"

Emma nodded.

"Still with Lucas Anderson?"

"No, she's with Naomi now."

"Oh, what happened with Lucus? Still friendly?"

"No, not so much. Let's just say he didn't take her promotion very well."

As they came up the deck, the younger generation was returning with breakfast plates in hand.

Emma and Anay slipped inside and loaded their plates before returning. They joined a group of cousins at a table. Across the plain, to the south, dark clouds were gathering. At her side, Emma's grandfather was peering out in their direction.

"Where are you being stationed, Anay?" one cousin asked.

"Copernicus," he said brightly.

"Another science ship? Aren't the two of you in the Navy."

"Oh, we are, but they only have three combat vessels and no real need for them."

"And they're all under UN control," another cousin added.

Anay nodded. "That too. The science vessels don't fall under that umbrella."

"So, the two of you can finally be together … in space," Chloe said.

"I'm sure you know how ridiculous that sounds," Anay chided.

"Of course I do," she said with a malicious smile.

"It's not as bad as it sounds," Emma said. "There are not that many projects. Both ships could be sent to the same planet … or rock."

Anay smiled at Emma, nodding. "And we'll be free to communicate, voice, messages, files … The science vessels have no restrictions."

"I didn't know the Navy had any restrictions," Chloe said.

"They do," Emma said. Everything on and off a combat ship passes through a filter, or filters. Personal traffic is limited to plain text messages, and each needs to be approved."

"I didn't realize that security was that big of a concern."

Anay exchanged a glance with Emma before he spoke. "Security is an excuse. They don't want us to be distracted."

"They don't want us wasting our time," Emma added.

"You do have free time on those ships, as in time to do as you choose?"

"We do, but many years ago, they realized that that time should be spent with crewmates rather than distant friends."

"Distant friend, distant enemies, or just random acquaintances." her grandfather said as he turned from the approaching weather and centered himself before the group. "A ship's crew needs to be tightly knit. Of all the freedoms you sacrificed when you joined the service, that one has been far more important than any other."

"Honestly, I don't see the need," Chloe said.

"To be honest, the need has waned, but 80 years ago, the sea service was crippled … For a ship to properly function, the micro-society that forms around its crew needs to be healthy. More so with smaller crews and, given the increasing use of automation, every new class of ship needs fewer people. They had little choice. What was amazing for those at the time was the effect it had. After the inevitable wave of bitching and complaining passed, morale skyrocketed ... That lesson was not lost on the greater society. Soon after, most corporations implemented similar restrictions, ours included." He looked pointedly at Chloe. "The rapid advances we've seen in the last 60 years may never have come if the world had continued down that path. We needed a new paradigm."

"Up-tempo," Emma whispered.

"His favorite phrase," Chloe added in the same hushed tone.

Anay smiled nervously, keeping his attention on Emma's grandfather.

"Up-tempo," he said, looking between Emma and Chloe. "With limitless energy and near limitless materials, the notion of waste has changed. Time and focus were the two resources in short supply. People smarter than I am realized this before it was too late."

Her grandfather looked over the sympathetic, bored faces and held up an apologetic hand.

"Just adding my two bits."

"Enjoy your breakfast." He added as he walked around the table toward the door.

Chloe pulled herself closer. "Still makes you nervous, Anay?"

"He makes everyone nervous ... outside of this family."

Emma gave him a friendly shove.

Emma and Anay quietly stepped down the stairs. Filtered sunlight from a pair of east-facing rooms showed them a path to the kitchen and the pot of coffee that had brought Emma out of her slumber.

"If you're not carrying the biggest bat, you had better be friends with the guy who has it in his hands."

The voice from the family room was unfamiliar.

"I agree, Ray, but no one will be impressed if the bat comes out of the factory broken."

That was her grandfather.

"All the same, Alexander, I'd like to accelerate the schedule. Weapons development can catch up. We need to start pushing out the hulls."

At the bottom of the stairs, Emma carefully guided Anay to the right, away from the voices.

"Let's grab mugs and head outside," she whispered.

"Our miners are always happy to deliver the materials, but bad press is not good for any of us."

"I don't think we need to worry about that. My people can spin this so many ways that the press will never notice the small deficiencies."

Emma peered around the corner, seeing only Chloe sitting on a couch in a formal red dress, her usually unruly blonde hair falling straight over her shoulders.

"How does the admiral feel about this?" Alexander asked.

"If he has an opinion, he's kept it to himself."

Chloe turned her head toward them and smiled. Emma started to raise her hand in a small, discrete wave when Chloe greeted them in a voice loud enough to carry across the room.

"Good morning, you two."

Emma winced as she heard the creak of a chair, followed by the sound of footsteps. Chloe stood and joined Alexander, who was as casually dressed as always, and a younger man, mid-thirties, Emma guessed, dressed more like a cowboy, without the hat.

"Nice pajamas," Chloe said.

'Too late,' Emma thought as she lifted two thick mugs from the counter and handed one to Anay.

"Good morning, Emma … Anay," Alexander said.

"You seem to have recovered." He was looking at Emma.

"Let me introduce Senator Raymond Park. Ray, this is another of my granddaughters, Emma, and this is Anay Mason, Jonathan's son."

"Ensign Stewart," the senator said from across the coffee station. He nodded briefly toward Anay and returned his gaze to Emma. "I've been following your adventures since you lifted off for Mars. That was great work you did up there, and I understand you've returned to us as a pilot?"

Emma glanced at Chloe and then back to the senator. "Thank you, senator —"

"Please, call me Ray."

Emma nodded to Ray as Anay exchanged her empty mug with one filled with black coffee.

"I'm not sure how much you heard from our conversation," he continued. "But I'd be interested to hear your opinion."

"On the Navy's construction schedule?" she asked, taking a long draw from her mug, giving herself a chance to think.

"Well." She looked at Alexander. "I'm inclined to agree with you, senator. The modular design of hulls should, within limits, allow us to upgrade the internal components as time passes."

"Within limits," Alexander said.

"Absolutely. We'll —"

There was a light tapping on the front door. Through the glass, a young woman waited.

"Time's up, I'm afraid. Alexander, Chloe, a pleasure, as always. Emma, Anay, I am honored to have met you both."

"I'll show you out," Alexander said as they approached the door.

The three watched in silence until the two disappeared around a corner.

Emma yawned widely, having stifled the same impulse twice before. "He seems to like baseball."

"I'm not sure about that, but I believe he's a fan of Al Capone," Chloe said.

"Who?"

"The gangster," Anay said. "Early 20th century. He liked baseball bats."

"Oh, that's just wonderful. What shady business are you and Alexander getting us into, Cthulhu?"

She looked pointedly at Chloe's dress.

"It's not shady. He wants a supporting voice for a more aggressive shipbuilding program … you know, keeping ahead of China and Europe."

"Of course."

"And I was just going to change — It wouldn't be me in this dress if his favorite granddaughter had not run off and joined the Navy."

Emma sneered at her older cousin with lidded eyes looking over her steaming mug.

"Sorry, not my color."

Chloe squinted darkly and flexed her hands. "I wish I had real tentacles." She then turned toward the stairs.

Emma looked up at Anay and gestured toward the back door. "Take a walk?"

July 5th 2123

The display said, 'Welcome to Saint Peter and Paul Docking Port.'

Below were listed details of the command staff and then the message of the day, 'Go with the Flow.' It was a popular paradigm for many in the military, but Emma realized its more literal intention. Together, the green arrows pointing to the right and the airflow coming from the left told her which way she would need to go regardless of the location of Galileo. Getting stranded in zero-gee dead air was not something she wanted to try again.

A baggage handler wrapped the retaining strap of her larger bag around a convenient handrail in front of the last few passengers who had exited the elevator. Most had disembarked at the hub station, heading down into the rotating ring. Above the construction noise, she could hear the angry voices of dock workers coming from below as they struggled to unload the much larger cargo chamber of the elevator.

"Ensign Stewart?"

Emma turned with a light nudge of the handhold. The woman floating before her was far too young. She belonged in a classroom somewhere on the surface. Her voice was soft, barely audible above the distant screech of a saw cutting into steel. Short dark hair showed below a tight ball cap, a common choice, but shorter than regulations required. With her feet further from the floor and her body slightly angled with respect to the deck, her eyes sat level with Emma's.

With a glance at her name tag, Emma said, "Petty Officer Harris. You're my guide?"

"Yes, ma'am. Is this yours?"

"Yes ... Carol?" She asked, recalling the ship's roster.

Harris nodded as she detached the bag in front of them. Emma kept a hold on the two smaller ones.

"This way out to the tram." She pointed to the right and kicked off with more energy than needed, forcing her to make a quick correction with a passing handhold. Emma floated along with practiced ease. As they passed out of the central shaft that housed the elevator cables, the passage narrowed, speeding their transit. However, the change was barely noticeable, with all points of reference external to the tube being so distant.

She could see the bare bones of the giant docking port through the clear tube, nearly a kilometer in every direction. Along with the Vaadhoo Elevator, construction was started on Saint Peter and Paul two years after the Jarvis Island Elevator began operations. A completion date was still several years into the future. Eventually, the space they were passing through would be filled with support facilities, four large internal docks, and spare parts storage. Now, the empty void gave them an unobstructed view of the berths from the inside, a rotunda comprised of two rings, one above and one below. Galileo was attached to two, oriented vertically, but there was no way to tell which from the tube.

A year earlier, the entire space had been exposed to a vacuum. The effort to ship compressed air up had been significant, but it greatly simplified the construction that was taking place around them, as well as future repair and refurbishment activities. A partially assembled structure was being pushed toward an obvious destination ahead and to their left. A free-floating assembly team waited with tools in hand.

Far below, she recognized the distinct blue physical training gear of an academy class in the middle of an exercise.

"They've been down there since I arrived on the station," Harris said, noting the direction that Emma was looking. "It looks fun."

"That's not my recollection … looks like second-year cadets. Once you puke yourself dry, they force you to make that crossing." Emma pointed from right to left. "But it's never straightforward. The instructors will disconnect cables, loosen panels, or set entire structures free. That group of nine moving along the guy wire is almost to the end, but they left three behind. They're about to find out that that was a mistake."

The three cadets had lost their grip and drifted into empty space. Ignored by the instructors, they had a long and embarrassing wait before rescue. Emma remembered that feeling all too well.

"They'll need to go back and devise a means to rescue the three before they drift beyond reach. If that happens, if they require help from one of the instructors, the entire class will have another chance to get it right."

Emma let the feeling of nostalgia pass and then turned back toward Harris. "What do I have for a sensor division?"

"Well … there's me, Lieutenant Smith, and Petty Officer Calvin, but they're specialists here on temporary assignment. So, I guess it's just me in the division."

"Specialists. Hmm, what're they doing on Galileo?"

"No one knows. The captain will brief the crew once we're underway."

The tube expanded as they passed into the outer structure of the docking port, and their forward motion slowed. Harris crashed gently into the door of a small elevator that would take them to the upper ring.

After exiting the elevator, they pushed toward a small car, one of eight that made up a train that ran a complete circuit of the port.

"How long have you been aboard?" Emma asked, maneuvering through the door of the car.

"Five days. Does it show?"

"You'll get used to it." Emma gave Harris a sympathetic smile as she nestled her back into a standing rest attached to a vertical pole. A retaining strap and counterweights, out of sight above and below the pole, guaranteed that she would remain comfortably in place as the train made its frequent stops.

After they had circled nearly three-quarters of the rotunda, Harris separated from her rest and grabbed the larger bag. "The next stop is ours."

As they slowed, Emma saw a banner for Galileo running the length of a ceremonial brow. She drew a deep, nervous breath.

"Seaman Jones," Harris called to the topside watch once they had stepped out of the car. "Ensign Stewart has arrived. Contact the officer of the deck."

"Sure thing, Harris."

Over 20 years in space, and the Navy could not make the obvious change from seaman to spaceman. Emma gave the smallest of shrugs.

Captain Ryan Hanson, a commander by rank, found her on the bridge, receiving a brief tour from Harris. He was tall and thin, with a dark complexion, closely cropped dark brown hair, and radiant blue eyes.

"Ensign Stewart, welcome aboard. My office, please." There was a note of humor in his terse request.

"Thank you, captain." She followed, dropping one level to a tiny office just aft of the bridge.

It would function reasonably well when the ship was under acceleration, with a desk, chair, small bed, and wash facility, but now, with the ship docked, it was a cramped, awkward place.

He reached into his desk and grabbed a small box as she drifted through the door.

"First things first, congratulations. You've been promoted."

Emma's eyes widened as he pulled her new insignia from the box.

"If you would." He pointed toward her collar.

She removed the ensign's bar, and he deftly replaced it with that of a lieutenant junior grade and then offered a hand that she earnestly shook.

"And now the bad news; you're the sensor officer on Galileo, but for our upcoming trip, full control of your sensor suite is in the hands of a pair of riders. I expect you to learn all you can from them, but don't interfere with their mission."

He continued as Emma opened her mouth to speak. "And no, you may not ask. We'll get underway tomorrow morning. I'll brief the crew shortly after."

"Have you checked in with the doc yet?"

"No, sir. I'm scheduled to visit medical in about ten minutes."

"Ah, good. I won't keep you."

Harris was waiting just out of earshot. The smile on her face grew as Emma approached.

"Congratulations, ma'am."

"Thanks, Harris. I need to find medical. That's on the ring, right?"

Harris nodded. "I'll show you."

Under a comfortable half-gee, the ship's doctor, Commander Klein, opened the door.

"Harris, you're dismissed, and ... Lieutenant Stewart, please come in and have a seat."

Forty-five minutes later, Emma returned to the passage with final clearance to remain a member of Galileo's crew.

After several aggressive course changes, a brief sprint that reached four gees, and more sustained runs at three and two, Galileo settled to a pleasant one gee. Free to leave her bed, Emma headed around the stationary ring to the crew's mess. The loud crashes she had heard from her room were part of the reason for those maneuvers, revealing poorly stowed items under a controlled situation. No injuries were reported.

She joined other junior officers near the front to wait for the captain to step behind the small podium and give the much-anticipated brief. The curved wall left of the podium, the outer bulkhead of the ring, was covered with collapsed bench tables, flush with the surface. Under rotation, it would become the deck. Looking down, she could see grooves under the table where she sat.

"You were on Rosalie before this?"

She looked up at an older lieutenant sitting next to her. Sandy blond hair fell across his forehead, turning gray at the temples. His once solid build appeared to be settling.

"As a passenger to and from Mars ... Lieutenant Martinez."

"Quinn Martinez."

"Emma," she said, filling in what her name tag did not say.

Quinn gave her a wry smile. "That may be the most unnecessary introduction I have ever heard."

She returned the smile with a hint of irritation. "My fault. Everyone has been acting pleasantly unaware since I checked aboard ... until now."

His smile widened. "I noticed your interest in the benches. I imagine this is a bit different from how they handled the gee shifts on Rosalie?"

"A bit." Emma mimicked his understatement. "They did their best to make every piece of furniture bidirectional, and the spaces were kept small." She shook her head. "The ring was small, too small, and the British spun the thing too fast ... for me anyways."

Quinn chuckled. "I take it this is more to your liking?" He patted the table.

Emma nodded. "What division are you running?"

"Navigation and Weapons. You're the sensor officer?"

"Yes, but sorry, Weapons. Do we have weapons?"

"One, aside from our tailpipe, but its purpose is not for combat."

Emma narrowed her eyes and waited for a better explanation.

"Sorry, you'll understand in a moment. I don't want to steal the captain's thunder."

A yell from behind, "Captain on deck," brought everyone to their feet.

"At ease, have a seat," Captain Hanson said after he worked his way through the narrow room and stepped behind the podium with a lieutenant and first-class petty officer at his side.

"I'll get right to the point. We'll spend the next five days flying to a location far below the ecliptic plane, about the same distance from the Sun as the outer belt. Distance from Earth is slightly less this time of the year. Once there, we'll attempt to form a physical connection between the Solar System and the Alpha Centauri System."

He paused, allowing gasps and stifled conversation to erupt.

"Attempt," he emphasized. "The 17th, to be exact, but the first to take place on an actual ship. Test barges were used previously."

He paused again to silence the muffled voices.

"Lieutenant Smith and Petty Officer Calvin have about ten minutes to give the details."

He stepped down and was quickly replaced by Lieutenant Smith.

"Thank you, captain. About eight years ago, one of our research barges, beyond Ceres Station, was experimenting with three independent technologies away from prying eyes. A quantum communications system using standard paired particles, a sensor, leveraging some of the same science, and an incoherent beam that used a ridiculous amount of power but turned out to be ineffective as a weapon."

"Quantum sensors?" Quinn asked quietly.

Emma shook her head. "I think the signal processors use quantum chips. That's not new."

Smith raised his voice with his eyes on Emma. "Standard range protocol requires weapons to be fired directly away from any populated regions of the Solar System. In practice, the team chooses a convenient star as a target. At that time, Sirius was an obvious choice. The test performed that day on the beam was only meant to stress the capacitors, combining light across the full spectrum, exceeding its normal high and low. Nothing unusual was noted, and all testing was concluded after two days. I'm sure the data was useful to the manufacturers, but otherwise, not particularly interesting."

He paused to look over the audience, taking a sip of coffee.

"Testing of the communication system failed like all previous and subsequent attempts. The sensor tests provided data but nothing that appeared useful. All data was sent to our laboratory at the Naval Warfare Center in Virginia, where it sat for six months before an engineer noticed an odd effect in the recorded images from the optical sensors. All that was expected was a field of stars and the beam, barely visible down its path of travel because of its interaction with dust from the belt. The engineer pointed out some unexplained points of light, short-duration speckles. They soon realized that some of those points were showing light from Sirius. That's when they called in my team."

He paused again, taking another sip.

"Is he expecting us to cheer?"

Emma pinched her lips together and kept her eyes on Smith.

"We spent about two weeks looking over the data and were about to declare the effect an unusual case of refraction, a result of gases expanding out from the path of the beam. It was only a stroke of luck that one researcher noticed that the tiny contribution made by Sirius B, the white dwarf companion, was not in the right place relative to Sirius A. In fact, it appeared about 8.7 years ahead of where it should be within its orbit ... With Sirius sitting 8.7 lightyears away, the interest in this minor mystery exploded. A quick check confirmed that the displacement of the light from the white dwarf was an exact match to the distance between the two systems. The only possible explanation was that the light we saw had not traveled the 8.7 light years to arrive at Ceres. It had found a shorter path. Following this, I convinced the community that the communications system had nothing to do with the effect. We focused on the interactions between the beam and the failed sensor experiment."

He cleared his voice to silence a murmur at the back of the room. "Attempts to recreate the effect with Sirius have not generated any additional data of interest, more or less the same results. Other star systems, however, have been more promising. We've tried the same combination with the eight closest. Data coming back from Alpha Centauri, Barnard's Star, and Wolf 359 has been interesting, to put it mildly. Best results appear around 550 million kilometers from the Sun. Alpha Centauri sits 60 degrees below the ecliptic. We'll head in that direction first. After that, we'll swing past the equivalent point for Luhman 16, with no real expectations, and then to Barnard's Star. Upon completion, all data will be returned to Earth for analysis."

He paused to look over the audience. "This will be our 17th attempt and the first aboard a ship. I thank you all for your impending support."

His eyes settled on Emma. "One last note for the sensor department. Along with the upgrades to Galileo's power plant and the addition of a triggering beam, the sensor suit has been fully replaced — I'm afraid they'll need to relearn all they know about its operation."

Emma held up a hand as if to wave, meant for the speaker and all the eyes that had turned her way.

"Ouch," Quinn said a little louder than his earlier comments.

"Jokes on him. I haven't learned anything yet," Emma added under her breath.

"He and I had never met before today; why —"

"I think that covers it," the captain said with a sharp tone. "All personnel are reminded to stay clear of the sensor space with the exceptions of Lieutenant Martinez, Lieutenant Stewart, and Petty Officer Harris. We'll provide regular updates as permitted."

Officers and crew started filing out of the mess.

"Want to head down and see what we're in charge of?" Quinn asked.

The sensor space was more over and up now that the ring was stationary and the ship was accelerating, but she left it alone.

"Sure, but do you want to grab lunch first? I've only eaten once since checking aboard."

"Sounds good. I never miss a meal, and they're serving stir-fry today."

With bowls in hand, they found a couple of seats in the small officer's mess.

"How was the trip up?" he asked before taking a mouthful of noodles.

"Miserable," Emma said after swallowing. "I was worried about my time on the surface, but that went perfectly, or better if possible."

"I'll allow it."

"But the ride up," she shook her head. "Over three days on that little car with its passenger compartment full. The cubbyhole I had was tiny, even for me."

"Sounds awful; I managed to catch a shuttle from the surface. Have you ever been in an atmospheric shuttle? It's a hell of a ride, but I understand the exciting part is the descent."

Emma gave a big smile with a mouth filled with rice.

"I'm familiar. I spent most of the last year piloting one on and off Mars."

"You're kidding. How did you get that assignment, or —"

"No!" she pointed at him. "I earned that assignment through hard work and, to some degree, because I had no usable skills," She finished coyly.

"I don't believe that."

"Linguist?"

"It was a multinational effort."

"Everyone there was speaking English."

Quinn waved off her last point. "Good for you anyway. A handy skill ... the piloting."

Emma shrugged. "The flight computers do all the work."

Quinn narrowed his eyes for a moment and then glanced around the room. "So you know, Smith isn't famous for his grace."

Emma shrugged. "I've seen worse, technically brilliant but clueless in a conversation."

Quinn winced but stopped short of saying anything.

"What?"

"Uh ... Sorry, I'll let you figure it out."

He gave her a sympathetic smile. "Finished?"

"Yep, and you were right. This was very good."

They met Petty Officer Joe Calvin coming out of the sensor space. The door clicked behind him as he stopped before them.

"Lieutenant Stewart, I'd like to apologize now for Lieutenant Smith's final comment at the brief and all future gaffs he's bound to make."

Emma almost laughed aloud. As did so many of the crew, Calvin looked young, but he was a first-class petty officer, which gave him at least five years of service. That made their ages about the same. He appeared average by most measures, although his jet-black hair and blue eyes stood out. Like all other enlisted, his underway uniform was back to blue, light over dark. It had been very different when she arrived at the Academy, and she was confident it would change again.

"No need. We're here to review the changes that he mentioned." She glanced past him at the door.

"Ah, yes … he's asked me to keep the space clear … at least for the moment."

"Oh, what's going on?"

"Nothing," he said, shaking his head. "Absolutely nothing."

"This is ridiculous," Quinn said. "Give me a moment," he said as he walked out of earshot, keying his communicator.

Calvin waited patiently, the start of a smile on his face.

"Okay," Quinn said as he returned. "The captain should be explaining how this ship works."

Emma nodded, understanding the reason behind Calvin's smile.

After a long, uncomfortable moment, Lieutenant Smith opened the door and stood aside, allowing them to enter.

"Come in, but don't touch anything. I meant what I said at the briefing; this is very different from anything you've seen. The settings need to be precise. If you fuck them up, Calvin will waste a day resetting the system. We don't have the time to spare — I'm going up to speak to the captain." He stepped out and let the door close.

"Called up for a personal dress down. I'd hate to be in his shoes," Quinn said.

"Don't worry about breaking anything in here," Calvin said. "I've set it up to store every setting and all state variables to a file. It can be restored in an instant."

"What's his purpose?" Emma asked.

"He knows the theory pretty well … seems to, anyways. I'm no expert."

He waved a hand, lighting the fabric that stretched from chest height to the ceiling.

"I can show you the basics."

Midway into the flight through the empty space generally found off the ecliptic plane, Galileo cut her drive and rotated 180 degrees. Returning to a single gee, she started decelerating toward a point on a line, directly between the Sun and Alpha Centauri A.

Three days later, she arrived, cutting thrust to a barely sustainable level, just enough to offset the pull from the Sun and maintain the desired motion. Ring rotation was started to provide the crew with a healthy, comfortable environment. After a heated discussion with Lieutenant Smith, Calvin was allowed to route the displays and controls to a secure space on the ring.

For the better part of the first day, Calvin worked the sensor and trigger controls, producing results very similar to the recorded images he had shown to Emma and Quinn. The main display showed the now familiar, speckled pattern over a stable field of stars. It was not a camera image, but similar. The intensity oscillated, colors shifted, and occasionally, a stable representation of a star appeared before winking out. The surging intensity had an irregular rhythm and was overlayed with random spikes that Smith called noise. Calvin monitored four other displays that Emma was only beginning to understand, each showing a set of data traces that fluctuated wildly as he adjusted the controls. A fifth display, off to the side, was for the camera. It showed the star field and nothing else of interest from what Emma could see.

"We're getting more data than we did in past experiments, but we're not seeing the predicted convergence," Calvin said.

"No, we're not ... The pattern really hasn't changed much either," Smith said.

"Although the timing of it is identical, just under five seconds. Let's push further out."

"I'll contact the bridge," Emma said.

A moment later, "All hands prepare for one gee acceleration. Secure the ring," sounded overhead.

Shortly after, the deck started to tip as breaks were applied to the ring structure. Unnoticeable to anyone on the ring was the vibration of maneuvering thrusters firing to eliminate rotation of the center hull. Outside the door, they heard a coffee cup bounce on the deck and roll past. "Damn it," followed.

"Let's eat and then try again. It will take a few hours to see any difference," Smith said. "Do you understand what we're looking for?" he asked Emma.

"I'm starting to, but please."

Smith nodded as they carefully exited the room, avoiding the cup, lid, and small floating spheres of coffee. Safely past the mess, they used a rail to pull themselves toward the crew's mess. "In case you were unaware, Alpha Centauri is a ternary system. The largest of the three is Rigil Kentaurus, a little larger than the Sun. Toliman is a little smaller than the Sun, and Proxima Centauri is much smaller, a tiny red dwarf.

The interface we're trying to form is a two-dimensional surface, at least when considered in isolation. It's like a window. We sit on one side with the opposite side in empty space within the Alpha Centauri system. When viewed with respect to the space around us, it has a very slight curve following a surface of equal gravitational potential that approximates a sphere around the Sun. Same story on the other side, the gravitational potential is the same, needs to be the same, but the curve is in the other direction, around Rigil Kentaurus."

"Why do they need to match?"

"Good question; you're learning. Matching several conditions between one end and the other is necessary, but matching the gravitational potential is the most important. Anything else would break a basic law of physics, creating energy when moving to a higher potential and destroying energy when moving lower. It has been a fundamental assumption of all theories developed so far."

"And there have been plenty of those," Calvin added.

Smith nodded. "Without a doubt. I suspect we'll have settled the neighboring star systems before they figure out how it's possible."

"So that covers the conservation of energy," Emma said. "What about the conservation of momentum?"

"Another good question. I'm sure you noticed we're still moving relative to the Sun."

"I have."

"The reason for this has to do with the conservation of momentum. Our current speed and direction of travel fall between that of the Sun and Rigil Kentaurus. For several reasons, we believe the two ends of the interface and the ship will remain fixed in space relative to one another … no motion between them. If there's no motion between them, then there must be motion between each end and one or both local stars. Don't forget that every star is in motion relative to the stars around it, some more than others. Now that we're running the experiment from a real ship, we can adjust our direction and speed. Hopefully, we can find a sweet spot, some compromise between the conditions we're trying to match on both ends."

Smith exhaled slowly, obviously, as they continued down the passage.

Emma nodded. "Sounds difficult."

"Uh, yeah … confidence isn't very high back home."

Halfway to the crew's mess, the engines fired. For the crew's sake, acceleration was slowly ramped up to one gee. Walking was awkward at first, but as the inertial force increased — once each step did not launch them upward — they were able to assume a normal stride.

"Now you recall, I said the surface approximates a sphere around the Sun. A perfect sphere would only be possible if the Sun was the only source of gravity in the Universe. Any other source will deform it: planets, surrounding stars, the galaxy as a whole, and clusters of galaxies beyond. We believe the chance of forming a stable interface is related to the shape of the two spheres. The less deformed, the better."

They arrived at the crew's mess and used the small handholds as a ladder to climb into the space.

"We're not worried about the surface on this side. It's a single-star system. We're also not concerned about Proxima Centauri; it orbits far outside the other two. The concern is with Toliman; it's in a tight orbit with Rigil Kentaurus. Deformation from its mass may be too much for an interface to form. Right now, it's about halfway to apoapsis, time-wise, and will continue toward that point for the next 20 years."

As they stepped into line, Smith surprised Emma with a slight apologetic shake of his head. "We're really not sure if it's better to have them close or far apart ... On top of that, there's a chance of a small undetected planet passing near the far end of the interface ... a small chance."

"Will we attempt to connect to Proxima Centauri or Toliman?"

"We will, but expectations are even lower. Toliman is currently further away than Rigil Kentaurus. Its larger, closer sibling will heavily influence its connection point, and Proxima is probably too small."

Emma drew a deep breath and nodded.

"A difficult task," Smith added. "In summary, we're moving outward, hoping to find a less deformed sphere on the far side. Once there, we'll look for a speed and direction that allows us to create a stable interface … and all of this is based upon unproven theories … obviously."

"Difficult," Emma repeated. "Thanks."

They each grabbed lunch and stepped around one of several messes still being mopped up.

"Harris," Emma said to the one member of her division.

"Oh, hey, lieutenant," she answered, mop in hand.

"Eighty more days?" Emma asked.

"Eighty-one"

"Hold steady. The Sensor Division will be waiting." Emma gripped her shoulder.

Mess duty was a time-honored tradition and for the best in Harris' case. At Smith's request, her access to the sensor spaces was removed for the duration of the experiment.

After lunch, Calvin initiated another session that quickly yielded better results. The intensity had increased, and the repeating pattern became very regular. Improvements continued over the next hour and then started to drop off.

"Damn it, this was our best chance," Smith said from a small desk built into the back wall.

"Should we move on to Luhman?" Calvin asked.

"Not yet. We should give it the rest of the day … Let's try connecting to Toliman and Proxima."

Calvin shrugged. "Sure."

As Smith had predicted, the connection attempts to the two stars repeatedly failed, showing little promise that a change in Galileo's position would help. After an hour, Calvin switched back to Rigil Kentaurus.

As he manipulated the controls, Emma stared over his shoulder at the display, the familiar pattern repeating with the same random noise popping up. Something about it was bothering her, triggering a memory that was just out of her reach, although annoyingly close.

Quinn came through the door.

"Still no luck?"

"No, sir," Calvin said with his eyes on the larger display.

"What causes that?" Emma asked. "The noise between cycles."

"No idea," Calvin said. "It is more noticeable than it was with previous experiments."

Quinn stood over Calvin's other shoulder, looking where Emma's finger pointed, but the spike had faded. "Are we ready to move on to Luhman?"

Calvin gave him a small node.

"No, and stop asking," Smith said

"Lieutenant Martinez has been at the navigation station most of the day," Emma said. "He —"

"Stop asking as a group," Smith snapped.

Quinn held up his hands. "Fine, that's fine. Should we push out further?"

"Yes, we'll try again in five hours and then five after that."

Returns at the next stop were no better. At the one after, they had noticeably degraded. It was clear they had passed the optimum point. A consensus was reached to move on to the Luhman 16 point.

After four long days transiting to that point and the better part of another looking at a blank display, the level of frustration grew noticeably. The improved equipment had not helped with the tiny brown dwarfs.

"I told them it was a waste of time, but that idiot, Kaplan, insisted."

Emma shrugged at Quinn. Kaplan was not known to either.

"It was on the way to the Barnard point," Calvin offered.

"Just turn around and keep your eyes on the display."

Calvin opened his mouth and then shut it before swiveling around.

"I hesitate to ask, but are we done here?" Quinn asked.

"Yes, let's move on. Never should have come here in the first place."

"Great, the Barnard Point is a four-and-a-half-day ride. We could use another break."

Smith made a few short entries on a keyboard. "We could cut that time in half."

"Well, we could if we want to lay in our beds at four gees for the duration."

"Do we have the fuel for that kind of acceleration?" Calvin asked.

Emma nodded. "Fuel isn't a concern. Reaction mass will run out long before fuel, but we have plenty of that also." She looked at Quinn for confirmation.

"Yeah, we're fine. Used just over 20 percent so far. We can always cut the drives and coast if we start running low, although nobody would like that."

Quinn looked over Smith's shoulder. "Oh, how do you work with that crap?"

He tapped on the display. "Hours, minutes, seconds — or worse — degrees, hours, seconds. Why can't you stick with degrees?"

Emma and Calvin exchanged smiles.

Smith's face went sour. "It's served the community for hundreds of years. Can we get moving?"

"Sure, one gee."

"You've been quiet the last couple of days," Quinn said to Emma as they found a pair of seats in the officer's mess. "Smith bothering you?"

"Eh, no more than anyone else. No, I've been thinking about Calvin's display, what we saw back at the Alpha Centauri point."

Quinn shook his head. "I couldn't make head or tails out of it. Did you see something useful?"

"I don't know, something about the noise spikes, a vague memory. Since we left for Luhman, I've been trying to understand some of the theory."

"Better you than me," Quinn said with a big smile. "I'm just an old chief who usually knows his place."

Emma looked at him in surprise. "You're a mustang. I should have known."

"Damned right. I had just made Senior Chief and then decided that life as a junior officer would be so much better." He pointed at Emma's collar insignia.

"Anyways, you have a better chance than Smith of figuring it out."

"Aw, thanks, chief."

"I'll consider that a promotion — Eat your meal."

Following dinner, Emma tried reviewing the material Smith provided but couldn't keep her eyes open. "Oh, I'm going to regret this." She left her quarters and turned down the short passageway, returning to the mess for a cup of coffee. Harris was ahead of her, dragging a standard mop and sealable bucket into the crew's mess. Its wheels were not cooperating.

One of the advantages of a closed system was that no moisture escaped. That which was injected by climate control, exhaled, or spread across the deck to evaporate eventually returned to storage tanks that lined the interior structures. The ring's structure in this case. Emma recalled that the center hull had an independent water supply.

She didn't want to say anything because Harris would immediately step aside and let her pass.

Following slowly behind, she watched the water slop higher with each step and drag. It finally reached the lip and splashed on the deck. Harris stopped and turned.

"Oh, sorry, lieutenant. This bucket sucks."

She ran the mop over the small puddle as Emma stared at the bucket.

"Lieutenant?"

Emma stared for a moment longer and then looked up in surprise. "Oh … sorry, Harris. I need to go."

She turned around and stepped into the main passageway that curved around the ring. Moving as fast as she could without running, she returned to the interface control room, a name that Calvin and Quinn had agreed upon when there was little else to do.

Calvin was alone, his head on a desk, sound asleep.

"Calvin."

Over an arm that was acting as a pillow, he peeked at her with a single eye.

"Oh, hey, lieutenant, what's up."

"I have a thought."

He sat up fully, looking at her. "Okay."

"The noise on the main display, running under the primary pattern … is it possible there's a feedback loop driving it?"

He twisted his face slightly. Sleep marks were fading.

"I don't know. It seems completely random, but we can take a look."

Calvin brought up the display and loaded a recorded session from the Alpha Centauri point.

"Okay, here is the primary pattern … and there it repeats. What're we looking — Ah, there was a noise spike."

They watched intently until the noise spiked again.

"That was a little stronger, right."

Calvin nodded, "yeah, maybe. That was about seven seconds."

A third spike appeared after another seven seconds.

"Definitely stronger."

Another seven seconds brought nothing.

"Did I miss it?" Emma asked.

"Don't think so."

Another cycle passed.

"It was more noticeable than it was at Ceres, but I still think it's just random noise — No, wait, there it is, very weak, but right on time."

They watched the spike return four times, each stronger than the one before, with each separated by seven seconds.

"And then it goes away," Calvin said. "Two cycles, I'm guessing."

Twenty-one seconds passed. "Yep, looks like seven cycles and then a reset. That does look like a feedback loop with something resetting it at the high end."

Lieutenant Smith came through the door. "What're you two doing up at this hour?"

He was in a better mood than they had seen since Galileo left the Luhman 16 point behind.

Calvin waved him over. "Look at this. Lieutenant Stewart noticed another pattern under the primary sequence."

He pointed out each of the spikes as they repeated.

Smith pushed close to the display as the noise pattern started again.

"Hmm, I imagine the spike is still present in that gap; just too weak for us to see."

"Does it mean anything?" he asked Calvin.

Calvin shrugged. "I don't know. I can think of one limiter that may be cutting it off after the seven cycles, but I've no idea what's causing it in the first place."

"Show me that limiter. Maybe we can figure something out."

Emma backed away, giving them room to work.

After a half hour, she found herself drifting away.

"Coffee, anyone?"

They both nodded.

When she returned, they had called up schematics and were busy tracing paths.

Five hours passed.

"Okay," Smith said. "We have a plan. We'll keep the standard configuration to start. Barring anything unusual with that session, you will then reconfigure. If we figured this right, it should eliminate the noise spike entirely."

Calvin nodded and stretched, yawning widely. The two lieutenants followed his example.

"Just over a day to go," Smith said. "Get some sleep."

"I didn't think the XO would ever stop," Emma said as she and Quinn pushed weightlessly toward the inner ring access chamber.

"You mean shut up, don't you?"

They stopped just before the chamber, gripping handholds attached to the center hull, watching handholds attached to the inner ring pass slowly, each labeled with a letter and number. D4, D3, and D2 at the moment.

"Hard to believe that only grease stands between us and the vacuum," Quinn said.

"Oh, not that hard," Emma countered and then noticed the smile on his face.

"Nice try, but I don't scare that easily — Here comes 'C'"

They pushed into the inner ring, grabbed hold, and immediately started to drift outward/down.

Feet first, they maneuvered into spoke 'C' and started to drop. At first, with help from their hands. It quickly transitioned into a gentle free fall and then a typical descent down a ladder, bringing them to the outer ring. The interface control room was just down the main passage.

"You're late," Smith said as they walked through the door.

"We're also just observers," Emma said to Quinn's mild surprise.

Smith shook his head. "Sorry, you lost that status yesterday. You're now a contributing member of the team." He shifted his gaze to Quinn, who shrugged mildly.

"Calvin has started the first session using standard settings. Once we see the expected results, he'll reconfigure and hopefully eliminate the noise."

For the next hour, the intensity increased, and the primary sequence became regular. The noise spike appeared but at a slower rate than what they saw with Alpha Centauri. As Emma watched the noise strengthen, a thought occurred and quickly turned into a relationship.

"The period of the noise spikes is inversely proportional to the combined mass of the stars."

She followed this with a series of numbers to support her statement.

As Calvin's fingers danced over the keyboard, Quinn and Smith stared silently, questioningly.

"It's accurate to two decimal places," he said. "Interesting, but I'm not sure if it helps us."

"Not here," Smith said. "But for other stars, it will allow you to calculate the configuration in advance."

"Right, that would be handy."

"Yes, it would," Smith said with a note of condescension. "Let's stop this session and reconfigure."

Calvin needed about ten minutes to enter the new values. Once in, he restarted. A display of static slowly coalesced into the familiar pattern, strengthening and weakening as he made minor adjustments. They were waiting for the secondary noise pattern to show, but as each moment passed, they grew confident that it had been successfully eliminated. The primary pattern cleared as Calvin tweaked the controls, clearer than any earlier attempt. A small speaker — that had only made white noise previously — now produced a distinct repeating sound that matched the display.

Emma was leaning closer when the display went blank.

"Oh, for fuck's sake," Smith cried out.

Calvin shook his head. "Haven't seen this before."

Emma stepped back to stand at Quinn's side, arms crossed.

Silence fell over the four. Calvin's hand hovered over a control, but he wasn't sure what to do with it.

"Damn it," Emma said.

"Sensor, Bridge, report."

"That was the captain," Quinn said with surprise.

"The camera," Emma shouted, pointing to their right.

That display showed the same star field as before, but at the center, Barnard's Star was much brighter.

"Pan out," Smith said quickly.

Calvin swiped at a control, pulling back from the center, drawing additional stars from the edge of the display. As they watched, a dim, ghostly ring of light appeared near the display's edge, hovering in space ahead of Galileo. It appeared as a perfect circle of defused, unfocused starlight centered around Barnard's Star. Outside of it, the star field continued. Emma approached the display, trying to understand what she saw within the border.

Years later, she would know that it was a series of rings; light from Barnard's Star filled the inner ring, light from the Sun folded back to form the second narrower ring, light from Barnard's Star passed through to form a third outside of the first two, and so on. The pattern continued, an infinite number of rings with widths diminishing toward zero. There would be a ratio, a limit, and eventually a new branch of mathematics to justify a generation of theorists but do little to explain the border of that region.

"How big is that?" Smith asked.

"Almost a kilometer across," Calvin said after a pause. "Sitting about a kilometer in front of the ship."

"What the hell are we looking at, Smith?" Quinn asked.

"I believe that is a stable interface," he answered slowly.

"Any data?" he asked Calvin.

"Some." Calvin looked from display to display. "Different from before. I'm not sure what any of it means."

Emma pointed at the camera display again. "Is it starting to move?"

As they watched, the circular region blurred and started collapsing inward.

"Zoom in," Smith said, but the interface's boundary dissolved completely before Calvin could act. The pattern reappeared on the main display and then quickly faded into static.

"Extraordinary, truly," Captain Hanson said.

The four sat at the wardroom table with all off-duty officers and a handful of enlisted personnel. They had easily reestablished the interface and watched it disappear like the first. That had been at the captain's request before reporting to the wardroom.

"All data has been transmitted to Virginia?" He looked at Smith.

"Yes, sir. They have it, and they've recalled the entire staff; it's almost midnight for them. Currently, we're authorized to reproduce the interface and send through drones at our discretion, but we'll need to wait on orders before proceeding any further."

"And that's why we're here, to ensure we're ready to proceed. Chief Blackrock, are the drones ready?"

The ship's Coxswain, Chief Warren Blackrock, gave a slight nod. "Yes, sir. Blue Drone is in the launch bay, primed to go. Red is on standby."

"Good. Lieutenant Stewart, to the best of your knowledge, will we be able to send and receive from the drone once it passes through the interface?"

"Yes, sir. We believe the interface is a physical connection between separate spaces and will allow the free passage of all mediums … until it destabilizes after two minutes."

"Chief, can you get Blue in and out in two minutes?"

"That's possible, captain, but it can't complete a full spherical scan within that time. If we allow it to stay, it can complete the scan and transmit what it finds. We'll have to reestablish comms and bring it back once another interface is opened."

"Thank you, chief. Lieutenant Martinez, will two minutes be enough time to fly the ship through, assuming that order is received?"

"Aye, captain," Quinn answered with more vigor than he intended. "We can get through in less than a minute. I do recommend that ring rotation is secured in advance."

"Agreed. After we adjourn, shift operations back to the center hull."

"Aye, captain."

"Clearly, returning will be difficult inside of a two-minute window. I've reserved the most important question for you, Lieutenant Smith — How confident are you that we can establish an interface back home?"

"We … we are confident. There's no source on this side to complicate the gravitational potential, and we believe the same is true near Barnard's. The drone will be able to verify that, but regarding the drone, if we allow it to stay as the chief is suggesting, there's a good chance that the next interface will be tens of thousands of kilometers away from it. Barnard's Star is unique in that its motion relative to the stars around it is very large. The interface will destabilize before it can return."

"Can we test this?"

"We can fire a target drone through," Chief Blackrock said. "See where it is relative to the next interface. They're disposable."

"Good idea, chief. We can do that while we wait for word from Virginia."

He briefly looked at each person around the table for concurrence.

"Captain," Smith said. "They'll need days to make the obvious decision. After the drone test, I'd like to experiment with varying locations and speeds. I expect to find an ideal combination where the time to form is shorter and the duration of the interface is longer. It would also be valuable to see how far we can move from this location and still form an interface."

"Very well, Smith, but we won't wander too far. I want to ensure that the duration stays above two minutes for the sake of our navigator."

He glanced over the group once more. "Anything else? … Okay, I think we're — What's on the far side of that interface?" he asked Smith while pointing at the displayed image.

"As discussed previously, we expect that it will be identical to what we see on this side, only facing outward from Barnard's Star."

"No, you misunderstand," Captain Hanson said neutrally. "What's on the other side of that interface within the Solar System? What will we see if Chief Blackrock flies a drone around it, a kilometer behind?"

A silence ensued.

"And a more pressing question — What will happen to Galileo if it's in the middle of that when it dissolves?"

The silence continued.

"The four of you get down to the sensor space and make sure the … the experiment will work from that location. After that, I want you to learn all you can before we send Blue or Red through."

All stood and started to exit the wardroom.

"Sir, we were leaning towards 'interface drive,'" Quinn said.

The captain narrowed his eyes at Quinn and then shrugged. "That's fine, lieutenant."

Outside the wardroom, en route to spoke 'A,' Emma nudged Quinn. "Interface drive?"

"It was discussed."

"I don't recall."

"Neither do I," Smith said. "And in no way, shape, or form does it qualify as a drive."

"What then?"

"Interface … creator," Emma suggested.

"I like the biblical note, but no."

"Establisher," Calvin offered without conviction.

Smith looked back at him with mock disgust. "I believe 'generator' describes it best."

There was no argument.

"Now watch this," Calvin said, replacing the image with another.

"Those two stars shifted," Smith said, pointing to the right.

"Let me get this straight; the two stars right next to Barnard's Star, showing through the interface, are also the two stars we're seeing just outside the interface?"

"Yes, but the light outside the interface is six years older … I would guess, based on the distance."

"And the first image was from the portside camera, and this is from the starboard camera?"

"Yes, sir."

"So, the older light is being split around the interface?" Emma asked. "The portside camera sees it to the left, and the starboard camera sees it to the right. — Is that lensing?"

"It's like lensing," Smith said. "In the true starfield, those two are in the center, nearest to Barnard's Star ... and it looks like there's a copy of all other stars within the boundary, showing just outside ... but their shift is smaller from image to image, and they're remaining on the same side as you switch between cameras."

Smith drew close to a console display, scanning a list of numbers. "So, the stars outside the boundary ... You're certain they're showing older light?"

"It's the only explanation I can think of." Calvin switched displays. "All we know is that it matches the original light, and the light inside the boundary does not."

"I don't see a second copy of Barnard's Star," Quinn said.

"No, it's unique in that respect," Smith said.

Quinn shrugged. "Are we ready for the drone?"

"I am," Calvin said quickly. Both Emma and Smith nodded.

"Chief Blackrock, deploy Blue. Once an interface is established, take it to the edge, 200 meters out, and keep all sensors trained on the interface. From there, send it 10 kilometers directly behind and then fly it straight back to Galileo. Give yourself a minute and forty to complete the entire maneuver."

"Roger that, lieutenant."

The time needed to generate an interface was much less than the first and a mild improvement upon the second. With each, Calvin recognized more of what was necessary to bring convergence out of the chaotic patterns.

The drone's image of the interface shifted across the background of stars as it moved toward one side. As expected, its circular shape became oval, narrowing with each passing second and disappearing altogether when seen on edge.

"No surprise here," Smith said.

"Nothing, not even a disturbance," Quinn added.

The drone continued around, accelerating heavily and showing only empty space between itself and Galileo. As it came to a stop, Galileo's bow shield was centered on the display from a perspective that was offset from the center by a small degree. Nothing else, aside from the field of stars, was visible. From the cameras aboard Galileo, the drone appeared just outside the interface.

As they watched, it accelerated toward Galileo. The camera aboard the drone showed that it was moving directly toward Galileo but remained off the same side.

"Can you push it closer to the center, chief?" Quinn asked.

"It's going straight up the middle lieutenant, by dead-reckoning. I can't explain what we're seeing."

Quinn let out a short laugh. "Don't worry, chief. None of us can."

"I'm giving it a nudge."

The drone's image popped from one side of the interface to the other. The image of Galileo from the drone also shifted its perspective.

"That's curious," Quinn said.

"That's the best I can do, lieutenant."

"No problem, chief."

The drone continued along the same path through empty space straight back to Galileo. From the cameras aboard Galileo, it followed a slight curve around the interface, ending up directly in front of it. Shortly after, the interface destabilized and collapsed.

Emma, Quinn, and Calvin turned questioning looks toward Smith.

He looked back, shaking his head and smiling, but the expressions on the three faces remained intent. "Oh, give me a break," he finally said. "You'll be lucky to get that answer before you die."

A single target drone was used to prove Smith's assumption regarding the relative motion between Sol and Barnard's star. The target drone coasted through, sending a limited data stream until the interface destabilized. With the following interface, a link to the drone was quickly re-established. The drone was seven thousand kilometers closer to Barnard's star than the interface, which matches his prediction well.

To address the captain's greatest concern, Lieutenant Smith and Chief Blackrock conjured a set of tests to safely demonstrate the effects upon an object caught between two star systems when the interface collapsed. It required two target drones, the entire inventory of 10-millimeter line, and a set of free weights from Galileo's gymnasium. What the tests showed was both unexpected and encouraging.

Previous interfaces had collapsed inward, but with weighted, connected drones on both sides, the interface would collapse directly away from the star system that held most of the combined mass. Both drones would remain in that system with the line still attached. This was true regardless of the distances between the drones and the interface, tested to the limits of available line. Like many other aspects of the interface, Smith had no answers to the questions that followed.

After the results of all tests were compiled into a concise report, they briefed the captain, and he agreed to send the first sensor drone through the interface. Blue Drone passed through without issue. Data returned, showing empty space around the far end. A quick check of star positions verified that it was sending from within the system of Barnard's Star. Chief Blackrock was able to turn it around and bring it back through within the two-minute limit. Over the next hour, Blue and Red made two trips each to complete a scan of near space on the far side.

Analysis allayed initial concerns, showing that the position of the interface was predictable to within a few hundred kilometers. This and other data were sent to Virginia as the ship accelerated in the direction of Barnard's Star. Smith's experiment varying the distance and speed, provided valuable insight. An optimal point was found after six hours of stop-and-go motion. They continued the tests for another day, coming about as the interface duration dropped back to the two-minute mark set by the captain. From there, they returned to the optimal location and waited as discussions and debates continued day and night, out of their reach. They had little to do beyond responding to the occasional request for data or insight. Four more days passed before word came. Galileo was to travel to Barnard's Star and return immediately. Rotation was secured, and the ship was placed at battle stations. Red Drone waited on the other side, having reported all clear. Lieutenants Stewart and Smith were in the sensor space with Petty Officer Calvin. Quinn Martinez was on the bridge.

Calvin established an interface with practiced ease, and Galileo quickly accelerated, passing through 30 seconds later.

"Like walking through a door," Captain Hanson said.

Displays around the bridge reset to their new surroundings, rotating to a new north-south axis. Navigation flip-flopped briefly and then reported their new position. A quick sensor sweep confirmed the empty space reported by Red Drone.

"Dock control, bridge, bring Red back."

"Dock control, Aye."

"Navigator, bring us about and prepare for a return trip."

Quinn gave Captain Hanson a look of concern. "Sir, we'll need about five minutes to recover Red."

"Ah ... understood. How is our position and velocity?"

"For a return trip, our velocity will be perfect following the next maneuver, and, from Smith's assessment, our position will be adequate for the next day at the least."

Quinn adjusted the ship's velocity to match the previous interface and paused as Red returned. After a minute had passed, Emma, Smith, and Calvin emerged from the sensor space with questioning looks.

"What's wrong?" Smith asked in a voice louder than necessary.

"Recovering our drone, Lieutenant Smith," Captain Hanson answered. "Let's wait until it's in the hangar before we try anything."

"Yes, sir," Smith said and followed Emma and Calvin back into the sensor space, where the three waited nervously until the order came from the bridge.

"Okay, back to the Solar System," Smith said as he placed a visibly shaking hand on Calvin's shoulder. "Establish a session and verify that the noise spikes match with Lieutenant Stewart's observation on mass. If so, reconfigure and run until convergence."

"I hope this works," Calvin said quietly, although loud enough to draw concerning looks from both lieutenants behind him.

The first session verified that the noise period matched expectations, matched what they had seen on the jump from the Solar System. With that data, Calvin began to reconfigure the generator. When complete, he started a second session. The noise spike was filtered out as expected, and the primary sequence quickly grew in strength but failed to converge as expected. The three exchanged worried looks as he started a third session.

Quinn banged through the door.

"The captain is doing an amazing job maintaining an air of calm, but what the fuck."

Emma looked up at him with a look of serenity, working hard to hide the pain in her stomach. "No worries, Lieutenant Martinez. Petty Officer Calvin is establishing an interface as we speak."

"It's starting to converge," Calvin said with excitement.

"Gotta go," Quinn said as he exited toward the bridge.

As the three watched the camera feed, a circular interface opened a kilometer ahead.

Thirty seconds later, Galileo passed through the interface, returning to the Solar System.

August 1st 2123

"Can you believe that guy? I was just starting to like him, and then he pulled this crap."

Emma peeked over a steaming cup of coffee at Quinn. In an enclosed environment, most people will fall into a predictable routine. Limited choices, she guessed. Since the first day aboard Galileo, she had spent most of her spare time with him. He was likable enough, but she felt no other attraction. His role with the interface generator had been relatively small, so there was no professional reason for them to be together, but there he was, complaining about someone.

"What are you, 40 years old?"

He stopped what he was about to say and gave her a bemused expression.

"No, but thanks for asking, and thanks for your woefully inaccurate guess ... 45. What brought that up?"

She put her cup down so he could see the sympathy on her face.

"You seem awfully worked up, so I thought I'd push you just a little further."

Quinn laughed aloud, interrupting the breakfast of the three other officers in the wardroom.

"Oh, I like that; you'll go far in this navy."

He sipped on his coffee. Neither were hungry after waking.

"You've changed in the last ... Has it been four weeks?"

"Almost ... I'm sorry, I just had the best night's rest since boarding, and I still feel groggy. Night, is that what we call it out here?"

"That's what Galileo calls it. Routines are important."

Emma smiled. "Right … I believe you were complaining about Smith."

"Yes, have you seen that brief he prepared for the captain?"

"No."

"Well, I guess I shouldn't be surprised. He paints it as a singular effort, his, obviously."

"You didn't get mentioned?"

"Yes, I did, in one sentence, right next to you. I believe the words 'with assistance' were in there too. Don't get me wrong; I played almost no role, but you were critical. We'd still be out there flailing about if you had not pointed them in the right direction."

"It was a tiny observation; I noticed an interference pattern. He and Calvin actually fixed it." She reached back to refill her cup. "I was just a fresh set of eyes making a small contribution, just like hundreds before me. It was only luck that it turned out to be the final piece to the puzzle — I think they would've noticed it eventually."

"Maybe, maybe not, but it was you who noticed it, and that deserves more recognition than he gave."

"I'm really not a fan of recognition. He mentioned us by name?"

"Yep, Lieutenants Quinn Martinez and Emma Stewart."

"This was for Admiral Richie?"

"No, the captain briefed her earlier. I believe this one was for the public."

"Oh … no," Emma said, head slumping.

"What?"

"I have a bad feeling about this."

Quinn was mystified, but before he could ask further, the head of engineering, Lieutenant Commander Fedorov, entered with Lieutenant Shaw. They were laughing loudly.

"There she is," Fedorov said with glee.

Emma let her head drop to the table.

"You heard?"

Emma kept her head down. "No, ma'am, but I can guess."

"What?" Quinn asked again.

"Well, we've gone public. The captain just finished a near real-time briefing with the press."

Galileo was less than a day from Earth.

"Maybe five of the questions had technical content, the others … well, the final question, or answer, says it all."

"What did he say?"

"Khakis. Or, to quote fully, 'Khakis. Lieutenant Stewart was wearing khakis, the underway uniform for all officers.'"

Quinn burst out laughing along with all the others in the wardroom. All but one.

Emma sat up and glared at him, which only made him laugh louder.

"I'm sorry, It's not —"

The room fell silent as the captain stepped through the doorway. Emma stood.

"Ah, good," he said, looking around. "We have our orders."

"We'll dock at Saint Peter and Paul tomorrow at 9:30. A team from Virginia will board to inspect the interface generator in its new configuration. We'll remain for three days to resupply and enjoy a little R&R. They're providing a shuttle, a real shuttle, so we'll need to schedule surface visits."

There was a murmur of approval.

"Following the break, we'll complete the circuit. Lalande, Wolf, Wise, Sirius, Luyten, back to Alpha Centauri and Luhman, and, finally, Ross 154; the remaining systems inside ten light years. Same plan as before, in and out, assuming we connect."

"What's the expected flight time?" Quinn asked.

"About eight weeks if all works out. We'll also be refueling … and taking on additional riders, 20, bringing the total to 22."

He glanced over the gathered officers and then settled his eyes on Emma. "Some will get an extended vacation to make room."

"Sir?"

"You'll be staying behind, lieutenant."

"Sir?" A note of concern was evident.

"Sorry, Admiral's orders, but I don't think she was given a choice. They want someone who understands what we've been doing for the last four weeks, can put together two words without stumbling, and can do this in multiple languages."

Emma stared back at her captain, silent, frozen.

"You're going on a victory tour, Lieutenant Stewart."

September 10th 2123

South, toward the Forbidden City, the lights of Beijing were bright and inviting, but the most Emma could manage was a brief look out the small window before she collapsed on her bed. The sheets had the feel of silk, and the mattress was hard and unyielding compared to what awaited her at home. It was as she had requested.

Five weeks had passed since her return to Earth. Within that time, she attended twelve speaking engagements, with almost every minute between rehearsing in a different language or reworking Lieutenant Smith's slides to satisfy the admiral's concerns. As a career builder, the five weeks could not have worked out better: five weeks traveling with Admiral Grace Richie, the commanding officer of the Naval Space Command, and her staff, twelve events around the world, giving a short inspirational speech at each before introducing the admiral.

The last, three hours earlier, had received the warmest reception. Her portion, as always, was met with applause, but Admiral Richie's speech and promises of cooperation delivered the desired message.

Emma wanted an uninterrupted night of sleep before taking the staff shuttle to Jarvis Station and Anay. Three days with him on the station would be followed by a visit with her family in Montana. Despite the exhaustion, she feared that sleep might not come easily. Before she could try, there was a final out-brief with the admiral in the penthouse suit.

Despite her immediate intentions and fears, she dropped into a brief slumber. An unmeasurable moment later, she sat straight up and queried for the time. More relaxed, she stood, straightened her dress whites, freshened up, and left her room.

The atmosphere was light and celebratory. Most of the staff had a drink in their hands. All were feeling relaxed at the end of a grueling schedule. Emma could not. The room was filled with admirals and captains. The lowest rank after her was a commander, and he was keeping his interactions under tight control.

"Here's a good Scot," an older captain said to Emma as she approached the admiral.

"You must try this." He handed her a glass.

She sniffed and then took a small sip and nodded with appreciation.

"Oh, wonderful. Bright girl."

She smiled politely as he stepped away to join others. The drink was less vile than some her grandfather had encouraged her generation to sample.

"Lieutenant Stewart," the admiral said as Emma approached the inner circle.

"I hope you don't mind the change in format for this last brief."

"Not at all, ma'am." She held up the glass.

The admiral took note of the drink. "You too?"

"It was a gift." Emma sipped carefully and grimaced.

With a nod of approval, the admiral cleared her voice, a small, distinct action that quickly silenced the room.

"A quick note for those who don't know. Galileo's attempt to connect with Luyten A has failed. This was not unexpected since it's farther out than Lalande … With the only successful connections, to date, being to Barnard's Star and Wolf 359, we're assuming that mass and distance are the primary factors in the formation of a connection. We can place the maximum range between 7.9 and 8.3 light years and a minimum mass between three hundredths and 14 hundredths of a solar mass. We have no idea about a minimum range or maximum mass, and please understand that this is entirely observational. We don't have a theory to explain any of this, but these estimates allow us to make a reasonable plan going forward."

She paused, taking a slow, deliberate drink.

"That plan falls upon us. We need to act quickly to capitalize on this discovery. Up-tempo."

Emma recognized her grandfather's mantra.

"The entire line of Batfish class corvettes will be converted into a new explorer type. With stealth in mind, the hull of each will be modified to lower its signature across the spectrum. The cyclotron and coils will be replaced, and the synchronizer will be adjusted accordingly. This will bring a welcome increase to the propellant's relativistic mass and allow those ships to range much further from Earth without refueling. Finally, space will be made to fit each with an interface generator. Right now, we're planning for a crew of twelve.

Most haven't been commissioned or even launched, so the transition should be relatively easy. We're unsure what we'll discover out there, so these ships will lead the way. Our three science vessels, Galileo, Copernicus, and Kepler, will be fitted for planetary exploration. The search for habitable planets will be their top priority. Any questions on this?"

The small audience remained silent.

"Naval Space Command is about to enter a period of very rapid growth. We'll be cannibalizing the sea service, stealing from Space Force, and starting an aggressive recruiting campaign. The shipbuilding program will also be ramping up. Our engineers are working on specs as we speak. Once complete, we'll put out an open request for designs. We're considering both a destroyer and cruiser class but will remain open to new ideas."

The audience, her staff, for the most part, remained silent.

"Enjoy your evening because tomorrow is going to be busy."

Groups reformed around the minor questions that some had held off asking.

"Lieutenant."

Emma looked up at the admiral. "Yes, ma'am."

"You have new orders that will keep you busy until Galileo returns."

A nervous look passed over Emma's face.

"No, not recruiting, although it was discussed."

"These are from Captain Hanson. Sorry about the chain of command, but it works poorly in these situations."

"Yes, ma'am." Relieved, she waited.

"You're being given another role on Galileo. They're going to need a shuttle pilot that's familiar with alien environments. Mars, for example. I honestly can't think of anyone in the Navy with more experience. That said, you'll need to qualify. Space Force has a class that flies out of Colorado, converting civilian shuttle pilots. You've already missed the first week but should be able to complete it in three. I certainly didn't hear any complaints when I forwarded the request."

"Yes, ma'am. That sounds great."

Emma slipped out of the brief after a minimum stay. No one noticed her leave, although that had not been a concern. Her exhaustion was gone, replaced by a growing excitement. She had plans to make and plans to cancel. She wanted to get past the latter as soon as possible. She nearly ran down the short hallway, but once in the elevator, she paused, staring at the column of buttons as the door closed. Her guilt surged, and tears welled up.

She bowed her head and whispered, "I'm sorry, Anay."

November 5th 2123

Eighty berths had been added before leaving Earth, but the living spaces aboard Galileo were still above capacity. At that, hundreds had been turned away. Every flavor of researcher had argued with conviction that a berth was essential. Essential for what was the question that most failed to answer to the satisfaction of the board responsible for assembling the planetary exploration team. It was another unenviable task for a group of senior scientists and politicians that, by the nature of their role, would not join Galileo. Emma recalled her uncle's description of the hours spent deciding between 'exploration' or 'evaluation' within the team's name.

Despite her family connections to that board, she had no input into the team's selections. On the other hand, Captain Hanson had sought her help filling the crew's berths. As with the research team, there was no shortage of volunteers, but the pool was very shallow once the unqualified were filtered out. Emma had been surprised when he asked for her help and found it more surprising when her friend Niko had initially balked at the offer. The billet's description had given her pause. She was to act as a liaison between the captain and crew of Galileo and the planetary exploration team.

"Niko?" Ahead of Emma, an officer and three enlisted were awkwardly maneuvering two large crates through a narrow passage in upper-level berthing just aft of spoke 'D.'

"Emma. Give me a moment. Let's take a break, guys."

With the crates on the deck, the crewmembers disappeared around a corner as Niko turned to Emma, her dark hair tinged with gray dust. She shook some loose with her hands and brushed it from her face with limited success.

"What are you doing?"

Niko shrugged mildly and smiled. A year on Mars taught Emma to recognize the irritation behind the smile.

"The stellar team complained that delta berthing is too crowded … and it is. We're shifting supplies so we can pop out a wall and give them a little more space."

"Are they the same ones that complained there was not enough centripetal force … acting upon them? Or was it centrifugal? I keep forgetting."

Niko's smile became genuine. "Yeah, they wanted us to spin the ring faster."

"That would be cruel for everyone." Emma looked past Niko at the two crates. "You do know we'll be cutting acceleration in another hour. It would make your task much easier."

"I've been aboard for two weeks, and you want me to start breaking the rules already?"

Emma nodded with her eyes wide and inviting. "We'll you finish in time? I don't want to wander into the Mouse Hole alone."

For unknown reasons, the lower-level ring section allotted to the research team, officially called the Planetary Exploration Center, had placards above each door declaring it the Lion's Den. Galileo's crew had adopted an alternative name.

"Hopefully. Want to help?"

Emma looked back at the crates and dropped her shoulders. "Sure."

With ten minutes of zero-gee, they managed to get the supplies moved and stowed. This was followed by a hurried transit down spoke 'D' to the lower level and into the Mouse Hole. Emma wanted a tour but did not want to wander into the space alone and endure the questioning stares. In addition to her curiosity, she needed a good reason to avoid the sensor space. After weeks of training, Petty Officer Harris would attempt her first interface. Calvin was there to guide her, and both agreed that Emma's presence would not be helpful.

Galileo's circuit of jump points within the Solar System had resulted in just two successful connections, Barnard's Star and Wolf 359. Distance or mass explained all but one set of failures. Each attempt to connect to the three stars of Alpha Centauri had failed. Proxima Centauri was the closest star to Earth and had a greater mass than Wolf 359. There had been hopes that its distant orbit around the other two would allow a connection, but that had not come true. A connection to the tightly bound pair of Rigil Kentaurus and Toliman had garnered less hope due to the complex nature of the gravitational potential surrounding two sol-sized stars so near to one another.

All the lessons learned from those initial attempts were incorporated into upgrades and an operational guide. All but two of the riders had returned to their positions at the research center in Virginia. Lieutenant Smith had leveraged the success aboard the Galileo into a promotion and a posting at the Pentagon. Petty Officer Calvin had requested and received a transfer to Galileo.

Plans for further exploration were set. Galileo received orders to jump across a string of four stars leading to Epsilon Indi, with limited hope of finding a habitable planet in that system or the system before, Lacaille 8760. En route, they were tasked to attempt a connection into Alpha Centauri through Barnard's Star.

All in the room watched the same display. One moment, it showed a field of stars centered upon a barely discernable white dot, tinged red. The next, that dot had grown into a bright red-orange star surrounded by a ghostly ring sharing that same color. A brief cheer filled the room before everyone scrambled to secure themselves against one gee of acceleration. A minute later, Galileo was in the Alpha Centauri System, near the smallest of that system's three stars.

The problem connecting to Proxima Centauri from the Solar System became apparent, if not fully understood, and there was little chance of improvement. The debris belt around the star would remain an obstacle for thousands of years. A few in the room had expressed concern, but not enough to put it on the agenda. There was only one reason for the small gathering in the wardroom, and that reason was less than a day away.

Galileo had come about 14 hours earlier and was on a decelerating path toward Proxima Centauri B, a planet that had held the interest of many on Earth for the past hundred years. Prospects that the planet was habitable were thoroughly squashed in the first half of the last century. Advancements in the technologies used to view distant objects and advancements in the sciences used to understand those objects had dashed the hopes of all but the occasional dreamer. Hopes of finding evidence of past life were more realistic, although still small.

The three drones of the exploration team, Gemini, Orion, and Taurus, were in orbit around the planet. The hope of habitability was put to a final rest as they began streaming data back to Galileo. Raked by a regular barrage of solar flares, coronal mass ejections, x-ray bursts, and gamma-ray bursts, the atmosphere was gone along with any water that may have once been on the planet.

Niko brought a detailed relief map up and stepped back to await the proverbial storm. Nothing in the details rendered from the drones' data would be questioned. It was the additions made by the research team that had her worried.

She looked down the length of the table at Captain Hanson, at the expression on his face, and cringed inwardly.

"Lieutenant Sasaki, I realize I placed you in a difficult situation, but this is why you're aboard this ship." He made his annoyance obvious to all in the room. "Please take this advice to heart. Once I give a firm 'no,' there will never be a reason to repeat the same question. You are here to filter out this nonsense."

"Yes, captain —"

"Captain, I insisted."

Silenced, Niko turned her attention to the paleontologist team lead.

"These locations have the highest probability of showing signs of past life. They are not negotiable."

"No, they are not … Smith, is it?"

Emma raised a hand to hide her smirk.

"It's Sanders, captain."

"Right … Lieutenant Sasaki, please explain the danger in Mr. Sanders' suggested landing sites."

"Yes, captain … Based upon data from the three drones, the unpredictable levels of x-ray and gamma-ray emissions from the star will make any landing site facing the star dangerous to the health of those in the party. They will be unprotected without an atmosphere over their heads, without a magnetic field of any consequence around the planet."

Niko displayed a set of traces to emphasize her point.

"Yes, you showed me those very same charts this morning. What I see when looking at that data is a tiny chance of harmful exposure." Sanders' agitation was growing. "More than ninety-nine percent of the time, we'll be perfectly safe."

"Yes, but over the time required to visit those five sites, the chance of exposure approaches 20 percent." Niko glanced toward the end of the table and received an affirming nod from Commander Klein, Galileo's doctor.

"It's a risk I am willing to take."

"It's a risk you will not face." Niko spoke quickly, anticipating a response from Captain Hanson. "The three sites on the dark side will suffice."

"Captain." Sanders pointedly ignored Niko. "The only chance of finding a hint of past life will be on the bright side of that planet. Those three sites will be useful to the geologists, but not me."

Captain Hanson remained stone-faced. Niko responded.

"Your colleague, Mr. Crane, disagrees." She looked across the table.

"His data is preliminary, at best."

Mike Crane rolled his eyes and turned to face Sanders. "The simulations are looking better at every iteration. Before the planet became tidally locked, its rotation was at some resonant frequency to its orbit about the star. Three to two, two to one, were not sure, but my point is that it would have been over those hundreds of million years when the water was boiled away. Before that, when life had a chance, both sides of the planet were receiving equal exposure."

"And won't anything left behind be better preserved on the dark side?" Emma looked down the table at Crane.

"Without a doubt."

Sanders twisted around to face Emma. "What's your role, exactly?"

Emma smiled back. "I'll be your pilot."

"You will … You don't look like Galileo's senior pilot?"

"No, that would be Chief Warrant Officer Rashidi."

"Do you have any experience flying on or off the Earth's surface, or is the sum total of your experience with an orbit runner?"

"I've never flown an orbit runner, but I do have some experience in Earth's atmosphere … during my qualification runs … five weeks back."

The look on Sander's face was a joy for Emma to behold.

He turned his attention to the captain. "You do understand the difficulties of flying a shuttle through an extremely thin, extremely cold atmosphere?"

Captain Hanson shook his head slowly and then let his eyes rest on Emma. "I do, and so does Lieutenant Stewart. Five weeks ago, she received her qualification and, apparently, a sense of humor. Before that, she spent a year with the Royal Fleet Auxiliary, flying on and off Mars. You'll be fine."

"The op is canceled. Alpha team is heading back."

"Roger that, Sanders. I have bravo team in sight. They'll be aboard in ten minutes."

"Right behind them, Stewart."

Emma could not sit. With her nails digging into the fabric of the headrest of her seat, she stared out the cabin window. The shuttle sat on its tail. The electro-props were useless in a vacuum, so it was the only option when landing. From the flight cabin 90 meters above the dried bed of an ancient ocean and 600 kilometers from the day/night terminator, Emma looked out at the fiery display emanating from the north pole of Proxima Centauri. It was the only source of light besides that of distant stars and galaxies. Red-orange coils unfurled across the dark sky, filling her field of view side to side and rising 40 degrees above the horizon. Loops within loops reached upward toward Ursa Major, outward along the horizon, and forward toward the planet and its panicked visitors, loops in precise detail stretching, bending, twisting, and eventually reconnecting in showers of plasma. One such shower had washed over the far side of the planet, scraping the thin atmosphere from the surface and casting it above the team in sheets of brightly charged particles. That had started the panic.

Galileo was safe, hovering directly behind the planet, not far from the surface but well above the wisps of gases that wandered the valleys below. Emma had delivered the drill teams to two of the three locations on the dark side of the planet. They had spent about twelve hours at each before returning to Galileo with the core samples. Analysis would start after the last collection, once Galileo was en route to the jump point back to Barnard's Star. Three-quarters of the way through the final collection, warning of an impending flare had come. Less than an hour later, the first wave of plasma struck.

"Emma, we're on the elevator and coming up."

Niko and bravo team were back.

Emma looked to her right, out to the western horizon, seeing faint details in the landscape that had been invisible an hour earlier. Bathed in the flare's light, it reminded her of Mars four and a quarter light years away. It was an unsettling mix of fear and nostalgia.

"Damn it!"

The bouncing headlights of the second buggy appeared, carrying alpha team.

A shout came up the ladder. "Can you see them?"

Emma looked down the ladder and shouted back. "Two hundred meters out and moving fast."

After the long climb, Niko pulled herself into the cabin and then dropped into a seat to catch her breath. Gravity was higher than that on Earth.

"Can we get out here?"

"I'm not sure. That last sheet was just three kilometers up. We may have to wait this out."

"I'd rather not ... Wasn't this flare supposed to be a non-event, safely over the star's pole?"

"That's what we were told."

"Any word from Galileo?"

"No, we lost comms when they recalled the drones."

As she spoke, the cabin lit up when another sheet of particles passed overhead.

"That was three kilometers?"

Emma looked down at the console and scanned the shuttle's physical controls.

"Closer to two and a half," she said, distracted and nervous.

The set of controls acted as a backup to the computer-controlled navigational system. Precise control of a flight was impossible when using muscle.

"Did you lose control of the buggy when you were coming back?"

Niko nodded. "Once with that second shower of particles."

"Same here. The navigation system rebooted itself."

"Can you fly?" Niko's voice came out a note higher than she intended.

"With these." Emma looked back down at the controls. "At least they're still fresh in my mind ... But up there, our DNA is just one concern ... if the plasma hits us, every circuit on the shuttle may fry. We'll fall like a rock."

They locked eyes briefly and then looked out the window as the landscape brightened. A distant line of hills showed along the shore of what was once a shallow sea.

"That was two kilometers above," Niko said.

Emma did not respond. Her eyes remained on the hills even as the light faded.

"They're coming up," Niko said, watching a feed above the elevator.

She grabbed her friend's shoulder. "Emma … Emma."

Startled, Emma looked at Niko and then keyed the intercom.

"All hands prepare for launch in 60 seconds. Secure your gear as best you can, and then strap in."

"Stay up here." She said to Niko as she dropped into her seat and snapped the restraints in place. "I'll need some help."

She then put her hands on the controls and drew a deep breath.

"Everyone's secure," Niko said as she shifted to the co-pilot's seat.

The shuttle lifted slowly until it was 200 meters above the ocean bed.

"We'll need to hug the terrain most of the way back … Let's take this nice and slow."

"That's almost ten thousand kilometers."

Emma nodded silently as she dropped the nose of the shuttle ten degrees and started moving forward, using the maneuvering thrusters to maintain the angle. Slowly accelerating across the flat surface of the dried bed was relatively easy, but her immediate destination was a narrow valley that would take them south, around the planet, and away from the storms of charged particles and plasma. Following the meandering contour would be much more difficult.

On approach, she turned the shuttle about a vertical axis and cut their speed in half.

"That's is how you plan to maneuver through that valley?" Niko asked as she studied the relief map.

"Yep, one slow turn at a time … It's not as bad as it sounds. I was able to chart a course, and we have access to all the sensors. I just don't trust the navigation computer to stay up."

"Just let me know what you need."

"Will do."

Midway through the first turn, the valley was illuminated by another shower of particles.

Emma completed that maneuver and two more, remaining perfectly centered through each. As she entered the fourth, Niko's warning came a fraction of a second before she saw the problem.

"Damn it," She shouted, swiveling the shuttle to stop her turn. "The map is wrong."

The side-looking radars used by the drones to create the map had missed a hill of rubble hidden in the shadow of the valley wall. Avoiding that hill put the shuttle on a direct course for the opposite wall.

"Can you make the turn?" Stress was evident in Niko's voice.

"Nope … hold on."

Emma pulsed the engine briefly, lifting the shuttle above the valley wall.

"Too much." She cut thrust as the shuttle continued to climb over the valley.

Among the sensors she was monitoring, one showed that the flare behind them was still very active.

"Thirty seconds," she said as the shuttle started to drop, as she aligned to the next section of the valley.

A moment later, they went blind. Every feed they had been monitoring was cut off as a shower of particles engulfed the shuttle.

"We've lost everything," Niko said.

Emma nodded with her eyes locked on a horizon shrouded in twilight.

"How are the controls?"

"They're okay ... but our sensors ... they're not coming back."

"They're all fried — What can I do?" Niko's voice was firm.

"Keep an eye on the altimeter," Emma said after a pause. "And check underside feeds; maybe they survived."

Emma inserted the shuttle into the next leg of the valley with Niko's guidance. Forty minutes later, after several successful maneuvers, another shower passed overhead.

"I'm not sure, but that was much higher," Niko said. "And weaker."

"Good. Let's get out of this valley." Emma lifted the shuttle just above the lip of the valley and dropped its nose another five degrees. Their speed increased modestly. In this fashion, she slowly increased their altitude and speed, placing more of the planet between the shuttle and the star. When Galileo appeared ahead of them, she made a direct ascent. The flight down had taken forty minutes. The flight up required six hours. By that time, the flare had subsided.

Once the shuttle was secured, Galileo fired its thrusters and accelerated away from the planet and star. Both Emma and Niko stepped from the shuttle, shaking with exhaustion, Emma more so. Quinn stepped forward from a small greeting party to catch her hand as she stumbled.

"I feel sick."

With his support, she crossed the bay to a small restroom.

Near the shuttle, Doc Klein had corralled the passengers. "I've queried your dosimeters, all but you, Lieutenant Sasaki." He looked at Niko and then toward the restroom. "And Lieutenant Stewart." "It's not great, but you're all fine. I recommend you take it easy for the next few days." He stepped up to Niko and stared intently. "The same, you'll be fine. I'm taking you off duty until we leave this system. Get some rest."

Niko nodded and turned her eyes back to the restroom door as Emma came out looking worse than when she had entered. Quinn grabbed one arm as Doc Klein ran over to support her other.

"I take it you never left the shuttle?" he asked.

Emma nodded.

"It shows. Yours is only modestly higher than it should be ... all the same, I'd like to see you in medical."

Emma was unsure what he was talking about but forced a weak smile. "Sure thing, doc."

Galileo's flight to the jump point was uneventful. The planetary exploration team quickly assessed the core samples taken from the ocean beds. No indication of life was found before the samples were packaged up and prepared for transfer to a small corvette. Months later, they would receive confirmation of their initial evaluation.

Upon return to Barnard's Star, Galileo immediately turned about and attempted a connection to the binary pair of Rigil Kentaurus and Toliman, the two larger stars of the Alpha Centauri system. After three days of rest, Emma and Niko were full of energy and anxious to return to duty.

"Looking good, Harris. Just give it another minute to converge."

Petty Officer Carol Harris' eyes lingered on Joe Calvin as he spoke. Emma smiled inwardly and then shifted into her field of view.

Harris returned her attention to the interface generator as the chaotic patterns coalesced into a single clean signal matched by the sound from a small speaker. The noise spikes were a concern of the past, permanently eliminated with one of the many upgrades to the generator.

"Nice work," Calvin said as an interface formed ahead of the ship. Establishing an interface from Barnard's Star had proved trivial and a third successful connection for Harris.

Emma pushed back to allow Niko a closer view of the camera feed.

They watched Red fly through the interface and flip about to bring its relative motion to a stop.

"All clear," Calvin reported from the sensor console.

The ship accelerated through immediately after.

"As simple as that," Emma said to Niko. "Shall we head down to the Mouse Hole?"

"Lead the way." Niko opened the door for Emma.

They returned the way they had come, through the hull's central passage, through ring access, and down spoke 'C.' They were pulling themselves head-first through the spoke when warning of ring rotation was announced. In response, Emma gave Niko a brief smile and sped her transit, forcing Niko to match. Only when rotation began, when their direction of travel turned into a headfirst drop, did they grab hold of rungs to spin about.

At the ring's lower level, Niko drew a deep breath and gave Emma a questioning smile. "What has gotten into you? I believe the mentor program in place to teach safe behavior?"

Emma smiled broadly and shook her head. "The last thing you need is a mentor, and the last thing I should ever be is a mentor."

"Clearly."

She and Niko stepped onto the curving passage leading to the Mouse Hole.

Niko stopped her just before the entrance. "Before we go in, I want you to know that I had everything to do with it."

"It?"

"Yes, but please understand, I did it entirely out of malice."

Emma cringed … and smiled, and pointed to the door.

"Let's get this over with."

Niko pushed through the door and ushered Emma through.

The room was crowded, more than when they jumped into the Proxima Centauri half of the system. All were standing back, facing the door.

Applause started in the center and then spread outward.

Emma turned about and met Niko's warm smile with a cold, piercing stare, which lasted a full second before a smile slipped out. "Thank you," she mouthed.

The crowd collapsed toward them, with Emile Sanders leading the way. He stopped before Emma and Niko and paused as the room became quiet.

"I am speaking for all of us, some more than others. We owe you a debt that can never be repaid … both of you." His pointed look at Niko surprised her. "I won't cheapen the moment with thanks, so let me just say that it's an honor to have you on our team. Both of you." He smiled and turned his attention to Emma.

Applause erupted once again.

"There is a tradition," he shouted. "Within our community to commemorate accomplishments with the minting of a coin. I am happy to say that Galileo's fabricator shop was up to the task."

Emile held out two brass coins. Emma and Niko accepted. On one side was a flaring star, labeled below as "Proxima Centauri." Across the top, it read "USS Galileo - 2123." On the other was a likeness of the shuttle, framed by another inscription.

Emma smiled at the words and then raised the coin above her head. "Damn the Plasma," she shouted with bravado and then sighed deeply and lowered her voice. "Let's take this nice and slow." The crowd laughed and cheered and then fell upon the two young lieutenants.

Slowly, as the congratulations waned, those in the room returned to their workstations and began to analyze the data pouring in from an array of five drones and the ship's sensors.

Nothing the team saw was a surprise. Sitting forty-five degrees below the ecliptic plane, it was evident that the eccentric orbit of the two stars had rendered the system uninhabitable. Buried in the dense debris belt of the larger star, Rigil Kentaurus, they spotted one rock that barely qualified as a planet and another that was clearly a dwarf planet. Both were heavily cratered, and neither had a significant atmosphere. Another dwarf planet orbiting within the debris belt of Toliman had similar characteristics.

Future expeditions would be sent to verify their findings and to survey the debris belts for their mineral content. Expectations for the latter were very high. Hope remained that conditions for a successful connection between the Solar System and Alpha Centauri would improve as the orbit of Rigil Kentaurus and Toliman further separated them.

Three hours after midnight the next day, Harris established an interface, and Galileo returned to Barnard's Star. After a brief exchange with the waiting corvette, they turned toward the jump point into Ross 154 en route to Epsilon Indi.

October 22nd 2124

"Niko, I'm five minutes out. Doc Klein is monitoring stats. Move the patient to building Alpha."

"Copy that, Emma. Patient is in building Alpha. Storm is subsiding."

"We're coming in hard. Clear the pad."

"Pad clear."

The shuttle rose briefly and then dropped like a rock as they raced past dark clouds on the right.

Emma winced as the young corpsman sitting behind her emptied his stomach on the pitching deck.

"Oh hell … sorry." He retched again.

That patch of wind shear was unavoidable, but the direct feed of Doppler data gave Emma a 3-D image of surrounding wind speeds, allowing her to maneuver past the last of the turbulence.

They broke through the final bank of water-filled clouds, and she vectored the electro-props under each wing downward, bringing the shuttle's flight level with the ground. A field of narrowly spaced yardangs passed beneath, long strips of gray rock separated by gray sand. Far to the left, an ancient impact crater spread to the horizon, holding a sea of drifting sand. Ahead was Research Station Atacama, three rows of Quonset huts sitting at a high latitude in the northern hemisphere, wedged between the high desert they were flying over and the Kalunga Sea. Both were devoid of life. The entire planet was devoid of life. It was an extraordinary find for Galileo.

The planet, 36 Ophiuchi-C Two, orbited its parent star at seven-tenths AU, a little less than the orbit of Venus, centered in the habitable zone but safely outside the tidal lock radius for Ophiuchi-

C. It had a thick atmosphere of nitrogen and carbon dioxide, with a hint of oxygen; a strong magnetic field that promised to keep the atmosphere in place for millions of years; surface gravity that was nine-tenths of Earth's; and temperatures that were livable across the latitudes, although high compared to Earth. Niko called it a clean slate, a near-perfect environment where life had never developed.

Sand-filled water surged through a wide gorge above the research station, cutting a channel through the dunes and across the beach before pushing into the heavy surf. The gorge had been dry for several years, according to the geology team. The flash flood surprised two researchers returning to the station from the foothills above. One was unharmed; the other was the reason for the hurried flight down from Galileo.

Emma came in fast, blasting water and mud in all directions. She cut the engines as soon as the shuttle settled on its gear. Doc Klein and Corpsman Craig raced under the opening hatch and into building Alpha. Niko exited the building and stopped at the edge of the landing pad to adjust her oxygen mask. Emma powered down and stepped out into the cool mist that had followed behind a driving rain. Washed-out sand and small stones covered much of the pad. Small rivulets were still running through the mess. A small earth mover was returning to scrape the pad clean.

"How is he?"

"Alive and stable. We have him in an oxygen tent." Niko took a deep breath, fogging her mask as she exhaled. "Commander Klein should know more in a moment."

Her tropical uniform was soaked, her hair a tangled mess, and her bare legs were coated in the fine sand that had formed the dunes around Atacama.

"They were bringing back core samples when the storm hit. It was not supposed to be that strong. We were all surprised."

Emma gestured toward the building. They both started in that direction.

"We're four jumps from home and an actual medical facility. That's twenty days, ten if we want to kill ourselves. Doc is the only option."

An ensign handed Niko a towel as they stepped through the second door into the dimly lit space and

popped off their masks.

"Damn it. We need lights."

The ensign nodded quickly. "They're running another line now."

The compact fusion generator worked flawlessly through the storm, but the supply lines and supports had torn loose as the winds peaked.

"Commander Klein?"

He turned toward Emma and Niko. "He'll be fine, beat to hell, but nothing that won't heal."

"Oh, thank God," Niko said. "I was afraid we had killed him with that sedative."

"No, no, you made the right decision. I'll let him sleep for another hour before we move him to the shuttle."

He looked at Emma. "I'll contact you when we're ready."

Emma let out the breath she was holding. "Thanks, doc. Standing by."

She and Niko passed through the mudroom into a small mess. The room was empty. They sat down next to a bank of windows facing out toward the sea. The thunder of crashing waves easily penetrated the prefabricated structure. Off to the right, an electrician had reconnected a line to the generator and was attaching it to a supporting pole.

A wave of relief passed over both.

Emma smiled at her old roommate. "Keeping busy?"

Niko shook her head at Emma, eyes narrowed. "Yes, but not with anything interesting, none of what you promised."

"Did I promise?"

"Yes, you did. Join me on Galileo, be the first to see new life forms, blah, blah, blah."

"I definitely didn't say that last part … and that was over a year ago."

Niko shrugged. "It's nice to see you."

"Sorry, I don't get down that often. The station seems pretty self-sufficient now."

"Well, not with food." Niko looked pointedly at Emma.

"Galileo is suffering alongside you, but supplies are on the way. New staff also."

"Don't get me wrong," Niko said, looking out at the clouds. "This planet is a dream come true, and there has been some interesting work figuring out how to make it habitable. That supply ship should be carrying cyanobacteria samples engineered from the data we sent back."

"Algae," she said to answer Emma's questioning look.

"It's a nice challenge, but this is the fifth planet that humans have visited, and still not a hint of life, current or fossilized. I'm spending most of my time helping Commander Davis run this station, and trust me, it's not fun."

Emma smiled knowingly.

Niko gestured toward the electrician, who waved and pointed toward the generator. She gave him a thumbs up as he reset the breaker. The lights in the mess came back up.

"Have you heard about Naomi?" Niko asked with a smile that bordered on a laugh.

"No, nothing recently," Emma said, curious.

Niko waited to speak, teasing.

"This must be good," Emma said.

"She joined the SEALs."

"Naomi?" Emma practically shouted.

Niko nodded. "Well, she's in training now … the odds are she'll fail out."

Emma bent her head in thought. "She was always in better shape than the rest of us, and didn't you tell me once that she was frighteningly good in basic combat?"

"I did … it's weird; she's a bit of a klutz."

"How are the two of you doing?" Emma asked soberly.

"Oh, we're great," Niko said sincerely. "Not together, if that's what you're asking. She mentioned some guy a few messages back, before SEAL training, a civilian — Oh … check the weather."

Emma paused briefly. "Damn it. Looks like we'll be cutting our visit short."

She sent a note to Doc Klein, and he confirmed.

"Hopefully, Copernicus has no better luck finding any life," Niko said, returning to the previous conversation.

Emma laughed aloud. "Okay, I did promise that you would be the first. We'll wish for an engine failure." She thought of Anay.

Niko looked out at the surf. "Maybe a small one. I'm not overly concerned that they'll find anything; the chance of life around Sirius is slim. Same for Epsilon Eridani."

"Ah, right. That's next on their list."

"Any word on funding for the next phase?" Niko asked with a mischievous smile.

Emma had an inside track for all information regarding the rapidly developing plans to terraform Ophiuchi-C Two and was aware of the broader discussions regarding the greater solar neighborhood. It wasn't a simple case of having access to data unavailable to those outside her family. Emma's grandfather insisted that she keep an active, if remote, role in the family business. He called her the perfect field representative.

She returned Niko's smile. "I certainly do."

No one within her command had complained about her side job. She suspected her careless protection of family secrets had more to do with that than anything else.

"Only five nations have signed on so far, with China taking on the greatest burden. Debt from Mars is keeping many others on the sidelines, that, and the distance." She rolled her eyes and pitched her hands up. "It's a few days further. I don't see the problem … Anyway, my family will have a greater share than we had on Mars. In fact, there should be a pair of transports coming our way, based on yesterday's message drop. I think they're banking upon your success here." She pointed at Niko.

"Lieutenant Stewart, prep the shuttle. We're bringing him out. If he wakes, he wakes."

They both received. Emma acknowledged Doc Klein as they stood and started fitting their masks.

Emma had the shuttle powering up and the rear door lifting as they exited the building.

After crossing the sand to the edge of the landing pad, she paused awkwardly and shouted to Niko through the mask, "Gotta go."

Niko's laugh was muffled but audible. "You know you sound a lot like Quinn."

Emma opened her mouth to speak but chose to shake her head as she continued across the pad.

Emma attached the shuttle to the starboard dock and remained in the cabin until the patient was offloaded. She was powering down when she received a message from Captain Hanson.

"Lieutenant Stewart, join me in the wardroom as soon as possible."

With Galileo in a stable orbit, the ship's ring was rotating. She pushed her way forward through the center hull and then dropped down spoke 'A,' skipping hand grips until the increasing gee force made that dangerous. She entered the wardroom to find the captain, most officers, and several enlisted in the middle of a discussion.

"Stewart." The captain waved her to a seat.

"To bring you up to speed, the supply ship is missing. They were supposed to follow Sunfish through the jump from Gliese 674 but failed. Sunfish popped back and found nothing."

"Uh-oh," Emma said with a small smile.

The captain nodded, "Yes, uh-oh."

"You already know what happened?" Lieutenant Commander Fedorov, the engineering officer, asked.

Emma nodded. "Yes, ma'am, the only thing that could have happened. They mistakenly jumped to Ophiuchi-A, maybe B, probably not."

"Why haven't they returned?" Now, the captain was testing her.

"Probably the same reason we struggled. It's a binary in an unfortunate arrangement. We were lucky, lucky that Petty Officer Calvin joined our crew."

Calvin sat at the end of the table with Petty Officer Harris at his side. Emma nodded in their direction. "Sad to say, the state of the science makes us dependent on an individual's skill, and I have no confidence in the training handed out to a civilian operator on a small supply vessel … What's her name, sir?"

"The …" The captain looked at the floor, shaking his head. "The Rum Runner."

Emma let out a laugh and was joined by many in the room. "That is, at least, part of the problem."

The captain waited a moment for the noise to drop. "Okay, we were discussing the options we have available. One requires you and Petty Officer Calvin to take the shuttle, meet Sunfish, and go to their rescue. That has some obvious problems."

Emma nodded. "Maybe a trip isn't necessary. The interface generator creates files —"

"Stop right there," the captain said. "Lieutenant Martinez made that suggestion, and Calvin was explaining why that won't work when you walked through the door."

She looked at Quinn, and he gave her a big cheesy smile. The captain gestured for Calvin to continue.

"The problem with the data is that it's only useful to the ship that created it. It can recreate a previous state of that ship's interface generator. If you want to execute a previous jump, all you need to do is load that state, and you're set. However, the data, the values, are of no use to another ship."

Calvin was looking at Emma as he spoke. Now that he was silent, the rest of the wardroom turned their attention her way.

"Um"

"Uh … what would it take to convert the numbers for Rum Runner?"

"We would need the factory measurements for their generator and all deviations after installation. If we could convert our data to a generic set, we could combine the two and make something they could use. That gives us two problems: we don't have their factory data, and I have no idea how to convert our data. It would take a programmer, a good one."

"Don't look at me," Quinn said as he held up his hands.

"Anyone?" the captain asked. "Anyone aboard?"

A moment of silence passed before Emma spoke. "There is one on the planet, quite good, I'm told. Sam Nowak. He's been helping the research staff."

"That could solve the easy part, but we'd still need Rum Runner's data," the captain said.

"Maybe not," Emma said. "Sam should be able to create something that accepts and converts a data set in any direction. Our data could be converted to generic data by removing any deltas, and the crew of Rum Runner could take that generic data and convert it for their use by adding the deltas from their drive."

She turned her attention to Calvin. "Will they have access to that information?"

"Absolutely ... but we should probably include detailed instructions."

"Was Sunfish able to contact them?"

"No," the captain said. "They were having trouble forming a connection."

"Hmm, we should give them the data also."

"Sounds like we have a plan," the captain said. "Calvin, contact Sam Nowak and see what he will need. Thank you all. Dismissed."

She and Quinn stepped aside as people filed out of the room.

"How do you think of these things?" he asked.

"Oh, you were heading in the same direction."

"Maybe, but I gave up as soon as 'no' came out of Calvin's mouth."

"Eh, it's my system. I should know a little more about it than most."

Quinn shook his head. "Feel free to take credit when it's due," he said with a hint of admonishment.

Three days later, Rum Runner jumped into the system and set course for the second planet.

"Sensor, bridge, we've received a request from Rum Runner for a full set of … Calvin files?"

"Bridge, sensor, Aye?"

The sensor space was usually empty. Galileo had adopted a long-term, stable orbit. Any debris that posed a threat had been identified months earlier, and Sunfish remained near, acting as an extra set of eyes. Emma was there with Harris, reviewing the maintenance logs after a discrepancy was noted. Petty Officer Calvin was assisting.

"Calvin files? I thought you renamed them."

Calvin looked apologetic. "I did … they were called 'calvin1, calvin2,' and so on. I removed the numbers and appended the system names."

Emma smiled and shook her head. "I'm not sure that's what I meant at the time. Will they be useful to them? Most of the jumps are straightforward."

"Sure, I use that information whenever possible, although we haven't repeated many jumps. They shave a few minutes off the convergence time … and probably a lot more for a ship like Rum Runner."

"Do their operators need more training?" Emma asked.

"Well, probably, but I was thinking of the equipment. No ships outside the Galileo class have better sensors, not even the explorers."

Okay, package them up and check with Sunfish. They may want them also."

"Yes, ma'am." Calvin pushed back from the terminal where Emma and Harris were reviewing logs and pulled himself to another.

"And try coming up with a better name," Emma said.

January 19th 2125

Emma banked the shuttle in a slow, lazy curve, protecting the booms extending outward near the back of each wing. Four more passes and her shift would be over, but with Atacama Station on the far side of the planet, the return trip would add significantly to her air time. Nine kilometers up, with Ophiuchi-C on the horizon, the planet was beautiful. A winding coastline of inlets and peninsulas marked the border between a rugged land mass of brown and gray and the deep blue of the Karkinian Sea. Scattered islands reached out toward deeper water. She gazed downward, regretting the day she had volunteered to pilot a shuttle back on Mars.

The routine had not varied for two months. Take the shuttle up, ladened with nitric acid, go to her assigned region in the higher latitudes, and release her cargo as an aerosol, usually between seven and twelve kilometers up, wherever the meteorologist said. It was painfully dull and likely to continue until Galileo returned to Earth for refurbishment in another three months. A month earlier, the experiment was nearing its scheduled end date as the supply of nitric acid shipped from Earth dwindled, but her hope of an end fell apart when a small refinery came online at Atacama.

She couldn't complain about the success of the experiment. Three shuttles and six pilots had brought the temperature in the upper latitudes of the northern hemisphere down almost two degrees. It was noticed and appreciated by everyone at Atacama Station, but the effect would disappear as soon as they stopped; the clouds would thicken, and the temperature would return to its miserable normal.

A quick query to traffic control gave her the position of two inbound heavy-lift shuttles that had just arrived aboard the Rum

Runner. Both were as large as the smaller space-based ships that moved personnel and materials between Earth, the Moon, and occasionally Mars. Disassembled, several shuttles sized like hers could be carried in the bay of one. Their capacity was close to that of one of the freight cars that made continuous runs up and down the elevators of Earth. Growth within the Ophiuchi system was accelerating. With it came an unquenchable need for material. A survey team had arrived a week earlier to select the locations for three planned elevators. Like Earth, two would remain in the planning phase until the first was operational. Until that time, they would rely on shuttles.

The pilots servicing Ophiuchi had adopted the same rules used on Earth when approaching or leaving the surface. Never fire the main drive until you are over open ocean. Numerous grass fires and several forest fires had not been enough, but after a family of four was lost while driving home from vacation, those practices had become rules and were enforced with a vengeance. It was the final shuttle launched from the short-lived facility near her family's ranch.

Emma looked upward. Hidden behind the deep blue, the two would pass overhead in another minute. With a deep breath, she cast away thoughts of a career change and checked the starboard camera monitoring the boom on that side of the shuttle. It was okay, but as she watched, an aurora flared on the horizon. The pinks and blues were faint against the sky, barely visible, but the purples showed clearly. Together, they were a shocking sight during daylight hours.

As she watched the little display, a sheet of purple fell across the path of her shuttle.

"Damn it."

She shut off the flow of nitric acid and ordered the booms to retract as she put the shuttle into a steep descent.

"HL-44, check your six. I'm in the middle of it."

The purple sheet, above and below, disappeared as HL-25, the second of the two shuttles, broke atmosphere in the distance.

"This is HL-44. Who … oh … Sorry, Miss Stewart. We have broken off descent."

She heard a hint of panic in the message.

'Miss Stewart?' Nobody called her that besides her mother, and that was a rare event. Her brother, Ian, had always been the troublemaker.

It took only a moment for her to realize the cause of the pilot's reaction.

"Traffic control, please confirm ownership of the shuttle that just tried to fry me."

"Hi, Emma. It's yours."

"Yeah, that's what I figured. Thanks, Jake."

"But don't blame them. It's all on us … or the software team. They pushed an update twenty minutes ago, and we haven't been able to establish new links."

"They pushed an update with two inbound heavy-lift shuttles?"

"They did, and once they back it out and get everything working, they'll be visiting Commander Davis."

"Good. I may have a few words for them when I get back."

"If you could, find me first. I'd love to listen in."

"No problem."

"While I have you, are you free to break your pattern? Leonardo has requested a passenger pick-up, mother and daughter. I've uploaded the course."

"I've already broken the pattern and would happily do anything else."

A moment of confusion passed quickly as Emma set the shuttle on course and considered the request.

"Jake, did Rachael just give birth?"

"She certainly did, Emma. You'll be meeting Rana Karkinian Zhōu, three kilograms of healthy, happy baby."

"That's a first. I'm on my way, ETA 38 minutes."

"I'll pass that on."

It was a first. The first birth on Ophiuchi and, more significantly, the first birth outside the Solar System, outside the orbit of Earth. More than thirty years on Mars had not resulted in one, although restrictions at that time had discouraged pregnancies on that planet. Such restrictions were unreasonable within the Ophiuchi System. A level of independence was necessary for a colony so far from home.

Emma circled the small maritime research vessel with electro-props only. They had dropped anchor a hundred meters from a small island, more like a large rock. The landing surface looked smooth, likely due to waves washing over it, but neither wave nor wind would be a problem for the landing. A mild, overland breeze had flattened the sea as far as Emma could see.

As she shut down the engines, a small launch detached from the Leonardo and crossed the short expanse of water. She met them at the water's edge, catching the nylon line and bringing the nose snug against the rock.

"Hey, Emma." Rachael waved with one arm, holding Rana with the other.

The coxswain hopped to shore, set Rachael's bags down, and rolled out a length of non-skid before using a second rope to bring the stern against the rock. Rachael stepped out and climbed to dry rock before Emma could lend a hand.

"I take it Rana isn't yet ready for a life at sea?" Emma asked as the boat motored away.

"Oh no, she was perfectly content. It was the captain that felt differently … and the doctors back at Atacama."

Rachael turned to bring Rana close to Emma. "She's going to be famous, and they don't trust her in the hands of sailors."

Emma peered closely at the sleeping face, smiling warmly. She was impressed by the situation but did not feel any of the maternal instincts that Rachael was showing. She had been the same around her younger cousins, considering them more of an annoyance, particularly when she had been pressed into service as the babysitter.

"Ready to go?"

Rachael nodded vigorously as they turned toward the shuttle.

May 21st 2125

The promotion ceremony transitioned into its fourth hour. Thankfully, they had provided chairs; sadly, they were only offered to the spectators. Emma, Quinn, and Irene Fedorov were waiting behind the last of a long list of enlisted personnel. "Last but least," Quinn had said. It was understandable; they had been away from Earth for an extended period, while the Navy had been rapidly promoting as part of the expansion.

Those from Galileo had spent most of the last year on a half-gee ring and were still recovering the strength in their legs. It was a cruel reward, standing at parade rest for the duration of the ceremony. Both Galileo and Kepler were attached to Jarvis Station. Each had only a skeleton crew, with the remainder at the ceremony on the station's habitation ring. It would've been even longer if most of the research staff had not remained on Ophiuchi-C Two.

As a full commander, Irene was to be the executive officer aboard the USS Fredericksburg, one of the new destroyers. Lieutenant Commander Quinn Martinez was to be the commanding officer of the USS Batfish, a much smaller ship. Both ships would fall under the United Nations Space Force umbrella. Emma, a full lieutenant, had yet to be reassigned, but new orders were inevitable.

"Abby, I didn't realize you were on the station."

The reception was growing more crowded by the minute. Emma led her old friend to a table where Quinn waited comfortably in a chair, talking with another lieutenant commander.

"I'm assigned to Fredericksburg," Abby said. "We just returned from our shakedown cruise."

"How did it go?"

Abby shrugged and smiled narrowly.

"Lieutenant Stewart," Quinn's friend said with surprise. "Congratulations on the promotion."

"Thank you, commander."

"Have you received new orders yet?"

Emma suspected she was about to receive an offer.

"We were just about to talk about that," Quinn said quickly.

"We were?"

He nodded.

"I met Anay here last October," Abby said in Emma's other ear. "He was with Lucas, getting ready for their trip to Sirius."

"Oh, that's great; I do miss him. How was he?"

"Okay, I guess. He was looking forward to the trip."

Emma nodded and turned back to Quinn with a questioning look. "I'm listening."

"Well, that's good. You have Captain Hanson's recommendation for this position and, obviously, mine."

"Batfish?"

He nodded. "Executive officer."

Abby grabbed her shoulder.

Emma shook her head. "I don't have the experience."

"Sure, you do. She has a crew of 12; the position calls for a full lieutenant, and we do require a pilot."

Emma looked back at Abby, who nodded excitedly.

"Think it over," Quinn said. "Take your time. I'll give you a minute."

Emma smiled. "Uh … uh … how much time do I have left?"

Quinn said nothing.

"Sure, it sounds fantastic. Thank you ... sir."

"You're welcome, XO."

"Congratulations, Lieutenant," Abby said, gripping Emma's shoulder and arm.

"Thanks, Abby."

"We'll be meeting Copernicus," Quinn said. "Who knows."

Emma's smile tightened. Ensign Anay Mason — This is never going to work.

September 18th 2125

"Who has eight?" Captain Quinn Martinez turned his head toward Petty Officer Angela Brown. Her tall, lanky figure stretched horizontally to the comm station, and her long dark ponytail floated freely behind her head.

"Miller has eight; Mascord has nine."

"Only counting those on first look, right?" Mascord asked.

"Right, any found after the first hour won't count."

"How about habitable planets?" Quinn asked.

"The usual: nine zeros, one for Lieutenant Stewart, one for Ensign Zhào, Five for Petty Officer Mascord, and a no vote for Chief."

Chief Ezra Andersen met Quinn's glance with narrowed eyes and a hardened jaw.

The combined fleets of interstellar ships from Earth, sixteen in all, had visited 43 systems to date. Limited by a jump distance near eight lightyears, the pattern of stars visited looked more like a pair of trees than an even sphere, a pair of trees branching at a right angle to each other, with Barnard's Star forming one trunk and Wolf 359 forming the second.

Since Ophiuchi, no planet had been found with even the remote possibility of being made habitable, and not one had been found with any evidence of life, past or present. The scientific community was not surprised. The consensus opinion painted the formation of Ophiuchi-C Two as an unlikely fluke, and they consider the chance of a similar find this close to Earth to be very small. The crew had higher expectations, but those were waning. With each barren, lifeless system that they visited, hope faded.

"Chief, when you're ready."

"Aye, sir. All stations report."

"Engineering is ready."

"Drones are ready, both Red and Blue."

"Sensors ready," Emma said, looking at Chief Andersen from her station.

"Comms ready," Brown said.

"And the helm is ready," Mascord said.

Andersen returned his attention to Quinn. "The ship is ready, captain."

"Very well. Helm, open a connection into 82 G. Eridani."

Mascord triggered the interface generator and started the long process of opening the first connection into a star system. Quinn eventually broke the silence.

"82 G dot Eridani. Who thinks of these names?"

Three of the other four on the bridge turned questioningly toward their captain. Mascord's eyes and hands were busy.

"Is there a complexity requirement that nobody told me about? Must start with a number; must have at least three spaces."

"It's more a designation than a name, sir," Brown said.

"We should come up with something better. As the first visitors, it's our right … our responsibility to give it an appropriate name." Quinn waited for the argument that never came.

Batfish had similarities to Galileo but was easily differentiated by a dark, non-reflective coating that made her difficult to spot against a field of stars and by her overall dimensions. Without a rotational ring, her protective hull was narrow with respect to her length but kept the teardrop shape. The length was less, but not by as much as Emma had expected on the day she first crossed the ship's brow. The long, linear array of magnetic coils, stretching fore to aft, was necessary for their mission, providing both range and increased acceleration when needed. It was a very large ship for a crew of twelve.

The lack of a ring was a regular complaint among the crew, particularly when the ship was in orbit. Without a ring, they relied on acceleration to provide a semblance of gravity. No one ever fully adjusted to zero-gee, and the longer it lasted, the longer the transition when the ship resumed acceleration.

Complaining, good-natured complaining, was part of life aboard a ship, although not something Emma had noticed to the same degree aboard Galileo. Perhaps it was the missing ring, the limited meal choices, or the added responsibilities that fall upon a smaller crew. Perhaps it was a captain who wholeheartedly encouraged the practice, a captain who wholeheartedly engaged in the practice. It was rare to hear a set of discontented words not first uttered by Quinn. The phrase 'A bitching sailor is a happy sailor' had become a paradigm aboard Batfish.

Unspoken was the loneliness that Emma sensed in those aboard the ship. They were far from home, further than anyone had ventured to date. They were far from any other ship in yet another lifeless system. These were good reasons but not the overriding factors. Twelve was a tiny number on a ship the size of Batfish. Empty passages and empty spaces were normal, something she had only seen on Galileo at a late hour.

A twenty-four-hour clock was a standard for all ships, regardless of nationality. The crew maintained a day-night schedule with regular business hours aligning with the day. Drills, maintenance, administrative activities, and meals were kept to those hours, leaving sleep, exercise, and leisure for the nights. Simultaneously, the crew followed an 18-hour routine set by a three-section watch, six hours for each. This continuously shifted a section's watch around the twenty-four-hour day, providing change essential to morale. Meals, breakfast, lunch, and dinner were scheduled to overlap the change of the watch. This encouraged the crew to gather. Emma looked forward to each meal, more often for the company than the food. The oncoming and off-going sections were often treated to a meal by members of the third section. If nothing else, it was a regular source of additional complaints.

Movie time was the only other reason for the crew to be together, always at the same time after the evening meal. Three large screens covered the walls within the combined mess. They were set to scroll through images and videos throughout the day and night. The scenes from the natural world had gradually ceded to those from urban environments. A thoroughfare, crowded with pedestrians, had become a welcome sight. At the selected hour, a film was sent to the larger display centered on the back wall while the side displays were shut down and the lights dimmed. The ritual attracted all free crewmembers, usually the eight off-duty. Part of that ritual was the discussion that followed; the worse the movie, the better the conversation.

Emma kept silent as Quinn spun about in zero gravity, unwilling to give him the satisfaction of an argument.

He looked at her and then toward the others sitting at their battle stations. "How about —"

"It's converging," Mascord said, sharp enough to cut off the sentence.

"That was quick." Quinn keyed the intercom. "All hands, stand ready."

As they watched, the familiar ghostly circle formed in front of Batfish.

"Chief, send in the drones."

"Yes, sir. Red away … Blue away."

"All clear," Emma reported a moment later.

"Take us through, helm; two gees."

Batfish passed through the interface without issue. Quinn allowed the navigation and sensor systems to reorient up and down to match the ecliptic plane.

"Spread the drones, chief. Let me know what we have, Stewart."

Emma waited as the streaming data from the two drones combined with that from Batfish's sensor suite.

The ship sat far above the ecliptic plane with barely a trace of dust within 300 million kilometers. From that vantage point, the planets and belts were clearly visible to the spreading array of sensors.

"I see … twelve planets and two significant belts."

"Did anyone have twelve?" Quinn asked.

"Petty Officer Howard. That makes three in a row for her," Brown answered.

"So unfair," Mascord said, exaggerating his anger as he smiled at Brown.

"The inner planets match predictions," Emma said as she continued her analysis. "Three in a tight orbit about the star and three larger planets outside those. Beyond the smaller belt, I see a gas giant, three ice giants, and two smaller rocks in outer orbits, one inside and one outside the larger belt."

"Do both of those rocks qualify as planets?" Mascord asked.

"Sorry, Mascord. They do."

"So close. I —"

"Spectral analysis shows an elevated oxygen level around the fifth planet."

The bridge fell silent.

"How elevated?" Quinn asked.

"Over twenty percent," Emma said, flashing bright eyes toward Quinn.

"How about chlorophyll."

"I ... a ... never mind that. The planet is green."

Emma brought up an enhanced image for the bridge crew. The northern icecap was centered. On one side of the cap, they only saw darkness, but on the sunny side, a large wedge of green and blue showed south of the ice.

The bridge crew exchanged excited glances, waiting on Quinn.

"The Copernicus is three systems back, wrapping up in Epsilon Eridani." Quinn unfastened his restraining belt and floated free from the captain's chair. "They'll rendezvous with a supply vessel in Luyten and then head our way. That gives us about ten days before we need to jump back through this point and give our report. Helm, how much time will we need to make orbit and return."

"At one gee? Just over ten days, captain."

Quinn did not hesitate. "One point two gees it is. We'll make a single pass, return, jump into Gliese 1061, and pass the good news to Copernicus."

No one complained.

Batfish assumed a polar orbit around 82 G. Eridani Five, the fifth planet from the star. She had dropped down the dark side and was about to break into the light of day over the southern pole. By Terran standards, the planet was huge, 4.5 times the mass of Earth and 2.7 times the surface area, with a surface gravity of 1.65 gees.

On approach, they had only glimpsed the biosphere south of the northern cap, but what little they had seen had every crew member, on and off watch, staring at a display. Those not on watch were gathered in the mess, watching the ice of the southern pole pass below the ship as they approached the day/night terminator.

Both drones had dropped below the ship to assume lower, decaying orbits parallel to that of Batfish. They would use their thrusters to avoid the planet's atmosphere. At that distance, their optical sensors would closely match those on the Batfish when surveying the surface, and their Lidar would give the crew a view under the thick forest canopy and the ocean surface.

They were not at battle stations, but Quinn had assumed the conn so Emma could operate the sensor station and train Petty Officer Howard on the unique set of routines she had loaded for the pass above the planet.

"The ice cap is small, giving way to tundra already."

Emma had routed the optical feeds from the two drones and Batfish to displays on the bridge and mess. All but the lone engineering watch had access to a display.

Ahead, the solid white was replaced by a mottled green and brown landscape with veins of stark white forming a fractal pattern stretching out to the horizon.

"What's causing that?" Quinn asked.

"Frozen rivulets," Emma said without bothering to zoom the ship's telescope. "It's summer at this end of the planet."

Pattern recognition software was added to Batfish's array of tools before leaving the Solar System. That software would process the broad images from the ship's telescope for signs of life and prompt the drones to focus on any detections. Emma intended a hands-off approach until something of greater interest was found. Her wait was short.

"What's Red looking at?" Howard asked. The feed on the left display showed an empty parcel of the tundra.

Emma zoomed until tracks in the mucky ground became obvious. She followed them for several kilometers until six four-legged animals appeared, plodding eastward.

"About the size of elks."

As Emma spoke, the second drone was directed to a pair of cat-like creatures trailing a half-kilometer behind the group. That feed quickly split to show a second pair waiting ahead behind a small grass-covered hill.

The crew watched and waited as the elks approached the trap, and the scene grew distant, drifting behind the ship and drones. Without warning, the drones were redirected to a much larger herd of the same four-legged animals to the north.

"Damn it," Mascord said.

"Bad luck, Mascord." Emma afforded a quick look in his direction.

The feeds shifted again and then again. The program was designed to capture brief snippets of life and then move to the next. The landscape was transitioning from a relatively flat tundra into one comprised of hills covered in evergreen trees. The numbers and varieties of life were rapidly multiplying.

"Can you gauge the size of those trees?" Quinn asked, pointing at the feed from Blue.

"One moment," Emma said as she directed Blue's Lidar.

A clear, multicolored image of a small section of trees appeared. As she rotated it to view from the side, it lost its sharp contrast but provided an easy answer to Quinn's question.

"They're short, between five and ten meters ... not surprising on a high-gravity world."

Quinn nodded absently as his eyes darted from one display to the next.

The continent continued without interruption, although a distant coastline could be seen to the west. The hills had dropped down to a vast plain, and the rate at which images flashed by on the displays grew to a dizzying pace.

"Stop there," Quinn said, startling the others on the bridge.

The image that had caught his attention had already passed, but Emma had no trouble finding it. She took manual control of Red and directed it back to a herd of animals crossing a wide river. They numbered in the thousands, with most being the size of young elephants, with coloring that had a likeness to that of a tiger, although muted. Each broke into a charge near the water's edge, splashing across the shallow water and then leaping forward as it became deep. From there, their awkward, panicked crossing kicked up a white froth. The reason for their panic showed a moment later. The head of a much larger creature emerged from the water, grabbed one of the striped elephants in its mouth, and disappeared below the water.

"Oh, shit," Mascord shouted.

"Glad we're in orbit, Mascord," Quinn said, keeping his eyes on the screen.

As they continued to watch, a second from the herd was taken, and then a third. Emma returned the control of Red to the program, and it switched away from the carnage and joined Blue, rapidly cycling through images. A long silence was broken by the voices of four on the bridge shouting "Stop" simultaneously.

It was unnecessary as Emma was already returning Blue to the image of interest.

"I thought things were supposed to be smaller on this planet," Quinn said, his head twisted slightly in Emma's direction, but his eyes locked on the left screen.

"Are those dinosaurs?" Howard asked.

"They're the size of … No, they're much bigger," Emma said. "This one is standing almost twenty meters above the ground." She circled one on the display. "Four legs like every other animal so far … That's curious on its own." She relinquished control of Blue as the expansive plain ended abruptly at a ridgeline that stretched from the western coast to the eastern horizon. The ground climbed into a thick but sharply-define bank of clouds, obscuring all surface details under Batfish and its two drones. Looking ahead, Emma saw that the clouds were growing thin and disappearing. Beyond was the deep green of a tropical forest.

For several minutes, not a sign of life was detected. All three feeds showed the billowy clouds passing below. When Blue finally snapped to a new location, all heads turned to its display. Nothing but a few wisps in the upper atmosphere and forest below could be seen until Blue zoomed in on a flight of birds just above the treetops based upon the shadows they cast.

"I hate to ask, but how big are those, Lieutenant Stewart."

Emma met Quinn's concerned look with a playful smile.

"Each wingspan is greater than 15 meters."

"I was afraid of that … Feeling relieved that we don't have a shuttle on this ship?"

Emma shrugged, maintaining the same smile. "I'm not so sure. Nothing I have ever seen can compare to this. I —"

She returned her eyes to the display as the five birds tucked into a dive and disappeared under the canopy. Moments later, all five rose above the leaves. Three twisted away, each holding a human-sized tree climber in a claw. The empty-clawed two pursued. One of the three made a clean escape with its prey. The other two were left with dismembered scraps.

"You were saying …"

Emma turned wide-eyed and silent toward Quinn, keeping her mouth shut, fearing what might come out.

"Sorry," Quinn said with honest sympathy. "Get a scan with the Lidar … I'm guessing the trees will be much taller than we saw in the last scan."

Emma turned away and triggered the Lidar on Red.

Half the crew had watched the birds pull apart the primates with indifference. It was gory but not beyond the realm of what they had seen on Earth, just at a larger scale. What they saw under the canopy could not be dismissed as easily and would not be forgotten. As Quinn suspected, the trees were much larger. The canopy sat 140 meters above the floor of the forest.

In addition, the Lidar showed some of the inhabitants living below the cover of leaves. The one that had captured the crew's attention was nearly as large as one of the trees. From image to image, like a many-legged insect from home, it wound its way through the forest, 50 to 80 meters above the floor, with a meal the size of a school bus struggling and failing to break its grasp.

With some relief, Batfish and her drones passed over the coastline. Offshore, a pod of whale-like creatures was detected. A final Lidar scan before the drones returned to Batfish showed that the ocean dwellers dwarfed the nightmare they had seen in the forest. This worried no one.

Once the drones were secured in their bays, Batfish accelerated toward the distant jump point.

November 11th 2125

"82 G dot Eridani Five. Who thinks of these names?"

Emma floated silently just inside the small bridge, waiting to relieve Quinn. Almost two months had passed since their discovery of the world below.

"There must be some complexity requirement that nobody told me about. Must start with a number; must have at least three spaces."

Still waking up, she gave Quinn a weak smile. "This sounds familiar."

The crew of Batfish remained in a three-shift rotation, with one officer and three enlisted for each shift. They were hovering far above the planet's north pole. From there, they maintained continuous communications with Copernicus as she followed a low orbit above the equator.

"It's a valid question," Quinn said.

"Are you certain, captain?" Petty Officer Brown asked. "Nothing has changed since the last time you asked it."

Emma smiled at Brown and then shook her head slowly in Quinn's direction. "I've known you for two years now? Just over, and I still haven't figured out how you were given command of a ship, given your … unique personality."

"Oh, that should be obvious. I reserve this personality for only the most deserving, those who have earned my pity."

Emma stifled a yawn.

"Yes, sir. Of course."

"And don't you think 'Aye, Captain' sounds better?"

Emma took a deep breath. "This sippy cup isn't going to be enough. Has Sunfish arrived?"

"Yes, a couple of hours ago. They're holding at the Gliese jump point for the initial evaluation. Copernicus should have it ready soon."

"Satellites deployed?"

"One. They're preparing the others."

Emma's section floated in the passage, waiting as she took the command seat from Captain Martinez. The main display was looking down on the planet. It was late spring in the northern hemisphere. Light from 82 Eridani bathed a tiny icecap and the surrounding forest, dark green like most other landmasses on the planet; blue oceans and swirling patterns of white clouds filled the image. A small icon showed the position of Copernicus.

"So, they're actually going down?"

"That's the plan. They selected a small barren island 300 kilometers east of the large continent. That's about five hours of flight for one of those birds."

"Captain." There was a note of alarm in Chief Ezra Andersen's voice, not something Emma had ever heard. All talk stopped.

"Something is rising from the planet."

Quinn spun about and looked toward the image.

Emma did the same.

It showed a small section of the planet, a forested region just south of a line of mountaintops.

"I see five contrails ... ending now. It looks like they're breaking clear of the atmosphere."

"What the fuck," Quinn said to no one. "Send this to Copernicus and Sunfish. We're still on laser comms?"

"Yes, sir. They're rising to match Copernicus' orbit, still on the far side of the planet."

"Wake section three," Quinn said over his shoulder. "Sound general quarters."

"Captain White, did you receive?" The message was to the captain of Copernicus, but Quinn included that ship's bridge.

"Martinez, I did. What's your evaluation?"

"They're coming around the planet and will be on your tail in about ten minutes."

Quinn called up a route map.

"Recommend a full burn toward the GJ-1068 jump point."

Copernicus immediately turned from the planet. The stream of particles from her three drives created a multi-colored pattern of lights in the atmosphere below.

"That's taking us away from Earth," the officer of the deck on Copernicus responded.

"Remember protocols," White said.

"Brown, what's the lag out to Sunfish?"

"Fourteen minutes."

"Good; tell them to hold position and keep streaming our sensor data to them. They need to report everything we see."

"I see a mix of ions and chemical propellant in their exhaust," Andersen reported to all.

"Good, their range must be limited; Copernicus may be able to outlast them," Quinn added.

"Their acceleration is still climbing, approaching six gees."

Sooner than expected, the five ships obtained a direct line-of-sight on Copernicus and adjusted their flight paths, maintaining six gees.

"Can we assist?" Brown asked, only vaguely aware of the conversation going on.

"No," Andersen said. "Out of range. Our only responsibility is to send what we see to Sunfish so that they can get it to Earth."

"With what, Brown?" Petty Officer Mascord asked quietly.

"How big are they?" Captain White asked.

"Estimate 120 meters, half the length of Batfish," Quinn answered.

"They've launched. Looks like a missile," Andersen said, his voice tense but tightly controlled.

Copernicus fishtailed. Invisible to the eye, the three thrusting beams narrowed into a sharp pattern as they were directed at the incoming missile. A brief flash was followed by an expanding cone of debris.

"Hit that ship," Quinn sent as Copernicus shifted its tail.

"They've focused their exhaust," Quinn said. "It's as good as any weapon they could carry."

The nose section of the attacking ship flared white as it flew through the exhaust from Copernicus, now up to full thrust. The ship slowed rapidly under the pressure. A quick maneuver allowed it to escape, but only briefly. The thin armor of its starboard flank flared and then caved inward; its hull material turned into a hot plasma that raced through the ship's interior. Thrust cut off, and it began to tumble, a result of its last maneuver and pressure from the particle streams.

"Another missile. No, count four. One from each."

Copernicus swiveled her tail, catching one missile early in flight and another midway, but it was too slow for the last two. The first struck the armored shell around the tail section, peeling back 20 meters of material. The second struck the tail section under the shattered armor. Thrust stopped, and the communications link went down. Copernicus drifted forward, on course, but without thrust. The four remaining ships were rapidly closing the distance between them.

'Anay.' Emma gripped the armrests of the captain's chair as fear caught in the back of her throat.

It was the first thought she had given him that day.

"We've lost comms to Copernicus," Quinn said.

She tried recalling thoughts from the previous day, but the fear was spreading. A cold sweat blossomed on her forehead. Her stomach tightened. She wasn't sure when she had last paid him any thought.

"The tail of Copernicus is glowing," Andersen said.

She and Quinn switched focus to the thermal sensor display just as the drive exhaust burst through the twisted mess at the tail end of the ship. Acceleration started to climb, although more slowly than before.

"Any chance of reestablishing comms?" Quinn asked Brown.

"Waiting on a link."

"Four more missiles in flight," Ramirez announced.

Growing hope was dashed. Emma watched as Copernicus tried maneuvering the streams to intercept, but with the aft maneuvering thrusters blasted away, the attempt was futile. Like a wounded beast, she thrashed about, trying to protect herself from circling predators. The first missile struck under the armor, again shutting down the drives. The next three struck the armor along the port side, further exposing the internal structure. Emma's mind remained blank. Thoughts would not connect, past and present.

"Auxiliary spaces are wrecked," Andersen said. "I don't think they can get the drives back."

"Fuck," someone yelled behind Emma.

All watched as the four ships approached Copernicus, which showed no signs of life, tumbling slowly. Two minutes passed, and the ships turned about, decelerating as the distance between them shrank.

After ten minutes, the details of the ships became difficult to see as they continued on a course away from Batfish. All five formed a single shape.

"What's happening?" Mascord asked.

"They've matched the tumble of Copernicus and are slowing it," Ramirez answered.

"They've attached themselves to the hull," Andersen said.

"The tumble is almost gone."

"Ramirez, shut down the thermal sensors and switch in the scope's sun filter."

"Yes, Captain."

He looked at Emma, sorrow and sympathy together. Tears welled in her eyes.

The flash overwhelmed the filtered telescope. The display blanked out for a moment and then returned, quickly gaining focus. An expanding sphere of plasma was all they could see, dissipating as it moved outward.

Ramirez removed the sun filter, revealing an empty field of stars.

A long silence was finally broken.

"What the fuck happened?" Brown whispered. "Did their plant blow?"

Chief Andersen looked down at the young petty officer. "No, read your god damned manuals."

Brown looked up at the chief with surprise and then over to Emma.

With her eyes on the field of stars and tears on her cheeks, Emma answered with her tone precise, clipped, and condescending. "A fusion plant can never blow, not by act or accident. If anything disturbs the confinement fields, all reactions stop."

She turned to face Brown. "As the chief said —"

"Stewart, Chief," Quinn said sharply, drawing the attention of all to him and stopping any further discussion.

He let the silence stretch into a long moment.

"A set of protocols were developed to guide the crew of any ship that encounters extraterrestrial life. You're familiar with some, those applying to the life below, but there's also a set written for an encounter with intelligent life. Copernicus was following one, running towards GJ 1068, away from Earth. They were following another when they ignited two fusion bombs attached to their inner hull. The capture of any ship represents a grave threat to the human race."

"Whose idea was that, and are we carrying one of those?" Mascord asked.

"Not the Navy's," Quinn said. "And yes."

Another long silence followed.

"Petty Officer Brown, has all data from this encounter been sent to Sunfish?"

"Yes, sir."

"Good work. Order them to jump through to Gliese 1061. Have them hold at the next jump until we're in that system. That's almost three days … If they don't hear from us after three days, they should return to Earth as fast as possible. You know how to word it."

"Yes, sir." Brown turned to her console.

"Chief, has there been any more activity on the planet?"

"No sir, but we have no visibility over the southern hemisphere."

"Message sent, sir."

"Thank you, Brown."

"Anything from the satellite, Chief?"

"No, it hasn't been activated … let me try something."

"No, nothing," he said after a long moment.

"Hmm, well, we need to retrieve it … or destroy it, but I don't want to get any closer to the planet. No telling what else is down there."

"It's in a low orbit. We can hit it with our exhaust. Any of it that survives intact will fall into the atmosphere."

"Good, we'll need to reposition for that. Once done, it's back to Earth, four gees, I'm afraid."

"Yes, sir." Andersen paused to enter a course and then turned to look past the captain into the passage. "Looks like we're all here; prepare for one gee. Helmsman, the course is set; once the ship is rigged, take us down across the daylight side. Let me know when we reach the first waypoint."

"Captain, the first ship is still intact," Emma said with anger and urgency showing through her tears.

Quinn paused. A moment of confusion passed quickly, replaced by grim determination.

"Damn it … The XO is right. We need intel; we can't pass up this opportunity. Chief, where is it now?"

"It's approaching apoapsis on the dark side of the planet. The orbit is eccentric but stable."

"I don't like it," Quinn said. "How close is it to the planet at periapsis?"

"Uh, very. Just above the atmosphere."

"And that's on the daylight side?"

"Yes, for the next few days anyway."

"Damn it … Chief, plot an intercept. We'll take our chances."

"Captain, will we jump in time to contact Sunfish?" Brown asked.

Quinn froze for a moment. "Uh … no. Tell them we'll be investigating the wreck and to proceed without waiting for word from us. Send quickly. I hope they'll still be in the system to receive."

"Aye, Captain."

Quinn looked over the gathered crew.

"XO, your section has the bridge. Ensign Zhào, prepare a boarding party, your section, and … chief, you'll also be going. The rest of you, get some sleep. The next few days are going to be long."

A series of hard burns brought Batfish down close to the planet, above the equator, near the burned-out hulk. Unfortunately, stopping the tumbling motion and inserting the boarding party took longer than anticipated. Their orbit brought them to the dark side of the planet, easily visible from the surface.

"Ensign Zhào, how are you receiving?"

"Voice is clear; the relay is working."

"Good. We have ten more minutes in the shadow of the planet. How is your timeline?"

Marina Zhào exchanged a look with Andersen. He shook his helmet in response.

"Sorry, captain. We just pushed through the blockage where the hull gave way and appear to be in a central passage. We'll need more time than that."

"Understood."

The passage had a familiar design, slightly wider than those on Batfish, but with the same set of handrails/ladder rungs. The spacing of each was similar. The coloring of the surfaces was the exception. Unlike the familiar dull gray favored by the Navy since they stopped using wood for construction, the sides of the passage were garishly colored. Bright red, green, orange, and yellow patterns stretched forward as far as the light would reach.

"That must be decorative," she said, keeping her audience to the four behind her.

The channel was also forwarding all audio and video to Batfish.

When the ship was under thrust, Marina realized they would be ascending a ladder toward the forward end of the ship. The remainder of the boarding party was standing by, all having cleared the blockage. Bright lanterns affixed to their helmets and chests flooded the immediate area with light. Three held jury-rigged sidearms. No one had considered the complexities of using a pressure suit in an armed action.

With quick hand motions, she pointed in the six cardinal directions and made some quick assumptions. "Port, starboard, overhead, deck, aft, and forward." She turned toward the last and kicked gently off a rail, propelling her straight up the passage. The varying, colored patterns and wildly shifting shadows from the lights behind made it difficult to see the physical structure of the passage. The sudden appearance of a crossing passage startled her.

"Halt." She grabbed a rail, bringing her motion to an awkward stop.

"I'll push past. Chief, Egebe, take the starboard passage. Howard and Miller hold."

She kicked past the crossing and stopped. Andersen and Petty Officer Femi Egebe proceeded down the starboard passage.

"There's a non-pressure door, ajar, deck facing," Andersen reported.

"Looks like sleeping quarters, no occupants, four standard-looking beds, no exit. Moving past … We're near the end. There's a thick window and a small panel. The controls appear to have melted."

"Roger, Chief. Return and then proceed down the port passage."

Marina kept her eyes forward as Andersen and Egebe passed behind her.

Within a minute, Andersen reported, "Same story: empty quarters, window, and a melted panel. Returning now."

"Does anyone hear that sound?" Spaceman Hal Miller asked.

Andersen and Egebe stopped just short of the central passage.

"Sound," Andersen said. "How are you hearing a sound?"

"Press your boots to the deck … there it was again."

Marina maneuvered around and pushed her boots against a flat surface.

"I'm not hearing a thing," she said.

"Oh, the hull is popping," Egebe said. "Still cooling since Copernicus' attack … or from the planet's shadow."

That reminded Marina of the timeline. "Pressing forward."

She kicked off. A few meters further, a pressurized hatch came into view, latched open.

"I'm going in."

The fear of an ambush was at the back of her mind. There was no way of hiding the bright light coming from each member of her team. Each would be an easy target, but it was unlikely that any of the ship's inhabitants could have survived the stream of plasma that raced up the passages.

"I see bodies … six. Chief and Egebe enter. Howard and Miller hold."

As Quinn watched the image of floating alien bodies from Ensign Zhào's camera, Batfish flew into the light of Eridani.

"Okay, here we are for all to see. Stewart, Ramirez, don't take your eyes off that planet."

Below, the darkened surface revealed little, but Emma was confident that Batfish's thermal sensor array would immediately detect any launch.

"Yes, sir. All clear."

"Two are strapped into chairs. The others are floating free. This must be their version of a bridge."

Consoles and displays lined the room's outer wall, all oriented to indicate that 'up' was in the direction of the ship's bow. The colors were the same: red, green, yellow, and orange, somewhat muted on the walls but not on any of the chairs or consoles. Marina found the complex, tortuous combination of colors challenging to focus upon and painful to the eyes.

Andersen secured his sidearm and kicked to the port side, grabbing the top of a chair with one hand and a body with the other. He slowly turned it in a visual inspection.

"The skin is badly charred; looks like any exposed clothing that they were wearing was burned off; some damage from decompression. It appears to have a beak, or the shape of one, large eyes … The spine is curved. A little shorter than us, I'd say. Five fingers; the index and ring are … long. The other three look like thumbs."

"Ensign Zhào, finish inspection of the spaces and grab anything that looks useful, including a couple of the bodies, and then get your team back to Batfish." Quinn sent.

"Aye, captain."

They pushed out of the bridge. The central passage continued forward, meeting another crossing passage.

Both were identical to those before the bridge. Two more bodies were found on the starboard side.

"I believe those are grappling stations at each of the windows," Andersen said. "Probably a backup control."

"Aye, Chief. There's another hatch ahead, latched open like those for the bridge."

Marina pushed into a large space that had the look of a warehouse. Stacked crates were secured with straps. The exteriors of most were scorched. Little remained of those near the hatch. Debris floated in the vacuum, and she spotted another body clinging to a wall, likely one of the outer bulkheads. She pushed around a stack of crates and stopped.

"There are cages up here, rows of them, different sizes."

She pushed forward. "It looks like they were carrying animals … All appear dead."

"Captain, we're at the bow of the ship. I believe this is the final living space. We still need to find engineering, and I think we should take as many of these crates as we can … Just a sample of what we're seeing will require multiple trips."

"Captain?" Andersen paused.

"Go ahead, Chief."

"If we can deploy the grapples, I think we should take the entire ship."

Quinn floated silently at Emma's side, staring at the image of the dark planet.

"Is that even possible, chief?"

"It should be. We'll need to use maneuvering thrusters to fly straight. Acceleration will be limited; I doubt we could do better than a single gee … and I'm sure it will damage our hull."

Quinn continued to stare at the planet.

"Still clear?" he asked Emma, knowing the answer.

"Yes, sir."

"Fuck."

"Captain, I concur." Zhào sent.

The engineering spaces had been exposed to a vacuum but were in much better condition. Most of the plasma, created as the exhaust from Copernicus bore a hole through the ship, had passed aft to forward through the living spaces. One body was found in the engineering spaces, well preserved, except for damage from violent decompression.

It required three trips around the planet to firmly affix the Birdies' ship to the hull of Batfish. The term 'Birdy' started as an insult and quickly spread. It was the first non-vulgar term they thought of to describe their new enemy. The ship was attached near the aft end of Batfish's teardrop hull to keep the combined center of mass as close to that of Batfish alone. Even there, as Andersen predicted, acceleration would be limited to one gee plus a small fraction. Any more would overwhelm the maneuvering thrusters and curve the ship's flight path.

The thrust of the drives was a welcome relief to all. The planet would soon be a distant spec, lost among the stars.

"How's she holding, Chief?"

"Perfect, those grappling cables have a nice bite on our hull. I'd hate to be the one who explains it to the hull techs at Jarvis."

Quinn laughed. "That's going to be an interesting conversation, one of many."

He glanced at Emma, desperate to bring her into the conversation.

"Bring us up to a half gee, Mascord."

"Aye, captain."

"All quiet, XO?"

"Yes, sir. Not a peep," she said quietly.

Emma was trying. Quinn took that as a good sign.

"Three-quarters, Mascord."

Ensign Zhào popped her head through the hatch. "Samples all negative, captain."

"Good news. Thank you, Zhào."

The decontamination had been a lengthy, improvised process. Fear had been low, but the effort was warranted. A final set of samples taken from the suits showed no new lifeforms.

"I have no idea what I was thinking when I suggested bringing one of those corpses aboard. The vacuum and cold should keep them preserved. Hats off to you, Chief. This was a brilliant idea. One gee, Mascord."

"Thank you, captain. In this case, I'll accept your compliment without complaint."

Quinn gave him a firm nod. On the main display, the northern polar cap approached.

"A quick nod to 82 G dot Eridani Five for a hard lesson, and we're on our way, but don't worry; we'll be back." Quinn looked around the bridge, seeing agreement. Emma smiled weakly, nodding her head with the rest.

"Of course," Quinn said. "We would be a system away, running empty-handed, if not for our XO."

Emma gave a short, dismissive laugh. "Thank you, captain, but to be perfectly honest, this was not my idea — You never let me finish."

Quinn gave her a curious look and waited.

"I said that the first ship was intact ... I intended to finish with something like 'There may be survivors; we need to go down and melt those mother fuckers.'"

Quinn knew Emma well enough to know when she was joking. He smiled anyway.

The crew burst into hysterical laughter that lingered far too long as her words were repeated.

November 23rd 2125

Niko Sasaki looked up from the magnified image and rubbed her eyes. "They're all dormant like you predicted. They just shut down as soon the temperature drops below your limit."

"And that's good," the biology team lead, James Thompson, said. "These little guys are toxic. When it comes time to populate the oceans with higher-level organisms, we won't want them around, but they can run amok for now."

"So, we'll need to replace them?"

"Eventually. Current conditions are perfect for them; they should thrive. Most of the models agree that they'll need at least 20 years to enrich the oceans to a level that will support our cool water variants and another 20 for enough carbon to be extracted from the atmosphere to start bringing down the temperature. If all works out, we can start introducing their replacement to the polar regions around that first 20-year mark. After that, they're free to compete, but the dropping temperature will favor the cool water algae."

Niko pushed through the gray tent flap and peered into the sky. A pair of robotic crafts circled the site as they did every morning. The effect upon the thin veil of cirrus clouds was difficult to measure, but the resulting temperature drop had been noticed and appreciated by all at Atacama. Unfortunately, the benefit from that effort had collided with the law of diminishing returns. Ophiuchi was still low, but the heat rising from the lifeless, unshaded soil was already distorting ground-level air.

"Will our cloud thinners change the timeline at all?"

James stepped out to join Niko in the harsh light. Sam Nowak remained in the shade at his terminal.

The remainder of Niko's small team was spread around the artificial lagoon, tending to various experiments.

"Maybe a little. I'm afraid they're showing their limits already."

Niko popped her head under the flap. "Sam, we're going to continue our tour. See you at lunch?"

Sam nodded enthusiastically.

Niko dropped the flap of her legionnaire's hat over her neck as she and James walked toward the next tent. She felt sweat running down her back and beading on her upper lip, inaccessible under her face mask.

Halfway to the next tent, a message came from Commander Lily Davis, head of the Atacama Research Station.

"Lieutenant Sasaki, we have a problem. Gather your team and head back to the station ASAP."

"Gathering now." She put a hand up to stop their progress. "James, something has come up. Grab Sam and anyone in tents five and six. Bring them to the head of the path. I'll get the rest. We need to get back to the station now." The concern in her voice was unmistakable.

"What's up?"

"I'm not sure. Commander Davis messaged for us to return but gave no reason."

"Another storm?"

"No," Niko said, checking quickly. "She just said to get the team back."

"Getting Sam and the others," James said, walking away.

The artificial lagoon was carved from sand and loose rock, extending a natural inlet. All algae cultures were maintained in separate pools that drew water from the lagoon. A tent sat between every two pools. Some were empty. Others held members of the team buried in their research. Shutting down ongoing activities took more time than Niko had hoped. Then, it took 15 minutes to walk over a set of dunes back to Atacama Station. That time could have been reduced, but Niko had no desire to push the researchers. Between the heat, soft sand, and face masks, she would have invited injury.

Commander Davis looked at her with mixed emotions as she led her team into the mess. Niko was expecting irritation, which was present, but fear and confusion dominated.

"Finally," she said to the larger group. "I wanted all present for this."

Niko and her team found seats in the back as Commander Davis continued.

"Rum Runner jumped into the system two hours ago and relayed a message from Sunfish. Eleven days ago, five ships of an unknown origin rose from the surface of 82 G Eridani Five and attacked Copernicus. After a short fight, they disabled Copernicus and attempted to board. At that moment, the crew of Copernicus issued a self-destruct. The five attacking ships were destroyed, along with Copernicus. All hands were lost."

A stunned silence was interrupted by a few gasps and whispers of disbelief. One whisper grew into a shout. "Commander Davis, that makes no sense. Nothing on that ship could have acted as a self-destruct mechanism."

Commander Davis paused, her irritation more obvious than before. "There was ... let's leave it at that."

She quickly cut off the same individual as he attempted to argue. "There is more."

With a silent room, she continued. "Batfish was present in the system during the attack. She survived and was expected to come out three days behind Sunfish and make contact. Sunfish never heard from her and is assuming she was lost."

Niko's head dropped. Her eyes focused on the damp sand scattered across the floor, tracked in by those around her. "Emma," she said under her breath.

"As you know, the first reports of that planet said nothing about intelligent life. So, it's unlikely to be the home for those ships. This means they could have come from anywhere. We need to prepare for the worst; assume that we will not receive any help from Earth, no further supplies, and no evacuation. Water and oxygen aren't a problem, but the cargo aboard Rum Runner will only feed us for the next five months. Our gardens are doing extremely well but aren't producing much with nutritional value."

"Commander, our sweet potatoes in plot C are looking promising," a civilian researcher said near the front of the room.

"Also, the pineapples, and don't forget the arugula," another said.

"I'm aware, but I also know those are the only three that will be useful to us. I'll be shifting most of you to the horticulture team, those not already a member. Fertilizer is not a problem, but we'll need to increase the production of oxygenated water. Let's assume that our stay will be greatly extended and plan accordingly. I'd rather not be dependent on arugula for survival."

Niko heard a few small, nervous laughs in response.

"Lieutenant Sasaki, you'll continue your work at the lagoon; just keep our samples alive. Nowak and Thompson will help you."

Niko stood to be seen above the group. "Yes, ma'am. May I suggest that we place the satellites in standby? Their transmissions are the only sign of activity that could be detected from the jump points."

"Good idea, Lieutenant. I'd also like to reduce our visible footprint, consolidate as much as possible. Rum Runner plans to stay in the system after shuttling the supplies down. They want to avoid jump points for the immediate future. We'll all have to wait and see what comes our way — Let's get busy."

November 24th 2125

Lacaille 8760 was three jumps from Earth and safety. As usual, there were no planets near their path. The star, bright and orange-red, could be seen starboard. Batfish had come about an hour earlier and was on a long decelerating path to the Ross 154 jump point. Emma, Marina Zhào, and Angela Brown were alone in the mess. Her apologies to Angela had been thoroughly rejected. Their friendship had grown.

Marina had come off watch a few hours earlier. Her section had finished preparing dinner and the cleanup afterward. Once again, movie time had been canceled due to waning interest. The three enlisted members had wandered away to enjoy their free time. Emma woke early and would take the watch in a few hours more. Angela had drawn the short straw and was fetching coffee for the current watch.

"I keep drawing a blank," Emma was saying. "I mean on everything. I can't remember my last thought of him, and when I try, everything else blanks out for that day; whom I talked to, what I ate ... where I ate." She smiled weakly.

"I think I can answer the last one," Angela said warmly and then set the tray of empty cups on an adjacent table and sat next to Emma. "I remember that feeling from school every time I was forced in front of an audience."

Marina looked across the table with tired, sympathetic eyes, her chin resting on a hand, straight dark hair touching her shoulders. "Well, I hate throwing cliches at you, but it will take time; don't dwell on it; distract yourself."

"No trouble remembering your time together?" Angela asked.

Emma shook her head. "None at all."

"Stick with those memories, they —"

"General quarters." Quinn's voice surprised the three. "All hands, crew your battle stations. Inbound, unknown ship detected. This is not a drill."

Their startled looks disappeared. All three raced to the central passage. Emma and Angela dropped to the bridge; Marina clambered up the handrails to engineering.

Petty Officer Janice Howard surrendered the sensor station to Emma, remaining at her side to hand over the watch.

"We've detected the signature of a ship ahead, burning hard. It's typical of any number of ships, all Terran, and it's coming from Ross 154. That's our next jump towards Earth."

Quinn leaned over Emma's other shoulder. "Mass estimates place it in one of the destroyer classes ... if military."

"It's doing four gees," Emma said. "I doubt it's civilian."

"Agreed, but Fredericksburg is still fitting out, and I don't think the Chinese have deployed yet."

"Beagle?" Emma offered.

"Must be; only choice. I'm guessing they've received word of the attack."

"That's good."

"Yeah, it is." He stood back, concern on his face.

"Is there a problem?"

"Not sure. Comm, identify ourselves to the approaching ship. At the end, attach ... attach this video of us ... okay everyone, smile, and wave for the bridge camera."

The mystified bridge crew complied.

"Sir?" Howard asked.

"We're about 12 days late. Sunfish would've tried contacting us in both Gliese and Luyten. After that, they would've assumed the worst … and then we show up. The crew of Beagle can't imagine a reason for our delay."

"Transmitted, sir."

"Thank you, Brown."

"I'm not sure," Andersen said. "It looks like a hostage video to me."

Quinn laughed aloud and then went silent. "It's not that bad … anyways, I was just grasping for an idea. No one considered … imagined the need for duress codes out here."

He sat back in his chair and turned to Brown. "We have a little less than a day before we rendezvous. That's more than enough time to work it out. What's the delay comm?"

"One way, 148 seconds, sir."

"We'll give them eight minutes," Quinn said. "They may want to board, especially when they see the Birdies' ship riding on our back like a space-born parasite."

Ten minutes passed.

"Batfish, Beagle sends greetings. We'll be coming about and slowing for rendezvous. Please prepare for boarding; please explain your delay; please explain the discrepancy we're seeing in your delta-v, and please, no more videos. We're nervous enough over here."

The crew stared at their captain in silence.

"Okay, you were right, Chief."

"Sir, what discrepancy are they talking about?" Howard asked.

"Our drive output is unexpectedly high for our current change of velocity. They're not aware of the extra mass on our back. Comm, send all data from our inspection of the Birdies' ship and the images from our drone when we attached the grapples."

He looked at Emma. "That should raise some eyebrows."

"Include the following Comm; 'Preparing port dock for boarding. Starboard blocked. Reason for delay was the retrieval and transport of souvenir. Reason for delta-v discrepancy is the transport of souvenir. Please review attached video and images of souvenir, and please accept our apologies for any discomfort we may have caused.'"

Five minutes passed.

"Batfish, Beagle, data received. Please stand by."

Five hours passed.

"Captain, message received from Beagle. I'll let you read this response."

Quinn drew close to the communication display.

'Batfish, Beagle, holy *@#$%. We are truly impressed. Please understand that the following is necessary. If possible, you will increase your burn to 1.2 gees to allow rendezvous; precise timing will follow this message. You will secure your drives on rendezvous but continue toward the jump point. Beagle will remain at distance with weapons trained. Our shuttle will hold at ten meters from your port dock. Lieutenant Stewart will traverse to the shuttle for medical tests and interrogation. Following the tests, we'll board and perform a visual inspection of Batfish and her prize. You will not be allowed to reach the jump point until this is complete.'

Quinn exchanged a questioning look with Brown. "I don't know about this." He waved over Emma.

Emma read the message and smiled warm and happy, then wistful, and then her smile was gone.

"Do you know what this is about?" Quinn asked. "I don't feel inclined to follow this one."

"No worries, I know Beagle's shuttle pilot, well, one of them, and I'm sure he'll be flying. Chief Walker; he taught me how to fly when I was on Mars … I think they're looking for a known quantity."

"Makes sense, but it's your choice."

"I'll go."

Quinn turned to the helm. "Mascord, bring us up to 1.2 gees very carefully."

"Aye, captain."

"Chief, keep an eye on our … prize."

"Aye, captain."

Emma sat in a jury-rigged isolation room aboard Beagle's shuttle for almost a full day. They ran every meaningful test on her that they could, limited by available resources. They retested the boarding party's blood samples that she carried. They gave her a bank of questions to create a psychological profile, and when her patience had reached an end, they freed her from the room. Only then was she allowed to speak with Chief Walker. Brief out of necessity, the net result of her conversation left all in the cabin speechless.

After returning to Batfish, she had a long shower before throwing on a fresh uniform.

By this time, the two ships were a few hours from the jump into Ross 154. Beagle would escort Batfish and her prize back to Earth.

Quinn found her in the mess and invited her to sit.

"They've finished their inspection of Batfish and our prize and remain impressed, to put it lightly. The shuttle is returning to pick up the inspection team, and then we're good to go."

Emma nodded, exhausted.

"So, explain this to me, Lieutenant Stewart, Emma. A warship three times our size is off our port bow, prepared to destroy us. They are heavily armed. We have four sidearms. From their point of view, the fate of the world is in balance. In response, you float over to their shuttle, they run a few tests, and then they have a short conversation with you. What was it ten minutes?"

Emma shrugged, dreading Quinn's next question.

"Ten minutes talking with you, and suddenly they're apologizing profusely and sending us on our way."

He waited a moment. "What did you say to them?"

Emma hesitated, an embarrassed look on her face.

"He asked me about Copernicus, and I started to cry and couldn't stop. I tried, I really tried. It was so embarrassing — I did manage a few words with Chief Walker before they brought me back."

Speechless for a moment, Quinn finally shook his head. "God, I wish I could think of a smart-ass comment right about now."

Emma burst out in laughter and then broke down in tears.

January 4th 2126

Fear and terror brought forth anger and hate. The mere existence of another intelligent species would have overwhelmed the sensibilities of some, those taught from childhood to cast a suspicious eye toward all that was different. The attack at Eridani drove much deeper, shattering the psyche of the ordinary and those they had labeled extraordinary. A cry arose, and the most predictable of shouts answered.

Calls for fleets of warships were sounded from every nation. The focus of research shifted to technologies that would be useful in the wars that most believed inevitable. Recruitment began in earnest for the armed forces, many religions, and the causes that arose in the ensuing confusion.

The ship retrieved by Batfish brought concerns and relief. The ion thruster impressed the team that disassembled it, but it couldn't match the acceleration produced by the ships of Earth. They had relied on chemical propellants to chase Copernicus and had burned a third of their supply to get as close as they did. The missiles were the only weapons found and were not deemed a serious threat. Computing systems were of interest but badly damaged.

The fact that they did not have an interface generator drew the greatest concern, raising questions about their origin. There had been no signs of civilization within the system. No transmissions were detected by any of the deployed sensors, and surveys of the inner six planets had found nothing of concern or interest. The five outer planets had not been surveyed, but distant observations showed all to be cold and lifeless. The five ships were delivered into the system, and it was inevitable that those responsible would return. Their absence would be noted.

The autopsies allayed other fears. Physically, they did not appear threatening, shorter than the average human, and much weaker in bone and muscle. Their nervous system was different, but not in any way that would give an advantage. Some concern arose as the examiners delved into the physiology of the aliens and realized that they would thrive in environments like Earth. There were notable differences, but their oxygen needs appeared compatible, as did their need for water and a similar temperature range.

The difference in their physiology had one significant benefit, one that brought great relief. It was determined that none of the microbial life forms found were compatible with life on Earth. Over millions of years, they had developed to target a very different set of weaknesses. They would quickly die if they made their way into a human body.

The original intent of the five ships appeared to be benign. They were collecting animals from the Eridani system for an unknown purpose. The fact that each ship was equipped with grapples implied something less benign. The fact that they didn't hesitate to use them after detecting Copernicus in orbit led to assumptions that were easily extended to their point of origin.

Niko was drenched in sweat. It was an unusually warm day on an unusually warm planet, at least, unusual for a habitable planet. It was midday, and she was returning to Atacama Station from the lagoon. A meal and air-conditioned sleeping quarters brought her back every day, but it was a trek she usually made in the evening, just before dinner, when Ophiuchi was low on the horizon.

This day was special. Two weeks after Rum Runner had jumped into the system with news of the attack, the harvest of the sweet potatoes and arugula had started. A week after that, the fruit from some of the pineapple plants that had survived a journey of 19 and a half light years and transplantation into an alien soil was declared ripe enough. By the commander's orders, every meal would be supplemented with local products. Provisions from Rum Runner needed to be conserved as long as possible. A tradition had started. The chore of turning the local produce into something edible would rotate among the researchers and Navy personnel. Today was Niko's turn, she, Nowak, and Thompson, the lagoon's caretakers.

The sweet potatoes and arugula were similar to what she had tasted before, but an Ophiuchi pineapple had a much stronger bite than any she could recall. Uncooked, it was almost inedible. Several had tried and failed to include it in a cake, and several others had worked it into a stir fry with mixed results. No one had attempted to combine it with the other two local products in a single dish, and all were growing tired of the repetition, so it was with trepidation that she stepped through the barrier into the mudroom.

"Hi Niko," Sam Nowak said as he shed his boots with a basket of sweet potatoes at his side.

Niko removed her mask and wiped the sweat running down her face. "Hi, Sam. Any trouble with the harvest?"

"Oh, these are from storage. We have an abundance, to put it mildly."

"Just shoot me now," James Thompson said from the doorway leading into the mess. "Are you serious about this, Niko? I thought today was curry day."

Niko nodded with confidence that she didn't feel. "This is going to be great. Do we have everything we need?"

"Sure do. The arugula is washed, and the pineapples are sliced, awaiting your magic touch. I've lined up the spices you requested … a little different from yesterday."

Niko sat to remove her boots and avoid the mud covering them. "That was an experiment."

"And the five before that?" James asked.

"All experiments. Perfection only comes through hard work, trial, and error …"

"Inspiration," Sam added. "Fortitude and —"

"We have contact," a voice shouted from the mess.

Startled, Niko looked up from her boots at James as he turned back through the door.

She accessed the feed from the communication frequencies as Sam ran across the room, following James.

Fear quickly turned to joy and relief. A Chinese cruiser, the Shenzhen UNSF, was in the system requesting status from Atacama Station.

"Lieutenant Sasaki, are you monitoring the comm feed?" Commander Davis sent.

"Just started. Have we answered yet?"

"No, and I'm 10 minutes away. How close are you?"

"In the mudroom."

"Good, get to the comm station and answer. After that, find out what's happened out there."

"Yes, ma'am. Heading there now."

She ran through a single door and down a short passage.

"Shenzhen, this is Lieutenant Sasaki of the US Navy. Atacama Station is operational. All personnel are present and healthy. Rum Runner is in the system, although their exact location is unknown."

"Acknowledged, Atacama, and glad to hear that all is well down there. We have contacted Rum Runner; they're doing well. We apologize for the delay. It has been a hectic month, and we delayed contacting you after entering the system until we had some confidence that it was clear. We'll enter an orbit by day's end."

"Understood, Shenzhen. What news do you have of recent events? We are only aware of the destruction of Copernicus and the disappearance of Batfish."

"It's good news then, Atacama. Batfish survived."

Through a thin wall, Niko heard a loud cheer erupt from a growing crowd in the mess. The sorrow she had quietly carried for the last month faded to a distant memory.

"The crew delayed their return to retrieve one of the enemy ships and are all now back on Earth."

"I know whose idea that was," Niko said without keying the transmitter.

"We'll remain in the Ophiuchi-C system providing security. In addition, the space fleet combined is forming a three-jump bubble about Earth. Ships will be available in Gliese 674."

"Thank you, Shenzhen, your presence is greatly appreciated. What do we know of the enemy?"

"They haven't been seen since, but much is being learned from their ship. We expect a fleet will form for a return to Eridani, but that's only speculation."

"Your ship is new to me. I was unaware of any in service of its size."

"As you can imagine, timelines have been accelerated, all timelines. Earth is responding to this threat … Are you in need of any assistance?"

"Do we need anything, Commander?" Niko fully understood that Commander Davis and every other person at Atacama were monitoring her conversation.

"Just mail, Lieutenant. Did they pull our drop before leaving Earth?"

"Did you have a chance to upload our mail drop?"

"We did … transmitting now. If that's all, I'll sign off. When Commander Davis becomes available, have her contact us."

"I will, Shenzhen."

Niko met Commander Davis in the mudroom, removing her boots. A handful of researchers came from the mess, their excitement obvious and matching what could be heard from those still in the mess. It was the start of a celebration.

"Finally," one of the researchers said.

Niko nodded and gave her a supportive smile.

"You do understand," Commander Davis said, shaking her head slowly. "Rum Runner's schedule brought her to us every month and a half. Shenzhen's arrival was just ahead of that schedule. Our worries may have been overblown." She pivoted away and stepped through the door toward the communication station.

The researcher looked at Niko and shrugged. "At least we can take sweet potatoes and that god-awful pineapple off the menu."

Niko's head dropped. "Right … After tonight?" She looked at him with hope.

"Are you crazy?" Two others looked at her questioningly.

"Damn it," she said, brushing past them into the mess.

"The explosion was extremely bright. Even through the filters, it reached the limits of the display."

Emma pantomimed a person facing a blinding light.

Chloe nodded encouragingly.

"It was not important in any way. We were far away. But it's something I can't forget. Two weeks later, just after we had met Beagle, the lights came on in my cabin after a long sleep, the best I had had since. They were blinding, and the first thing I thought of was Anay and why my last thought of him was so negative."

"It wasn't negative; you were concerned about the growing disparity between each of your ranks; you were acknowledging the difficulties of maintaining a relationship with another in the Navy," Chloe said.

"More than that. I was ... I am questioning my reasons for joining the Navy. I thought I was following Anay's dream, but I'm not so sure anymore."

"No kidding." Chloe's sarcastic tone met only confusion. "You've been looking for an escape from this family since you were twelve years old."

"Maybe, but that was not Anay's fault ... and I was wondering if we should break up. I was wondering if we already had ... Regardless, it was just a passing thought, but the next morning, that same thought popped into my head right after I opened my eyes, and since then, it's the first thing that comes to mind when I wake."

Chloe's smile was not sympathetic. "Well, that sounds familiar."

Emma gave her a questioning look.

"Flowers!"

Emma's closed her eyes as she put her hands over her ears. "Mr. Granger — Did you have to bring that up? I felt so bad about trampling his flower bed."

"Of course. You always have and always will ... and you always forget the most important detail."

"The throw?"

Chloe nodded. "It was perfect. You caught Uncle Jon at second."

"I never saw where it went. Mr. Granger must have been waiting at his door to start screaming."

"You do know that he's dead now?"

Emma nodded solemnly. "I heard."

"A sad ending to a sad life." Chloe snorted derisively. "He lost what few friends he had because he couldn't shut up about you and the flowers."

"It wasn't that bad."

"Yes, it was; I mean ... I suspect there was a lot more behind his hate, but once you trampled the bed, his focus turned on you alone. People did not want to go near him. Every conversation would eventually turn to you, the privileged little brat."

"Aren't you here to cheer me up?" Emma asked with a deep, questioning look. "I'm never going to forget those flowers now."

Chloe shook her head slowly. "You already have perfect recall of every bad memory in your life."

"More of every mistake I've made ... those dealing with others, now that I think about it. I could make the same mistake in math over and over and forget what I was doing wrong, but I say one thing that I regret, and I'm stuck with it."

"Am I in any of these eternal twisted memories?"

"Sure, several at least — Do you remember bringing your boyfriend here when you were 17? It was in the summer."

"Uh ... no, you may need to be more specific. What was his name?"

"I don't remember that, but I do remember gawking at him until you noticed. It was embarrassing, and I thought you were mad at me."

"Oh right, it's coming back now; a 14-year-old beanstalk was trying to steal away my love."

"Really?" Emma asked, matching Chloe's tone.

Chloe narrowed her eyes and started raising her hands, immediately eliciting a smile from her younger cousin. "No, not at all."

They heard the crack of a bat through the screen door leading to the deck. The youngest of her cousins could be heard with friends in a field adjacent to the small lawn. She and Chloe were alone in the sprawling home with the afternoon sunlight pouring through the open windows. Every adult in the family, minus Emma, had been drawn into the changes sweeping across the world. Alexander was not allowing them to relax.

Following Anay's memorial service, Emma had been content to do nothing. She had had almost no free time since she left for Mars four years earlier. Batfish was being repaired and refitted as the world outside the ranch exploded, figuratively. Politicians and doomsayers were screaming. The pacifist factions within the government favored the phrase 'We told you so.' The more hawkish were saying the same. Business and academic leaders were maneuvering for a position in a rapidly changing order, while the ordinary just wanted to lay low. Emma placed herself with the last group. She spent most of the time alone, hiking, running, baking, and eating. It was nice to see Chloe. She was spending what little time she could afford with Emma.

"Any interest in meeting a senator?" Chloe asked, shaking her head at the same time.

"Eglin Shaw wants to stand by your side and … I don't know, declare war on all aliens."

"Not today … or ever."

"Then back to your not-negative thoughts of Anay. You were sitting with Abby at the time. Can you recall any later thoughts of her? Maybe they're tied to him in some way."

"We were outbound; I don't remember what system. We were talking about Fredericksburg, and I mentioned Abby and —"

"Emma, this is Quinn. I'm afraid your vacation is over. Sturgeon has found something. We're deploying."

Chloe waited for a moment as Emma stared into space.

"Is that a breakthrough?" she asked excitedly. "Did you remember something?"

Emma gave a short, distracted shake of her head, and Chloe realized she was in another conversation.

"A shuttle is heading down to you now, at the ranch. All crew should be aboard in two hours. We leave then."

"Getting ready now, Quinn. See you in about two."

She looked up at Chloe, who was showing obvious concern.

"What's up?"

"Gotta go." She stood and started toward the stairs and her room above.

"Now, when is your flight?"

"Soon, they're coming here. I need to pack."

"Here? The ranch?"

Emma nodded over her shoulder.

"I'll make sure the pad is clear," Chloe said.

Emma stopped on the first step. "Thanks for everything, Chloe."

"Our destination is Groombridge 1830, six jumps, a 27-day transit at one gee, 13 plus at four gees. I'm not sure what our orders will be on that. Our first jump will be into Wolf 359."

Quinn had gathered the entire crew in the combined mess, all but one in the underway uniform. Emma was at the back, wearing a bright yellow and black shirt above a pair of yellow shorts; red curls were floating freely about her face. She maintained a light grip on her bags to keep them in check. Batfish would undock from Jarvis Station following Quinn's brief.

"Sturgeon captured radio traffic in their sweep of that system. Some of it was audio that they were able to demodulate. We can hear words but have no idea what's being said."

He looked at Emma, briefly considering a comment about her outfit. "XO, we have over 12 hours of recorded voices. I'm hoping they will keep you busy for the ride out; finally, make use of your education."

"Looking forward to it, sir." She gave him a haughty, self-mocking smile.

"It came from the first planet in the system. No other activity was seen, no ships or stations. Sturgeon avoided getting any closer after detecting the signal, but they were close enough to verify that the planet's orbital regimes were empty. We won't be letting our guard down, though; the system has five other planets, so the presence of ships is a reasonable assumption."

"Are any of the others habitable?" Marina Zhào asked.

"No, the first planet's orbit is centered in a narrow habitable zone. The rest are far beyond.

There is preliminary consensus that the inhabitants are Birdies, but this isn't the home of those that destroyed Copernicus."

"Why not?" Petty Officer Brown asked.

"Well, first off, the scientists feel it's unlikely that we would find multiple alien species this close to Earth, meaning they must be Birdies. To answer your question, there are 13 jumps between

Eridani and Groombridge, and the Solar System sits on that path. It's very likely they would've been seen in transit, and they certainly would've seen us. Avoiding the solar system would take 23 jumps."

"This is assuming they have the same 8-light-year limit that we have," Emma said over the heads of the seated crew.

"That's right, XO. We'll know better in a few months."

"Sir, are we planning to melt those mother fuckers?"

"Mascord," Quinn said with annoyance, suppressing any laughter. "The answer is no; we'll be scouting for Fredericksburg. Sturgeon is inbound, preparing to dock at Jarvis Station. They'll refuel and resupply and then follow behind. A tanker will follow behind them — We've been fitted with an antennae array tuned to the frequency that Sturgeon was picking up. The signal should be clear at the jump point."

"One final note; command has provided us with a two-seated trainer, although some assembly is required before it flies. The surface of the planet will be accessible."

Emma wrinkled her nose at Quinn.

"I thought you would like that, XO."

He eyed Mascord. "Any further questions?"

January 26th 2126

"One last chance," Quinn said to the bridge crew. "Chi Orionis waits for us a couple jumps back … an island paradise."

"XO?" Petty Officer Jason Ramirez asked with a puzzled look.

"I'm sorry, Ramirez," Emma said. "Captain Martinez discovered the new routing software that came with the last upgrade. He found a void in space a few jumps back that's home to seven isolated stars. All are more than eight light years from the surrounding stars, preventing any jumps and forming an island of stars. His words, not mine."

Quinn stood near the bridge's entrance, smiling earnestly.

"Chi Orionis is one of the seven," Emma added as she scowled at him.

"A system we must visit," Quinn said. "It's said to have an eccentric companion that destroys all that come near."

"It's a binary," Emma said when Ramirez twisted his head upward. "And, as the word 'isolated' implies, we can't go there … that said, I believe our captain would be in good company if he did find a way." She returned her attention to Quinn.

"So … no interest?" he asked.

The bridge remained silent.

"Very well. Mascord, open an interface between Xi Ursae Majoris and Groombridge 1830."

With the Calvin file loaded beforehand, Mascord only needed to trigger the interface and sit back. All on the bridge watched the set of displays over his head, anxiously awaiting the formation of the jump point, but as time passed, it became apparent to all that something was wrong.

"What just happened?" Quinn asked as the displays flashed briefly and then went blank.

"I'm not sure, captain. Trying again."

After two uncomfortable minutes, the interface formed in front of Batfish precisely as it should have on the previous attempt.

"Everything good, Mascord?"

"Aye, captain. Reading all green."

"All right, send in Blue."

A drone painted dull blue accelerated through the interface. "Reporting all clear," Ramirez said.

"Uh ... Roger that," Quinn said.

"Captain?" Petty Officer Mascord was waiting on his order.

"Very well, helm. Take us through ... and run diagnostics on the generator ... once we secure from battle stations."

"Aye, captain."

Batfish passed into Groombridge 1830 without further incident.

Sturgeon followed and would remain at the jump point. Fredericksburg stayed in Xi Ursae Majoris, three hours from the jump point at maximum acceleration, hidden in the outer region of a debris belt.

"We're receiving a signal," Emma said. "This is speaker two."

Emma spent most of the journey analyzing Sturgeon's recordings. In the twelve hours of audio, she identified three speakers. Most of their speech was in the form of reports. News broadcasts, Emma assumed. One very insightful segment featured a pair of speakers in a conversation. Within a small database, she had collated words, phrases, and individual phonemes from all recordings, finding 63 of the last. It was significantly more than the English language used, and she was confident she had not heard all. She attempted to place the words into one of the standard categories used to distinguish the languages of Earth but encountered regular exceptions as she worked through the list. Unfortunately, the lack of context kept her in the dark regarding the meaning of any of the words.

It would be a difficult language for her to understand and almost impossible to speak. Nearly a third of the phonemes could not be produced by human vocal cords, although she came close with a few, using her lips and tongue to emulate the sound. Among the repeated phrases, she identified two as possible greetings or introductions. Her attempt to reproduce one was a dismal failure, but she did come close with the other, contorting her mouth until it hurt. Computer-generated speech would probably be needed for auditory communication, but a written language would work much better.

"Sounds like another news broadcast."

"Very well, XO. Let us know if there are any significant changes.

Ramirez, do you see anything else, radar or any other active sensors?"

"Nothing active, sir."

"All right. Mascord, execute our first maneuver."

"Aye, Captain."

"We're maneuvering to put the star between us and our target, planet one. It's in a near-perfect polar orbit around the star, so we'll drop below the ecliptic. XO, you'll probably lose the signal at that time."

"Aye, Captain."

Quinn stopped what he was about to say and raised his eyebrows at Emma, flashing an approving smile.

Emma shrugged. "Okay, I agree; it does sound much better than 'Yes, sir.'"

Quinn nodded and continued. "Once below the star, we'll burn hard until we're inside the planet's orbit. From there, we'll approach the sunny side. We'll also time the release of a drone to put it on the far side of the planet as we approach."

"Captain, will the gravity well of the star be a problem if we need to run?"

"Not at all, Mascord," Quinn said. "It's somewhat counterintuitive. The well of a planet does present a concern. Copernicus, for example, probably would've survived if they had been in a high synchronous orbit around Eridani Five instead of the much lower one they had assumed. They were fighting a full gee and a half when they started running. It would've been a different story if they had been 50,000 kilometers higher.

On the other hand, the well around this star will never be a problem. Put another way, we would toast our exterior if we ever flew that close. We may feel a hundredth of a gee on the coming pass. That said, we'll keep a hyperbolic trajectory to minimize the threat of intercept. If anything rises, we'll continue past and then head straight to the jump point. If they pursue, Fredericksburg may have a chance to break in her cannons."

Mascord nodded enthusiastically.

Brown snorted derisively and looked at Mascord. "Really ... gravity well?"

"Hey, at least I paid attention to Professor Allen's lectures."

Quinn laughed aloud. "Allen is still teaching orbital mechanics? He was there when I went through basic ... not all that long ago ... back in my enlisted days."

"He is, captain," Brown said. "Worst week of basic."

"Ugh, just two days for me. The only part I remember was a chief's introduction before Professor Allen entered the room. 'The most important thing you need to know about orbital mechanics is that they take too fucking long.'"

The enlisted on the bridge joined him to finish the statement.

Emma looked around the bridge with a bemused look on her face. Her eyes stopped on Quinn.

He smiled back. "At the time, I thought he was talking about the effort to solve the problems by hand. Only later was it explained to me that the actual gravity-assisted maneuvers took too long. It's a science better suited for a fuel-conscious platform than one capable of sustained high-gee thrust. I know it's not always true; I know they're part of every calculation Mascord makes, but we made you smile, so it was worth it."

Emma shook her head, holding her lips tight for a moment. "That wasn't a smile."

Quinn shrugged affably. "Regardless, we'll make the chief's point in this system. On approach to the planet, the usual options will not be available. Orbits of any size are off the table. They're too slow and would take us around to the dark side. Hovering would give us away instantly with bright, beautiful displays in the atmosphere. For now, I'm planning a series of low elevation fly-bys but standby for change ... Any questions?"

The bridge remained silent.

"Good, let's secure from battle stations until close approach."

The inner system appeared safe. Two minor debris belts circled the star, but they were nowhere near Batfish's planned course. They had a clear view of the planet's far side from the drone's sensors, and Sturgeon was reporting all clear on both sides of the jump point. Emma was behind Petty Officer Ramirez at the sensor station, controlling Batfish's telescope via hand gestures while watching the display above the console.

"The drone pinpointed the signal to a position near the equator. That point will come into view in about ten minutes."

The display showed a single large body of water with islands of various sizes scattered across. "The southern ice cap is prominent." She zoomed in on one of the larger islands north of the ice. "Not much here. Looks like low shrubs over most of the ground. Biodiversity is minimal."

She panned northward. "Same on the coastline."

She zoomed out and panned to an island near the equator. "I think that's a strip of grass there … and it looks like the same shrubs inland."

She panned again.

"This landmass ahead, the signal must be coming from there … still over the horizon."

Only a few moments passed, and they were crossing over the coastline of the larger island.

"Same grass, same shrub." She panned and then stopped abruptly. "Are those buildings?"

Quinn stepped closer as she zoomed in on a row of structures.

"Looks like crops to the right and trees across the top," he said.

"Hmm, the scope is at its limit," Emma said. "Can we get closer?"

Quinn drew closer to the display, concentrating on the fuzzy image of the buildings.

"Do we have anything else, Ramirez?"

"No, sir. Still clear all around."

"Let's wait until the signaling location comes into view, XO."

"Aye, captain."

The landscape rolled steadily by, initially distorted by the atmosphere and then coming into focus.

"This looks like a town," Emma said. "It's nicely kept ... that looks like a park, and the land around it all seems ... agrarian. They're farmers."

"Not many roads," Quinn said.

"The signal is back," Ramirez said.

"A new speaker," Emma said. "I recognize that phrase. I think this is the start of a broadcast."

"Good morning, Groombridge?" Quinn asked.

"Not sure yet," Emma answered impassively as she panned to the signal's origin. "That's a radio tower."

She turned and looked over at Quinn with an incredulous look on her face. "This place looks like Earth 200 years ago."

Quinn stood back and considered for a moment. "Hard to believe they have space flight ... Okay, helm, take us in close, but keep above 300 kilometers and keep us on the sunny side ... and don't create any atmospheric displays."

"Aye, captain."

"Captain, I'm fairly certain they're not Birdies."

Emma had the telescope trained on a group of four walking down a wide, centrally located road.

"The color is wrong; they're walking more erect than I'd expect, and the tall one in that group must be two and a half meters tall, based on the shadow. The Birdies were well under two meters, a little shorter than us."

"Well, score zero for the scientists," Quinn said. "It looks like the galaxy may be more populated than they thought, or at least our neighborhood."

Emma zoomed out. "This central section reminds me of a shopping district, warehousing over here ... It looks like housing is distributed, assuming this unit is for housing." She circled a building on the display.

"Any sign of technology?" Quinn asked. "Besides the tower."

"There was a vehicle." Emma quickly panned the display and zoomed in on what could be a truck.

"And here, at one of the farms, these buildings must house something like a tractor. The crop rows are too neat to be maintained by hand … and these tracks coming out of the building look like they were made by wheels."

"Could be housing animals," Quinn said. "And a wheeled plow pulled by those animals."

"Maybe."

She then zoomed out until the entire town was in view and then panned along a road leading toward a smaller town until several moving vehicles appeared at the leading edge of the display. "Here they are on the move."

"Well, they don't look like a threat," Quinn said. "That's good news."

"Captain," Mascord said. "We're getting close to the 300-kilometer limit."

"Aye, helm, take us … take us over open ocean and then straight up to 10,000 kilometers. Spread the beams; I don't want to risk damaging anything down there; we'll have to risk the light show. Once up there, I'd like to survey the entire planet. There must be towns larger than this one."

The on-again, off-again nature of the thrust they had endured for the last two hours gave way to an uncomfortable two gees.

Lost in thought, Emma only noticed when she turned to speak and realized all others had found a seat.

"Testing your legs, XO."

"Ha, barely noticed." She started to sit when her knees buckled, dropping her unceremoniously into a chair. "I was thinking; Groombridge 1830 is considered a super flare system. The development of life here is unlikely."

She paused to adjust herself on the chair and then to adjust the chair itself to a higher gee position.

"So far, I've counted twelve varieties of flora: two spread wild across the planet, eight crop types, and two different trees in town. Adding at most a few farm animals ... there isn't enough variety — I doubt any of what we're seeing is indigenous to this planet. Furthermore, what is the chance of an intelligent species developing within such a tiny biosphere?"

"I'm sure there's much more down there than we've seen, but I see your point," Quinn said.

"So, if not from here, where did they come from, and how did they get here?"

"Mascord, that's far enough. Take us straight up, three gees."

"Ramirez, where's the drone now?" Quinn could retrieve the data instantly, but maintaining crew cohesion required involvement by all, a notion drilled into him at Officer Candidate School under the heading of 'Delegation.'

"It's 42 hours from the L2 point. It will arrive with a small reserve of reaction mass, enough to maintain position."

"Very well." He adjusted his chair and turned towards Emma, waiting for an answer.

Emma opened her mouth to speak but was cut off by Quinn.

"Mascord, did the diagnostics find any problems with the generator?"

"No, sir."

"Eh, collect the data. We'll have Sturgeon pass it on to Fredericksburg. Something else for the designers to look at." He motioned for Emma to continue.

"Sir, in addition to 'where' and 'how,' I suppose we could add 'when,' 'why,' and maybe a 'who' to the list of questions."

"Who?" Quinn asked.

"Well, they do not appear to be a space-faring race, far from it. So, who brought them here?"

"Perhaps the Birdies?" Mascord asked. "They could be a slave race, producing food for their masters."

Emma shook her head. "Nothing we've seen so far supports that. Those fields are about the right size to support the town and not much else. In addition, I'd expect to see some level of infrastructure to support spaceflight, runways or landing pads, and some way of refueling. The system has no gas giants, and I don't think we'll find a refinery down there."

"There are the outer planets. No one has looked at those yet."

"And there are the eight adjacent systems we haven't visited," Quinn added. "Those make me nervous."

"Ease thrust to two gees. That will put us up there in twenty minutes. Soon enough."

"Sir," Ramirez said. "There's a new signal. Much stronger than the other."

"It's directional," Emma added. "And … it's now centered on us."

Quinn's eyes widened. "Damn it. Belay my last helm. Keep us at three gees."

He accessed the intercom. "All hands prepare for seven gees."

With the ship at battle stations, the responses were nearly instant.

"Max thrust, helm."

With a flick of Mascord's wrist, the background noise of the drives grew in volume, taking on a musical tone as the long, linear arrays of magnets approached their capacities.

"Passing five gees, Mascord yelled."

"What do you have, Emma?" Quinn asked.

She ignored the use of her first name. "It's voice, but in another language … and there's a second signal from the same direction. I'm playing with it now."

"Sensors, do you have a location?"

"Aye, captain," Ramirez answered. "It's about twenty kilometers north of the town, right on the horizon."

Emma directed the telescope towards the signal.

"Yep, too close to the horizon to see anything. We'll need to move closer."

"We're not doing that," Quinn said.

"Helm, take us directly away. I don't want to be in their line of sight."

"Aye, captain."

"XO?"

"Captain, the language is different, but I'm convinced it's the same race."

Quinn tried twisting under the heavy acceleration. "And it's being directed at us? You're sure?"

"Absolutely. The main lobe was centered on us, although it's breaking up now due to the horizon."

"What about the second signal?"

"It's gone now, but … I'm looking at the recording … there."

An animated, cartoonish image appeared on a secondary display. Three short vignettes repeated in a loop. The first showed a circle representing a planet with a ship in orbit. A smaller ship separates from the larger one and descends to the planet. The second vignette showed what appeared to be a happy greeting between three nondescript figures on the ground and a nondescript figure standing next to the smaller ship. The third showed a physical map with a location marked by a plus sign. Emma quickly found a matching location from the recorded imagery and put it on another display.

The bridge was silent, minus the drives, as the recording repeated.

"Helm, this is killing me. Reduce thrust to one gee."

The force that was pressing all into their chairs dropped off immediately.

"Comm, are we able to respond?"

"Aye, captain. Our transmitter can be configured for both the audio and video, although the surface transmitter is currently over the horizon."

"Thanks, comm. We're going to keep it that way for the time being. Send all to Sturgeon. Request they pass on to Fredericksburg immediately with a request for orders ... Lieutenant Stewart, anymore on the audio."

Emma broke her train of thought and met Quinn's gaze. "Uh ... the signal is a simple message, perhaps three phrases repeating like the video. My guess is that the text matches the video, an invitation to meet on the surface. The language is ... is simple compared to that from the tower, although three phrases aren't much to go on. Specifically, the human vocal cords can correctly produce 64 percent of the phonemes from the tower and 95 percent of those in this message."

"Anything else?"

Emma paused, gathering her words.

"They're trying to communicate with an unknown ship in orbit and chose a language other than their own. There may be another race in the vicinity."

"Not what I wanted to hear, Stewart — If true, why did they send the video?"

"I'm not sure. Perhaps they were guessing which language to use and added the video to ensure we understood their request." Emma shrugged.

Quinn put his head in his hands. "So, there may be multiple races in the vicinity. Great."

"Comm, send Lieutenant Stewart's theories along with the rest."

"Aye, captain."

Two hours passed, and nothing of interest was found on the planet, although they had yet to see all.

A second populated continent-sized island was found, centered just north of the equator. It was like the first, scattered farming communities with a few large towns.

The northern pole matched the southern in size. Life in the highest and lowest latitudes would be difficult.

Quinn called up statistics:

- Surface gravity: .7 (Earth standard).
- Axial tilt: 4.5 degrees
- Atmospheric content: 19% oxygen, 79% nitrogen, 2% trace gases
- Average sea surface temperature at the equator: 13.5 C
- Average overland surface temperature at the equator: 17.8 C

"Livable but cool," he said to no one in particular.

"If we go down, the contagion protocol will be in effect until we sample the environment ... To be honest, I would not be upset if Fredericksburg says no. Environmental sampling kits were never designed to test an entire planet."

"If all sampled microorganisms are as incompatible with our physiology as those we found with the Birdys, then we're safe ... probably."

Emma realized that she had greatly simplified the problem and didn't care.

"How many kits do we have, chief?" Quinn asked.

"Eight."

Quinn nodded. "Take them all. Test the air, water, and soil near the landing site and around anything alive within the vicinity.

"Yes —"

Brown interrupted. "Captain, we have orders from Fredericksburg."

Quinn stepped to the communication station to read the message. "We have a go," he said with a heavy sigh.

"Lieutenant Stewart, you're both our pilot and interpreter. Obviously, you're going. Chief Andersen, I'd like you to accompany her down. You will stay with the trainer, and both of you will stay in constant contact. We'll load provisions for an extended stay, although you may return after an hour. You'll have enough reaction mass to get you there and back with plenty to spare. Just make sure the batteries are fully charged in case you need to run."

"Aye, captain," they said together.

"The atmosphere is thin, and the surface temperature is on the cool side, so take something warm. We'll load additional oxygen bottles in case you need them once you're out of the environmental suits. Hopefully, you can shed those after we analyze the samples.

Make sure you use sunblock; the magnetic field is weak compared to Earth ... Finally, you will take firearms but keep them locked in the safe until needed."

Andersen nodded slowly. "Yes, sir."

"Any questions?"

"Batfish will remain in orbit?" Emma asked.

"We'll adopt a low-elevation orbit to assemble the trainer and then hover just off the coastline until you make contact. If your stay gets extended, we'll park ourselves in a fixed orbit, right over your head."

Emma smiled broadly. "Sounds good to me, sir."

As Batfish transitioned to the lower orbit, details of the planet were revealed. The population was spread across five large islands and eight smaller ones. The layout was the same as the first two: farms, small towns, and no indication of any technology more advanced than that of Earth two centuries before. Additional radio signals were detected, emanating from scattered towns, all much weaker than the first. Emma confirmed that all used the 'broadcast' language that Sturgeon had detected. The language of the message sent directly to Batfish remained unique.

February 1st 2126

The trainer shuttle was engineered for simplicity and flexibility. A modular design allowed its components to be stored in the void spaces aft of Batfish's primary hull and forward of the auxiliary spaces, very close to where a full-sized shuttle would be housed on a larger ship. Emma had flown this model exclusively during her abbreviated qualification course, three weeks that were part of a distant, disconnected past.

She and Chief Andersen sat side-by-side with storage behind and below, crammed with gear, food, water, and breathable air. A retro burn brought the trainer out of orbit and into the upper atmosphere. Aerobraking slowed their descent until Emma could roll the craft, put the nose down, and enter a glide path.

Batfish responded to the invitation by repeating the three phrases, using Emma as the speaker, and sending an edited video clip. A representation of the local star was added to the planet's depiction to imply a time of day. The landing craft was made to look more like the trainer, and they showed a pair of nondescript figures emerging rather than the one. The inhabitants of the planet responded quickly, re-sending the images from Batfish. This was taken as an acceptance.

"Idling the main drive," Emma said. She followed the predetermined glide path's circular descent. To the south, she could see the outskirts of 'Tower Town,' Quinn's designation. Small white clouds were scattered across the western horizon with light blue sky in all other directions. The yellow-tinted star hung above the eastern horizon.

The trainer could land on its tail, but that was only recommended on a prepared surface. The landing site was just a flat patch of sandy ground, recently cleared of brush to form an oval. The possibility of a super-heated pocket of moisture sending molten sand in every direction was too high.

On the final approach, Emma flared the electro-props under each wing, sending a cloud of sand into the still air. As the wheels touched, she cut power to avoid pulling more of that sand through the spinning blades.

The landing site was placed off-center in an unused field. Around that field, row crops extended in all directions, some a few inches high, others towering over her head. The land stretched down and away to the south. Beyond the planted fields, she saw the same low-lying vegetation that covered most of the planet, clinging to the rolling hills right to the horizon. That vista, combined with the cool air, brought memories of the Scottish Highlands, memories from any of the numerous trips that were forced upon her as a child. She could see what looked like a barn and a pair of large sheds sitting atop a small hill northwest of the landing site. Beyond that were two neat rows of buildings. All appeared to be of brick-and-mortar construction. Halfway between the barn and the shuttle, three figures approached. Their gait was slow and ponderous, but the distance covered by each stride gave them a pace to match a human in a slow run.

First contact was not a course at the academy when Emma attended. Still, there were many opinions on how to conduct oneself at, possibly, the most important introduction in the history of the human race. None offered reasonable answers to the trivial difficulties that Emma faced. The practice sessions on Batfish raised a handful of concerns. Quick-thinking crew members developed solutions, but without time to test them, all agreed they would have to see what would happen. Emma hopped from the trainer into the soft sand, regretting that flippant approach. With her first step, the boot of her loose-fitting environmental suit caught in the sand and almost brought her down.

"Fuck," she muttered, taking further, careful steps.

"I'm on the surface," she sent to the bridge.

A small amplifier in her backpack would maintain a connection to Batfish through the trainer. The suit was rigged like a standard uniform with both audio and video pickups.

"They've stopped near the edge of the landing pad. Two are setting up a canopy."

"Damn, they're tall."

Chief Andersen remained with the trainer, preparing a test kit to sample the air for dangerous pathogens. Emma, below average in height, with a slim figure encased in an environmental suit, a pack on her back, and a large portable display under an arm, walked carefully toward the three towering aliens.

Their legs reminded her of those on an elephant, thick columns supporting the weight above. Their bodies were a match for the legs, a solid block extending upward, narrowing where Emma expected a neck. Their heads appeared more like extensions of their bodies than separate entities, but the motions of each said otherwise, easily twisting and turning as they looked between each other, Emma, and the trainer. A pair of large eyes appeared in the right place; they had small dark pupils surrounded by bright green irises with only hints of yellow-white around the edges. Two nostrils were spread wide, but Emma suspected a connection underneath. They were bipedal, standing more erect than the Birdies would have, more like a human. By that same standard, their arms appeared slightly shorter but were as solid as the rest. The five-fingered hands could easily wrap around Emma's head.

Their exposed skin appeared leathery with mottled colors of gray, green, and brown. They were hairless, as far as Emma could see. Each was clothed from ankle to neck. The designs appeared very familiar, pants reaching from relatively small shoe-less feet up to a waist and a shirt covering the body and arms. All appeared to be of the same material and well-worn. The colors did not match, although all were as subdued as their skin coloration. The tallest of the three opted for a red shirt and gray pants. Another chose dark green with a lighter gray. The third wore gray over lighter gray—the opposite of the Birdies' preference for bright and gaudy.

One of the two stopped erecting the canopy and stepped to the side of the taller one. An image of the famous painting 'American Gothic' flashed in Emma's mind. Thankfully, there was no pitchfork.

Emma came to a stop two meters from the three. The tallest, Red on Gray, stepped forward, paused briefly, then said "talmahk" and followed with a slight bow, keeping his arms at his side. Emma thought the word contained a note of surprise, knowing that her perspective lacked the relevant context to draw such a conclusion from the observation. 'Tal,' the first sound, was new. The second, 'mahk,' was familiar, having been used in the message three times.

Her suit clearly amplified any external audio, but it had no external speaker. All communications were expected to go over a network. "Talmahk," she shouted loud enough to be heard through the face mask, and then she mimicked their bow.

The three looked down upon her with what she felt were bemused expressions.

She took a deep breath, stepped forward, and rotated the display to show an image of the building that had sent the message to

Batfish. She could only hope that their eyes could interpret the pattern of pixels as humans did.

The one with gray-on-gray clothing stepped forward and then turned to point at the structure behind them.

"Off to a good start," she said under her breath.

No one replied. It was agreed that she would provide regular updates, but they would not disturb her meeting needlessly.

She repeated the beginning of the message, which sounded like a greeting to her, and followed by pointing to the structure and nodding. All three immediately imitated her nod within the limits imposed by their thick necks. Red on Gray spoke a mix of words that Emma had just used and others new to her, all part of the simple language directed at Batfish.

She then called up an image of the tower in town and attempted to repeat a regularly used phrase from those broadcasts. The language used was much more difficult for her. She was confident she mangled most of the words but hoped they would understand what she was attempting.

Their bemused expression grew. Green on Gray stepped forward, carefully held a hand near Emma's face, and reached out to touch the mask. Emma took the gesture as a question and called up the agreed pair of animated images. One showed oversized microorganisms attempting to get inside the mask and failing. The other showed the opposite, microorganisms trapped inside the mask.

Green on Gray repeated the nod that Emma had shown them.

"I think they understand the masks. They're intelligent."

"That mask does not come off until Andersen has all his samples and each has been analyzed," Quinn sent.

Emma turned and waved over Andersen.

"We'll need to sample what they exhale."

Facing the three, she tapped on her mask and pointed to the test kit in Andersen's hands.

As he started a waving pattern with the intake wand, Green on Gray stepped toward him and blew toward the wand's end. The other two followed suit.

"Very intelligent."

Emma then called up an image to demonstrate the passage of time, showing Groombridge rising from mid-morning to high noon. The three nodded, and Emma held a hand up, waving as she stepped back, but Red on Gray held up both hands, an apparent sign for her to stop. She did, turning to face the three as Green on Gray lifted a clear glass container from a satchel sitting near his feet and held it out. Emma accepted the gift with her free arm, firmly pressing it against her chest. The three then stepped back and bowed in their unique way. Emma returned the gesture as best she could and followed Andersen to the trainer. The three began an animated discussion as they finished setting up the canopy. She heard enough before moving out of range to recognize it as the language of the broadcast from town rather than in the message sent to Batfish.

Interestingly, the word 'talmahk' was used several times. When finished, Gray on Gray unfolded a small table and centered it under the canopy. After which, they all returned to the nearest structure.

"How are you feeling, Stewart?" Quinn asked.

"Much better now. I was afraid my knees visibly shook when I first greeted them, but after that first bow ... I was fine."

"Any idea about the word 'talmahk'?"

"They use it in both languages, making it a proper noun or an indication of shared words. Either would make sense."

She handed the container to Andersen's outstretched hand.

"Water, I'm guessing."

"That would be a shame," Quinn remarked.

"Well, if you need anything, don't hesitate to ask. We have the data from Chief Andersen's first kit and will need another hour to evaluate it. The suits stay on until then. I want to see zero compatibility or something very close."

"Roger that, Captain." She accepted the folding chair offered by Andersen.

An hour and a half passed before Quinn sent a message down to Emma and Andersen.

"You should be safe … may be safe; It's the best we can do. We have zero compatibility with any of the sampled bugs, and while it was a small sample, I am told that it should be representative of the planet. They are fundamentally different from Earth's bugs, or, for what it matters, the Birdie's bugs. Using the same logic, they should be safe from ours … The water looks good also, H_2O with a few minerals. This said, don't stop testing."

"I won't, captain," Andersen replied.

"The virologist aboard Fredericksburg also told me not to expect the same going forward. He's calling this planet a poor example … sparse, he said."

"Sounds like good advice."

"Agreed … Also, it looks like you may have more visitors. We're tracking a dust trail from the road between the landing site and the town. Probably a truck. Maybe for you."

"Maybe," Emma responded.

"We've seen a few workers in the fields and some moving between buildings. I'm not sure what all the purposes are for this site, but farming is one."

Emma had unlatched the suit's headpiece. Holding her breath, she lifted it over her head to let it hang behind. She exhaled and then took a careful breath through her nose. The air was cool, with the distinct odor of old pine needles. She breathed a little deeper and then promptly sneezed.

"Oxygen seems okay. Does that kit look at pollen?"

"It does. You should be fine," Andersen answered.

"It looks like they're coming." He pointed toward the closest structure on the far side of a small gully.

The same three had exited the building and were walking down the shallow slope.

"Round two," Emma said as she stepped out of her suit and handed it to Andersen.

She then slipped on a light jacket and started toward the original meeting spot past the edge of the pad.

"You should see the truck," Quinn replied.

To the left, a vehicle was coming over a rise.

"It looks more like a minibus, and it looks full."

"Full? Do you have a count?"

"Eight or ten."

"Chief Andersen, stand ready," Quinn ordered.

"Should I pull a weapon from the safe?"

"Not yet, just be ready. Are they accessible?"

"Yes, sir."

Emma refrained from comment. Her strongest feeling was curiosity as the original three came from her right, and the minibus stopped on the dirt road to the left.

Two climbed out of the bus; one was female. Her shape was not as exaggerated as some human women, but it matched in form. She appeared slightly shorter than the male at her side, and both were shorter than Red on Gray. The bus continued toward the row of structures with the other riders. The three males stopped short of Emma at the side of the canopy. Red on Gray indicated with an arm that Emma should turn her attention toward the new arrivals.

"I'm getting the impression they took one look at me and called in a woman to do the talking."

"Well, you did say they were similar to Earth 200 years ago."

"Yes, I did. I'm calling her Yellow on Gray; the other is Green on Green."

"Chief, you can stand down."

"Yes, sir."

"Green on Green has a package. I'm not sure what's inside."

"They're here. Wish me luck."

Unencumbered by the environmental suit, Emma felt more comfortable and confident.

She stepped under the canopy and set the display on the table. Placing both hands on her collar, she said, "Talmahk?"

Yellow on Gray stepped closer, pointed at Emma, and repeated "Talmahk" and then a second time while pointing at Andersen.

She then put a hand over her midsection and said "Odishi," and then the same as she gestured toward Green on Green and once more while pointing at the original three.

Emma repeated, bringing what was likely a smile to Yellow on Gray's face.

"Good guess," Quinn said.

"Hush."

Yellow on Gray bowed toward the three. Red on Gray returned the bow, and then they turned back toward the structures. Green on Green then handed Yellow on Gray the package and followed the other three away.

From the package, she pulled out two small cakes, small even for a human, and handed one to Emma, keeping the other for herself. She then just stood before Emma, waiting.

"She's waiting for me to take a bite. I'm going to trust her," Emma said.

"I wish you wouldn't, but it's your call," Quinn said.

"Need the water?" Andersen said.

"Yes."

Emma turned her head and nodded to the chief. He grabbed the glass container and jogged over as Emma continued to wait with the cake in her hands. Once he was at her side, she took a moderate-sized bite and nodded to Yellow on Gray as she chewed.

"Tastes like low sodium cornbread, with some interesting notes. Not bad."

Yellow on Gray nodded back and bit into her cake.

"I believe this is a ritual."

She accepted the open container from Andersen and took a small drink before handing it to Yellow on Gray, who took a much larger drink and bowed to Andersen.

"I believe I've been excused," he said.

"I believe I'm about to start a lesson, but I'm not sure if I'm the teacher or the student," Emma said.

She and Yellow on Gray finished their cakes and the water in silence, after which Yellow on Gray assumed a position on one side of the table and invited Emma to the opposite.

After a mid-afternoon break, they continued until the light started to dim and the temperature became uncomfortable. Groombridge was low on the horizon when Emma returned to the trainer.

"The two of you appeared to get along fine," Andersen said from a chair he had set up under a wing. "How was your first lesson?"

"Great, although there's no doubt I was the student." She climbed into the cabin and then came down with a blanket. Warmly wrapped, she accepted the offered chair.

"Six hours of standing. I'm not used to that."

"I'm guessing the three of you did not listen to the entire conversation."

Andersen shook his head.

"All," Marina Zhào said.

"Most," Quinn said. "If you have the energy, I think it would be helpful to discuss what you learned."

"I'll do my best to summarize. Feel free to toss in any observations," Emma said.

"Her name is Adashi, and yes, they did choose her because of my sex. They believe that the similarities would speed up our communication. I'm not going to argue that point. That said, she was one of only three in the town that could act as an interpreter. They were surprised that we did not understand a common language, and that's when it became interesting."

Emma sat under the wing with Chief Andersen until darkness and cold air drove them back into the trainer. The four continued to dissect her conversation with Adashi long into the night.

Most of that first day was spent learning a few basic facts about the Odishi. They had three dialects of their own or possibly separate languages; Emma was not sure. In the broadcast, they heard the standard dialect used by all their citizens, but they also had a dialect for leaders and diplomats when acting within their role and a third for use by engineers and scientists. Separate from those three dialects was the language heard in the message sent to Batfish. It would be the focus of Emma's lessons to come.

It was a language common to the Odishi and five other races. Appropriately, Adashi referred to it as 'Common.' It was created specifically to match the speaking abilities of each. One of those races, the Talmahk, was human or very close. All memories of the races were almost 500 years old and had been passed down over several generations. Those memories were somewhat vague. To Quinn's great relief, the other races were not local. The Odishi had left their home and traveled to Groombridge 1830, when the people of Earth were sailing across the Atlantic, willing or unwilling, for a new life on the American continents. The reason or reasons for their move had not been discussed. Neither had there been any explanation of their current state, a backward farming community rather than the space-faring race that had traveled a great distance to find a new home.

Emma was in no rush to question Adashi on those details. The answers would come much more quickly when she better grasped Common. What she had learned so far, a set of facts that would take about five minutes to recite, had required Adashi the entire afternoon to explain.

Curiously, Adashi had expressed little interest in Emma, Batfish, and why this group of 'Talmahk' was so illiterate.

The next morning, Red on Gray met her under the canopy. A light rain was falling, and the air had an unpleasant chill. "Emma," he said clearly and then bowed. She would have to learn his name. For now, she simply bowed. He indicated the nearest building with an arm and said, "Adashi."

"They've moved my lessons inside."

"Be careful, Stewart. You will need to maintain your connection. That's not an option."

"Yes, sir. Chief, I'll be fine, right?"

"Not a problem. The relay should have no trouble."

She followed Red on Gray across the gully to the first building. Its walls were of gray mortar, the roof an intricately woven, watertight thatch, light brown for the most part. She would learn that it was part of an observatory that had detected Batfish maneuvering above the town. Inside, a set of well-thought-out visual aids were being set up by a small group of Odishi. One was Green on Green, the bearer of cornbread from the past day. Unfortunately, like their meeting under the canopy, not a chair was in sight.

"The connection seems fine. I believe everyone that was on that bus is here for my benefit. Look at this setup."

As it had been the day before, she was sending all that she saw and heard up to Batfish. The stream of images put Quinn at ease. It looked like a classroom back on Earth, although grade school at best. Red on Gray pointed her toward a table holding a small selection of cornbread cakes and two water containers. Not having suffered from the cake she had previously eaten, she felt brave and chose one with green lacing throughout.

"This is delicious; still needs salt, but it has a great flavor otherwise."

She nodded to Red on Gray and smiled.

He returned what she was now certain to be the Odishi equivalent of a smile.

"Enjoy your exotic dishes, Stewart," Quinn said.

"We're about to break out the dehydrated meals here, but don't worry about us. We also have news from Sturgeon. They'll jump into the eight adjacent systems to ensure we're alone out here.

Fredericksburg is moving into the system and will remain at the Xi Ursae Majoris jump point."

"Roger that, Captain, and rest assured, I'm not worrying about you at all."

"Adashi is here."

Emma greeted her teacher with a smile and an Odishi bow. Adashi returned the bow with grace but looked exhausted.

"I think she was up all night creating these displays. I'm guessing they have about the same sleep requirements that we have."

"No coffee pot in sight?"

"Sadly, no."

That night, like the night before, like many nights to come, Emma analyzed what she had learned with Quinn, Zhào, and Andersen.

The day had been discouraging. Most of her lessons had centered around numbering systems, mathematics, and the array of methods the Odishi used to keep time.

Initially, she was surprised by the amount they managed to teach with her limited vocabulary. The Odishi used a base-12 numbering system. Thankfully, they had a common numbering system that accompanied the common language, and it was base-10. That reduced her math lesson to one of terms, learning different wording for familiar concepts.

The various methods of timekeeping led to a more convoluted lesson, although, in this case, she was confident that the language barrier added to her struggle. Days and years were used, and they were derived in the same manner as those on Earth. That made sense. Local time was based upon the planet where they stood, but what had confused Emma were Adashi's references to other systems of time and her frequent attempts to explain how those differences fit into everyday conversations.

The use of three dialects and base-12 numbers had complicated Emma's understanding of the Odishi, but the use of six additional definitions for a day and year was inexplicable. Adding further confusion, each of the six was interwoven with its unique lore.

Emma was convinced that her repeated failures to grasp any of what she was hearing led Adashi to pivot to a straightforward explanation of a common timekeeping system. The length of a day and year were averaged values derived from the home planets of the five races. Both were longer than a day and a year on Earth. There was no concept of a month, week, or minute, but a hundredth of a day made for a short hour, and a thousandth of an hour made a second that came very close to that on Earth.

Quinn was encouraged by the use of common systems. It would greatly simplify interactions with any of the five other races. The identity of those other races remained an open question. More specifically, were the Birdies one of the five?

Over the next day and then many to follow, she enjoyed greater success, although she was confident that they had adjusted their methods and pace to avoid the difficulties of the second day. Her time was devoted exclusively to learning the Common language. Adashi led the effort, but as time passed, individual lessons were handled by other Odishi. Their methods appeared perfectly tuned to her personality and capabilities. Each lesson reinforced a previous one while adding additional content. Each varied just enough to avoid overwhelming her with the excessive details from a single line of thought.

Upon return to the trainer, she spent the first hour or two reviewing her notes from the day and recording what she had learned. To the limits of her memory, she stored every word, defined or not, each new phoneme, phrase, name of places, and name of individuals, adding details and comments where needed. After which, she chatted with the crew over a simple dinner. Later in the evening or early in the morning, she would package all information into a lesson and send a copy up to Batfish.

March 23rd 2126

Weeks passed. Emma made periodic trips to and from Batfish to take from their dwindling supplies and to switch out her companion. Boredom aboard the ship had grown to the point that there was always a volunteer. It was a chance to get out of a cramped environment, visit an alien world, or at least feel the force of gravity. Once on the planet's surface, the excitement, or at least curiosity, lasted a day at most. Emma felt guilty, but Quinn insisted that the trainer was continuously guarded and that she was never left alone on the planet.

Sturgeon reported that all adjacent systems were clear of any threats, as clear as they could determine from the jump points. A small research team had been assembled from the crew of Fredericksburg. That ship would soon be in orbit with Batfish. The researchers would study the Odishi, the planet, and, significantly, the star. Concern was growing over its stability.

Galileo was en route to the system and would assume control of all research. When that ship arrived, Batfish, Sturgeon, and Fredericksburg would return to Earth for refurbishment and then deployment to 82 G. Eridani. Emma and the other researchers would be temporarily assigned to Galileo. Hammerhead and Puffer would accompany Galileo, providing reconnaissance and security. Both had been provided missile batteries in the voids where Batfish had stored the parts of the trainer shuttle. Emma informed Adashi of the ship rotations in a general sense, numbers of ships but not capabilities.

Adashi and her team eventually described the five other races that spoke Common. No actual images were available. The artwork shown to Emma had been recreated from very old memories passed from generation to generation. The depiction of the Ki Ti Tor Mahk matched that of the bodies on the captured ship. This gave Emma some confidence in the memories of the Odishi.

The Sal appeared to be a cross between a human and a mouse. At least the faces depicted in the images had some human characteristics. The similarity ended there. Their ears were very mouse-like, and short fur covered their bodies.

The Mahkee appeared to be, at most, a meter high with a muscular build, smooth yellow-green skin, and a thick mane running down their back. They had oversized eyes like the Odishi and the Ki Ti Tor Mahk, but their irises were shown as dark brown, almost black. A close Relation to the Mahkee, the Porta Ree, shared the same facial characteristics, skin, color, and mane but appeared to be of human height and extremely thin.

The one other race that shared Common was the Talmahk. The recreated images looked exactly like humans. Emma could not explain it, and neither could the Odishi. Their memory did not extend much beyond basic descriptions of the races. They had no references to territory or political boundaries. They were not even sure where their own home had been before they traveled to Groombridge.

April 19th 2126

The wet season for the equatorial band of the planet had arrived. It was the third day of rain following an on-again, off-again mix of showers and fog reaching back another week. Emma ran along the edge of the narrow, muddy road that stretched from the landing pad to the farm yard, her display under an arm, carefully shielded from the rain. The klackish to her right was chest-high and would not be ready to harvest for another month. It was the source of the small meal that she found herself looking forward to every morning. To her left, the ground sloped downward across a fallow field, reaching the road connecting the observatory to town. Beyond that was lost in the mist that filled the air.

A pair of radanks stood in the farm yard, oblivious to the steady drizzle or perhaps enjoying it. Docile, comfortable in Emma's presence, they didn't react as she passed in front of both. Siljay, formerly Red on Gray, was standing in a large puddle packing a small bus. Emma greeted him as she climbed the oversized steps leading up to the schoolhouse door, once office space for the observatory, once a barn. Adashi met her at the door under a small overhang that shielded both from the rain.

"Good morning, Emma." It was a human greeting but spoken in Common.

"May this day bring you joy," Emma answered with one of several Odishi morning greetings but spoke in Common.

"We have no lessons planned for today," Adashi said.

Emma looked up at her expectantly.

"Would you like to visit Maklay?"

That was the town to the south. To date, Emma had met 13 Odishi, perhaps seen another 20 in the distance, working the farm, and spoken with only 8.

"A field trip. That would be wonderful."

Adashi looked at her questioningly.

Emma winced. "Bad joke. The word 'field' has other meanings, and we are going on a trip, so …"

Adashi slowly shook her head, a gesture she had learned from Emma. "English?"

"Yes." Emma sighed. "The term used in the other languages of our world is more appropriate."

"That was very funny, Emma. We'll need to learn more of your humor, and then, perhaps, you can learn of ours."

Emma gave Adashi a wry smile. Odishi humor was deeply sardonic and, when appropriate, made liberal use of irony and occasional sarcasm.

Adashi continued. "We have scheduled several visits to give you a better understanding of how we live. The farm and observatory are incomplete representations of the Odishi. We have commerce, markets, a government, and even a younger generation."

Emma had never met a young Odishi, or she had never met an Odishi that didn't tower over her. She understood that their process was the same as humans: a mother, a father, and a child or children. In the Common language, the term 'child' only referred to the offspring of an individual. Emma was unaware of a specific term for younger Odishi.

Two of Adashi's assistants, Rork Akane and Tormond, followed her out the door. Each had been responsible for some of Emma's lessons.

"Captain, I'm visiting Maklay today and will be out of communication range."

There was a short pause.

"Oh, right, Tower Town. Any idea how long?"

"Not at the moment."

"I'm not worried. Have fun."

"I may have a good opportunity to discuss the attack by the Ki Ti Tor Mahk, although I'll be out of range before you can get authorization from Fredericksburg."

"If a chance comes up, take it. I'll inform Fredericksburg."

"Roger."

Emma ran behind the three as they quickened their pace through the rain and over the puddle blocking an open door at the back of the bus. She paused momentarily and then took a running leap to avoid the deeper water. Rork reached out, shut the door, and waved to Siljay, who sat behind the large steering wheel in the front.

She felt like a small child, shifting on the oversized seat to find a comfortable position. It was the first Odishi seat she had used or seen. The material was from an animal hide, likely that of a radank, stiff and somewhat abrasive. The window behind her head appeared no different than a vehicle's window on Earth. The bus's body reminded Emma of plastic, although she knew it was not derived from fossil fuel. That didn't exist on the planet. As they accelerated out of the farm yard, she could hear the soft whine of an electric motor coming from under her feet. Siljay maneuvered around the larger potholes and bounced over the smaller ones as they started up the first hill on the road toward Maklay.

"Tell me about your home," Adashi said from the seat across from Emma.

Emma nodded vigorously. She had learned much about the Odishi over the past ten weeks but spoke little about humanity. Her only restrictions were the discussions of system locations, military capabilities, and deployed assets. Discussions of Fredericksburg and Sturgeon were limited. The pending arrival of Galileo was acceptable.

"Our world, Earth, as I've mentioned, is like Iburak in many ways."

Iburak was the Odishi name for their planet and the star that it orbited. From their mythology, 'Ibu' made sense to Emma, 'home' or 'mother.' The Odishi society was nominally matriarchal. No rules enforced the sex of the leaders, but personal preference led more females into the role. The suffix rak had limited use. Its meaning, 'lost,' alluded to their arrival into the system. Discussions in past lessons had talked around the subject.

"We have caps of ice over that cover our north and south poles; most of the surface is covered with water; and life is present on every landmass and at all depths of the oceans. Earth has a much greater tilt to its axis, which causes local temperatures to vary greatly over a year. Snow will cover the land at one time of the year, and steam will rise from the soil at another."

Emma's confidence grew. It was the longest uninterrupted statement she had made since starting her lessons, and she completed it without mistakes, to the best of her knowledge. "Life on Earth is diverse compared to Iburak, although I understand that all I've seen here was brought by your ancestors."

"The original settlers go back only four or five generations," Adashi said.

Emma understood that the Odishi were long-lived, but they had not discussed that either.

"But you're right, the only native life was in the oceans, and some very low forms in the soil — How diverse is life on Earth?"

"We count plant species in hundreds of thousands and animal species in the millions."

Rork and Tormond showed clear doubt on their faces, but Adashi smiled. Mischievously, Emma thought.

"I suppose it would make sense for a race that has names for thousands of colors to parse the species of its planet so finely."

Emma smiled warmly at Adashi's playful jab.

"Then again," Adashi continued. "Limiting ourselves to 12 colors has been a regular source of confusion."

"Perhaps a reasonable compromise was found with Common?" Emma asked.

"Perhaps. It's more than 12, although I'm unsure of the actual count."

Adashi paused for a moment. "Perception varies with every race — In this respect, you're very much like the Ki Ti Tor Mahk."

Emma's smile dropped from her face. She realized too late that it would raise questions but was frozen by indecision. Was this a good time to mention the attack?

All three Odishi noticed her discomfort.

"How does the diversity on your planet compare to others you have encountered?" Adashi asked quickly.

Emma started to speak, but words would not come out. She met Adashi's concerned look and felt a cold sweat across her forehead. The only other planet they had found with life had hidden the five Ki TI Tor Mahk ships before they attacked.

The bus leaned side to side as it drove through a small ditch. Emma grabbed the sides of her seat only to distract from the conversation.

"Let's try the cakes that Siljay brought," Adashi said with a light, calming note. "They smell wonderful."

Emma nodded quickly and reached into the basket offered by Tormond. Her motion felt mechanical, forced. Given the passage of time, she had thought the coming discussion would be easier.

"Oh, this is stupid," she finally said.

The Odishi turned their attention from the basket of cakes to Emma, a mix of surprise and alarm on their faces.

"I'm being stupid," Emma clarified, tapping her chest.

"I would like to tell another story from my recent past ... not a happy story."

"Yes, certainly," Adashi said. "But have a cake first. Collect your thoughts."

"Thanks, yes." Emma felt the fear drain away as she looked over the cake in her hand, one with a deep yellow hue. One she had not seen before. Her choice held the attention of both Rork and Tormond. She looked up at their curious faces and then back down at the cake in her hand. "Did I just make a mistake?"

"The value of a distraction should never be dismissed," Adashi said enigmatically.

"Okay, fine," Emma said and enthusiastically bit into the cake.

It was hot, painfully so, with a flavor like horseradish missing the fumes that fill the head.

She chewed and swallowed with determination and then bit into the cake again. Her older cousin Chloe, Cthulhu, had slipped her so many spiced morsels that she had developed a taste for them. The cake was not the hottest she had eaten, but close.

She gave the three an appreciative smile and let it fade as she set the cake in her lap.

"Before we came to your system, we, the crew of Batfish, were investigating a world like our own, full of life. This was about 140 of your day ago, 170 of ours. We were with a science … ship." She only knew of one word in Common for a vessel.

"They were in a low orbit around the equator when five ships rose from the surface and attacked her with … projectiles, self-propelled projectiles?" She was unsure of a word for a missile.

"The Ki Ti?" Adashi asked with a new emotion that Emma took for anger.

Emma nodded gravely. "They were small ships, but our science ship, Copernicus, was unarmed. They destroyed one of the five using the drive's exhaust, but the other four crippled her with the projectiles. After that, they attached their ships to her side. It was at that time that Copernicus blew herself up to avoid capture. The explosion destroyed the four remaining ships."

Emma lifted her display from her side and called up images from the captured ship.

"Here is what we found aboard the first ship."

She allowed Adashi to scroll through the images. When complete, she returned the display to Emma and paused for a long moment. "My first question: Why did the crew of Copernicus blow up their ship?"

Since the incident, Emma had never been in a conversation that considered capture as an alternative.

"It was a requirement that was imposed upon our ships. I believe you understand that we're reluctant to reveal the location of our home world. We also don't want our people or technology to be captured. That's also considered a threat to our world — From what you know of the Ki Ti, would they have harmed the crew?" Emma swallowed hard, wishing she had not asked the question.

"Probably. More so after you destroyed the first ship, but that's based upon very little, very old information. They were violent and angered easily."

Emma looked up and nodded, relieved.

Ahead in a broad valley, she could see the distant town through the clearing mist. A narrow river cut through cultivated fields from the right and passed through the town. It exited on the left, wide, tidal in nature. A few delicate wisps of smoke rose from buildings. Bakeries, she guessed and then picked up the cake for another bite and then looked pointedly at Adashi. "Your second question?"

Adashi stared back for a moment and then answered. "The question is, 'Would it be possible for the Odishi to meet the race or races that live in star systems beyond 82 G Eridani?' I understand that this is not for you to answer, but we are hopeful that you can relay it the leaders of your people."

Emma nodded solemnly. "I will."

It was not a request that would be welcome on Earth, and Emma was sure that fact showed on her face. It was an awkward moment that she wanted to pass quickly.

"Since we arrived in orbit above your planet, your existence here has been a mystery." You came here from a distant place, but you have no ships. You're brilliant by our standards, but we see no signs of an advanced civilization. Technologically, you are as we were hundreds of years ago.

On Earth, there are groups that isolate themselves from others and avoid using technology. Several have claimed land on planets that we're attempting to make habitable. The most popular explanation of your existence here aligns with the behavior of those groups ... I disagree with that assessment."

Adashi met Emma's gaze. She was both somber and hesitant. Melancholy, Emma thought.

"You're right, of course. Let me give you a brief history of the Odishi on Iburak. That should fill our time until we arrive in town."

"We were once part of a union of seven races. I have mentioned five in our discussion of the Common language: The Ki Ti Tor Mahk, the Sal, the Mahkee, the Porta Ree, and the Talmahk." She gestured to Emma on the last, then twisted her face in confusion.

"The other, the Kochpotat, were quite friendly but incapable of articulating any of the sounds of the Common language. We, the six other races, were equally incapable of speaking their language, but the written form of Common allowed us to communicate.

"Between members, the union was relatively peaceful. There were disagreements and small acts of violence, but nothing like the violence of another race. The <Malanxm?> lived far beyond the borders of Union space."

Adashi paused, knowing the final sounds in the name would be beyond Emma's capability. Regardless, Emma made several attempts, with the final causing pain in her throat.

"How about 'Malum,'" she said after a moment of thought. "It's the term for evil in one of our oldest languages."

"That works well," Adashi said. "Only one of the six had full command of the language, and it was a common practice for the other races to modify pronunciations to match their abilities."

"Only one?" Emma asked, narrowing her eyes at Adashi.

"Not the Odishi. The range and quality of Ki Ti Tor Mahk speech was … is almost perfect."

Emma frowned.

"Don't worry; it's one of their few strengths."

"Regarding the Malum, they were a violent race. For hundreds of years, they would raid Union space, destroying ships and installations but leaving the planet-bound populations alone. Something changed; we don't know what; either we never knew or that knowledge was lost. It doesn't matter. They turned their wrath on the planets and then, more specifically, on the Odishi planets. We fought. Some in the Union fought at our side. Others did not. They had either lost the ability to resist the Malum or chose to stop out of self-preservation. After several years of war and slaughter, it was decided to send a group of Odishi to safety, far from Union space, away from the Malum. Unseen, we had hoped, a fleet of transports and an escort of combat ships left the second planet in the Ika system with more than two million settlers. They passed out of Union space and through a sparsely populated region, mostly Sal and Ki Ti, who did not want to live within the Union. Many were criminals; others just felt constrained by our common laws."

"Pirates," Emma said, using the English term.

Adashi gave her a questioning look.

"Before space travel on Earth, before air travel, we used our seas to travel great distances, riding on ships blown by the wind."

"As we do now," Adashi said.

Emma nodded. Batfish had reported several sailing ships passing between the islands.

"Groups of criminals would use their ships to capture passing merchants. They would steal the cargo and often kill the crew. The attack by the Ki Ti reminds me of those pirates."

"That's a fair description," Adashi said. "Although I'm not sure they were as violent, at least the Sal were not. We had no trouble from them, although we believe some eventually betrayed us to the Malum.

We passed through that region into space considered empty but did not stop. We believed that safety could only be achieved with distance, so we continued until our provisions were low. Scouts had been searching for a viable planet without luck. This system was not considered in the initial search. I'm sure you know that the star is unstable."

Adashi paused.

"We do," Emma said. "Old observations have shown great flares coming from the star, although nothing recent."

Adashi continued. "Eventually, they did investigate and found this world. It was not ideal, but the air was breathable, and we could begin agricultural production without reforming the surface. Our goal at the time was to make it a temporary home until we could find a better world. The star would remain quiet for many years, so we felt safe in that decision. Settlements were established on all major islands. We were building two small cities when the Malum found us. They destroyed our ships as they attempted to flee, then turned to the planet. Ground strikes annihilated the two cities. After that, they struck smaller towns and then individual farms."

"We were convinced they intended to exterminate us, and then their attacks stopped. We don't know why, but we hope it was an act of decency, in the end, a reluctance to eliminate another species. This, at least, gives us hope that others survived."

"I'm very sorry this happened to you," Emma said.

Adashi nodded. "Over half of us were killed in the attack, most of our leaders and nearly the entire technology class."

"Is that what stopped you from rebuilding a fleet or at least a few ships?"

"It would have slowed the effort, but no, this planet is responsible for that failure. We found that the topsoil had healthy levels of metals but soon realized there were no significant deposits to mine, at least none accessible by any means available to us following the attacks. What little we had was brought down when we settled the planet. Construction of even a single ship would have been impossible. Now, even the required knowledge has faded."

Adashi paused and looked out the window. Emma followed her gaze.

The ride had become smooth and steady as the small dips and occasional potholes disappeared outside Maklay. That changed suddenly as they crossed onto a road of brick. A steady chatter ensued from the wheels and the frame of the bus.

This continued for several minutes before the bus slowed. Ahead was the town center. The rain had left the road and buildings with a freshly cleaned look. Like the buildings at the observatory, construction was of brick and mortar, although the buildings before her had a finer finish and were adorned with plants and flowers. The center had the feel of an urban garden. Trees provided shade at equal intervals, although the need for shade was small. Well-kept bushes lined most buildings, small relative to the buildings and the Odishi. Sidewalks were the only thing missing compared to many towns on Earth, but the placement of the trees encouraged vehicles down the center, leaving a path for pedestrians on each side.

They stopped in a small, three-slot parking lot. It was, otherwise, empty. Vehicles were a rarity. Emma had noticed one other, a truck parked in front of what she assumed to be a warehouse. Due to this rarity, they had drawn the casual attention of a pair of smaller Odishi walking along the side of the road, small compared to all other Odishi Emma had met but taller than the average human adult and much taller than her. That attention turned to awe as she hopped down from the open door in the back. Both stopped and stared in silence. At her side, Rork barked a command in Odishi Standard. Emma recognized the language but didn't understand what was said. The two gave him a look that Emma categorized as defiance and then slowly walked away, returning their eyes to her. She raised her hand in an Odishi wave, which they immediately returned.

"Go," Rork shouted. Emma recognized that word.

"How old are they?" she asked after Adashi exited the bus.

"Nine or ten."

She was using Common years. Using the local year, a standard adopted by the Odishi, they were all over 15. Using the Terran year, their ages were between eleven and twelve.

"Do you have an organized system of education?"

Based upon the last ten weeks of well-orchestrated training, Emma knew the answer.

"We provide guided education to all young Odishi. It continues until they show a willingness and ability to guide their education or achieve a suitable level of functionality. Those two are still very young. Our first visit will be to their school."

She gestured ahead to a small building that the two young Odishi were entering. Siljay remained with the bus. Emma and her three instructors cut across the road diagonally. They were met at the doorway by an adult. He was younger and taller than Adashi.

"Emma Stewart, our Ika." He performed a formal bow, which Emma repeated. "Welcome to the Maklay School for young persons. I am Aren Token."

"I am honored by the time that you give me today," Emma said, pulling from a list of common formal greetings Adashi had provided.

Adashi seemed pleased with the exchange.

"Ika?" Emma asked.

Ika was a prominent character in Odishi mythology—one of five sisters, all children of Ibu. To the best of Emma's limited knowledge, Ika represented weakness within Odishi society.

"It's a great honor."

The problem with Odishi humor was that it could be very dry and delivered with patience not seen on Earth. Days could pass before the intent was fully revealed. Admittedly, she was small by comparison. She was confident that any of those in her company could toss her onto the roof of the schoolhouse.

Aren Token, the schoolmaster Emma assumed, led them inside. The structure of the building appeared very basic. A single hall stretched back to a typical Odishi unisex restroom and a tiny office by Odishi standards. Interestingly, the internal walls and doors were made of wood. She had only seen bricks, mortar, and plastics used in the buildings of the observatory. To the right and left, open doors led into classrooms, each with several rows of standing desks. This confirmed one of Emma's suspicions. The Odishi did not like to sit.

They passed four empty classrooms before finding the children or young persons. The last room on the left held five students, including the two Emma had seen on the street. The final room on the right held eight, clearly an older group. Aren Token led the group to the left to meet the youngest. After an introduction to the instructor and then the children, the adult Odishi shifted to the side.

"The students would like to ask you some questions," the instructor said.

The students stared at Emma with glee, which she recognized and with a less familiar look that she realized was curiosity. Each wore a uniform of a sort, or at least the patterns matched, dull red over dull gray. Like children on Earth, the five were much more expressive than any adult Odishi she had met.

"How far did you travel?" one asked. It was clear they were in the process of learning the Common language.

"Very far," Adashi answered for her. "Many star systems."

Their curiosity turned to excitement.

"Did you fly in a ship?"

They were very immature for their age and, more surprisingly, for their size, although when considering their long life expectancy, it made sense that their developmental period would be longer.

"I did, with 11 friends. They're in orbit around your planet." She pointed up.

"I flew down in a smaller ship."

"Are they holding their breaths?"

"No, the ship holds air for them to breathe."

They seemed pleased.

"What animals do you have on the ship."

"We have no animals on the ship, but many back on our planet."

This excited them, but the next question was not the follow-up that Emma had expected.

"Do all Talmahk have fur like yours." The child ran its hands over the top of its smooth head and down to its shoulders.

Emma suppressed a laugh but couldn't stop a full-toothed grin.

"No," she said with forced sincerity. "We call it hair." She used the English word, not knowing a Common word for hair. "Some have no hair like you. Some have short hair; some have long hair. Many have dark hair." She stepped to a wall and pointed to a darkly stained knot. "Some have light hair." She ran her fingers along a lightly colored strip of wood. "We call that color blonde while I am a redhead." She lifted curls on both sides of her head and then learned one more thing about the Odishi. They could laugh.

Her eyes widened with surprise, encouraging the children to laugh louder. The term 'redhead' seemed to please them as they repeated among themselves.

One finally commented, "It's not red." That raised comments from the adults behind her, leading Rork to retell Adashi's comment about the many colors defined by the human race. Aren acknowledged Rork and then gave Emma a small sympathetic bow.

Emma shrugged off Rork's comment with a smile and continued to answer an increasingly silly stream of questions from the young Odishi.

"Let's visit the older students," Aren said, taking advantage of a brief pause.

Across the hall, as with the younger students, formal introductions were made. Emma was still looking over the new faces when the first question was asked.

"What has surprised you since first coming to our world?"

They only appeared a few years older than the younger class, so that question surprised her. She was tempted to use it as an answer.

"I suppose," she said after a thoughtful pause. "Our similarities have surprised me more than anything else. We had concerns that we would never be able to communicate with you. Concerns that our thought processes would be so different that we would be incapable of understanding each other, regardless of language. That is clearly not the case; even the structure of our sentences is close.

I was surprised that your buildings look so much like ours, that your vehicles had four wheels like most of ours, and that you have schools for young people, just like us. Your personalities and your humor are very familiar. Perhaps it's common sense that two intelligent species would share many traits, but I still find it surprising."

"Perhaps that's common sense," Aren said. "But I believe one meeting with the Kochpotat would test your assumption as would a meeting with the …"

"The Malum," Adashi prompted.

"The Malum," Aren repeated. "I hope I never meet them, but our history tells us of an inexplicably violent race. The Kochpotat are also described as inexplicable but never violent. How about another question."

"Will more humans come to visit?"

Emma nodded vigorously. "Yes, another ship will be arriving today or tomorrow."

She was speaking of Fredericksburg.

"A small team of researchers from that ship plan to study your star system and planet. More will arrive in a few days aboard a ship dedicated to research. Some hope to meet your people and learn all that they can."

"What can we teach you?"

Emma exaggerated the surprise she felt upon hearing the question to benefit both the younger and the older Odishi in the room. "I would not be speaking before you if I had not learned the Common language from Adashi, Rork, and Tormond." She gestured toward the adults to her right and nodded at Adashi.

"Or if I were, it would sound like this."

In English, "Since I arrived, you have dedicated every waking moment to my education. I thank you."

The young were amused, as she had hoped. Aren Token was appreciative, as he had been since they met. Rork and Tormond both looked confused, which did not surprise Emma.

She turned to the subject of her statement with a guileful smile.

"You are very welcome, Emma," Adashi said in Common, as Emma had hoped.

She returned her attention to the young. "All that we know of the races that inhabit this region of space was learned from you. It's difficult to estimate the full value of that information, but I'm certain that the lives of many will be preserved as we travel further from our home."

She looked again to Adashi, this time questioningly.

Adashi nodded and then spoke. "Emma's race has met one other member of the Union, the Ki Ti Tor Mahk."

"Oh," Aren said with a pained expression.

"Emma, please tell us of your encounter," Adashi said.

Emma immediately stiffened. Before a classroom of students, Adashi's request was the last thing she had expected, but as she started to retell the same story she had told on the bus, the fear fell away. Every young Odishi in the room reflected her feelings with perfect clarity. Curiosity, fear, anger, and finally, sadness played across their young faces. The fear of embarrassing herself disappeared in that room, with it a host of other feelings that had tortured her since Anay died aboard Copernicus. On completion, Adashi bowed approvingly, and Aren thanked her and the instructor. They filed out of the room, past the empty classrooms, onto the street.

Outside, the light from the dim but not-so-distant local star bathed the brick-lined street, buildings, trees, and puddles in a distinct yellow hue. Emma closed her eyes and turned her face upward, enjoying the warmth on a perpetually cool planet. "Adashi, you once mentioned that you have a young daughter. Has she taken responsibility for her education?" Emma maintained her pose.

"No, not yet. She's in class at a school nearer the edge of Maklay. We have four in this town. She's eleven now but is already guiding some of her studies. I expect she'll finish classroom instruction in another three years."

Emma bent her head down and opened her eyes. Adashi sounded both proud and melancholy. Typical for a parent separated from a child, she guessed.

"I would like to show you one of our markets just over the bridge," Aren said. "Food from regional farms is brought to that location for merchants to purchase. Markets are at the center of our economy. Just beyond that is our local center of government. I'm hoping that you find it interesting."

"I'm sure I will," Emma said. "Every day since I set foot on your planet has been interesting, today more than any other."

"You are a very talented speaker," he said as they walked along the side of the road against a row of buildings. Above, a cloud passed quickly, followed by a cool breeze blowing from ahead.

"Thank you for the compliment, but these three deserve the credit." She indicated Adashi, Rork, and Tormond.

"No, I was referring to your skills before an audience. This was your first encounter with younger Odishi, but in each class, you demonstrated a surprising understanding of them while remaining cognizant of the four of us."

"Understanding the point of view of those in your presence is one of the more difficult lessons I've taught," Adashi said. "Most of my students have struggled to master the skill to deal with a single group. Successfully modifying speech to match multiple points of view is much more challenging."

"I should mention that much of the education I received before coming to Iburak was dedicated to understanding languages and patterns of speech. Most from Earth would have had the same struggle."

"Another similarity," Aren said as a pair of trucks drove past, their electric motors humming.

"It is," Adashi said. "But let's consider the reasoning behind your statements." She had turned to Emma.

"You show a reluctance to accept credit for your actions. The three of us were of great help to you, but I've never had a student who learned so quickly."

"It's true," Tormond said with sincerity.

Emma took a deep breath, feeling uncomfortable and unsure of what to say in response.

"A bigger question I hope to answer soon is if all humans act this way."

Emma was certain that Adashi was teasing.

"That's unlikely," Tormond said.

"That would be impossible," Aren said. "A society could not function, at least a government could not function."

To force a break in the conversation, Emma nodded silently and then stepped to the left, to the side of the bridge. Below, she could see solid stone arches meeting the river just upstream of a broken ledge. Water cascaded down the loose rocks, giving rise to a plume of mist. Below that, the river broadened. Calm, serene water stretched out toward the coastline. A small ship was tied to a quay that paralleled the river and a long building below the market. A distant pair of Odishi were pulling a net to the river's edge. Trapped within its folds, their struggling catch was evident even from where she walked.

"Aren," she said, looking over her shoulder. "I originally thought you were a school administrator, but now I suspect you have a higher role."

"I do … I am the administrator for Imaotak, this island." He gestured with his hand down the river and toward the market.

Emma's eyes widened slightly.

"This surprises you?" he asked with a kind Odishi smile.

"Of course it does," Adashi said teasingly.

"You represent more than a million Odishi," Emma said in her defense.

He laughed. It was a short, subdued laugh, but the first she had heard from an adult.

"Emma, you represent over seven billion humans from our perspective."

Emma started to shake her head.

"Are you not the chosen representative from your planet?"

"No, I'm not," she said quietly, just above the sound of the water below. "I'm the chosen representative from Batfish. One from a crew of twelve."

"What's your role on Batfish?"

"I am … responsible for our sensors." She was tempted to explain, but he appeared to understand, and beyond that, it was irrelevant to the point he was about to make.

"So, unprepared in any way to interact with another race, you came to our planet and opened a dialog."

Defeated, Emma decided not to argue the point.

"Perhaps it was fate that brought you to us, but that doesn't change the fact that you are the representative of Earth. What must be the most critical moment between two races, and the burden was placed upon you alone."

He placed a gentle hand on her shoulder. "And here we are, only 120 days later, walking through the streets of one of our larger towns, communicating with ease ... as friends."

Words failed Emma. She could not think of anything to say, anything appropriate to match his last statement. With effort, she met the eyes of each Odishi and then nodded to confirm their friendship.

A second, larger location within the confines of the fallow field had been cleared while Emma was in town. She stood at a safe distance, covering her ears. The roar of the shuttle's electro-props was deafening. A mix of wild klackish, dried grass, and shredded jokap bush, previously dragged to the side of the landing pad, was rising in a chaotic swirl before dropping around and behind her. She stood fast until the sound of the drives dropped to an idle and then vanished. The rear hatch dropped to the ground, and research team members stepped out, casting furtive glances in her direction and beyond where Adashi waited. Emma recalled her first moments on the planet, crossing the landing pad toward the towering figure of Siljay.

"Emma," one shouted as she carried one end of a cloth bag across the pad to a staging area.

It was Abby Webb. Emma had hoped to see her, but the shuttle's manifest was never transmitted to Batfish.

She walked toward the growing pile of baggage to meet her friend. It looked like they would be setting up a camp, although they would need to be much further from the pad. Once Abby had set down her end of the bag, she raced toward Emma with a lopsided grin offsetting her intense eyes. Others set down what they were carrying but remained in place, their eyes bouncing between the small reunion and the Odishi beyond. Abby wrapped her arms around Emma in an embrace and then backed away to look past her.

"Another pivotal moment for the human race, and just like Barnard's Star and Eridani, you're in the middle of it. Why does this keep surprising me?"

Emma rolled her eyes skyward, but not before a shadow had passed across her face.

"I'm sorry," Abby said quickly. "I —"

"Abby, don't worry. I really am okay now. You need to meet Adashi."

Emma turned around and waved Adashi forward. "How is your Common?"

Abby placed a hand on Emma's shoulder. "We'll know in a moment," she said uneasily.

"Don't worry about her. She'll be very nice despite your obvious shortcomings."

Abby relaxed visibly, but not for reasons that had anything to do with the approaching Odishi. She tightened the grip on her friend's shoulder.

"They made an interesting request today," Emma said, keeping her eyes on Adashi. Her question had been on Emma's mind since it was asked on the road leading into Maklay. "They want our help contacting the other races. They seem anxious to be reunited with other Odishi."

She looked up at Abby with a thin smile but saw only concern in response.

Abby locked eyes with her, but it was clear that she was hesitant to speak. "Emma, that request was made with more urgency than you realize."

Emma opened her mouth to speak and then closed it as the Adashi came close.

"Adashi, this is my good friend, Abby Webb."

"I am pleased to meet you, Abby," Adashi said in almost perfect English.

Abby paused momentarily and then said, "I'm pleased to meet you, Adashi," in somewhat broken Common, showing no discomfort as she looked up at the hulking figure.

The use of Common surprised Adashi, who turned to Emma with a questioning look.

"I've been forwarding all that you have taught me up to Batfish. From there, it's been passed to other ships in the region and back to Earth. I suspect hundreds of others have learned the basics like Abby."

"You're joking, right?" Abby's question was in English, but Adashi appeared to understand.

"About what?"

"Emma, that number is in the millions … probably hundreds of millions by now. I believe your lessons are being converted to every language on the planet. They've received some polish, but it's your work … or both of yours."

"I …" Emma lost track of what she wanted to say. From her perspective, such numbers were inconceivable. They needed further explanation, but all she wanted to know was what Abby was referring to before Adashi joined the conversation.

"It seems like only yesterday that the two of us were on Jarvis Station together," Abby said, covering Emma's confusion.

"Yesterday? That seems like a lifetime ago to me."

"Jarvis Station is in orbit about Earth," she added for Adashi's benefit.

"Of course, it was only yesterday," Abby said with natural humor. "Let me break down my itinerary. You and I were talking on the station, and then I was floating in the middle of nowhere, and now we're here, talking again … Okay, maybe it was two days ago."

Emma crossed her arms and looked at Abby, trying to think of an appropriate response. "It's nice just to talk to someone close to my height … and, I must say, your command of Common is impressive, given that you only had two days to learn."

Abby sneered at Emma and then looked up at Adashi. "With nothing else to do, Fredericksburg has been hosting lessons for the last two months."

"It's nice that they let you come down for a visit." Emma pointed to indicate Abby alone. "I would've thought your research was best conducted in orbit."

"They sent us all down. When Galileo arrives, a few of us will return with their first shuttle run. I'm happy. This makes three planets I've been on."

"Five for me," Emma said.

"Show off."

Abby paused before shifting her gaze. "I also have a few questions for Adashi, but they can wait until we've set up."

She turned around to see that the shuttle was empty, and the team lead was pacing the field for a suitable location to place their camp.

"I think they can manage," Emma said, still anxious for Abby to explain her earlier statement. "Would you like a tour of the observatory?"

"I would love one, although I was also looking forward to setting up a tent."

She grabbed Emma's arm and started walking toward the distant buildings of the observatory.

Adashi followed alongside the two.

"You have questions, Abby?"

"I do ... first let me ask about a debris field we found in orbit about your star. We have some long-distance images and were wondering if you or another could identify what we're seeing. It's clearly the wreckage of ships, many ships."

"I couldn't, but we do have some records of the ships that brought us here. I can arrange a visit to town if you would like."

"That would be helpful, thank you."

There was a long, silent pause in the conversation as they walked.

"And your second question?"

Abby started slowly, ensuring every word was correct before she spoke. "We've made an observation about your star and would like to confirm it with you."

Adashi nodded as a human would, encouraging Abby to continue.

"Stars have ... magnetic fields that periodically build and then release energy. Some, like our own, release on a regular schedule. Others, like yours, work on a much longer, irregular schedule ... Yours has not released energy in a very long time, and we're predicting that it will soon; six to twelve years is our estimate. The damage will be ... catastrophic to your planet if it's released in this direction."

Adashi stopped walking. They were near the bottom of the ravine between the landing pads and the observatory. A small stream trickling over rocks and sand made a sound that was clear over that of the mild breeze passing overhead.

"Thank you, Abby ... We've been watching our star for many years for that reason. It has been the primary purpose of our observatories. The flare, I believe you call it, will occur in about seven and a half of your years. It will not be the short-term event we saw 180 years ago but will last several days, emanating from both poles. Unfortunately, we'll be passing over the star's northern pole at that time … It's unlikely that any life on the planet's surface will survive the event, and any that does will not live long. Too much of the atmosphere will be stripped away."

The cold, emotionless delivery belied the significance of the words spoken. Emma stared up at Adashi, trying to understand what was just said. "Are you sure?"

"Yes."

"Can we help? … can the Ki Ti or Sal help? You want to meet them. We can find them."

Emma balled her fists to stop her fingers from trembling, but she could do nothing to stop the tears from welling in her eyes. She wanted to run, be alone as the true scope of Adashi's words flooded her mind. There were over five million Odishi. All ships of Earth combined would be pressed to carry 2000. With a two-month round trip, at best, they could evacuate 92,000 to Earth over the next seven years. Their birth rate over that period could be higher than that number.

"Your empty classrooms."

Adashi nodded. "We confirmed our worst fears about twelve years ago. The last Odishi birth occurred just over nine years ago … My daughter was one of the last. I was pregnant when we learned of our fate."

Vertigo struck. It felt like she was back on Rosalie. She carefully sat on a large rock at the edge of the stream. "Do you believe the Sal or Ki Ti can help?"

"We don't, but it may be our only chance. In truth, many of the old have accepted as fact that the Odishi of Iburak will soon be gone. We can only hope that others survived the Malum attack."

Emma bent her head to the ground as fear clouded her mind. "You asked … you asked me to ask for help finding them, but we're unsure where to look. Our best guess places them somewhere beyond Eridani, but we haven't ventured beyond that system."

Abby cleared her throat, capturing the attention of Emma and Adashi. "Another of my questions is regarding the location of the Ki Ti Tor Mak. Your journey here probably followed a direct course, so it would make sense that the Ki Ti and the Sal can be found somewhere along the path between this system and your original home — Can you tell me anything about your home system that could help us identify it?"

Adashi thought for a moment. "Let's continue moving," she said, indicating the observatory's direction with a hand.

They stepped over the stream and began climbing the steep side of the ravine.

"I'm afraid we lost the location of our home star when the Malum destroyed our ships and the first cities we built. That information was embedded in the technology that they so thoroughly eliminated. We have tried finding it with our telescopes, but we're not even sure of a general direction in which to start."

"Are you looking for anything that would stand out? Obviously, a single star would not."

"Yes, are you familiar with our stories that revolve around Ibu, the mother, and the sisters, Ida, Ima, Ina, Isa, and Ika?"

Abby shrugged. "I'm aware of the stories but not familiar."

"Well, the stories aren't important, but the characters may be, or what they represent. Ibu is the star of our home system. In the night sky of our home world, the brightest stars represent the sisters. Ida sits in the direction of the center of the universe, although we believe the center of the galaxy is the actual reference. Ima and Ina accompanied Ida in the front, while Isa and Ika remained behind Ibu. What's important is not that they were the brightest stars, but that they were close enough that we were able to settle four of the five systems before we had met any of the other races, before we had an … interface generator."

She looked at Emma for confirmation.

"That's right," Emma said softly.

They were out of the ravine and climbing the gentle slope toward the schoolhouse.

"How long were the… transits between the settled systems?" Abby asked.

"Several years at least, but short enough that some individuals were said to have made the journey out to one system, back, and then out again. We may have charts in the building ahead. If not, there may be some in town."

"I may be able to find it," Abby said. "We have the … positional data for many stars. I can search for small clusters and see if one matches your description."

Adashi led them past the school and into the observatory. She started to explain its operations when Abby interrupted.

"I found 22 clusters within 150 light-years that match my search. I can extend it further if needed. Looking at the shortest routes to each, none pass close to Eridani … Emma, is your MDU up here? Maybe a visual aid would be helpful."

"It's in the schoolhouse. I'll be right back." Emma exited the building and ran across the yard, scattering three radanks gathered around a trough.

"We may have some drawings of the night sky from Ibu or one of the sisters," Adashi said as she pulled open an elongated drawer. "It was all we had when we started searching, old memories."

The top drawer held large photographic images that stretched from edge to edge. She pulled out a corner of the stack and briefly flipped through each before shoving them back. The second drawer was empty, as was the third. The bottom drawer held a random collection of smaller photographs, drawings, and written documents.

"I'm not hopeful," Adashi said as she pushed aside a pair of drawings from a young Odishi's hands. She gathered the remainder in her hands and brought them to a table.

Emma came through the door with her mobile display in hand. "Here you go." She handed it to Abby.

Abby connected to the device and then swiveled it around to show Adashi a three-dimensional rendition of one of the clusters she had found.

"You can rotate it with a finger." She placed the display in Adashi's hand.

"The galactic center is in this direction." A vector appeared, stretching from the selected star to the edge of the display.

Adashi played with the display, shifting around the spheres.

"Can you move the vector to this star?" It shifted immediately.

"Do you know the orientation of these stars?"

A second vector appeared. "That's galactic north. The best you can do is assume the ecliptic planes of the stars all match that of the galaxy."

Adashi played with the image for another moment, then set it down on the table and started sifting through the sheets of paper. Abby and Emma stepped to her side as she pulled one sheet from the pile and pushed the remainder to one side.

Emma drew up on the tips of her toes and wiped a loose tear with the back of her hand before leaning toward the sketch. "Eastern and western skies?"

"Of Ibu," Adashi said.

The sheet held two sketches. One showed a diffused but obvious depiction of the Milky Way in the background. The foreground showed scattered stars, three brighter than the rest. The second sketch showed just stars. Several across the top were connected as if to form a constellation, but the sketch was centered on the two brightest.

"This is the best representation we're going to find here," Adashi said. She pointed and named each sister star on the sketches and then frowned at Emma's display.

"Can you show the other clusters?"

The image on the display was replaced.

"No."

Another popped up.

"No."

This continued for the remainder of the 22 images.

"Go back eight."

The requested image appeared.

"How far is this?"

"About 140 light years."

"And a light year is the distance that light travels in one of your years or about eight-tenths of the common year."

"Yes … yes," Abby answered, both apologetic and surprised.

"The shortest route would have required 43 jumps, taking about 190 days at one gee."

Emma winced. "We're not getting out there anytime soon, not at all, without refueling stations."

Abby lifted the display from Adashi's extended hand and set it on the table. "You believe space between here and there is mostly empty?"

"It was, and I don't imagine that has changed, but Union space is not our current concern."

"No, it's not. ... Does the flight duration match that of the fleet that brought you here?"

"Not very well. The exact time is well known, 174 of your days."

"That's close."

"Yes, but in the wrong direction. I don't believe we could have maintained your measure of a gee for that length of time, and I suspect there would have been some delays along the way."

"And it passes nowhere near Eridani," Abby added, bowing her head in frustration. "It looks like the path is deliberately avoiding Eridani."

"That makes no sense," Emma said.

"No, it doesn't — You know that we're still defining the limits used to determine if an interface is possible between systems, namely the distances between the two stars and their masses."

Abby picked up the display and spun it about; her eyes narrowed. "I'm going to broaden the parameters a bit and see what that gets us."

The room fell silent as Abby ran the calculations in her head. Emma wiped back another tear as she watched. The bleating of a radank just outside the building provided a momentary distraction.

"Nothing," Abby said, but the intense look on her face did not change.

A hoof scratching at the door momentarily drew Emma's attention.

"This is better," Abby declared. "Forty-one jumps and about a hundred and sixty days, and it passes directly through Eridani ... It all depends on one large brown dwarf."

Emma let her shoulders slump. "I thought it was impossible to jump to a brown dwarf."

Abby shrugged. "We had no luck connecting to Wise or Luhman 16, but this one is much larger, over twice the size of either of the Luhman dwarves and about ten times that of Wise … In fact, its temperature is more like that of a red dwarf. Its catalog entry is from a very old infrared survey. We'll call it Denis."

Abby met Emma's forlorn eyes with encouragement. "It's just two jumps beyond Eridani."

"And?" Emma asked.

"There's a new corvette class, the Pathfinder. Two have been launched so far. They use the same hull as Batfish, but their only function is to find optimal jump points and generate Calvin files for the fleet. If a jump is possible, one of those ships will figure out how to make it."

Abby turned to Adashi. "Assuming we get past Denis, assuming we find the Sal or Ki Ti, this brings up one final question; our leaders believe the presence of an Odishi will reduce the chance of miscommunication when we make initial contact."

Adashi bowed deeply. "I would be honored."

Abby's smile broadened. "You knew we were going to ask this."

"I did."

"But it doesn't have to be you," Emma said suddenly, her concern evident.

"It does. That decision was made shortly after you and I met, although I hope that one other Odishi can accompany me, Tormond or Rork." She turned her head toward Abby.

"That was expected," Abby said, trying to match Adashi's previous tone.

"And, of course, Emma," Adashi added.

Abby's eyes widened briefly, and then she turned to Emma questioningly.

Emma looked between the two. Her surprise gave way to a thin, tightly controlled smile.

"That was definitely not expected. I'll need to clear it with Fredericksburg."

With her orders changed, Emma made a brief tour of the observatory, thanking those she found and then saying goodbye. Abby followed her from building to building, taking the opportunity to greet the same individuals. Adashi had already taken one of the smaller buses to town. She would return the next day with the possessions needed for the journey. In the time between, she would make farewells, one to her daughter far more important than any other. Emma saw that on Adashi's face.

"This is all very sudden," Emma said. "I had hoped to spend more time with you."

She and Abby were walking down the slope toward the newly erected camp. "By the way, congratulations on the promotion … lieutenant."

"A little late, but thank you, lieutenant."

"Oh, no," Emma said, shaking her head. "I am now, Ika. They gave me a title … well, not really a title. I think they were making a joke about my size."

"A title? That's just great. Now you're royalty on two separate planets. Which of the sisters is Ika."

Emma cringed slightly and mumbled, "The weakling."

Abby burst into laughter. "Perfect. I like these people."

"Me too. It's hard not to … What are your plans?"

"I'm just here until Galileo arrives. I'll be working from there."

"Studying the star?"

Abby shook her head. "Not me; I've done what I could. They have an expert aboard that has already taken over that effort. He'll be interested to hear Adashi's estimate of the flare's timing. I can pass that on, but that will be it for me. I'll spend my time with the debris field, what's left the Odishi fleet."

"That could be interesting."

"I'm certain of it. While there's nothing close to the complete ship you dragged from Eridani, there will be more than enough to keep us busy."

Emma nodded, tight-lipped.

"One other thing on my list; I'm investigating that anomaly you reported when you entered the system."

Emma gave her a questioning look before recalling the event. "Oh, the hiccup with the interface generator. Isn't that a problem for the designers ... or the factory?"

"More than likely. Oddly, we've only seen that specific failure when entering this system, and just three times. Both Fredericksburg and Sturgeon had the same problem on their first attempt to jump in."

"Curious."

Abby nodded in agreement. "It is, but I'm much more interested in the debris field."

"I don't blame you ... I do have one question about Union space."

Abby nodded for Emma to continue.

"Was the travel time estimate that you gave to Adashi firm? We're working to reduce the time spent crossing systems, right?"

"That is one of the purposes of the Pathfinders." She smiled briefly and continued. "They plan to map four or five jump points between stars. Some much closer to each star, well ten, maybe fifteen percent is what I've heard."

"I'd be delighted to cut travel time by fifteen percent," Emma said.

Abby raised her eyebrows in agreement. "Another thought is to use automated stations to open the jump point, allowing the ship to pass through at a higher speed. For this to work, we need to make the creation time of the point more consistent. Otherwise, the ship is likely to miss."

They stopped at the edge of the smaller landing pad, past the trainer, looking toward the camp.

"Something smells good. Lunch?" Abby looked at Emma with hope.

"Sure, it should be a nice change … but I only have an hour before I return this shuttle to Batfish. They need to get it disassembled and stowed, and I need to get over to Fredericksburg."

Abby drew a deep breath as they continued toward the row of tents. "What then?"

Emma thought for a moment. "Adashi and … one of her assistants will join us, and we leave for Earth and then on to meet the Sal. Well, I hope we meet them first. I'm not sure how welcome we'll be if all we find are Ki Ti."

"Uh …" Abby stopped what she had started to say, looking uncomfortable.

"What?"

"Have you considered the possibility that Sal were aboard one or more of the ships that were destroyed alongside Copernicus?"

Emma stopped and gave Abby a pained expression. "No, not until now."

June 13th 2126

"Emma, I'm afraid we just missed you. We're breaking orbit, and I can see you're on approach to Jarvis." It was Quinn.

Fredericksburg had just joined the Jarvis network, making the connection possible. Emma was standing with Tormond before a set of displays currently showing live images of Jarvis Station and Earth. Adashi stood before another, reviewing details of the first of many scheduled meetings. The housing unit, explicitly arranged for Adashi and Tormond, was uncomfortably spacious. It was a conversion from eight two-person quarters meant for the crew, a square of four from one level and the level above. Emma was given an entire unit just outside of the Odishi space.

"Captain, or Quinn, if we're being informal, I'm sorry to hear that, but it's your fault for rushing ahead of us."

"Orders are orders. More importantly, you shouldn't call me captain. You left Batfish behind three weeks ago, but forgive me if I'm missing your point. Should I be calling you Ambassador Stewart or perhaps Ika?"

"So, you spoke with Abby before leaving Groombridge. I should never have told her about that. To answer your question, neither. I'm a liaison, not an ambassador, and I'm not sure what an Ika is yet."

"The weakling, right?"

"Yes, thanks for the reminder. How is my replacement fitting in with the crew?"

"Oh, Ensign Matthews? He's great, and Lieutenant Zhào is the acting XO. Clearly an upgrade."

Emma laughed aloud.

"So that you know, Captain Hoffman chewed me out on my first day aboard Fredericksburg. I have picked up some bad habits regarding etiquette and protocol. Commander Fedorov had to save me. She explained in detail whom I had for a previous captain."

"Oh, that guy. It's no wonder you got yourself into trouble. Hey, wait a minute. You're not under Hoffman's command."

"Not now, I was then, before I was made the liaison."

"Anyway, this is an official communique. Please inform the Odishi representatives that Batfish is proceeding on the agreed course. We'll join the fleet at 82 G dot Eridani. With a path through Denis finally established, we'll proceed in that direction at the pointy tip of the spear, one of the spears."

"Very well. I'll pass it on. Stay safe, Quinn."

"You too, Emma. We'll see you again soon."

August 8th 2126

Another pack of children raced past Chloe and her grandfather, with their teachers calling from behind. Alexander held up his hands as the last of the group brushed past. Ahead, a gentle but insistent cordon of secret service agents brought them to a stop or at least deflected their course. The objects of their interest towered above the agents and those they protected. Trailing behind, a separate group was crowded around one individual. Emma's dress whites were barely visible through the tight pack of young girls, animal balloons, and popcorn bags. Even some of the teachers were standing nearby to listen.

It was a cool, sunny afternoon in early August. The National Zoo had closed its gates to the public to host young children from schools across the greater Washington area. It was an unusual start of the school year that conveniently aligned with Adashi and Tormond's final visit before Fredericksburg departed. The president, her wife, and their four children were accompanying them on one leg of their tour of the zoo, past the big cats, pandas, and elephants.

Across the planet, accommodations were made to make the two Odishi comfortable. Meetings and gatherings were held outdoors or in larger rooms with high ceilings. It was understood that the Odishi preferred to stand, so chairs were a rarity. A shuttle had been configured before their arrival and served as their home, carrying them from city to city where they were shown the world's wonders. It carried all that they had brought, primarily food and clothing.

Not that they were afraid to sample the food offered at every stop, but they had found little to sustain their nutritional needs, and both had lost weight, although Adashi told them not to worry.

The world tour reminded Chloe of a theater: political theater, one city, one act. Politicians were playing to an audience but ignoring the visitors before them. While the plight of the Odishi was known to all, so was the backward nature of their planet. Their hosts were offering little in the way of help.

The group ahead was beginning to split. The president, family, staff, and Secret Service detail walked toward an exit. Adashi and Tormond had turned and were coming back toward Chloe and Alexander. Emma came from behind, waving to the unmoving group of well-wishers as she crossed the security perimeter around the two Odishi.

"More adoring fans, Emma?"

Emma smiled back at Chloe. "Children."

"Not all of them," Chloe said before Adashi stopped at her side.

"Anything promising?" Emma asked Adashi using English, as Adashi had insisted on their visit to Earth.

"We have established a good rapport with the leader of your nation. It's all I had hoped to accomplish."

Emma frowned. Adashi had said the same a day earlier.

"This process can never be rushed, Emma. I am confident that assistance will be provided, but now is not the time to ask."

"Why is that?"

"We have received warm greetings in every city that we've visited. The leaders have catered to our needs and taken great measures to ensure our safety." She gestured toward a pair of guards shooing away another group of gawking children and then toward patrol craft hovering silently in the distance.

"It has not escaped our attention that some are not as welcoming as others."

"It's not —"

Emma was interrupted by Alexander. "You've been gone for a while. There have been some ugly changes since you left. An old brand of politics has returned, one I thought we had grown out of many years ago. The attack by the Ki Ti Tor Mahk has presented an opportunity for a number of ambitious yet mediocre figures. Rather than performing the hard work needed to benefit their constituents, they've found it easier to use fear and hate to twist their moral compasses. Fear can be handled. Assuming the source is a misunderstanding or lie, honesty and persistence may counter its effects. The problem with hate is much worse as it will spread like a disease almost impossible to eliminate. Sometimes the best you can do is turn it aside, redirect it in a less harmful direction."

Alexander looked up at Adashi with an apology in his eyes. "There are many that would rather persecute the Odishi than help."

"For what reason?" Open hostility had replaced Emma's frown.

Adashi looked down upon her with sympathy. "It's an easy association; the Ki Ti, the Malum, the Odishi. As long as that association persists, there will be fear, and that fear will lead to hate. The association must be broken. That will only happen after the differences between the three races are established. The tour of your cities was a good start."

Emma drew a deep breath, mollifying her anger. "Your greatest source of hope is still with the Sal and Ki Ti. Correct?"

"More accurately, they may be the source of our greatest hope, a single hope that they may lead us to other Odishi that survived the Malum, Odishi that could assist with our evacuation. The Sal and Ki TI are unlikely to assist; they are, or were, as you say, pirates. Our relationship with them was never good."

Together as a group, they continued along the winding path toward the next exhibit, although not one paid attention to their surroundings.

"Unfortunately, that hope is fading. The distance to Union space is great."

Alexander nodded. "It's true. It will take at least four fueling stations to bridge the gap. That will be a multiyear effort once we find the appropriate gas giants, and this assumes that we don't stumble into a war."

"This is another reason that you should ask for help before we leave," Emma said, growing exasperated. "Allow time to plan. Find a place on Earth that would make a good home."

Adashi stopped to face Emma. "If we ask for assistance now, the assistance that we'll need, the request will be rejected."

Emma stared up at Adashi defiantly.

Adashi continued. "A wise commander will see any great victory of arms as a failure because the conflict was not resolved through concession. A wise diplomat will see any request for concession as a failure, believing that a difference of opinion should never have occurred. Applying careful pressure, a nudge, at the right time and place can be much more effective than a request for help."

"I'm — I'll give you credit for borrowing that cliche, but you are giving us far too much credit." Emma could not stop herself from smiling, if only for a moment. "I'm certain we operate on a lower plane than that … Whom will you nudge? In what direction?"

"We'll only know that once we understand all aspects of the problem. Regardless, I am afraid that Earth could never accommodate our population."

"A population of five million? That's a trivial number. We call it a drop in the bucket … Sorry, I didn't mean to belittle you."

Adashi smiled and waved off Emma's concern using a very human gesture.

"It's not an issue of numbers; you're not ready to accept any number of us as ... neighbors, not for several years at the least, more years than we have on Iburak. This is due, in part, to the attack by the Ki Ti, but even without that, acceptance by many on your planet would be unlikely."

There was a painful pause in the conversation.

"There is Mars," Emma said weakly. Interest in that planet was waning on Earth.

"Or Eridani, or Ophiuchi."

"Mars will not be capable of supporting life in the time we have, and the gravity on Eridani would kill us. If possible, I would like to visit Ophiuchi."

"That can be arranged," Emma said quickly.

"And what's the flight time between Groombridge and Ophiuchi?" Chloe asked.

"A month and a half, one way ... I know, we've done the math. Every ship in all the fleets of Earth could only move a small fraction of the Odishi population, but we can build more ships."

She looked up at Adashi. "When do you plan to start applying careful pressure?"

Adashi paused, looking down at Emma with earnest concern.

"As of today, my part has ended. Another will need to carry our request to a successful conclusion. It cannot be Tormond or me."

"A third party," Alexander said. "That will be the best approach, and you're right about the timing." He was addressing Adashi. "Once a politician says no, getting them to change their mind can be challenging or costly anyway. You're also right about the reception that you received on your tour. There is goodwill, and we can work with that, although the best results will be in your absence."

"Okay, that's good," Emma said. "Who do we convince to act as a third party?"

Alexander looked back at Emma for a long moment. "I —"

Adashi answered softly, barely audible above the distant voices of park visitors. "We chose you, Emma. I have been confident of this decision since your visit to Maklay. Now, I am certain. This is the reason that Minister Token referred to you as Ika." Adashi imitated a human shrug.

Emma shook her head, dumbfounded. "I'm missing something."

She kept her eyes on Adashi but received no answer.

"I … here on Earth, the weakling is not the one who bends others to their will. They're usually brushed to the side … or choose to remain out of sight."

"As does Ika."

Emma bowed her head, more to hide her frustration than any other reason.

"Let me explain," Adashi said.

Emma cleared her face of any emotion and looked up.

"The mother and five sisters are the basis for much of our literature and are referenced often in everyday life, more often … too often, in political settings, but the reference was made with the sincere belief that you will bring change."

Emma wanted to argue that point but was not sure where to start.

Adashi continued. "You believe that Ida, the strongest, the warrior, would make the better representative, that Ida would use her strength to bring about change, but that's never true. Ida leads and will never voluntarily alter the chosen path. She can't see or even imagine a better path. Ima and Ina have the single-minded purpose of following Ida's direction. They see no path at all. They live for the reward Ida will bestow upon them for faithful service. Isa, equally single-minded, equally blinded to the path, is dedicated to protecting Ika, fending off attacks or, more often, hiding her from the other three sisters. Isa lives for the sacrifice."

Adashi focused her full attention on Emma. "Only Ika can bring forth change. She is always reluctant, always unsure, but when events dictate it, she will be thrust to the forefront. There, she will define a new path and force Ida upon it, unwillingly, often unknowingly. The object of change, Ika's methods, and the final results vary from story to story, but in the end, Ika is always allowed to return to her desired station behind Ibu."

Emma blinked up at Adashi, unsure if she should laugh or cry.

"Adashi, I'm the only human that you truly know. You chose from a list of one. I think, with time, you will find a better choice."

"I'm sure we could find a good choice, but I'm not certain we would find a better choice. We indeed know you far better than any other, but more importantly, you know us better than any other does."

"You will see Emma. Give this time."

The driver for Adashi and Tormond was coming across the plaza, past the last small pack of students that couldn't take their eyes off the visitors.

"I'll see you again tomorrow aboard Fredericksburg. We can talk then."

Emma nodded silently.

Once the Odishi and their security detail were out of earshot, Chloe nudged Emma.

"I think she nailed it."

Emma looked at her with obvious confusion.

"You ... Ika. That is the perfect description of your entire life."

Alexander let out a short, sharp laugh. A gesture that was so rare that both of his granddaughters looked over in surprise. "I rarely agree with Chloe, but in this case ..."

He smiled at Emma.

"It's Cthulhu," Emma said. Her eyes were locked on Chloe for a long moment before she turned to Alexander. "You started to say something before Adashi dropped that on me?"

"Yes, uh, I had intended to suggest a third-party organization rather than an individual, but I think we can work with Adashi. The Navy would fit the role perfectly, and you've already earned credentials as their spokesperson."

Emma clasped her hands together and looked down at them in thought. "We'll need to convince the Navy first, ask them to shut down the production of warships to focus on transports. It would be an understatement to say that they won't be enthusiastic."

"Oh, it's much bigger than that," Chloe said. "We're not even close to the production capacity needed to build the numbers needed to move them here. Ophiuchi is double the distance, so we need to double that number. For Eridani? Triple it."

Emma brightened slightly. "The yards would need to be expanded — That they would support."

Chloe gave her a wicked smile. "Now you're thinking, Beanstalk."

"Are you still free tomorrow morning, Emma?" Alexander asked.

"The shuttle is scheduled for noon, but that's flexible. Fredericksburg will not depart without us. Our schedule is their schedule, and there's no rush. Ophiuchi isn't going anywhere, and we're still waiting to see what the fleet finds."

"Even better. Let Captain Hoffman know that you'll be delayed. Senator Park would like to meet with us at ten."

"I don't think I know him," Emma said.

"Sure you do," Chloe said. "He was at the ranch when you and —"

"Oh, right," Emma said quickly. "Likes baseball."

"Well ... bats anyways."

"He's an ally," Alexander said. "Skip Chelsea will be there also, another ally. It would be helpful if we could invite two or three more politicians that may actually need to be convinced to help ... if any are still in town."

"Should I invite Adashi and Tormond?" Emma asked.

"No, not to this. Better they're not present; better if they were off the planet."

Alexander hesitated, giving Emma and Chloe a pained expression.

"You should know that, as it stands, we do not have enough support. It's close, but if the polls are correct ... come next year, there will be no chance. The entire political spectrum has been thrown to the wind. Activist members who spent their lives fighting against the military are now calling for more warships; those that had once called for open borders now want to lock down the Solar System, and then there are those like Ray, seeking alliances with, as of yet, unknown parties — I guess what I'm trying to say is that we're coming up on one of the most unpredictable elections in our history. If it goes our way, we'll be set, but at this time, it's not promising."

"We can always hope," Chloe said before winking obviously at Emma.

Emma rolled her eyes, and then both cousins turned expectedly to their grandfather.

"Hope is an unreliable companion," he told both before focusing on Chloe. "Happy?"

Chloe nodded and smiled.

The three stood for another moment as the zoo continued to empty, and their security cordon maintained their distance. "I'm hungry," Emma finally said. "There's a steakhouse just up Connecticut Avenue."

"One last meal before you hit the proverbial road?" Alexander asked.

Emma nodded slightly.

Emma shuffled down the hall toward her grandfather's oversized suite. The one dress she had brought felt uncomfortable, baggy, and of a material too thin for her changing tastes. The floral pattern was subdued, but she still felt awkward behind it. She had spent too many years in a uniform. The burden placed upon her the previous day by Adashi had prevented any meaningful sleep. Just past midnight, she decided to stay up and research Senator Park and any other senators who were not out campaigning or on vacation. Her anguish was intermixing with anger, anger arising from hopelessness and the sudden responsibility to solve a problem that was thrust upon her, a problem that appeared to have no solution.

Chloe stepped out of the room as she approached. "Good morning, Emma. We received your message, and I have one question — Are you fucking crazy? Eglin Shaw is the last person we should be talking to. She's the mouthpiece for every senator ... every member of Congress that we want to lose this year. I'm surprised she's here and not back home shouting lies, trying to salvage a disastrous first term."

"She's only in town for the day," Emma said before yawning. "Coffee inside?"

"Of course — I know what you're thinking, but it won't work with her. She's not going to see reason; hell, she won't even listen to you."

Emma followed Chloe through the door and was struck by the smell of coffee. "Did Alexander pass it on to Senator Park?" she asked, pouring a mug.

"Yes, of course … I still think you're crazy."

"Maybe, probably."

Emma was happy to be on her feet near an end table against a wall of Ray Park's office. She was either too tired or too frayed to sit, and with the addition of Senator Shaw, the last convenient seat was taken.

"This is impressive," Ray said as he rapidly swatted at the display, jumping from image to image of the conceptual design for a carrier thrown together by a consortium that Alexander often supported in Washington. "Preliminary, I'm guessing. How many hard points is that?"

Chloe leaned toward the display. "Twelve there, but the design is modular. It's unlimited … within reason. The hard points can also vary in size and utility. A simple variation is all that we'll need to attach the personnel pods."

"And how does this help us?" Senator Shaw asked. "Our Navy, not the aliens."

Emma stepped forward, preparing to speak for the first time before the group.

"And you are?" Senator Shaw asked forcefully.

"Eglin," Ray said. "You know very well who she is."

"No, Ray, I don't. Are we speaking to another of Alexander's grandchildren, or is it the Navy lieutenant or perhaps the ambassador?"

"A fair question," Emma said. "For this conversation, I believe Emma will do."

Chloe twisted about to give her a look of warning, but Emma did not pause.

"Regarding your question ... Using a carrier to transport combat ships will provide the Navy with two significant advantages and a collection of smaller ones. For the ships it carries, eliminating an interface generator, capacitors, and other supporting equipment should allow for a 15 percent increase in combat effectiveness. Reduction of the reaction mass requirements could yield a 30 percent improvement."

"How, exactly, does the removal of the interface generator or ... reaction mass improve a ship's combat effectiveness?"

"Less mass means better acceleration and the ability to add additional weapons or armor. Lower power requirements and more available space give about the same."

"And if we simply add more weapons and armor to existing ships?"

The look on Emma's face flipped from confused to questioning. "To do that, we'll need to increase the size of the hull for the space, the engines to maintain the acceleration, carry additional reaction mass ... everything grows."

"I'm still not seeing a problem," Eglin said.

Emma looked down at Chloe's now smiling face and then back up to Eglin.

"Senator, you do understand that bigger is not necessarily better. A bigger ship is a bigger target, easier to detect, and easier to hit. Bigger costs more. Bigger requires a bigger crew."

Alexander cleared his throat and turned about in his chair, but Emma was not deterred.

"Some very smart people determined the optimum size for each class of ship. Every one of them would be pleased to know that those ships could go into combat with a 45 percent increase in effectiveness."

"Smarter than a United States Senator?"

Emma stared back at the senator, amazed at the sincerity behind the question. "On this? … Yes."

"Of course," she then added dismissively.

"Okay, that's enough on ship designs," Ray said loud enough to end further discussion. "Let's move on to the larger question that will not be asked today." He looked at Alexander, who nodded his approval.

"Are we in a position to commit existing resources toward a three-year program leading to a fleet of a hundred or so of these ships?"

Skip Chelea cleared his throat before Alexander could respond. "I'm no expert, but it does seem overly ambitious."

"I won't argue that point, Skip, but it's not without precedent. When our nation was dragged into World War Two more than 180 years ago, we accomplished the same, producing over a hundred carriers in the same three-year window."

"Is that a reasonable comparison, Alexander? Those ships were a fraction of the size of that." Skip pointed at the display. "Most would fit on one of those hardpoints with room to spare."

"Back then, our production capacity was a fraction of what it is today ... and we won't be alone —"

"I don't want them on Earth," Senator Shaw said.

"That's not the plan, Eglin." Ray shook his head reassuringly. "Not at the moment."

"I don't want them in the Solar System."

"Mars isn't a viable option, and the gravity of Eridani would kill them, so that leaves Ophiuchi."

Ray glanced questioningly at Alexander.

"Ray is right. Unless another planet is discovered in the next three years, one that supports life as is, Ophiuchi is our only option. And it's not a great option. Oxygen breathers will need assistance for another forty years. Back to your question, Ray. The answer is no; existing resources will not support an effort of this magnitude, but we'll have no problem ramping up production in the belts. I'm including the belts in the Alpha Centauri system now that we've figured out how to make that jump consistently. It's much closer than Kuiper."

"Why just us?" Senator Shaw asked. "I'm sure both of you understand that the cost of these ships will bust the budget ... To whom should we send this bill?" She maintained eye contact with Alexander.

"Not just us, Eglin," Ray answered. "If we take the lead on this, I'm confident that other nations will follow. If we don't take the lead, I fear someone else will."

"And what do we get for our generosity? Are they going to teach us a new way to farm?"

"The fleet, for one thing. When all is said and done, those carriers will make a worthy addition to our Navy, and I suspect the shipping industry wouldn't complain if a few came their way, but that's secondary —"

"When all is said and done," Senator Shaw snapped. "We may not be around. What we need now are more combat ships, larger combat ships."

"That is the risk that we need to evaluate. Our fleet is out there now trying to assess the threat we face. Trust me, Eglin. It is our top priority, but looking past this, as we venture further into the universe, I'd prefer to be known as the ones who saved the last of an ancient race rather than the ones who let them perish."

"They're not necessarily the last of their race," Senator Shaw said.

"And that makes it better," Emma said, not hiding the sarcasm. "When we encounter the ships of their long-lost cousins, and they ask us if we've seen any colonists, what should we tell them, senator?"

Ray quickly interjected. "This is beside the point. Last of their race or not, I'm fairly certain we will not be looked upon kindly if we let them all die. I, for one, hope to meet allies out there rather than enemies."

"And that would be much easier if Lieutenant Stewart's exploratory fleet had not blown up the first five ships they encountered."

Ray's head fell a notch. Alexander and Chloe turned their attention toward Emma.

"My fleet? Are you kidding?" Emma asked. "The explosion that destroyed four of those ships was the direct result of a protocol imposed upon the Navy." She glared down at the senator accusingly.

"Don't look at me that way. Issues such as that are not under the purview of the Senate. I had nothing —"

"No, they're not, but I know very well where the request originated. Should I call up the memorandum senator?"

"Are you calling me a liar ... Emma?"

The room fell into an uncomfortable silence, with all eyes on Emma as she considered her response.

"Oh, look at the time," Chloe finally said.

Emma snickered, regained control, and then stifled a full laugh.

"Ray," Senator Shaw said, just under a shout. "You've wasted my morning. If you're counting votes, you know in which column to place mine."

She stood and walked out the door, looking neither right nor left.

Ray stood, as a polite gesture, and watched her disappear into the hallway.

"Well, I'm pretty sure that did not help our cause," he said to Alexander, then turned his head to Emma. "All the same, I'm impressed. You held your ground nicely. Someday, when you're an admiral, that may be useful." His smile was warm and affectionate, but there was no room to misconstrue his words.

"Alexander, if I may have a few words."

Chloe, already standing, nodded silently and followed Emma out the door, letting it close behind.

"Oh, look at the time," Emma said with a wicked smile.

Chloe suppressed her smile, looking left and right, seeing a vacant hall.

"I've never seen you like this — As Senator Park said ... impressive."

"Thanks ... I'm so fucking tired."

"Adrenaline wearing off?"

"It showed?"

Chloe nodded. "Before you even spoke. Was it your intention to make a new enemy?"

Emma shrugged, noncommittal, eyes half closed.

Chloe continued. "Do you remember Mr. Granger? This is going to be much worse."

Emma nodded and lowered her voice. "Oh, I definitely remember Mr. Granger ... and his flowers. Just between you and me, don't let her forget while I'm away. Keep poking at her ... I believe we have a unique opportunity."

Chloe stepped back with her eyes on Emma, reappraising her younger cousin.

Emma smiled weakly and put a finger to her lips.

August 18th 2126

"All right… one last status before we open the jump," Quinn said.

"Bridge, engineering, all systems are green. Excess heat is radiating aft, showing hot. The nose is 30 degrees above ambient," Lieutenant Zhào reported over the intercom.

"Thank you, XO."

"All clear on this side," Ensign Matthews reported from the sensor station. "Drones are ready."

"Very well, Matthews."

"Two ships in system," Petty Office Brown reported from the communication station. "Sturgeon has refueled and is two days behind us. The Water Boy is taking up station in the belt."

Quinn frowned and shook his head. "Stupid name for a tanker, Brown."

"Not my decision, sir. That's democracy in action."

"Hmm, Valdez was the better choice. What do we have ahead of us, helm?"

"Gliese 167, Captain." Petty Officer Mascord said. "A K-class with three known planets and eight predicted exits, including this one."

"Thank you, Mascord … Open it up."

Mascord triggered the interface generator, an automated process since the drive was updated two months earlier. Being the first to enter the system, Batfish did not have a Calvin file to initialize the drive. The process would take considerably longer, and the timing would be less predictable.

Nine minutes later, an interface opened, connecting to space near Gliese 167, over seven and a half light years away, as the photon flies.

"Blue drone away," Matthews reported.

"Calvin files sent to Sturgeon and Water Boy," Brown reported.

The bridge went silent as the drone flew through the jump point and started streaming sensor data back to Batfish.

"All clear," Matthews reported.

"Takes us through, helm, two gees."

"Aye, Captain."

Those on the bridge were pressed into their seats as Batfish accelerated toward the interface. Twelve seconds later, they passed into another star system. The interface destabilized and collapsed a minute after that.

"Launch Red Drone and spread them wide."

"Aye, Captain."

"Good connections to both … near space remains clear … starting triangulation."

The two drones raced away from Batfish at a right angle to each other, streaming continuously.

"The star is currently flaring … no concern," Matthews reported. "I count seven planets and a single debris belt. No threats yet."

The bridge remained silent, waiting for the expanding sensor array to reveal the finer details in the system.

"I'm counting eight, nine … twelve comets in the inner system."

"Seems like a lot," Quinn said, unconcerned.

"One anomaly."

"Roger that." Quinn stifled a yawn. There were always anomalies.

"Directing thermal sensors and the big scope."

The larger sensors of Batfish focused on the anomaly, adding to the composite images generated from the drone data.

"I'm seeing acceleration ... just over ten gees, but coming down."

"That's noise; give the drones a chance to get in position."

"Three gees. Optical is up." An image appeared of the display above the sensor console.

"That's interesting," Quinn said slowly.

"Thermal is up."

"Cut thrust, helm," Quinn said with sudden alarm. An obvious image of a thrusting ship was showing on the thermal display, a dull red blob with a bright line extending from it.

Gravity aboard the ship dropped away.

"Let the drones coast, Matthews," he said sharply.

"Aye, Captain."

"How big is that?" Quinn asked no one in particular.

"It's big, captain," Matthews answered. "We'll know better in a few minutes."

"And how old is this image?"

"Twenty-four minutes."

"So, nineteen minutes before our light reaches them. Any danger of being detected?"

"By our standards, the odds of seeing us from that distance will be tiny," Matthews said after a short pause.

"However, the triggering beam for the interface will be hard to miss if they have a reasonable sensor trained on this jump point."

"Oh, right, damn it. When will that reach them?"

"Uh ... detectable breakthrough light should reach them fifteen to sixteen minutes from now."

"Helm, what's the travel time to their current location, using a single gee?"

"Four days, twenty hours, captain."

Quinn paused in thought, calculating possible scenarios.

"Do they have an obvious destination, Matthews?"

"On display, Captain."

A map of the system popped up with a blinking mark showing the jump point leading to a nearby red dwarf. The mark was labeled with the catalog designation for that system.

"And their originating point," Matthews added.

A second mark appeared along with a course between the two.

"Zeta Doradus ... A or B. Too close to tell which."

"Hmm, A is an F-type star. That could be interesting ... but I like either for the name alone."

"Captain, our measure of the ship's acceleration has settled to 1.4 gees. They should flip and begin deceleration in about three hours. That will allow them to jump in about two days."

"Assuming they follow the same rules we do," Quinn said. "Assuming they don't turn straight at us in another fifteen minutes ... All right, we're just going to have to watch what they do. Bring the drones to a halt relative to Batfish."

"Aye, captain."

Twenty minutes passed. "Captain, we have an enhanced image," Matthews' said. "Um ... estimated hull length is 1.2 kilometers."

Quinn spun about and pushed off his chair toward the sensor station. "Are you sure? That can't be right."

"That's larger than anything we have," Mascord said in disbelief.

"The estimate is good ... and I'm also counting five drives. That's a big ship."

"Well, shit. What are we supposed to do against something like that." Quinn went silent after pulling the collected data to analyze.

"Still no change in their course," Matthews reported. "I don't think we were noticed."

"Captain?" he asked in the silence that followed.

Quinn shook his head. "It's just a transport, a freighter, a very large freighter ... and based upon its delta-v estimate, I'd say it's running empty. Anyone see differently?"

He popped his results up on a display.

The crew remained silent as the nervous tension on the bridge eased slightly. The possibility of being detected by a passing ship, a freighter, fell dramatically after the light of Batfish's entry into the system had passed it by.

"Freighter or not, we'll let it leave before we use our drives. Then, we'll head to the Zeta Doradus A jump point and see what we can find in that system. We'll make it a two-gee run to limit our exposure — Any questions?"

Quinn waited the prerequisite time and was about to continue when Ensign Matthews spoke up.

"Sir, just a comment. Jumping in and out of binary systems can be difficult. We may need to make a manual jump, which may take several hours to reach convergence."

"And this worries you?"

"Yes, sir. Sitting for hours at a jump point into what may be a busy system should worry all of us."

Quinn drew a deep breath and nodded. "Good point, Matthews."

"Thank you, sir. There's also the possibility that we'll jump into the wrong system."

Quinn opened his mouth to speak, but Matthews continued. "And it may be difficult to return if we do miss-jump."

"Thank you, Matthews; anything more?"

"Uh ... the concentration of gas and dust in this system is higher than most. Due to collisions, our midpoint velocity on a two-gee run will make our nose cone obvious to any thermal sensors."

Quinn shook his head. "That would normally be true, but the Zeta Doradus jump point is far above the ecliptic plane. We'll pass through the bulk of that dust in the first few hours ... and at our midpoint, we'll be flipping about, and there's nothing anyone can do to hide three thrusting drives."

With eyes narrowed, Quinn stared at Matthews.

"That's all, captain."

"Good, but now I'm curious, did you ever receive a turn-over from Lieutenant Stewart?"

"No, sir. She never had a chance."

"Well, that is surprising — Where did you learn to be such a pain in the ass?"

Matthew's returned Quinn's inquisitive stare with one of doe-eyed innocence. "Since coming aboard, I've made every effort to learn from the best ... captain."

Quinn nodded his approval.

August 20th 2126

Two days passed, and the freighter jumped as expected. In doing so, it confirmed that the freighter was using technology like that of Terran ships, and it removed that ship from the system before it could see the light from Sturgeon's inbound jump.

Three hours later, Sturgeon popped into the system. Data was exchanged, and she assumed the role of passive observer, tracking Batfish and maintaining communications as that ship accelerated northward.

Four additional days under heavy acceleration and deceleration brought the exhausted crew of Batfish near the Zeta Doradus jump point. With difficulty, Lieutenant Marina Zhào stood to address her watch on the bridge. "Helm, reduce thrust to one gee. Captain Martinez is giving us a short break before we make the jump. Comm, inform Sturgeon of our new jump time. Battle stations in 30 minutes."

"This feels much better," Quinn said as he stood at the entrance to the small bridge, flexing his back.

"Still an empty system, Howard?"

"All clear, captain," Petty Officer Janice Howard reported from the sensor station.

"Everyone, call a relief if you need one. I suspect the next system will be far more interesting than any other we've visited."

Quinn backed into a small nook to allow the crew to get past him and access the ladder he was blocking.

"Captain." Chief Andersen nodded as he squeezed past to relieve Petty Officer Miller at the helm. "The launchers are as good as they're going to get, short of a visit to Earth. Feel free to add me back into the watch rotation."

"I will, chief, assuming we survive the next hour."

Andersen winced and then turned his eyes meaningfully toward Miller and Howard.

Catching the look, Miller smiled broadly. "Don't worry about us, chief. Mascord says the time to worry will be when Captain Martinez has nothing to say."

Andersen assumed the helm as Miller left the bridge. He kept his eyes on Quinn as he sat.

"Okay, point taken," Quinn said with a shrug. "And uh ... nice work with the launchers."

Andersen waved off the compliment. "Credit goes to Egebe and —"

"Lieutenant Zhào, I'm detecting breakthrough radiation ahead," Howard said, looking first at the officer of the deck and then at the captain. "Someone is forming a jump point straight ahead ... 7200 kilometers."

Zhào drew a deep breath but said nothing for a moment that stretched far too long in the minds of the bridge crew. "Chief, a new course is entered; execute, please. This will bring us parallel to the ecliptic. I don't want to fry them with our exhaust. Cut thrust to a half gee. Sounding battle station."

Quinn nodded his approval as he relieved Zhào. "Comm, you're monitoring the Ki Ti frequencies?"

"Always, captain."

"How is your Common?"

"Still learning. Brown knows it better than any of us."

Rapid footsteps on the ladder leading to the bridge announced the arrival of Brown, Mascord, and Matthews. After a quick turnover, Quinn positioned himself to address the entire crew via the intercom.

"In about one minute, we expect a ship to emerge from a jump point directly ahead. Our momentum will carry us within a few hundred kilometers. Since there's no way to avoid this encounter, we will embrace it."

"Captain, the jump point has stabilized ... and a ship is emerging," Matthews reported with dead calm. "Looks like another freighter, much smaller than the other."

"Brown, prepare a message, a simple hello from —"

"Welcome visitors," sounded from one of the monitored frequencies in the Common language. "Please hold your position for inspection. A Seemak Patrol ship will jump over to meet you."

Quinn held his tongue between his teeth, suppressing the string of obscenities at the back of his throat. "As I said, we're embracing this ... fully. Brown, send 'Thank you for your welcome. We'll bring our ship to a stop and await the Seemak Patrol'. Mascord, resume deceleration, bring us to a stop relative to the jump point, 1.5 gees."

Brown repeated the message as Batfish rotated and began to decelerate. Quinn returned to his chair as the added weight pressed him down.

"Captain, Seemak translates to 'free people.'"

"Thank you, Brown. It looks like we've found our pirates."

"Talmahk!" came over the same frequency. There was clear excitement in the voice. "Are you Talmahk?"

Brown twisted her head, seeking guidance.

Quinn cringed. It was a decision he would've preferred others to make. The Odishi believed they were Talmahk when they first met Emma a very long seven months before, but they quickly acknowledged a difference. The extent of that difference had been debated at length on Earth, debates that continued, Quinn was sure. The sketched image sent by Emma showed a remarkable physical similarity, but little else was known of the Talmahk.

"He didn't sound angry … so yes, we are Talmahk."

Brown nodded and turned back to her console.

"Yes, we are. Are you Sal or Ki Ti Tor Mahk?"

"We are Sal of the freighter Borgo Tandi."

"Borgo," Quinn said behind Brown. "That's a drink."

"Yes, sir, an intoxicating beverage. Tandi means transport."

Quinn let out a laugh. "So, another Rum Runner. This is good news."

Borgo Tandi cut its thrust just ahead of Batfish off their starboard bow.

"What news do you bring of the Union?"

Brown turned once again to Quinn.

"Aw, shit. Now I've stepped into it." Union space was very far away. The Navy did not expect to reach that distance from Earth for many years.

"Uh … send … sorry, no news. Our connection … to the old realm was lost a very long time ago. We have no memory of that time."

Brown did, and Tandi responded. "A shame, but I'm sure you'll be welcomed all the same."

"Captain," Matthews said. "There's breakthrough radiation about ten thousand kilometers ahead, away from our exhaust trail."

"Thank you, Matthews. That will be the Seemak Patrol."

A second ship arrived a long minute later. It was small and very similar to the ship they had carried back to Earth, grappled to their hull.

"Captain, we're receiving both audio and video."

Quinn stood and immediately felt the added weight from 1.5 gees of thrust.

"Mascord, reduce thrust to one gee. Brown, route to this display and activate the attached camera, and be ready to feed me answers if I stumble."

"Yes, sir," Brown said, smiling nervously.

A Sal appeared on the large display. Fine gray-brown hair covered a somewhat human-looking face and scalp. Large mouse-like ears and large, wide-set eyes spoiled any further comparison. He appeared to be male by the standards of which Quinn was aware, although he was confident those standards would soon be obsolete. The look on the Sal's face conveyed both curiosity and sincere warmth as if he was greeting an old friend that had been missing for years. He appeared to be wearing a uniform, navy blue, with traces of light gray. Behind him, Quinn recognized a Ki Ti Tor Mahk wearing a similar uniform. Her face showed the same curiosity with a hint of wariness but friendly all the same.

"Good. There you are," the Sal said as he pulled his hands back from the display. "I am Captain Juun of the Seemak Patrol. This is a great honor. A Talmahk has not visited us in over a hundred years."

"I am pleased to meet you, Captain Juun, and we look forward to visiting your home system. I am Captain Martinez, commander of this ship … the Batfish." Quinn felt awkward as he struggled to interpret his thoughts into Common words, but Captain Juun gave no indication of difficulty understanding his speech and showed no impatience with his slow delivery.

"You and your crew will be most welcome, but before you can pass into our system, we'll need to gather information, inspect your cargo, and perform medical scans. Can you tell —"

He stopped talking just as Matthews announced another ship was about to enter the system.

"Sorry, you've probably noticed that another jump point has formed. That will be Krekar of our defense fleet. Don't be alarmed. I'm sure they're just curious."

There was a pause as both captains awaited the arrival of the third ship coming from Seemak. The freighter had resumed its acceleration and was clear of the immediate space.

"He just called that a jump point," Quinn said to the bridge crew, smiling with a calm he did not feel. "Why can't we? 'Interface' is such a mouthful."

"Captain, jump points may refer to either end of an interface or to the large volumes of space from which, or into which, an interface may form," Mascord said.

"Thank you, helm, but I can read." Quinn did his best to appear annoyed rather than nervous.

Mascord returned a sour look. "And weren't you bragging —"

"The ship is coming through," Matthews announced.

The new ship emerged from the jump point, much larger than the patrol vessel and a little smaller than the departing freighter. Like the first two, it didn't have the protective shell that had become common with the ships of Earth, giving them the teardrop shape. It did have a ring, large in diameter but relatively narrow in width. A protective nose cone extended back to wrap the forward edge of the ring. Dotting the cone was an array of sensors and prominent weapon stations. Notable among those were four oversized, concave laser ports, each unsheathed. Amidships was a large non-rotating hull section. Aft of that, the hull narrowed steadily as it stretched back. Additional sensors and weapons showed on the thick portion. Its size came close to that of the new cruiser being developed for the Navy.

"Is that an exhaust port centered on the nose cone?" Quinn asked.

Matthews zoomed one display until the port was all that was visible. "It is; you can see scorching on the inside."

"It looks like a hornet," Mascord said. "I mean the ship itself."

Quinn looked at a second display that showed the ship end-to-end and winced.

"Now that you mention it … I wish you hadn't."

"Captain … Martinez." The Sal captain struggled with the name. "Sorry for the interruption. I was conferring with Krekar. It was only curiosity that brought them through. Before that, I was about to ask you for the location of your colony."

Quinn hesitated briefly before Captain Juun spoke. "Understood. We're all hiding out here, but please understand that our reputation is no longer an accurate description of our society. We're building a new union far from the Malum fleets. All are welcome to join."

Quinn's eyes narrowed, and a slight furl stretched across his forehead.

"You've seen Malum ships?" Juun asked, clearly worried.

The look on Quinn's face turned questioning. "No, we were told that they had once been in this region of space and then disappeared."

"Then you've seen the Odishi? They passed through this region just ahead of the Malum." Captain Juun appeared keenly interested in Quinn's answer.

"We have, less than a year ago. They … introduced us to the Common language … or reintroduced."

Juun exchanged a look with the Ki TI Tor Mahk that Quinn could not interpret.

"We were certain that they had perished. Our historians should be relieved." He finished with a hint of a smile. "They're doing well?"

Quinn nodded, not wanting to say too much. "Yes, they are."

Juun stepped to the side and brought the Ki Ti Tor Mahk forward. "Me Ka Tak and I will board your ship to perform the inspection and screening and then guide you through the jump point."

Quinn's eyes flicked to the display of Krekar, the silhouette of a hornet obvious. He nodded.

"Yes, certainly. You will find docking ports amidships, marked by lighting. They can operate in a vacuum or under pressure; it's your choice."

Juun glanced to his side. "Pressured … I'll contact you when we have a seal." The display went blank.

Quinn drew a deep breath and turned to face the bridge crew. "It appears that we've stumbled into the most complex of the scenarios we trained for, the friendly encounter. I suppose it beats the other extreme, but it won't be easy, and we all need to understand that 'friendly' is merely our current perception."

He looked again to the display of Krekar and shook his head. "Only curiosity? We're going to need some ground rules."

He connected to the intercom. "All hands, visitors will soon board to perform health screenings and to inspect our cargo, our pantry, I suppose. You're all aware of our restrictions, but I will repeat them for clarity. Do not reveal the location of any star systems, and do not reveal the direction of our travel. Do not discuss military capabilities, including the existence of Sturgeon in this system and our two missile bays, although they may not remain hidden. To avoid any possible hints of Earth's location, the displays in the mess will be disabled, and movie time will be postponed until they leave. Finally, avoid discussions of the Odishi. I mentioned that we've been in contact with them, so that bit of guidance has been complicated … On that note, be warned, they, the Sal at least, are very good at reading our faces, probably our emotions too — Lieutenant Zhào and Petty Officer Howard, report to the bridge to provide relief."

He looked toward Brown. "You and I will meet them at the docking port. I'll let you do the talking."

"Good idea, Captain," Brown said, stone-faced.

Petty Officer Howard, Batfish's most experienced operator of the interface generator, tried for the fifth time to establish a jump point into Zeta Doradus A. This followed a half hour watching the automated process rotate through the same five steps, always returning to the same failed state. Me Ka Tak, a pilot with years of experience navigating this particular point, floated just behind her, showing clear frustration. Petty Officer Brown stood at her side, doing her best to interpret the technical jargon of two languages.

Batfish's interface generator was unlike any Me Ka Tak had seen. It was a point of confusion that she mentioned several times. The communication gap also troubled her and finally drew a question from Captain Juun. Quinn explained that Common was not the first language for most within their Talmahk community. Juun accepted the explanation with a shrug.

"Here, now," Me Ka Tak said, motioning toward one side of a display. Howard followed her directions, bringing consistency to the pattern.

"Don't worry about the return jump," Juun said to Quinn with a casual air. "That one is always easy."

"More, more," Me Ka Tak said, pointing to a control.

Howard continued to turn the dial until the display blanked out in convergence, and the jump point appeared ahead of Batfish.

"Good, wonderful," Juun said. "I was about to ask Krekar to open a jump for you."

Quinn nodded silently to Juun. "Me Ka Tak, thank you for your assistance."

The Calvin file and several hours of recordings were sent to Sturgeon via a tight beam. Quinn had no illusions that it went unnoticed but was confident it would remain unmentioned. Based upon a first impression conveyed by two individuals, they would not openly question the action.

By plan, once Batfish jumps, Sturgeon will turn back and pass all information to the next explorer in what was becoming a chain of ships stretching back to Earth. With some luck in the arrangement of those ships, news of first contact with a militarily capable, possibly friendly world, empire, or union would arrive back home in about a week.

"Helm, take us in."

"Your ship is singing."

Quinn looked across the table at Me Ka Tak and listened carefully to the sounds he had learned to ignore over time. They were louder. They were always louder in the mess, but he heard more. "That's from our drive coils. The volume is unique to this class of ship, but it's getting worse. They should have been replaced during our last visit home."

He would not mention that none had been available due to the surge of new construction due to an attack by members of her race. That aside, she was not what Quinn had expected. Her face was predominantly yellow, with traces of red stretching from the eyes. A white scalp blended smoothly with the yellow, just above the eyes. The curve in her spine was nowhere near as pronounced as the corpses he had seen on the captured ship. Her beak was more rounded than he recalled, reminding him of a walrus without the tusks. Her eyes were still quite large, and the two long fingers on each blue and green hand were unsettling.

"It's a beautiful sound. Ours sound more like the grinding of gears when they need maintenance." She glanced at Captain Juun with an unrecognized expression.

Quite the opposite, Juun responded with an easily readable look. It was a smirk as apparent as those his crew occasionally shared with him. "I'll speak with maintenance when we get into orbit."

Batfish had flown through the jump point into a small reception party. The Seemak Patrol guarded each of the three entrance points into their system. Eight ships were spread over a volume of space greater than 30,000 kilometers across, about three Terran diameters. It was large by standards, only a few years old, but the human concept of distance had been radically altered since the visit to Barnard's Star. The missiles carried by Batfish could reach any of those ships in less than five minutes, although Quinn was confident that they could bring destruction to Batfish much more quickly. Three were identical to Captain Juun's small patrol ship. Five were larger warships, although none matched Krekar. All had hailed Batfish in a friendly manner, greeting the representatives of an unknown Talmahk colony.

They were en route to the one inhabited planet, only a two-day journey due to its current position in a large orbit on the inner edge of a massive debris belt and a favorable tilt of the system's axis. Small settlements were spread throughout the belt, mostly miners, but not all, Quinn was warned. They were thrusting at a leisurely eight-tenths gee to match the planet's gravity, a standard that the Seemak had adopted.

A shuttle from the planet was racing to meet Batfish with a set of antiviral, antibiotic, and antifungal medicines meant to protect the planet and a pair of vaccines to protect him. The Seemak were being more cautious than the Odishi. Me Ka Tak assured him that they would be targeted and fast-acting. Juun assured him that he would feel miserable over the last day of the flight.

"Be careful," Me Ka Tak said to Juun. "I don't trust the maintenance crew on Ra. Any other Patrol station would be better."

"Disreputable contractors? That sounds familiar," Quinn said.

The sharp sound made by Me Ka Tak could only have been a laugh of derision.

"Disreputable contractors can be found on all stations. I'm speaking of murderous contractors and murderous guards, and … the list is long."

Quinn's look of consternation was quickly interpreted.

"There's no danger to you, Captain Martinez, and no danger to Me Ka Tak, but this idiot needs to be careful wherever he goes." Juun was clearly indicating himself.

Quinn realized he was starting to like his fellow captain. He was even warming toward Me Ka Tak, but that would be a long process.

"He stole from the wrong family," Me Ka Tak said before he could ask.

"That was a long time ago, and I'm not sure there's a right family to steal from."

"Better, at least." She turned her head to Quinn. "And then he murdered the assassin that they hired."

"Murdered?" Quinn failed to reproduce the word, which Me Ka Tak stated with such ease, but both understood his question.

Juun nodded good-naturedly. "He was an amateur."

"Yes … and he was the young son of the head of another family." She looked across the table at Quinn. "I believe Captain Martinez is still worried."

"A little," Quinn said. "Does your government normally allow … powerful families to … kill their enemies?"

Juun and Me Ka Tak exchanged confused looks before Juun answered.

"We are Seemak. There is no government. We're free of that oppression. It's the powerful families that provide leadership. The council that will greet you in two days has a representative from the five leading families."

His look turned inquisitive. "I'm guessing your colony is under democratic rule?"

"For the most part," Quinn said.

"So, you have factions?"

"Yes," Quinn said slowly, realizing he was being interrogated.

Juun laughed. "Please don't worry about that answer. The council will welcome it. They … We don't believe a single entity should rule. When they do, it's usually through violence."

Quinn nodded his head and straightened his posture. "You showed a strong interest in the Odishi when we first met but haven't asked any more of them."

Me Ka Tak shook her head—a surprisingly common action used by both races.

"There is a shame that Captain Juun hinted at, felt by some but not openly acknowledged. It makes many … most of us, hesitant to speak of them. They could have used our help, but we chose to stand back and hope the Malum ignored us. They did, and it was the last we saw of either. Over the years, ships were sent in the direction they went, but nothing was found. A few of those ships were lost, leading to some wild speculation. It was assumed that the Odishi had been annihilated and the Malum had returned to their home until you arrived. Your words should have been greeted with excitement, or at least interest, but I've seen few discussions and have heard little in the broadcasts … And half of that has been of one family or another casting doubt on the truth in your words."

She was now looking at Juun with what Quinn could only interpret as a cross look.

"Me Ka Tak is attempting to shame me now — Captain, I see the truth in your face, but I'm in no position to defend your honesty."

"My honesty needs to be defended?"

"No, that's not a requirement. Your statement was to the two of us, and we believe you, but you'll need to be careful when you're down on the planet. To make such a statement before the council would require proof — Don't worry; they won't ask."

Batfish had a database full of images, but Quinn felt he had already said too much, breaking his mandate. "No one has heard from other Odishi out of Union space?" he asked.

Juun shook his head. "No, not a word."

Captain Juun's inquisitive look returned. "So, you've met the Odishi but appear ignorant of the Seemak, the Union, and the eight or more colonies between. I can only assume that your colony sits further from Union space than Seemak, in the direction they traveled. This is surprising. Seemak was always considered to be on the edge of occupied space. Not anymore."

Quinn lowered his head briefly and then looked up with a narrow smile. "Captain Juun, you are a talented interrogator. It's a shame so many want you dead."

"Exactly." He nudged Me Ka Tak with his hand. "I may be willing to accompany you back to your colony … if my skills could be of use."

"I'm not sure we'll need an interrogator, but a representative for your planet would be very welcome."

"That is a decision for the council," Me Ka Tak said.

"And of Captain Martinez," Juun added, his smile growing. "Few of us have wandered far in that direction. There was a group of Ki Ti Tor Mahk flying ships just like my patrol —"

"Captain," Andersen interrupted. "The meal is almost ready." He came through the galley doors carrying plates, utensils, glasses for the three, and a pitcher of water.

"Chief, thank you. Thanks for throwing this together."

"Glad to help, captain." He returned through the doors.

Juun continued. "They were flying five ships dropped off by a transport six systems from here and haven't been seen since." He looked at Quinn carefully.

"How long have they been missing?" Quinn asked, doing his best to look curious with a hint of concern.

"It's been almost a year."

"Do ships go missing often?"

"No, and to lose five implies that the cause was not an accident."

Quinn smiled disarmingly. "Trust me, Captain Juun, Me Ka Tak. If I knew something, I would tell you — Almost a year ago? I can request information when I return, but I'm reasonably sure it would've been mentioned before we were sent in your direction."

"Ah, don't worry about it. They were from one of the belt families."

"Criminals," Me Ka Tak added. "Whatever their fate, it was most certainly deserved."

Andersen entered again, carrying a platter, holding lobster tails, baked potatoes, and melted butter. Me Ka Tak immediately made a sour face as the smell filled the room.

"Something smells wonderful," Juun said. "And something does not."

He sampled the butter with a single finger and then made a face to match Me Ka Tak.

"Chief?"

"It's gone." Andersen scooped up the butter decanter.

"This, on the other hand …" Juun set the lobster tail on his plate, his attention drawn to the knife and fork.

"There are similarities," he said, staring at the tines of the fork. "I could visit every colony between here and the Union, and the inhabitants of each would make some use of this instrument, but in every case, it would have three points, not four. You truly have been apart from the Union for a long time."

"As I said, our history is long, and we have no record of any others before we met the Odishi."

"Amazing," Juun said. "As is this creature. At the least, you should try this Me."

"Actually, I find this quite good." Like an apple, she held a baked potato in her hand and was nibbling at it, wary of the heat.

"He just called you 'Me' … Is there a custom that guides the use of names?"

Me Ka Tak finished swallowing a larger bite of the potato and then washed it down with a drink of water. "Captain Juun is just lazy. When you meet the council, always use their full names, even if another is abbreviated. I doubt any would show offense to you, but it may be taken as that."

Quinn nodded. "Thank you, Me Ka Tak."

Andersen stepped into the mess. "Captain, please forgive my breach of etiquette."

Quinn looked up at him in confusion.

"I believe seafood calls for these." He set down three three-tined forks and smiled broadly.

Juun picked one from the table and held it up, facing Quinn.

"This is curious."

August 28th 2126

The honor of escorting a visitor from another colony went to the captain of the Patrol ship that first encountered them. Inspecting the ship, screening the crew, guiding them through the jump, and then accompanying them toward the Seemak home world were all part of this duty. Any successful outcome from the visit would bring credit to that captain. Credit that extended back through any family connections. The duty also extended to any planet-side visits. For that, Juun delegated Me Ka Tak as his ally before the council. All parties involved understood his reasoning. As the captain of Batfish, Quinn represented a lost Talmahk colony, at least from the local point of view.

Batfish was directed to a very high orbit, one outside of the planet's second moon, a small rock by Terran standards. Quinn joined Captain Juun and Me Ka Tak aboard their Patrol ship. He recalled that it was capable of atmospheric flight, but they would dock at a station and take a shuttle directly to a port facility that filled a harbor adjacent to the planet's capital city of Raygao. He carried a hand-held communications unit, an enhanced version of the phones that almost everyone on Earth above the age of six used. It could provide direct audio, video, and data links to the ship if it was in a synchronous orbit overhead. The current orbit placed her far out of range. Lieutenant Zhào would act as captain until he returned. She was to keep Batfish in that orbit until his meeting with the council was concluded.

With a crew of eight, Six Sal and two Ki Ti Tor Mahk, the Patrol ship dropped out of high orbit toward the station. Quinn studied a set of interactive displays they put up for his benefit. The displayed images were surprisingly grainy, and the controls somewhat clumsy, but it was more than sufficient for his immediate needs.

The statistics for the planet itself were reassuring. Eight-tenths of a gee with an oxygen level slightly higher than Earth. He would be comfortable. It was very young as planets go, having dropped out of the surrounding belt only a few eons earlier. The surface was rugged and geologically active. Oceans covered just over half. Mountains covered the remainder. With a local year nearly twice that of Earth and an axial tilt 50 percent greater, the seasons in the higher and lower latitudes were long and harsh. Life still thrived in those regions. Native species of both flora and fauna had adapted to survive the brutal extremes. His destination near the equator would be more pleasant.

The planet's population was just above 300 million, with most spread around the equator, filling the valleys and clinging to the sides of the surrounding mountains. The majority were Sal by a nearly two-to-one ratio. The Ki Ti Tor Mahk made up the remainder, except for a small community of Mahkee and Porta Ree. As Captain Juun had mentioned, the planet, or more completely, the star system, was controlled by a loose federation of twenty-one prominent families. Every inhabitant within the system owed allegiance to a family. A chain of allegiances connected those families to the twenty-one at the top. Rural areas appeared to be divided by geography, but the cities had more complex arrangements. The Mahkee and Porta Ree had a single voice, equivalent to a family. The Patrol did not have a voice but did have a seldom-used veto privilege. Their ships patrolled all space beyond the planet's atmosphere, including the belt and any nearby star systems that captured their attention. They were the system's largest military force, but many families maintained small fleets.

The Seemak Council comprised representatives from five families, although Quinn could not find any description of the process used to choose those families. The listed names did change irregularly as he looked at their history. From his brief conversation with Juun and Me Ka Tak, it seemed unlikely that a family would voluntarily give up a seat on the council. Quinn pushed his head back and closed his eyes. He had six hours and was still recovering from the two vaccinations he had received earlier.

Two guards stood before the closed double door into the council's chamber. Me Ka Tak presented her credentials as Quinn stood back. The high wall to his left was adorned with large placards, five for the current ruling families and one below for the Patrol. A nameplate sat in front of each, matching those he had read about on the flight down to the planet. Carvings were at the center of each. Those honoring the three Sal families depicted aspects of their natural world: a pair of finely detailed flowers framed by leafed plants that looked remarkably similar to ferns; an elaborate, but unlikely, bird soaring against the backdrop of a mountain with a fish hanging from its bill; and the third, a school of larger fish leaping over a wave with a billowy cloud in the background. Quinn would have used the word gaudy for each if the two honoring the Ki Ti Tor Mahk families were not so painful to his eyes. Wild geometric patterns of red, green, orange, and yellow filled each in a manner he could only call haphazard. Haphazard as a whole, but as he looked closer, he saw subtle coloring that revealed fractal patterns running through the veins separating the broader structure.

Me Ka Tak appeared to be negotiating with the guards, if not arguing, about what he could not hear or guess. In time, one guard opened the pair of doors, and the second passed through only to turn about and wave Me Ka Tak forward. She did the same for Quinn and waited until he was at her side. Together, they stepped into the chamber. Quinn expected to find the representatives sitting behind a high bench, reminiscent of a courtroom. It did feel like he was on trial. What they stepped into was far different, a casual gathering of close to thirty individuals clustered across several broad steps under a hemispherical dome of glass. The dome extended from the building, providing 180 degrees of view and allowing sunlight to pour in from above. A latticework provided some shade.

Most present were Sal or Ki Ti Tor Mahk, but a distinct pair stood apart. They shared some similarities: thick manes of blonde hair crowning small, pinched faces of yellow-green skin and tiny reddish noses. Those similarities ended at the neck. The Mahkee was short, perhaps a meter in height, with a muscular build. The Porta Ree was closer in height to the average human but unnervingly thin. That pair immediately locked their eyes on Quinn. All others in the room barely looked their way before returning their attention to one of several conversations.

The view behind the small crowd caught Quinn's attention. Through an uninterrupted, curved glass wall, he looked out over Raygao and down the coastline, a thin strip of land between the world's largest ocean and a towering range of mountains. Even from this distance, he could see the surf rolling onto shore. To the right, across the extensive grounds of the government center, he could see the top half of a shuttle sitting tail down, framed by a distant, snow-covered peak.

"Remember," Me Ka Tak said. "Everyone will be honored to meet you, and you are honored to meet them — I see the heads of three families; be careful. With them, stay with the truth, if possible. Apart from the Patrol, truth may be a ... fleeting anomaly on this planet, but the family heads will always expect it. They have a long memory or at least surround themselves with those that do, and they take great offense at even a hint of dishonesty."

"Can I lie in front of them to another?" Quinn asked with a sly grin.

"They may allow it, or you may find yourself on the run, like Captain Juun."

Quinn subtly gestured toward one Ki Ti Tor Mahk and then turned away. "The head of a family?"

"Yes, Freeholder Ta Tok, but don't confuse him with that family's representative, also Freeholder Ta Tok."

"I don't think I will. His robe is … very different." Quinn found the swirling mass of colors as difficult to focus upon as the placards outside of the room, although the patterns did have a more natural look as they flowed smoothly down to his feet.

"Beautiful, I would say. The difference is that he can wear whatever he chooses. The Ki Ti Tor Mahk on the council feel obliged to match the dull sensibilities of the Sal."

She turned him toward an approaching pair.

"Captain Quinn Martinez, we bring welcome and greetings from the elected of our humble confederation." The voice was guttural, unexpectedly so from the narrow-framed Porta Ree. His name was recognizable, but the other words required a moment to interpret. They were clearly part of the Common language, but something in the delivery had him confused. Cadence or inflection came to mind, recalling one of Emma's lessons.

"I'm Toregan Teen, and my partner is Ray Moold Jan, but you may call her Jan, and Teen would be an acceptable name for me."

"I'm honored by the welcome from your elected and greet you in the name of the leaders of my colony."

They looked back at him silently, questioningly, he suspected. He turned to Me Ka Tak to see a similar look.

"'Greet you in the name of the leaders.' What does that mean?" she asked, clearly poking him.

"Sorry," he said to her. "Sorry," he said to Teen and Jan. "I was trying to sound diplomatic. It's never been one of my strengths."

Teen nodded with understanding. Jan stifled a laugh and then looked behind her. "This is good," she said. "We will better trust what you say."

Her cadence was similar to Teen's, but he was already growing accustomed to it.

"Thank you, Jan. Going beyond my skills as an orator, with this language or otherwise, I'm still learning the intricacies of your society. You speak for the elected of your confederation. Am I to understand that a family does not rule over the Mahkee and Porta Ree?"

Quinn understood the democratic nature of their confederation from the research he was allowed on the flight to the planet, but he was anxious to pass the conversation back to them before he started to babble nonsense.

"Here, it's true," Teen said. "But not back in Union space. We are amused that the Mahkee and Porta Ree that came to Seemak were fleeing from a society ruled by a single family for hundreds of years … to this planet, ruled entirely by families."

Quinn smiled, acknowledging the irony. "The families accept your elected leaders?"

"For the most part. We hear complaints that the change of leaders from one election to the next makes us difficult to predict. Still, our patron has been perfectly happy with us and our contributions … Has your colony experimented with elections?"

"Absolutely. We have factions on our world." Quinn intended to remain vague on the subject. "Some use elections, others use inheritance to select leaders."

"Factions! More than two, I would guess, from your wording." Both were staring closely at Quinn. "Estimates of your population are spread between two and five million. Many factions would imply a fractured society." Both continued to stare.

"Fractured would imply weakness," Me Ka Tak said.

"Are those estimates or guesses?" Quinn asked, looking between Jan and Teen.

"A little of both," Jan answered. "Estimates of when you settled out here, like many of us, 500 years ago; estimates of the number of original settlers, 10 to 20 thousand; and estimates of your growth rate, which are more likely just guesses."

Quinn turned to Me Ka Tak, maintaining his small inquisitive smile and narrowing his eyes. "I … my face seems to be a source of information to everyone I encounter."

She bowed somberly, her eyes closed but a smile evident. "Word may have been sent ahead of our ship that you lacked certain skills."

"Well, certainly, I'm an explorer; we never intended to make contact — Aren't you supposed to be on my side — And did you mean that I lack the skills or that all Talmahk lack the skills."

Her smile grew. "Just you, your crew was perfectly inscrutable, and yes, I am on your side. I am your guide, your protector, and your advocate. Another sent that word — You may have met him."

"Ah, that I believe."

She continued. "It's important for you to understand that privacy is highly valued among the Seemak. Compelling an individual to speak against their will is considered inappropriate by most families and a crime by some. Quite the opposite, manipulating an individual into divulging information is considered an art. I tell you this now because …" She indicated he should turn around.

The representatives of the five families approached. Off to the right, the Patrol liaison observed. Another three stood to the left and back, certainly the family leaders Me Ka Tak mentioned. All others remained near the bottom of the broad staircase, where they had been when he entered the room.

"Captain Martinez, the Third Council of the Seemak Union welcomes you and welcomes the opportunity to hear tales of your travels and your colony. In turn, we'll share all you wish to know about the Seemak. Me Ka Tak informs us that your experience with the Common language is limited, so please stop us anytime if you don't understand what you're hearing."

Condescending storytellers were not what he had expected. He should probably interpret that as 'Tell us all of your colony's secrets and the best route we should take to get there.'

He looked briefly at Me Ka Tak and then at the Sal in the middle, who had made the introduction.

"Tales I can tell, Freeholder Jardin, although the information I'm allowed to share is limited." He was annoyed that the words were still coming out slowly. "Tales would be a welcome change to my expectations. Before entering this room, I was afraid I was stepping into a court of law." His smile was slight and solemn. He made sure it was evident to all nine within close proximity, but it may not have been to Me Ka Tak. Out of the corner of his eye, he was certain he saw a look of shock on her face. The Ki TI Tor Mahk council members were unreadable, but the three Sal initially showed confusion. That confusion gave way to tentative smiles.

"At times, this room is arranged to intimidate those who enter that door." He indicated behind Quinn. "Many do come through to receive justice, but most are simple beggars, hoping to reposition their family within the hierarchy. I don't believe you're either of these?"

Quinn considered for a moment. "The question of my colony's place within the Seemak Union will need to be asked by those that follow. I'm merely an explorer. Any question of justice would best be asked by the council, but I'm not aware of any need."

"We shall see," Freeholder Ta Tok said from the far right.

"You say you're an explorer," Jardin said, ignoring Ta Tok's comment.

"Yes, one of several. We have recently decided to expand our knowledge of the systems near our own."

"Could you define the term 'near' for us?" the Sal representative on the left asked.

"No, I cannot, Freeholder Rasaan." Quinn matched her smile. "I can say that our interests are entirely peaceful. We seek knowledge of available resources, habitable planets, and potential allies."

There was some truth in his statement.

"Wonderful," Jardin said. "Peace, prosperity, and strength are the central tenants of the Seemak Union." The representatives separated as Jardin invited him and Me Ka Tak down toward the glass wall, looking down upon the city.

"As you're aware, we're forming this new Union right here, far from the tyranny and violence of the past. A Talmahk colony would be a welcome addition, regardless of your size."

They stopped before a long, curved table of food. Elaborate serving dishes dotted its length. They were ceramic in appearance, and some had embedded heating elements. Between them sat trays of loose items. Finger food, he realized as others grabbed freely. Glasses filled with water were available at either end. A second table caught Quinn's eyes, beverages that were not water. Emma had mentioned a lack of alcohol on the Odishi world. From what he had seen and heard on this world, he seriously doubted that the races of the Seemak would follow that practice, and it was a good bet that their physiological response to alcohol would be like that of the people of Earth.

"I was assured that nothing before you will cause harm," Jardin said.

"But caution is advised," Me Ka Tak added, indicating one section. "Everything here is best left to the Ki TI Tor Mahk, and all should avoid these." She pointed to a tray of colorful vegetables or possibly fruit and then looked back at him.

Quinn smiled at her and then leaned over the selection. Only a rare moment of common sense stopped his hand from reaching out. "I'll take your advice on this."

"Of course, you will," she said with a modest bow before grabbing a cloth napkin from a stack and a flat round of bread from a tray and handing both to him.

He bit from one end. It was hot, not overwhelming, but close, most likely from capsicum or an extraterrestrial equivalent. He looked at Me Ka Tak, unable to hide his surprise.

"The fruit would've been much worse," was all she said.

He mimicked her bow and then turned to Jardin. "I should thank you for your hospitality."

Jardin smiled gregariously. "I'm glad that you're not a diplomat. There will be a time for that profession, but not now."

A glass of water was handed to Quinn. He used it to wash down the bread.

"I imagine you have a process for bringing new colonies into the Union, the new Union; exchanging diplomats, setting rules, discussing boundaries?"

"No process has been defined. Currently, we have an agreement with two other colonies. Yours will make three if your leaders are willing. With your visit, we hope to build a trusting relationship … one between you and those present. Once that's established, others can attend to the formalities."

Quinn found the notion of Earth joining an organization of families, criminal families by any definition he knew, to be laughable. It was not a request he could carry to anyone, not the nations of Earth, the United States alone, or even the Navy. Even his crew would question his sanity if he seriously proposed the idea. Nonetheless, he had seen more combat-capable ships on the short flight between the jump point and the planet's outer orbit than all the nations of Earth had produced to date.

"I will, of course, return with word of the new Union, the Seemak, and the good people in this room."

He realized at that moment that all other conversations had subsided, and the attention of most was upon him. He looked around to see nods of approval from the Sal, the majority in the room, and from Jan and Teen. The Ki Ti Tor Mahk were less readable and, he suspected, less amiable to the notion, less trusting of him, Me Ka Tak being the exception.

"Captain, I believe we're off to a good start today."

Me Ka Tak quickly slipped between Quinn and the new speaker, a tall, elderly Sal.

"Captain Martinez, I introduce Freeholder Rono Jass, head of the Jass family, patron of the Ka Tak, and sponsor of Freeholder Jardin, head of the Third Council of the Seemak Union."

Jardin stepped into the conversation. All others quickly withdrew from earshot.

"Freeholder Rono Jass, I am honored by your presence."

"As I am by yours. Your arrival here on Seemak is both unexpected and very welcome," he said conversationally. "Discussions of the new Union were limited to optimistic dreamers until a few short years ago. I believe great opportunities will soon make themselves available to those with the means and determination to seize them. Our Union will be at the heart of those opportunities, and I believe you see this as I do. I know Me agrees."

Me Ka Tak bowed deeply. Quinn was still confused over the polite use of names.

"I do," she said. "The new Union is our greatest chance to establish a secure, peaceful region of space where all can thrive."

"Peace and security are paramount concerns," Rono said. "For these reasons, I will allow this subject to be broached once."

He looked past Quinn toward the two other family leaders present, another Sal and a Ki Ti Tor Mahk. They both stepped forward to join the conversation. Quinn shifted to balance the members of the conversation and steeled himself for the questions he expected.

"Travel between the stars has always been a dangerous endeavor. Ships can break down; the vacuum of space is unforgiving. Ships can be attacked; concealment in any system is a simple matter, and ambush is difficult to combat … But far more often, ships just disappear."

Jass laughed, more to himself. "No need to mention the three failed attempts to reach old Union space; the foolhardy make poor examples." He glanced toward a small group near the end of a table and then returned his attention to Quinn. "There are, from time to time, losses that attract the attention of many." He addressed Quinn directly. "Most recently, as you're aware, five small ships of the Ka Kek family, a client family of Freeholder Ta Tok, disappeared." He gestured toward the Ki Ti Tor Mahk to Quinn's right. "They were far outside of patrolled space in a direction that has always been problematic. It's also the direction of travel for both the Odishi fleet and the pursuing Malum fleet 400 years past, and it happens to be the direction of arrival for your two ships."

They did know of Sturgeon.

"We may never know what became of them, but it would ease the fears of many freighter crews if the threat was mitigated. Knowing that we have an ally such as yourself on that … exposed flank would greatly comfort them."

Quinn nodded. "As an ally on our flank, would ease the concerns of many within my colony. As Me Ka Tak said, a secure and peaceful region will benefit all of us."

"I wholeheartedly agree, captain," Freeholder Ta Tok said. "I believe that's all that needs to be said on this subject."

Quinn nodded. Ta Tok responded with a short, formal bow but was otherwise unreadable.

"And now a drink to commemorate this occasion." Jardin's voice boomed across the room.

The staff anticipated his call. A table near the glass wall was covered with tumblers, each filled with a golden-brown liquid. Me Ka Tak looked there and then back to Quinn and grimaced in the unique manner of a Ki TI Tor Mahk. He felt the need to respond with a lopsided grin.

All present passed the table, picking up a glass and a memento from an adjacent table. Once past, standing next to the transparent wall, Me Ka Tak said, "Don't drink yet."

Quinn obeyed.

As the last had a drink in hand, including the staff, attention shifted to the three family heads, who had gathered, apart from all others. Together, they tipped their tumblers, downed the contents, and set the glasses down. The five representatives and the Patrol liaison followed.

"Now," Me Ka Tak said. He mimicked her action, the action of all others in the room still holding a glass, and downed the drink in one swallow and then set the empty tumbler on a table.

The bite of alcohol was barely noticeable, allowing the flavor to stand out. It was both cloyingly sweet and putrid. He thought of rotted flesh floating on honey. With eyes half closed in concentration, he fought his stomach until the flavor subsided.

"I'm sorry I ever doubted you, Me Ka Tak."

She grabbed his shoulder in a good-natured manner. "Only a Sal can appreciate it."

Quinn nodded and then held up his memento. "What does this represent?"

She looked at hers closely and then walked to the table where a few remained. Two others were at the table, looking in Quinn's direction. Both turned away as she approached. A placard rested in the center of the table. Quinn recognized the writing as Common but could not read any of it.

After a glance, Me Ka Tak held up hers. "The center represents our victory against the Malum. It's a small piece from the hull of one of their ships, destroyed when we encounter their fleet in the adjacent system ... so the story goes. In truth, there's no record of any ship from this planet opposing the Malum. Quite the opposite, the standing orders from those few days were to avoid that system and all Malum ships. The rear guard of the Odishi fleet most likely destroyed it." She rotated the memento to show the front. "The crests around the base honor the eight families that ruled Seemak at that time. Five actually ruled. Three were insignificant at the time but have since grown in power."

She glanced meaningfully in the direction of Freeholder Ta Tok.

Quinn smiled appreciatively and then twisted his head and glanced behind and down. From their height, 32 floors up, he could see crowds of pedestrians lining the walks and sleek ground vehicles passing between them in single lanes.

"I think this is going well," he said quietly.

Me Ka Tak swiveled around, meeting the eyes of others in the room before turning back to Quinn.

"I believe you will be abducted or murdered before this day ends. We should probably leave while there's still light, soon … perhaps now."

Her matter-of-fact delivery kept Quinn frozen in disbelief.

"Now," she said.

"Right, yes. Should we give our regards … anything like that?"

"No, they'll understand. In fact, I'm going now. Wait a moment and then follow behind. There are waste facilities to the right. Head that way. I'll call an elevator." She glanced briefly out the window and down and then turned and left Quinn alone. He watched her go and then shifted his attention toward the bar, noting those looking his way. With alien faces, it was challenging to separate curiosity from murderous intent. After a short count, he calmly turned about and walked up the steps and out the double doors. To his right, an elevator door was open. Upon seeing Me Ka Tak waiting, he walked toward it and stepped inside. She immediately pressed three for the ground floor and then four after a moment of thought. The elevator dropped a short distance before opening on the 25th floor. The young

Sal who had called it could only stare at Quinn in surprise until Me Ka Tak said, "Please take another," and closed the door.

At the fourth floor, she grabbed his arm. "We're getting off here."

They turned right and jogged past more surprised Sal. After a left turn, Quinn followed Me Ka Tak down a broad flight of steps. She was talking into what looked like an antique phone, making hurried, cryptic statements.

Why was he trusting her? No one within the council chambers had seemed threatening. He slowed. The staircase was empty of others but not silent; the din of the activity in the lobby came from below.

She slowed and then stopped, allowing him to catch up. "I should have warned you of the danger, but I wasn't sure it was real until we stepped into that room."

He stopped two steps above her.

"Wondering who your real enemies are?" she asked with no sign of humor.

Maintaining eye contact for a long moment, he considered his lack of options and finally decided to trust his stronger instincts. "Not anymore ... well, not you anyway. When you get the chance, could you explain who they are?"

"I will, as soon as I know."

They continued past the lobby, down into a sub-level.

"It's ... uncanny," Quinn said as they hurried down the stairs. "Your city, your buildings, and the buttons in that elevator are very similar to any number of cities, buildings, or elevators on Earth."

"What — Could you please focus on survival?" They continued past the first sub-level.

"On earth?" Me Ka Tak asked. "I'm not sure your rambling thought translated correctly."

Momentary confusion passed quickly. Quinn had not intended to reveal the name of the homeworld for all humans but saw no harm either.

"It's the name we gave to our colony … the name of our planet."

Me Ka Tak looked back at him as she pushed through a door, revealing an underground parking garage. Her face was twisted in a manner he had not seen before. "Earth? … Of course, you walk on both — That's very clever."

Sarcasm. She was becoming more readable with every conversation. Quinn smiled grimly. "Focusing on survival."

She nodded back, mimicking the Sal/Talmahk/Human gesture.

Quinn realized that one side of the garage was open, the seaward side. A moist air blew through, giving the surface under their feet a wet sheen. Me Ka Tak was peering left and right as they hurried from the stairwell towards a pair of signs he could not read. The squeak of tires could be heard coming around a corner out of sight. As he looked in that direction, a narrow silver car appeared, moving fast and rapidly decelerating. A Sal was looking past them out of the right-side driver's window. 'There's a difference,' he thought. The last of the cars on Earth with that configuration had been relegated to the museums many years before.

Me Ka Tak opened the door behind the driver for Quinn and then ran around to the front passenger seat.

Once seated, she said something indecipherable, and then Quinn felt his back press into the seat as the car pulled away, and then he practically fell over as they swerved around a corner toward the exit. She snapped into place what appeared to be a five-point harness as the next corner pressed Quinn against the window. A quick look around the back showed no safety belts at all.

Out of the garage, they slowed. The grounds of the government center had the look of a park, and several pedestrians, Sal and Ki Ti Tor Mak, were enjoying what Quinn would consider a beautiful day in any other place. They circled the building and then turned toward an open gate controlling access to the complex. The driver rolled down his window and waved to the Mahkee guards. Quinn remained motionless but was confident they could not see through the darkened window.

Once on the street, Quinn had his first close look at the populace of the capital city. They traversed several city blocks before he spotted anyone that was not Sal, a pair of Ki Ti Tor Mahk strolling casually down the inclined walk. The car turned right past those two, climbing a steeply graded road leading away from the shore.

The city gradually fell behind, replaced by large homes shrouded in lush green trees and bushes, similar and different from those on Earth. "Where are the flowers?" he asked, wanting to break the long silence that started shortly after the car left the garage.

"Not here," the driver said. "Only Sal live here. I could take you into a Ki Ti village, but that would be a bad idea."

Me Ka Tak twisted back to face Quinn. "Ki Ti Tor Mahk cover their homes in flowers. Therefore, most Sal avoid them entirely. Their loss. Raygao has one village predominantly filled by Ki Ti Tor Mahk."

"Two," the driver said.

Me Ka Tak gave the driver a sour look. "One that I'd be willing to show him when we get past whatever is happening."

The driver laughed. "That may be difficult since the most obvious way past this will be the death of your Talmahk friend."

"He's my charge. I am his escort. It's my duty to the Patrol to protect him."

"By running from the council? No one takes their duty to the Patrol that seriously."

"Who wants him?" Me Ka Tak asked. "Why? Is it revenge for the lost ships?"

"Which we had nothing to do with," Quinn added quickly.

The driver laughed again, loudly, derisively, more like a human laugh. "No one believes that."

"Then revenge," Me Ka Tak said.

"I'm not sure. What were the opinions of Freeholder's Jass and Ta Tok?"

Me Ka Tak paraphrased the introduction between Quinn and Freeholder Jass, emphasizing his desire to establish relations with the Talmahk colony. She then repeated what Freeholder Ta Tok had said, nearly verbatim.

"Then no, not revenge," the driver said. "Given what you just said, Freeholder Ta Tok would never authorize an attack for the sake of revenge, not against the wishes of Jass."

"It must be information they're after." She looked pointedly at Quinn. "You may still survive this."

Quinn would've preferred some hint of humor in her delivery. "How certain are you that anyone is after me? I saw nothing in the council chambers that worried me."

She said nothing, but her look told him how little she trusted his observational skills.

"There's no doubt," the driver said. "Jouh Nee, by the way."

"Huh."

"His name," Me Ka Tak said.

"Oh, sorry … Quinn Martinez or just Quinn. You said there's no doubt?"

"None. Several Ka Kek squads are already searching the city near the government center, and one is waiting near the shuttle … I did get a close look at one from that squad." Jouh briefly glanced at Me Ka Tak, enough to catch her attention. "He was marked."

"Can you describe it?"

"It looked like a small green claw to the side of his left eye."

Quinn looked at Me Ka Tak in the sudden silence, but her eyes were on Jouh Nee.

"Sorry, Quinn," she finally said. "That's the mark of an assassin, probably a member of the Ti Mak, a client family of the Ka Kek."

Quinn drew a deep breath. "Can we meet the shuttle at another landing site?"

Me Ka Tak looked at Jouh Nee for an answer.

He shook his head. "I don't know whom we can trust. I'm not even sure about the Patrol; not all members. I'll make inquiries, but right now, we need to hide."

Quinn turned away to look out the window. His ears popped. Outside, the homes and greenery had faded away. Small, scraggly evergreens slid past the window, clinging to rocky soil. The glass, he noticed, had become cold to the touch, and they continued to climb.

August 30th 2126

Emma was comfortable in her tropical uniform, shorts, and a light top. She was well-rested after an uneventful flight to Ophiuchi-C and looked forward to seeing Niko. Adashi and Tormond looked miserable, sitting across from her on the modified shuttle. They were unaccustomed to the wildly varying gee forces inherent to an atmospheric descent, and, in Emma's opinion, they looked gaunt. When asked, both would wave off concerns about their health, and, in truth, neither seemed to be suffering from their limited diet.

Their approach to Atacama Station showed on a display as clear as any window. It had grown enormously since Emma had last been there while stationed aboard Galileo 16 months earlier. It seemed like a lifetime. She could see twenty or more artificial lagoons lining the shore, stretching away until the ocean haze obscured the view. A pier reached from the station's edge straight out toward deep water. Moderate-sized watercraft filled several of its berths at the far end. The Quonset huts were gone, replaced by two-story and three-story buildings further from the shore, blocky and ugly but probably more comfortable. Tubes connected most into a network, a welcome addition with the air still unbreathable. Greenery filled most empty spaces between buildings and formed a ring about the small town. A narrow winding road connected it to a landing strip a kilometer down the coast. The shuttle was aligned to that strip.

Coming in horizontally, with assistance from the engines under each wing, the shuttle touched down smoothly. Emma quickly realized that her notion that Niko would be waiting outside the shuttle as they dropped the rear hatch was outdated. Only the ground crew was visible inside the fenced-off field, waving the shuttle toward a string of open-air structures, sheltering a handful of electro-prop planes. A shuttle bus was driving through a gate to meet them.

"How is the temperature?" Emma asked Adashi once she was seated on the bus, and the two Odishi were uncomfortably reclined upon the contraptions that had replaced the eight seats at the front. All windows were sealed to maintain a breathable oxygen level, but the temperature was much higher than on the shuttle, very close to that just outside of the glass.

"Terrible," Tormond said as the bus detached from the shuttle.

"Livable," Adashi said, "We can adjust."

They had come to Ophiuchi-C Two to determine whether the Odishi could make it into a home. The data from Atacama Station had been encouraging in some ways and depressing in others. Like all humans on the planet, they could only survive in a sealed environment, a building, a vehicle, or while wearing a breathing apparatus. The engineered algae released as part of phase one was now detectable in the warmer surface water of every ocean and attached sea, but the increase in oxygenation was barely measurable. Phase two releases were still years in the future and still under development.

Nutrition was also a concern. Looking out the windows, it was clear that efforts to adapt plant life to this world had succeeded, but that meant little if all turned out to be incompatible with Odishi physiology.

Passing through town, the empty streets were noticeable. A growing fear that no one would greet them immediately dissolved as the bus drove through an airlock into the largest of the buildings. Emma could see through an opening set of doors into a large room packed with people. 'The entire population' was her first thought, but that was also based upon out-of-date information. All the same, it was a larger greeting than they had seen in any city on Earth, although every one of those had been tightly controlled for security reasons.

As they walked through the doors, the shock of seeing two Odishi in person, their height, their bulk, and their very alien appearance, caused a hush to pass over the crowd, but its duration was short-lived. A loud, almost raucous cheer followed as if the crowd before them seemed anxious to cover its initial reaction. Before arriving on Earth, Emma had warned Adashi and Tormond of the human tradition of yelling and slapping their hands together as a positive form of greeting. Fortunately, or unfortunately, nothing of the sort had happened due to the subdued nature of most diplomats and advanced warning of the subdued nature of the Odishi. Glancing to her side, she saw Tormond stiffen slightly and slow his gait even further than its usual lumbering pace. If Adashi had any reaction, Emma did not see it and was sure no one else could have noticed it.

As the noise subsided, two came forward: the station's new commanding officer, Captain Renard Garnier, and the now-recognized executive officer, Lieutenant Commander Niko Sasaki. Emma felt her eyes grow damp. She was unsure if it was for the mass greeting or Niko and didn't care. Captain Garnier ignored Emma, as was proper, and addressed Adashi directly. His Common was precise and obviously rehearsed. Adashi responded in Common and then quickly switched to English. With a nod, Renard dismissed Niko and invited Adashi and Tormond to tour the building and several attached labs. A hand-picked group of scientists followed to provide the details he was also learning. Niko watched Adashi and Tormond disappear into a hallway before turning to face Emma, a look of delight and amazement still on her face. Anarchy returned to the oversized room and, with it, anonymity. Dozens of overlapping conversations formed an incoherent din, leaving Emma and Niko alone.

"Lieutenant Commander," Emma said as a greeting.

"Ambassador," Niko said in an obvious parry.

Emma rolled her eyes dramatically and then embraced her old roommate warmly. After stepping back, she gestured toward the center of the splintering mass of people.

"This place has changed — Is that everyone?"

"Almost … but you first. Those two are amazing. You need to tell me everything, and please include the details I haven't heard, especially the embarrassing ones — Let's walk and talk. I need to make sure everything is set for the celebration."

Emma recognized a few faces as they slowly walked around the mass of people, but no names came to mind. She realized they were in the mess; or was it a cafeteria? The civilians greatly outnumbered the military component.

Tables were being returned to their original positions, and food carts were rolling out from the kitchen.

"Embarrassing? That may be difficult, but let me think — Oh, right, do you know the first thing I did after planting my feet on their planet?"

"I don't know. Did you take a step?" Niko asked, smiling in anticipation.

Emma laughed. "Close. I tried, but the shoe of my baggy environmental suit caught in the sand. I almost fell right in front of the three waiting to greet me."

"That sounds about right."

"It gets better," Emma said. "Do you recall Neil Armstrong's first words when he set foot upon the Moon?"

"I do," Niko said slowly.

"Do you know what word was used to commemorate the first step upon a world occupied by another race?"

"Oh no. Just one word, right after you tripped?"

Emma nodded and smiled, allowing the moment to stretch out. "Fuck."

Niko's smile grew ear-to-ear. "Wow, I'm so proud to know you." She placed a hand on Emma's shoulder. "Who else have you mentioned this to?"

"No one. It just came to me — You did ask for embarrassing."

"I did. Please don't stop."

"Let me think about it — All this is for us?" Emma pointed toward food being arranged in and just outside an alcove used to serve the daily meals.

"Perhaps for your two friends, but also this." She pointed to a banner that stretched along one wall. It read, 'Two Years Down – Fifty to Go?' "The anniversary of Atacama Station is in two days. You gave us an excuse to start early. Let's wander into the kitchen."

As they passed through the doors, a young spaceman apprentice shouted, "It's just about ready, XO." He was pulling a large basket out of the air fryer.

"Thanks, Kane," Niko shouted back.

"Sweet potato fries," Emma said as they stepped closer. "For your salad?"

Niko looked back at Emma suspiciously. "How do you know about my salad?"

"Word spreads. It's a small … not world … region of the Orion Arm?"

"It's for the Odishi; I thought having a locally grown dish would be good."

Emma shook her head. "No complaints. That is one of the reasons for our visit ... Have you enticed any more humans? Any humans?"

"Maybe," Niko shrugged weakly. "Or they're just being nice."

Emma grabbed a fry from the basket and bit it in half.

"Sorry," she said under Niko's scornful glare. "I was checking for salt. The Odishi use very little."

Niko's face turned briefly to one of panic. "Damn — Stop right there," she said to Spaceman Kane, who was approaching with a pair of shakers.

"How about pepper?"

Emma nodded. "They do use spices."

Niko nodded, took the pepper shaker, and applied a light coating as Kane shook the basket. "Put these out between the arugula and pineapple, and don't forget the mango dressing."

"Yes, ma'am."

Emma and Niko passed through the kitchen and out a second door into the cafeteria. Emma told of her months on Iburak in the Groombridge system and gave details of her visit to the Odishi town and school house, becoming emotional on the last. Niko listened intently, amused, a little jealous, and then somber and supportive. At one point, she considered asking about Anay, expressing some sorrow, but it would've been a very awkward, poorly-timed question to ask someone so close to tears.

After a long tour, the towering forms of Adashi and Tormond appeared at the far end of the cafeteria.

"They've become so thin," Emma said with a sad note.

"Thin?" Niko asked incredulously.

Emma nodded. "If I had to guess, I'd say they've both lost over 60 kilos."

As the Odishi approached the spread of food, Niko shifted their position to see past the crowd, observing from afar. After a cursory look over some of the serving plates, Spaceman Kane stopped them before the salad to explain its local content.

"Is that Common?" Emma asked as they drew closer.

"One of the better speakers. Bright kid."

Tormond placed two pineapple chunks on a small plate and popped one in his mouth. His reaction was immediate and unexpected. After spitting the chunk back on the plate, he let out a low, painful groaning sound. Something Emma had never heard. Spaceman Kane looked chagrined, as did Niko at her side. Emma felt fear encroaching. A fear that Ophiuchi would not be able to support the Odishi.

"It burns," they could hear him say.

"Fucking pineapple," Niko mumbled under her breath.

As they approached, Adashi helped herself to a plate of arugula.

"This is good," she said, holding the plate toward Tormond.

He tentatively put a leaf in his mouth and then performed a human nod.

The sweet potato fries were next. Adashi sampled two at once, chewing slowly, and then calmly turned to Emma, unsurprised by her presence.

"These will sustain us." There was excitement in her voice, although Emma was certain no one else in the room noticed. She asked Niko, "May I see these in their natural form?"

Niko glanced at Spaceman Kane, who turned and ran back to the kitchen.

As they waited, Tormond tried several of the fries and then used the mango dressing as a dip. His approval was apparent, as was Adashi's, after trying the condiment.

Kane returned with two oversized sweet potatoes and held them up to Adashi. She accepted one and then snapped it in half with ease. She held the inside of one half to her mouth and sampled the flesh before handing it to Tormond.

"Could we see where these grow?" she asked Niko, then turned to Captain Garnier. "Please forgive our excitement, Captain. This is a very welcome discovery."

He quickly waved off her concern and then called over a technician. "Follow us," he said to the young petty officer. "We need to check the fit on those masks you cobbled together."

With an affirming nod from Adashi, the three left the vicinity as two civilians approached, each holding a tray of small cups.

"It's a little early, Johnny," Niko said with a pained expression.

"It is XO, but with two honored guests standing before us and the captain going that way, the time seemed right."

"XO, what is this?" Emma asked with mild accusation in her voice.

Before Niko could respond, Johnny held his tray out to Emma. "Lieutenant Stewart?"

"It is early," she said, regretting that she had stepped into the conversation. "What am I about to do to myself?" she asked, turning her head to Niko.

"It's Shōchū, locally distilled, obviously … another use for our abundant crop of sweet potatoes."

"Is this a cultural contribution of yours?"

"You're familiar? — Oh, of course, you are, but no. I had never heard of it before coming to this planet. Blame these guys."

"Is it good?"

"Awful," Niko said, wrinkling her nose.

"Well, in that case …" Emma poured the shot down her throat.

"Oh, God, you've never been more right in your life."

A growing crowd of onlookers burst into laughter.

"Emma," Tormond said directly over her shoulder. "Why did you drink it after she told you it was awful?"

"She's never been able to say no," Niko said.

"That's not it … or not all of it. Give me a moment; I want to get this quote right … 'To truly appreciate the good, you must fully experience the bad.'"

Tormond maneuvered around to stand before her. His face was as animated as she had ever seen. "Did Adashi teach you that? She has said the same to me many times."

The discovery of shared bonds was a source of excitement to the Odishi and a common theme in their literature.

"No, that came from my grandfather, Alexander. Something he said a long time ago."

"There's a lot of bad out there," Niko said. "I'm not sure I'd adopt that as a philosophy."

"Nor would I," Emma said. "As I recall, he did add a caveat. 'Only a … masochist can appreciate all the good that the world has to offer.'"

She used the English word for 'masochist,' realizing it had no Common equivalent. The same was true for the word 'sadist,' she realized.

"I don't believe any of what he said was part of a serious conversation."

The crowd separated and then broke up as the captain led Adashi through. She held two oversized breathers. One she handed to

Tormond. "There are small leaks around the sides, but it will be fine for a short walk." She showed him the locations on each side. "Miss Watkin assured me that the positive pressure will keep out the carbon dioxide."

"Shall we go?" Niko asked.

With quick agreement, she led Emma, Adashi, and Tormond toward the airlock.

"It's only been five days," Niko said, annoyed.

"And?" Emma asked, not letting her friend's agitation change her relaxed mood.

It had been five days. The first three she had spent worrying about the future of the Odishi, but on the fourth, hopelessly uninvolved in the work that was taking place around her, she had allowed her shoulders to slump in a comfortable fashion. The morning seemed no different, although it was her last on the planet.

No word had come from Earth of changes in the political tides, but word had arrived from another direction, from a greater distance. At the jump point leading into Zeta Doradus, Batfish had had a friendly encounter with ships from those that call themselves the Seemak. Their search appeared to have ended with a positive result. A fleet was being assembled, and Fredericksburg would leave orbit in one day to join, although she would remain safely within a trailing squadron.

"Didn't you tell me they were just simple farmers?" Her tone remained annoyed, but her eyes said something very different.

"I believe I called them peaceful farmers, but they do live a simple life. Why do you ask?"

"It's only been five days. During that time, we showed them the environmental data, our labs, and equipment; gave them a tour of the lagoons; and explained our methods and results. It was just an enhanced version of the new arrival orientation program. I was certain that we were boring them with details — I still can't read them very well."

"It takes time," Emma said and then waited.

"Well, very early this morning, Adashi came into the south lab with some ideas, improvements to our methods. The Ph.D. she found spent about 15 minutes looking at her suggestions and then had the watch wake me and about half the biology team. They're all there now. She and Tormond are giving a lesson to the experts. It's — She's not a farmer."

Emma nodded vigorously. "No, she's not. I've been trying to make that point for six months … but microbiology? I was certain she was a linguist. It made sense at the time … but come to think about it, she and Abby had an in-depth conversation covering physics and astronomy before we left Groombridge. She seemed quite knowledgeable on those subjects also — Is there anything promising with her suggestions? Can we move up the timeline?"

"It seems likely. At least she was confident that we could. It seemed to be her only goal in the conversation I witnessed. I wish I could have listened to more of what she was saying, not that I'd understand much."

"XO duties?"

Niko nodded. "And I wanted to let you know."

"It's good news," Emma said. "Ophiuchi is set. You have everything here they'll need to survive, and it sounds like your schedule could move up. As I see it, we're past one obstacle with two to go, or maybe just one, depending on Batfish."

"And Quinn," Niko added.

"Oh, right." Emma smiled, slight and pensive. "We're heading up to Fredericksburg later today. There's no give in the schedule this time. The captain wants everyone aboard in advance of our departure."

"Understandable," Niko said. "I'm going to miss you, but in this case, not nearly as much as I'll miss Adashi and Tormond."

Emma shrugged as she poked at her cold hash. "Naomi's coming out on the Kellen."

"I heard," Niko said. "She's the aid to a Marine colonel, command staff for a platoon of SEALs and a platoon of Marines, not exactly her dream. If you see her, say 'hi' for me."

"I will. Fredericksburg has orders to join squadron Kellen."

"Are you packed?"

Emma shook her head vigorously. "Are you kidding?" She picked up her half-full breakfast tray and coffee. "I suppose I'll need to do that soon ... and check on Adashi."

"And I need to ensure the potatoes get loaded, and then it's back to my routine."

Emma gave her a look of sympathy that lacked any sincerity.

Niko stood and turned toward the airlock. "Good luck out there, Beanstalk."

"Hey," Emma said to stop her friend from walking away. "Who did you hear that from?"

Niko looked back over her shoulder and mimicked Emma's previous expression. "Word spreads. It is, after all, a tiny region of the Orion Arm."

October 2nd 2126

Quinn turned to face downwind and let the hood of his coat shield him from the biting wind. Dried pellets of ice bounced off the waterproof material as others swirled around his face. He looked down a long snow-covered valley but could not see much past the start of the forest that delineated the property line for the mountain cabin that had become their hideaway and his prison for the past 15 days. Obscured as they were, the trees reminded him of evergreens back on Earth, a place he feared he might not see again.

An animal, barely visible, broke from the forest, ran along the edge, and then re-entered. Two smaller creatures pursued. The sound of their passage was limited to that of a single branch that was snapped from a tree by the first in its desperate attempt to survive.

Me Ka Tak remained inside, wrapped in a blanket, on the floor near the glowing embers of a fire. Her race had little tolerance for the cold climate of the highlands above Raygao, a blessing since no other Ki Ti Tor Mahk had been seen nearby. Any reassurance he felt was limited by the news of a pair of Sal, likely mercenaries, asking questions in the small village further down the valley.

Batfish remained in high orbit above the planet and was aware of the search that was scouring the planet. The Ka Kek and their allies were asking questions in almost every town and city. That was the limit to the information the Patrol had allowed to be sent up. Nothing was sent of his location. That had changed three times. He was now above a mountain village 200 kilometers from Raygao and 50 from the coast, by his reckoning. The air was thin and bitter cold at night, and he spent most of the daylight hours indoors, hiding.

The door to the large balcony where he stood swung open and shut quickly.

"Anything new?" he asked, twisting his head to face Jouh Nee. His command of Common had improved dramatically since he had uttered a few faltering words at the jump point into Zeta Doradus, but his phrase did not translate well.

After a short, confused pause, Jouh Nee answered. "I have news … new news if you wish. Bad news, I'm afraid. A small fleet has left a Ka Kek station and will reach orbit in two days."

Quinn turned full about, ignoring the sting of pellets on his face. "I need to contact Batfish or get word to them."

Jouh Nee held up a hand. "You will; a link is being arranged. You should be able to connect using your device."

Quinn placed a hand on the hard lump under his coat. "Could the signal lead the Ka Kek here?"

"Not likely, but ask the Patrol engineers when they arrive."

"They're coming here … actual members of the Patrol?"

"Yes, with the Ka Kek fleet en route, The Patrol has become concerned for the welfare of your ship. They believe an attack would risk open warfare with an external and unknown entity. They sent a warning, but your crew has been hesitant to trust them, understandably hesitant. The Patrol hopes they will heed your order to seek safety."

"I appreciate their effort … Will they intervene if the Ka Kek attack?" Quinn asked.

"They may, but only after less confrontational methods fail. Come in; a meal is ready."

Quinn was certain that the two from the Patrol, Greer and Jair, were more than simple engineers. Their line of questions said as much, perfectly reasonable questions he wished he could answer honestly.

"Why the belt?" Quinn asked. "Why can't they run for the jump point?"

Greer exchanged a worried look with Jair before answering. "There's a second, larger fleet heading toward the jump point. Your Batfish could not get there ahead of them, and the Patrol does not want them to try."

Quinn nodded. "Is it a blocking fleet?"

"No, it's not … We believe they're going in search of your colony."

"To what end? A raid?" Quinn felt annoyance, unable to act, unable to send a warning.

"Not likely — First, we believe their only interest in you and your ship is elimination. To prevent you from requesting membership into the Union for your colony."

"Okay … that doesn't … aw shit. Are they planning to capture our colony?"

Greer nodded. "It's the only model we have that makes sense."

"And if I make that request now, assuming I have the authority, would that stop those ships?"

He shook his head.

"In their eyes, you have the authority, but the request must be made at the government center. All negotiations with the council are conducted in person. To do this, you must request a meeting that includes all members, Freeholder Ta Tok included. He could delay for the better part of a year or simply wait until he had the assets in place, guaranteeing that you wouldn't make it there alive — If it isn't obvious, the Ta Tok family will benefit from the capture of your colony. The Ka Kek are clients of theirs. Your colony would become a client of the Ka Kek."

"How large is the Ka Kek family?"

"They claim control over five million of the Seemak. It's probably less, but don't underestimate them. Their fleet is one of the strongest, fielding over 50 combat-capable ships. Only the Jass family has a larger fleet … and the Patrol, of course."

It was ridiculous, Quinn thought. They believed the population of Earth to be under five million, making it an easy target. The reality was so much different. They could not hope to capture the planet, but a fleet of fifty ships posed a significant threat. If they managed to destroy the few ships that Earth did have, they could control the planet from above. In another year, the US Navy alone would have the numbers to match the Ka Kek, but numbers were only part of the equation. The Seemak were flying between star systems before the United States was a nation. Most spent much of their lives aboard one ship or another and would be very capable in combat. On the positive side, nothing he had seen to date had given him the impression that the Seemak were highly advanced. The ship they captured at Eridani, the Patrol ship that brought him to the planet, and what little he had seen on the surface all appeared old and worn; perhaps quaint made a good descriptor.

Time was an unknown factor. They could spend a year or more searching the systems beyond Eridani or, with a bit of luck, reach Earth in a few months. The list of habitable systems in the solar neighborhood was not that large.

"Captain?"

"Sorry, lost in thought. I'm just surprised their goal is not to capture Batfish or me. They do not know where to find my colony or what they will find when they arrive. A little intelligence would be valuable."

"I'm sure they would be delighted to capture you, but their primary goal is to keep you from the council. Murder is much easier than capture."

"And don't forget," Me Ka Tak said, still wrapped in her blanket. "The Ka Kek think very differently from other Seemak." She was addressing the two engineers as much as Quinn. He had no idea what she was talking about.

Greer nodded knowingly. Jair looked at Quinn. "Murder would be much more enjoyable than capture, more rewarding ... the first Talmahk in more than 100 years."

Me Ka Tak stepped closer, noting the concern and confusion on Quinn's face.

"We were all hunters long ago, before the Odishi. The five lost ships were on a hunting expedition, collecting trophies and live animals for a very profitable preserve they maintain on the planet."

"How are the Odishi involved in this? I doubt they had much to teach you by the time you found them, certainly not farming."

All looked very confused. It even showed on Me Ka Tak's face.

"Farming? — No, we only hunted for pleasure by the time the Odishi found us."

Quinn assumed a confused look of his own. "They found you?"

"Yes, of course, before we even had space flight. Same for the Sal ... and the other races of the Union. You seem confused."

"Yes," Quinn said, scratching his head. "I ... had assumed the opposite. They brought space flight to you?"

Me Ka Tak's face was, once again, unreadable. "Eventually, once our more barbaric tendencies had faded. To start, they introduced us to the Common language and —"

"They imposed it upon you," Greer said. "As they did with the Sal. It was their principal tool for eliminating those ... barbaric tendencies."

"The language?" Quinn asked.

"Yes, this surprises you?"

"Like so many other things that I've learned recently."

Greer continued. "They used it to mold our thought processes, make us predictable and controllable ... harmonious with our future neighbors. Assuming you have truly encountered them, they are doing the same to you now."

"No," Quinn said, slowly shaking his head, ignoring the question of their encounter with the Odishi. "Yes, they taught us the Common language, but I don't see how it will alter our thinking."

Greer gestured toward Me Ka Tak. "The Ki Ti Tor Mahk have over ten words that describe the taking of a life."

"Fifteen," Me Ka Tak said.

Greer dipped his head and smiled. "Fifteen. Many of those allude to the pleasure of the act. Common has a single word for taking a life and a single word for the narrower case of taking a sentient life, murder." The Common word had a grating sound.

Quinn tried again to repeat it and had no better luck than his first attempt aboard Batfish.

"Exactly," Greer said. "It's difficult to say and carries a horrible connotation. Ironically, the Ki Ti Tor Mahk is the only race that can pronounce it correctly."

He glanced at Me Ka Tak before continuing. "Using either word to convey any other idea has always been discouraged — Overall, the effect on the Sal world was miraculous. The rate of murders plunged from the time of the Odishi's arrival until all communities had adopted Common."

"I'd say the same for the Ki Ti," Me Ka Tak said. "But many would call me a liar — The Ka Kek will not speak Common by choice. Most of their member families living in the belt have never learned the language. They're very different from other Ki Ti, aggressive, cruel … they don't even keep spouses in the belt." Me Ka Tak shook her head in disgust. "The longest relationship that you'll find out there is between a mother and a child, and that usually falls apart near the age of ten, before the child enters adulthood."

"We do have a … proverb on our colony." Quinn shrugged. "'See No Evil, Hear No Evil, Speak No Evil' and maybe 'Do No Evil.' It was spoken long before we met the Odishi."

"It sounds like something they would say," Jair said. "Is this a practice of yours?"

"Mine? No … or not as it was originally intended. I believe it was practiced by the factions that initially adopted it, but over time, within my faction, at the least, a more cynical view of its meaning was adopted. In years past, I may have looked the other way when our rules were broken."

Quinn smiled. The three Sal smiled. Me Ka Tak's look of disgust turned into one of disappointment.

"Did this philosophy affect the people of your colony in any way?" Greer asked.

"Not all, but I mention this because some may have been … by this phrase and similar. There are factions within our colony that are much more peaceful than others; have always been. Perhaps they're just words, but I wouldn't be surprised if they had some effect on those that listened with sincerity … more sincerity than I have … until now."

"At the moment, you do not sound like the captain of a ship," Jair chided.

"Too thoughtful? As I've told my crew, I have many sides — So, you're telling me that the Odishi are manipulating us ... deceiving my colony?"

"Manipulating? Yes. Deceiving? Never," Me Ka Tak said.

"Our history is clear on that matter," Greer said. "The Odishi were known for their honesty, yet no one could trust them. Direct interaction with them was infrequent. Generally, they used others to express their desires. If they did come to your planet, all talks needed careful planning, a set of goals established beforehand, and observers put in place to reiterate those goals as the negotiation turned in an unexpected direction."

"For any interaction or just negotiations?" Quinn asked.

Greer shrugged dismissively. "With the Odishi, they were the same. There was always a purpose when they spoke to a member of another race. They were encouraging you to do something, and you would inevitably walk away from the conversation wondering why you had just agreed."

"Did anyone ever test their resolve?" Quinn asked.

"On occasion. Typically, it led into another long conversation in which further commitments were made."

"No violent opposition?"

"No ... nothing on a large scale."

"There was one confrontation I know of," Me Ka Tak said. "And, of course, it was with a Ki Ti colony. They had agreed to stop harassing a Mahkee mining operation in a neighboring system but didn't keep their word, and then they made the foolish decision to attack the Odishi ship that came in response."

"And," Quinn said.

"What do you think? … It was over within days. The colony lost every combat-capable ship and then found itself back in a negotiation, making further commitments toward the harmony of the region."

Quinn decided to keep his mouth shut and gave a simple nod of appreciation.

"I think I can speak for all Seemak on this matter," Greer said. "If you manage to survive your visit with us and do encounter the Odishi again, please express our desire for nothing but peace and harmony … and to be left alone. No one here wants to see them again."

"I know of some that would kill them on sight," Me Ka Tak added. "The Ka Kek have a long-standing order to do just that."

Quinn nodded slowly, unable to hide the exhaustion that was taking hold of him.

"The satellite is almost overhead," Jair said.

The three had moved to the balcony. The sleet had lessened. "All right, captain, you should be set. Send when ready. We'll compress it and then pass it on to your Batfish as a single burst. This should eliminate any chance that the Ka Kek detect our communication."

Quinn had typed a message on the small keyboard earlier. It was a series of random thoughts, insults for the crew, lyrics to very old songs, and complete gibberish when his creativity ran dry. The transmitter encrypted that message, but he was confident that his new allies would make every effort to break it. Attached was a second message that he had compiled and encrypted earlier. That doubly encrypted message, a personal communication to Lieutenant Zhào, would require her personal key. He could only hope that his effort was sufficient to confound any attempts by unwanted listeners to read what he sent.

"XO to the bridge" sounded over the intercom.

Before Petty Officer Brown could elaborate, Lieutenant Zhào came through the large hatch and grabbed a handrail to bring her motion to a stop. Breathless, having kicked her way from engineering while listening to the details in Quinn's message, she paused before speaking. "I've entered a course. Take us to one gee helm, and when the ship is rigged, take us up to four. We need to lose ourselves in that debris field." She was referring to the large belt circling the star just outside the planet's orbit.

"XO, the message is nonsense; I mean, it's obviously from the captain; he's talking about how the stars look very different today, and then he insults you, and me, and most of us, and then he says that this is the worst trip he's ever been on, and then it becomes unreadable. I think it's a code. At one point —"

"Brown, ignore all of that," Zhào said as she strapped herself into the captain's chair. "He sent a personal message. Briefly, 80 degrees of the belt spin ward is uninhabited. We need to lose ourselves in there. The smaller of the two fleets that we've been monitoring is, as we suspected, coming for us. I'll fill everyone in once we're on the move. For now, send 'Message received' and whatever you want to match his nonsense, but make it quick. Once you're done, attach the personal response I sent you."

The feel of a single gee was a welcome relief after a week of weightlessness, but it was short-lived. The sing-song of drive coils sounded through the hull as the mild pressure gave way to the crush of heavy acceleration.

"They're accelerating," Greer said, repeating the message sent to his earpiece. "And more so," he added after a moment. "I believe they've accepted your message … and we have a response."

Quinn let out his breath and looked down at his transmitter. 'Message received' followed by rambling nonsense to match what he sent. He ignored it and read Zhào's message.

"Quinn, we're following your instructions. For the last day, we've been tracking two fleets. Four frigate-sized ships are approaching the planet, and nine are approaching the jump point back into Gliese 167. In that fleet, we count two frigates, three destroyers, and four of cruiser size. I believe our lead over the four frigates is sufficient to find a hiding place. Once hidden, we'll await further word from you or Earth. We've identified your current position and will review the recorded conversations that you sent. Note that the Patrol had given us the same warning earlier today. We were waiting to act, unsure whom to trust. Supplies aboard are sufficient for an extended duration — many thanks to Captain Juun. Good luck."

"Good," he said to the transmitter and then looked at the two engineers. "Thank you for this and your earlier warning to Batfish."

Jair nodded solemnly as Greer opened the door.

"Me Ka Tak," Quinn said as he passed through. "Lieutenant Zhào sends many thanks to Captain Juun for the supplies."

"She does? Good." She turned a questioning stare toward Greer.

He waved his hand dismissively. "It wasn't authorized, but no one has complained either."

"We're passing another to the south," Petty Officer Second Class Jason Ramirez said with strain in his voice.

"I see it," Chief Andersen said as he zoomed a secondary display onto a robotic thruster nudging a small asteroid into a safer orbit.

With Captain Martinez on the planet behind them, he had assumed the role of a duty officer to reduce the load on Lieutenant Zhào and Ensign Matthews. Following a short one-gee break to eat, hydrate, and rotate the watch, they were back up to four gees, reducing their velocity relative to the belt, preparing to blend in with the surrounding debris. The pursuing fleet was a day and a half behind and not a concern. The time of their final maneuver was approaching, and once complete, he was confident Batfish would become invisible to their sensors.

It was a crowded belt, but that description was deceiving. The empty space between rocks could hold fleets of ships, but it was nearly perfect for their purpose. The search volume before the Ki Ti Tor Mahk held millions of objects. Batfish with tiny signatures of optical, radar, and soon thermal would be nearly impossible to find.

"Helm, the course has been entered. On the mark, give me 7.8 gees and maintain for 47 seconds." Andersen drew a deep breath just before the uncomfortable gave way to misery. The weight on his chest pushing against the air in his lungs was most noticeable, but no part of his body was spared. His vision narrowed even as his ears were filled with the sound from every drive coil aboard Batfish, all singing their own tune as they accelerated an intense beam of particles onto the surface of a small asteroid that they were approaching.

Forty-seven seconds later, the thrust stopped. "Give me a full nitrogen purge of the hull, engine space, and drive sections. Purge and secure the aft radiators; route coolant forward." He unbuckled from his seat and floated free to catch his breath. His vision was returning, and the discomfort in his extremities was fading. He triggered the intercom. "XO, I recommend a full suite of maintenance checks on the coils, skipping any active tests."

"We're on it, chief, or will be in a moment."

Batfish coasted out of the cover afforded by a larger asteroid on a new vector that closely matched the debris around them. With her jet-black hull cooled to a level that blended into the background, she was invisible to the still-distant fleet of four Ki Ti Tor Mahk ships.

October 8th 2126

Commander Samuel Strauss, captain of the USS Sturgeon UNSF, had been unsure how to interpret the first narrow beam transmission they had received three weeks earlier. No one was supposed to know Sturgeon was there, so its arrival had been a surprise, and the content had been no less alarming. The Seemak Patrol had informed them that a faction on the planet was pursuing Captain Martinez and that he was successfully evading them with aid from other unidentified individuals. They ended the transmission with a request for patience. From Batfish's final message before jumping into Zeta Doradus, he understood the role of the Patrol was to protect the inhabitants of that system, so his only guess was that they were trying to prevent an escalation.

In response, he had opened a jump point into Lesser Doradus C and passed the message to the fully established chain leading back to Earth. The first of two squadrons en route to Zeta Doradus had accelerated in response and was now three days out.

Concern for the welfare of Captain Martinez and Batfish grew, but they received no response to the periodic messages that they broadcasted toward the jump point into Zeta Doradus. Three weeks passed before a second message arrived, warning of the approach of a Ki Ti fleet. As he stared at the display, the breakthrough radiation from the jump points of those ships was detected by Sturgeon's sensors. The intense but short-lived light sources were quickly replaced by the steady, dim infrared of their thrust, vectored in the opposite direction, the glow of accelerated particles shedding heat against the background.

"That's 32 minutes old?" he asked.

"Yes, sir," Petty Office Nelson answered.

"Hmm, no choice now. Recall the drones, Nelson. Helm, open a jump point into Lesser Doradus C."

"Opening now," Petty Officer Nguyễn answered as his hands flicked over the console in a well-practiced motion.

After several months sitting at the same jump point, a very bored crew had found the optimal location to generate an interface, the sweet spot, cutting the time needed to establish it to less than a minute and consistently placing the far end near the same relative location.

"Jump point established."

"Thank you, Nguyễn. Nelson?"

"One moment, Captain … Drones are home."

"Thank you, Nelson. Take us through, helm."

For operational security, the paired repeater stations at every jump point in the systems from Sol to Eridani had not been deployed any closer to Zeta Doradus. Sturgeon passed through the interface to establish communications with the approaching squadron of 12 ships and Sunfish, sitting at the far exit toward Earth.

The tiny red dwarf was noticeably brighter than the dim speck of light that had sat before them a moment ago. A handful of other stars on the system display had shifted slightly and brightened; most had remained as they were. As he watched, the entire field of stars rotated around the red dwarf, aligning to the local north-south axis.

"We have a link from Squadron Redmar … and one from Sunfish."

"Thank you, Nelson. Pass on what we know."

"Message away."

The term 'link' was a misnomer. The link message was sent periodically with precise timing and positional information and a compressed data package, which held news from Earth, personal messages, and any change in orders. In this case, the data package from Sunfish was identical to that from Squadron Redmar.

"And now we wait for a response," Captain Strauss said to the bridge crew. The response to their message would come from Squadron Redmar, and the expectation was that orders would send them back to Gliese to monitor the approaching Ki Ti fleet.

That message arrived in less than an hour.

"Helm, open a jump point."

Sturgeon was back in Gliese 167 a minute later, awaiting the Ki Ti fleet.

'Finally,' Emma thought. The batch of personal messages had arrived unannounced and long overdue. It should not have taken ten weeks. There was mention of a failed repeater at the near end of Barnard's system, but she was fully aware of the low priority placed upon non-essential traffic.

They were passing through an unnamed system, only known by a string of random characters that comprised its catalog entry. The non-descript red dwarf would probably never generate enough enthusiasm for anyone to bother with a name or more interesting catalog entry. At the least, it had sufficient mass to avoid concern over the formation of the next jump point. Jumping in and out of Denis, the previous system, had been challenging even with the Calvin files sent from the Pathfinder.

Squadron Kellen was two days behind Redmar, decelerating toward the next jump point at a leisurely 1.2 gees. It was being kept low for the sake of Adashi and Tormond, but even 1.2 gees were taking a toll upon the Odishi. Emma could see it when they struggled to move about the ship, in moments of labored breathing, and in the steady decline of their health. Many aboard Fredericksburg were chaffing at the slow pace, anxious to participate in the coming encounter that was expected to turn violent. Word of Quinn's problems on the planet had reached them weeks earlier.

Emma immediately accessed the batch of messages from Chloe.

"August 10th: It took three days, but Senator Shaw's anger must have finally boiled over. She went on a rant, singling you out as she explained why 'children of privilege' should not be making decisions that affect all of us. Apparently, you lack the required experience and temperament. It was poorly received, but the negative reaction was short-lived, so I poked. No response from her, but a member of her cabal took the bait and made it personal, but not against you alone. I am, proudly, 'The least deserving of Alexander's lap dogs.'"

"August 15th: Sadly, after five days of back-and-forth, that obnoxious ass was muzzled. The drop in poll numbers may have had something to do with it."

"August 16th: Hurray! The conversation has restarted. It's now in the hands of their supporters to continue the downward trend. I find it particularly arrogant of you to predict this would happen."

"September 8th: Shaw managed to pivot the conversation away from you to Captain Martinez, Batfish, and, more broadly, the Navy. His bad decisions are the reasons for the dangers we face. I'm not sure where she's going with this; perhaps away from you is all she can hope for."

"September 20th: Their new line of attack has gained no traction, and their occasional potshots at you continue to hurt them. Very unfairly, I'm not receiving the same level of sympathy."

"October 1st: News of Captain Martinez has arrived. I'm hoping for his safety. So is the rest of the world. Attacking him was the final mistake for at least six campaigns. They have no chance now. I think you can chalk this up as a victory, Beanstalk. Congratulations."

"October 3rd: Emma, I'm sorry, but this is terrible news. Shaw doesn't matter anymore, but we have a larger problem. No one wants to divert resources away from a combat fleet. The perceived threat, even from a faction of the Seemak, has turned all but a few away from the Odishi cause."

Following Chloe's final message, Emma remained seated on her bed, staring at her toiletry bag, wrestling with the urge to hurl it across the room. In truth, her feelings were mixed. She would never admit it, but the pessimist in her agreed with those back on Earth. If the survival of the human race was at stake, any other concerns were secondary. She stood to dress, feeling sore and tired. It would be painful, but she needed to update Adashi and Tormond, assuming they had not already discerned the shift in opinions from the general news broadcasts that had arrived with the messages.

October 11th 2126

"Captain, the radiation is starting to measure on internal sensors."

"Thank you, engineering — Still no response, Comm?"

"Nothing yet."

"Sensors, are they aiming for us or our sweet spot."

Lieutenant Duncan twisted back toward the captain, shaking his head. "No way to tell, captain. They're on course now to make the jump but will need another ten minutes to get their speed down. That will put them right on top of us."

Captain Strauss squinted at the nine Ki Ti ships approaching Sturgeon. The display captured the intensity of the exhaust plumes with unnerving accuracy. No harm had been recorded yet, but that would change soon if they remained on approach or chose to focus their exhaust, assuming they had that capability. The blunt shield at the forward end of the ship faced the streaming particles, protecting those behind it, but they would need to turn soon to create a jump point. They needed to get out of harm's way, and, more importantly, they needed to inform Squadron Redmar of the arriving fleet and the lack of response to all hails. They were in communication with a Patrol ship shadowing the Ki Ti fleet. Their only advice was to jump sooner rather than later.

"Helm, turn us about and open a jump point. Once open, fly us through as close to the perimeter as possible. I want to get around the corner as soon as we can. I suspect we're about to get that response we've been waiting for."

He adjusted his seat until his body was nearly parallel to the deck. "All hands prepare for maximum acceleration."

The expected message came, a sharp and angry command, piped directly to a speaker on the bridge. "Intruders, hold position and prepare to surrender your ship. Do not attempt to jump into the adjacent system."

"Damn it — Helm, as soon as that interface forms, take us through."

He quickly accessed the communication system. "Seemak Fleet, we've received your message … Please divert your exhaust. It's causing harm … Once this is done, we are prepared to discuss —"

Nearly eight gees crushed the air out of his lungs as Sturgeon accelerated toward the open jump point.

The ship bucked sharply as a beam of energy lanced out from one of the cruisers and cut into the armored cone aft. Three more followed, and red appeared across a status panel for the auxiliary engineering space.

"they've come about," Duncan yelled.

"Missiles detected, ETA 93 seconds."

Captain Strauss glanced up to see that each of the nine ships had presented their broadside, bringing most of their arsenal to bear. Six seconds after the interface opened, they entered another star system. It placed them, by most measures, light years from their attackers, but no safer than they had been the moment before. Beams followed them through, peeling back the portside armor from the auxiliary space to the bridge. A high-pitch screech followed a deafening bang as the air on the bridge began to vent into space. Barriers dropped quickly, cutting off the flow, but there was nothing to stop the incoming fire. The drive shut down, and the lights dimmed momentarily as repeated strikes sliced away the overhead armor and tore into the aft structure. The ship shook violently as sections explosively separated from a shrinking hull. The red statuses from the auxiliary space turned gray, indicating a loss of connection.

Too late for some, the forward half of Sturgeon passed below the interface boundary and out of the field of fire. A large section that had separated, including the auxiliary space, a string of drive coils, and attached armor, remained visible for another three seconds. For three seconds, every beam weapon aboard the pursuing ships focused their wrath. Little of what remained was recognizable from the bridge.

"Redmar, this is Sturgeon. The enemy is hot. Missiles inbound, ETA 74 seconds. Expect entry of their ships into this system in approximately nine minutes. Expect an entry point near our own. We are incapacitated and … and we've lost three crewmembers, but do not need immediate assistance. All data from the encounter has been sent."

The forward section tumbled slowly away from the interface. The destruction stopped just short of the heavily armored bridge section. In addition to the auxiliary space and long drive sections, the docking ports were missing, and both missile bays were destroyed. Forward of the bridge, the damage was confined to the armored hull.

"Helm, stop this tumble and get us pointed back toward the jump point." If the ETA on the missiles was correct, the interface would close shortly before their arrival. If not, Captain Strauss wanted the heavy bow shield between the nine remaining crewmembers and the missiles.

As Sturgeon slowly corrected her tumble, using her two surviving thrusters, the ships of Squadron Redmar were rapidly deploying their missiles into space and placing them on a steady course toward the anticipated point of arrival for the Ki Ti fleet. All ships, but one, were arranged in a rough hemispherical shell approximately 30,000 kilometers out. Those ships were moving inward. Beagle was the standout. Already near the jump point, she was rapidly accelerating toward the back side, leaving a trail of unmoving missiles in her wake.

The interface collapsed with about ten seconds to spare.

Five minutes passed before Sturgeon gained some control over her tumble and managed to point the shield toward the expected point of arrival. Two more passed before breakthrough radiation appeared in five separate locations, very close to where Sturgeon had come through, about 200 kilometers from where the ship had drifted, a trivial distance in the context of space combat. Beagle, only slightly better positioned near 6000 kilometers out, cut thrust and flipped about to meet any attack head-on. All other ships accelerated inward and directed their missiles toward the opening points.

The first of several irregular waves of missiles rapidly closed the distance as the light of four additional jump points broke through, and the first five stabilized. To the crew of Sturgeon, they appeared as the dimly lit outline of five ovals, menacingly out of place against the unchanging constellation of Orion. Unexpectedly, the first objects to emerge were also missiles. They came through almost as one and then separated in every direction, splitting into many smaller missiles. Each of those targeted one of the Redmar missiles. The first wave was destroyed in this manner, a series of explosions between the squadron and the now emerging ships, the smaller frigates and destroyers.

The crew of Sturgeon could only watch with a growing sense of doom as the five Ki Ti ships came through the jump points and launched a second salvo that targeted Beagle. By Terran standards, the ships were squat and ugly. Each appeared different in shape and the attached weaponry haphazardly spread across the outer armor. Not one had a habitation ring, but the bulbous fronts gave the impression of a bow shield underneath. The gray-white hulls appeared mottled and dirt-covered, likely due to years of flying through a debris belt.

"One minute until impact," Duncan shouted.

Beams from Beagle targeted the incoming missiles, only visible on the hardened shell as incandescent points of deep blue, pulsing bright and dark as the ablative material vaporized. Beyond the show of light, the effect was minimal. This changed as they focused all on a single missile, but the pace of destruction was slow. More obvious were the beams reaching out from the Ki Ti ships toward the second wave of Redmar missiles; a mix of green and violet showed brightly as they passed through the expanding cloud of gas and debris left by Sturgeon. A second salvo was launched, again targeting Beagle.

Broad beams of laser light from the approaching but distant ships of Squadron Redmar flashed over the exposed but well-armored structures of the Ki Ti fleet, causing no damage. The streams from the particle cannons of the flagship battlecruiser Redmar and the cruisers Shenzhen and Haikou had a more significant effect, cutting through the armor but causing no noticeable degradation of the targeted ships. The second wave of missiles drew close, but counterfire rapidly depleted its numbers.

Six missiles launched from Beagle turned toward the approaching Ki Ti missiles and immediately exploded. Spreading cones of shrapnel swept outward, destroying all but two of what remained in the first salvo. The defensive beams turned one of those into a fireball, but the last struck Beagle head-on. As the blinding flash cleared, Beagle remained. Her forward armor shell had been stripped away, but the thick bow shield underneath had held. A dull glow on the port side was the only sign of damage.

The momentary relief shared by the bridge crew on Sturgeon faded as the second Ki Ti salvo started their terminal maneuvers toward Beagle. One flash was quickly followed by eight others. All had avoided the bow shield.

Few missiles remained in the second Redmar wave, but five reached their intended destination 300 kilometers from the Ki Ti Fleet. Three flashed blinding white light. The other two hit the fleet with a mix of wavelengths. The combined effect shut down their sensors and halted all counterfire long enough for the remaining missiles to reach the ships. Those missiles lacked the armor and acceleration of those launched by the Ki Ti but did carry large warheads. In rapid order, the five ships came apart. Glowing debris spun away as the four cruisers of the Ki Ti fleet emerged from their jump points.

Much larger and just as squat and ugly as the smaller ships, the four focused their fire on Redmar. Heavy beams turned the distant target into a bright speck of light against a dark field of stars. Defensive fire turned upon the third and fourth waves of Redmar missiles, but it came too late. Countermeasure missiles lit up the four ships as many others raced inward. Beagle had been destroyed, and by all appearances, the Redmar was suffering significant damage, but the end of the Ki Ti fleet was approaching. Sturgeon's bridge crew was staring intently at the screen, entertaining a growing hope, when a brilliant flash of light shut down every surviving sensor on the ship.

Squadron Kellen was a day and a half behind and decelerating toward the jump point. All understood that any contest between the approaching Ki Ti fleet and Squadron Redmar would be decided quickly, long before they arrived. It was also understood that the squadron's momentum would carry them within reach of the victors of that contest, regardless of any last-minute maneuvers.

On the eve of battle, from the ranks of the untested, a few pessimists can always be heard, whispering in dark corners, assigning blame, and discussing options they would never have the authority to execute. In Emma's presence, their fears went unspoken but were obvious all the same. Also obvious were their targets of choice. This had Emma depressed, as did the politics of Earth 40 light years behind and the politics of the Seemak two jumps ahead.

Batfish was hiding amongst the debris of that system's largest belt, and Quinn remained safe with aid from the Patrol, which was reluctant to extend its help to any of Earth's ships beyond passing warnings and messages.

One of those messages greatly interested Emma, Adashi, and Tormond. They had passed along the encrypted traffic between Quinn and Batfish just before Batfish ran for the safety of the belt. The first level of encryption, handled by a standard fleet key, had revealed a degree of nonsense that could only have come from Quinn, free of coercion. Emma was called before Admiral Walsh aboard the Kellen to testify to that fact. He had insisted before making a priority request to have Marina Zhào's personal key copied from a data vault back on Earth and sent to the Kellen. Expecting a delay of more than a day, Emma found a berth for the night and then went in search of Naomi. After spending a half hour wandering the ship aimlessly, marveling at the number of new faces, she found herself at the entrance to hanger delta, the reported home of the SEAL Team Four detachment.

"Lieutenant, how may I help you."

Startled, Emma spun about to face a first-class petty officer with questioning eyes and a genial smile, easily balancing a pair of oversized coffee tins.

"Ambassador?" His look turned to something closer to shock. It was a reaction she had grown accustomed to as Emma Stewart. It had become much worse over the last three years.

"I'll find the commander," he said quickly.

"Oh, no need, Jackson," she said after a glance at his name tag. "I'm looking for Lieutenant Medina?"

"No kidding? This is perfect; she's going to love this."

Emma narrowed her eyes as she pulled open the air-tight hatch leading to the hanger. "I'm missing something."

"Sorry, ma'am," he said, following her through. "Everyone knew you were aboard, so you may have come up in a conversation … like an hour ago. Lieutenant Medina mentioned that she had worked with you for over a year on Mars, and we all ripped into her … me included." He was full of cheer and not the least bit apologetic. "We may have implied that she was a name dropper and perhaps a few other things … She's on the other side of the shuttle, gearing up for an exercise."

Another first class was coming around the shuttle, his voice booming across the hanger. "Jackson, perfect. What did they cost us?"

Jackson handed over the two tins of coffee. "Four knives and a handful of those stupid coins."

"Not bad, I uh — Lieutenant, can I help you?" He had just noticed Emma and then quickly realized who she was. "Oh shit." His voice remained as loud as it had been when he rounded the shuttle. Another head looked around, and then a third, and then there was the sound of shuffling feet as a platoon of SEALs, half-dressed in pressure suits, came around.

"Emma," Naomi screamed and then attempted to run in her direction. Emma hustled to meet her friend, afraid she might fall. They embraced warmly, but as Emma backed away, Naomi wore a cheesy smile as she goaded the other SEALs in the room.

"I didn't think you were on a team."

"No, I'm still with the command staff, but they invited me to the exercise. I think they needed someone new to harass." There was general agreement from the sudden crowd. "We're about to —"

"Hey, time's wasting," A chief said, coming out of a small office with the team commander. "It's almost time to M-T-M-F, and all I see is a herd of barely dressed pups."

"M-T-M-F?" Emma asked.

"It means —"

"Gray, no; not appropriate." Jackson looked towards Emma.

"Oh my god, Jackson," Naomi said, stretching her words. "You have no idea where that phrase came from, do you?"

She placed an arm over Emma's shoulder, enjoying the confused look that Emma and Jackson were sharing.

"What?" Emma asked, inches from her face. "No … No, it can't be. It's been … almost a year."

She turned toward the chief, who had not noticed her until she spoke.

"Melt those mother fuckers, is it chief?"

Everyone in that hanger section, including the commander, burst into laughter.

"It's 'Melt the' … but close enough," Gray said.

Emma shrugged.

"Lieutenant Stewart," the commander said. "It's truly an honor to have you come down and break our schedule. I take it this is a personal visit?" He directed the question at Naomi, who promptly slipped her arm off Emma's shoulder.

"You're not a requirement for this exercise, Lieutenant Medina. If you wish …" He gestured toward Emma as she and Naomi shook their heads.

He nodded. "Now that that has been settled …"

Taking the hint, the platoon turned toward the far side of the shuttle.

"I'll see you after?" Naomi asked before following.

"I'll be here." Emma watched her friend shuffle away, a hand on her leggings to stop them from slipping down. Memories of a simple time filled her head, and then, just as quickly, others intruded, Eridani, Copernicus, and Anay, but unlike times past, the memories were warm, even welcome.

"Lieutenant Stewart." The chief interrupted her chain of thought. "They'll bounce around Kellen's void spaces for about six hours. Following that, we're having a get-together with the Marines right here. It's nothing special, but you would be most welcome. Burgers … no beer, I'm afraid." He looked hopeful.

"Burgers would be wonderful, chief."

They were. Emma had two. After many months of eating at the side of Adashi and Tormond, trying to match their near-vegetarian diet, she enthusiastically welcomed the change. The SEALs and Marines treated her as a celebrity, and, for once, she welcomed the attention. She and Naomi stayed together throughout the evening, reliving memories of their time on Mars and discussing their hopes and aspirations for an uncertain future. On that, the commander immediately rejected her one thought of Naomi's role on a security team. If required, if requested by the admiral, a single fire team of four experienced SEALs would accompany Emma. There was no room for a lieutenant just out of training.

Emma was called away as the gathering was ending. The key had arrived in a time that Emma considered impossible, but the admiral's staff showed only disappointment. The combined transit time for the request and the returned key was just over 12 hours. Six billion kilometers of travel back and forth required five and a half hours. A handoff between ships and repeaters cost less than two hours; this included the creation of 22 jump points. The only delay had occurred in the basement of a nondescript building on a base in Colorado Springs, where a security manager had fought tooth and nail to stop the transfer.

Side-by-side with the admiral and his staff, she reviewed the information pulled from the message and the recorded conversations that Quinn had included. The admiral was greatly encouraged by the actions of the Patrol, their honesty, and their apparent desire for peace or, at the least, their desire to avoid a confrontation. Even Quinn's meeting with the council had seemed positive until Me Ka Tak informed him of the peril he faced.

Emma was less encouraged by Quinn's conversation at the cabin with Me Ka Tak and the Sal who were helping him. Even the most reasonable among the Seemak did not want to speak with the Odishi or have them anywhere near their planet. Me Ka Tak was the one unlikely exception. The remote possibility of help from the Seemak had all but vanished. This she realized before the battle at the jump point had started.

Back aboard Fredericksburg, she reviewed the message and recordings with Adashi and Tormond. They studied the council members and the three family heads at the gathering to welcome

Quinn. They also discussed the expressed interests, similarities between members, personalities, and even facial traits. Tormond shared Emma's negative opinion. His despair had been growing since word of Quinn's troubles on Seemak had reached Fredericksburg. It worsened as they listened to the conversations between Quinn, Me Ka Tak, and the Sal Patrol members. Adashi remained cautiously optimistic, seeing vague possibilities. Emma was unsure if she was presenting a brave front or was just incapable of acknowledging the difficulty faced by the people of her world, possibly the last of her race.

This was when the light of the confrontation at the jump point between Lesser Doradus C and Gliese 167 reached Squadron Kellen. Initially, that light raised more questions than it answered. Sensors reported breakthrough radiation but no indications of numbers. The emanations from weapons acting upon unknown hulls were obvious, but the results of those strikes could not be determined. Only when the streaming data from Shenzhen arrived did they learn the details of the battle. Sturgeon was lost, although most of the crew had survived. Beagle was lost with all hands. Emma recalled without any display of emotion that Chief Walker had extended his tour of duty to take part in the expedition. She watched as the frigates and destroyers of the Ki Ti fleet came apart under the pounding of heavy missiles, and she watched with growing hope as waves of missiles closed in upon the four cruisers, and then the image flashed briefly and disappeared.

Fredericksburg's optical sensor, trained on the distant jump point, provided an explanation. The source of radiation was evident to all aboard except Adashi and Tormond.

True to its name, the postmortem brief was kept short and remained on point throughout the discussion. Squadron Redmar had been lucky, and the lessons learned were many. The Ki Ti fleet had been overconfident. They underestimated the opposition they faced and failed to use scouts to reconnoiter the far side of the jump point. They made their jumps at the most obvious location and did not plan for the mass of missiles that waited on the other side.

A positive note was made of a contribution from the intelligence community. The dissection of the Ki Ti ship captured at 82 G. Eridani revealed several exploitable weaknesses in the passive and active optical sensors used aboard that ship. The countermeasure missiles had been designed around those discoveries, although there had been no guarantee that the ships of the Ki Ti fleet would share the weaknesses.

The fusion warhead had been a desperate attempt to eliminate some of the inbound missiles. It had destroyed the closest and incapacitated some further out, but most were unaffected. The four ships suffered far worse following the intense blast. As their sensors reset, the remainder of the third wave and then the entirety of the fourth wave slammed into their hulls. Twelve survivors were pulled from one cruiser and two from a destroyer. All others were lost.

The stealthy hull of Sturgeon had been detrimental to the ship's survival. The gloss-free, pitch-black material had readily absorbed the laser light used to cut the ship into pieces. Future designs would balance the need for stealth versus survival in combat.

The crew of Sturgeon was rescued, and the bodies from Beagle were recovered. The bow shield of the Redmar had worked as intended, absorbing an enormous amount of energy while protecting those behind it. Relief valves for the tanks of reaction mass, an integral part of the shield, had let loose, sending a super-heated plume of gas into space. The shield was a loss, and the tanks were heavily damaged, but the Redmar had sufficient reaction mass from longitudinal storage to return home. The squadron commander moved to Shenzhen, and Seahorse, another Batfish class ship, jumped into Gliese 167 to monitor traffic in that system.

At the end of the brief, it was noted that the Ki Ti Tor Mahk fleet had not used their fusion warheads against a ship, but it was uncertain if this was by choice or if they had been unable to deliver them on a target.

"Captain Martinez, wake up."

Quinn opened his eyes to see Me Ka Tak's face hovering over his.

"What's wrong?" he asked as he sat up.

"Five vehicles are coming up the road. You need to run."

Shaking off the fatigue he was feeling day and night, Quinn slipped into his pants and reached for a heavy jacket. "What about you?"

"It's too cold out there — I'm Patrol; I'll be fine. Jouh Nee is waiting at the back."

He pulled on socks and the boots Jouh Nee provided. Outside, it was dark and bitterly cold. He could hear the crunch of snow from a single pair of approaching feet. The sky above was filled with tiny points of light from distant stars and larger, brighter points reflecting from the debris belt just beyond the orbit of Seemak. He craned his neck upward and scanned toward the eastern horizon, wondering how far Batfish had flown around the great circle before losing herself.

A small rock entered the upper atmosphere and broke into multiple streaks, falling silently. The sound of the feet stopped just ahead of him.

"How close are they?" he asked a grayish figure.

"They're Patrol," Jouh Nee answered with a note of confusion.

"At this time?" Me Ka Tak asked from the door. "Unannounced?"

Quinn followed Jouh Nee back inside. It was clear that they were not running.

"This should be interesting."

"Most certainly," Jouh Nee said with deliberation. "Let's see what they want."

With armed guards positioned around the house, Greer, Jair, and a third Sal sat down with Quinn and Me Ka Tak. From his uniform, Quinn knew that the new individual was a senior captain of the Patrol. Nothing of consequence was discussed while Jouh Nee served a mildly caffeinated tea, sickly sweet as was the highland style.

"Thank you, Jouh Nee." He sipped politely before turning his attention to Quinn.

"Captain Martinez, events … a change of fortunes has brought us here at this hour."

Quinn nodded in silence, waiting for the captain to continue.

"I am Vice Commander Joba of the Intelligence Branch, and I'd appreciate anything you can tell us about your colony."

He was accommodating. That was a good sign. "A change of fortunes?" Quinn asked.

"Yes — The Ka Kek fleet completed its transit across the Bi Kan system late yesterday."

Quinn knew Bi Kan as Gliese 167.

"At the far end, they attacked your companion ship as it escaped through a jump point and then followed it through. Our observer was certain that your ship was destroyed, but it returned a short while later. Either it did, or an identical ship. It's difficult to say with the smooth, dark exteriors that encase your ships."

He paused, waiting for Quinn to comment.

"They're explorer ships. Scouts."

"Yes, you mentioned this when you arrived in our system. Scouts, small and not well armed … if armed at all."

Quinn nodded, calmly lifting his cup of tea. It was an effort to keep his hand steady.

"So, we're certain you have more ships at the far side of that jump point, enough to make short work of a very capable fleet."

Quinn hoped it was true, but he was not aware of any fleet that size, either from a single nation or a combined fleet under the United Nations banner. The existence of one wouldn't surprise him, either. Shipbuilding programs had become closely guarded secrets since the attack at Eridani.

"A colony of your size would have difficulty fielding a fleet of that size and strength."

"You're basing this on estimates made regarding my colony," Quinn said.

Joba nodded. "Estimates that we can both agree were low."

Quinn remained silent.

"I should explain what's at risk," Joba said. "The Ka Kek are aware of their loss and will call upon all their ships to form another larger fleet. They'll also call for allies to join them — The council has been recalled. Freeholder Jass has given the members a single day to return to Raygao. He wants this conflict to remain between the Ka Kek and your colony, much like the disagreements that families have had in the past, but without guarantees, he must act to protect all Seemak."

"Guarantees from me?"

"No, it has been acknowledged that you are who you say, simply the captain of a scout ship. He hopes that the head of one of your families or a member of your governing body has accompanied your fleet and is prepared to discuss options. Failing this, the council is likely to call for a fleet, one much larger than anything the Ka Kek family could raise."

What little joy Quinn had taken from the likely victory vanished, as did his confidence. "Would the Patrol join that fleet?"

"The Patrol remains independent unless compelled by a unanimous vote of the council … So, probably." His voice carried a note of warning.

"Would the presence of an ambassador help ease his fears?" Quinn asked. He thought of Emma and how she disliked that title. He thought of the Odishi and realized they could not enter the system.

"It would help, but honestly, I don't think it would be enough. Your colony now represents a grave threat to the Seemak."

"If that's the case, why are you here? — How can I help?"

"You could let us know what we'll encounter on the other side of that jump point, what we would encounter if we were to find your colony — I understand these are questions you should not answer, but your answers may dissuade any … militant actions by the council."

Quinn stared back at Joba, holding up a hand after a moment to give himself a chance to think.

"I'm not sure what to say. Would it be best to portray my colony as weak and of no threat to the Seemak, or should the portrayal be one of overpowering strength?"

Joba looked at Quinn curiously; a thin smile showed beneath questioning eyes. "Captain, we were hoping to hear the truth. The council is expecting the truth. On this, the consequences for you will be severe if it turns out to be anything less."

Quinn shifted in his seat and slid his cup of tea to the side. "I would break a vow of our Patrol, Navy is the term we use, if I were to tell you anything about our ships or fleets, but I can correct one of your misconceptions about my colony. I believe that may tell you enough."

"Anything would be helpful."

"You must understand that when I said that we have no memory of the Union, I was reaching far back into our history. You believe we arrived on our planet in small numbers about 500 years ago and have grown modestly since that time, but the truth is very different. Our ... written history reaches back many thousands of years. Our natural history goes back millions. We've been on that world growing and spreading for a very long time — Our population exceeds seven billion."

He glanced around the table, seeing only disbelief.

"I'm a member of a single faction, one of many. We are powerful but not the largest. I tell you this because a war on this scale would be terrible for both of us."

Joba's head dropped, and a pained look crossed his face. "Captain, we need the truth."

"It is," Quinn said with a pleading, desperate tone.

"Captain," Jair said. "You were just asking us which lie to tell. Don't be ridiculous."

"Captain," Joba continued. "When you first arrived, you told us of the Odishi, and there was skepticism. It may not have been as obvious to you because you've been on the run with, perhaps, the only person on this planet that hopes it's true."

Me Ka Tak gave Joba a sour look as he talked.

"The records of their passage through this space are clear. They were refugees, running from the Malum with what little protection that one of their last fleets could offer. The Malum fleet that passed us by was far more powerful. They had been hunting down the Odishi for years, and they were fully aware of the direction that they were headed."

Me Ka Tak's expression turned angry and possibly guilty.

Joba continued. "They could not have survived, and yet, you are aware of them, and you did come here with knowledge of the Common language. Captain, your origins are clear, and — I'm afraid I can no longer help you."

Joba stood, and with him, Greer and Jair.

"If you allowed me to contact my ship, I could provide proof of the Odishi and certainly some indication of the size of our civilization." Quinn felt defeated as he spoke. They were not willing to listen.

"Describe this proof."

"We have images of our —"

"Don't waste our time, Captain … Your ship in Bi Kan has politely discouraged our ship from passing through the jump point. We'll request they send your ambassador … and you will come with us."

The suite in the government center was meant for a high-level visitor, specifically a Sal. The bed was soft, and the kitchen was stocked with more choices than Quinn was willing to try. He stood near the edge of a large, well-furnished balcony, looking out over Raygao.

Despite the accommodations, it was apparent that he was not a guest. The entrance to the room was locked from the outside, and he was standing 42 floors above the ground. It was very much as it had been in the mountain cabin, with one exception. There, he had considered the Patrol to be an ally. He was afraid that that was no longer true. It made little difference.

He heard his title from behind and recognized Greer's voice.

"Greer, call me Quinn if you wish. I think we're familiar enough."

"We were some time ago, but varying customs can be confusing and dangerous ... Quinn, we need you to make a message for your Batfish and bring them into a high orbit above Seemak. The ... Fredericksburg is en route with your colony's ambassador. When the council session completes, the Patrol will escort both of your ships back to the far point in Bi Kan."

"Have the Ka Kek ships stopped their search?"

"No, they're still in the belt. We're tracking two, but the other two remain hidden, like your ship. The Patrol has sent a small fleet of ships. Yours should be safe, provided it doesn't materialize close to the hidden Ka Kek."

Quinn nodded. "Will the ambassador remain?"

"That's a decision for your colony and the council, but I believe the answer will be no. The session will be short. They're only meeting your ambassador to deliver a formal declaration of intent."

His meaning was clear; Quinn felt sick.

"By intent, you mean war?"

"Not necessarily. War can be avoided if you do not resist. The intent is to take possession of your colony."

"The ambassador will bring proof of my claims."

"Proof that you've encountered living Odishi? Proof of the claims you made of your population? Even if they find your ambassador credible, even if the Odishi survived, even if you live on a planet that's home to billions, they will not alter their plans. They intend to test your claims in combat."

"They have no idea what opposition they'll face." Quinn didn't know either. "The losses will be terrible for both."

"What they do know is that your fleet is hiding on the other side of the Bi Kan jump point. That's not the behavior we would expect from a powerful opponent. The only explanation is that you're attempting to deceive us. If you had the strength you're implying, your fleets would be above Seemak, and our conversation would be very different."

"They're hoping to avoid further bloodshed — The Patrol has been very generous with the treatment that I've received and with your actions toward Batfish. I find it difficult to believe that you would turn so easily to violence."

"I appreciate your sentiment, but you did limit your statement to the Patrol because you are fully aware that it stands apart from most Seemak in this desire for peace. We do understand the cost, but it's a foregone conclusion that, following their meeting with your ambassador, the council will compel the Patrol to lead the way through the Bi Kan jump. Have no illusions; we will follow that order — We are honor-bound to ensure the safety of your two ships, but after that ... I'm sorry, Quinn."

October 19th 2126

Lieutenant Marina Zhào checked the status of Batfish's crew one more time. All were ready for a sustained four-gee maneuver. The ship was in better shape than she had been since leaving Earth. The time spent coasting through the belt had not been idle. They were to join the closest ships of the Patrol, which meant the two passing just north of Batfish, still deep within the belt.

They had not responded to the Patrol's broadcasts but would as soon as they fired their engines. The broadcast included a message from Captain Martinez, basic instructions to accept an escort back to Seemak, and the location of two of the Ka Kek ships, far away and of no concern.

Two others remained hidden and were Marina's greatest concern. She estimated that they would need about an hour to reach the safety offered by the weapons of the Patrol ships, making several assumptions regarding those weapons and assuming that they would join Batfish on the same course toward Seemak.

"Comm, send the message. Helm, execute the maneuver." Marina sank into her chair, an unpleasant but familiar sensation. The minor imperfections in the material made their presence known, the same ones she had intended to fix after the last high gee run. She ignored the bridge crew for the moment, viewing returns from the sensors as they scanned the region for another engine flare.

Twenty seconds passed. The Patrol ships had maneuvered to join them, accelerating heavily. She was about to relax and turn her attention back to the crew when an active sensor sweep detected three high-doppler objects. She bypassed the helm and maneuvered the ship from her chair, but it came too late. The hull clanged with an impact as the ship bucked sharply onto a new course.

"Howard, where did that come from?"

"Tracking back. Nothing is showing up."

She maneuvered the ship again.

"Brown, tell the Patrol that we're under attack."

"Three more," Howard shouted. "Near miss," in a lower voice.

"Mascord, when ready, I'm giving the helm back." She turned the ship again. "Maneuver every three seconds. Keep it random."

"Ready."

"It's yours. Brown ... Howard, find anything yet?"

"Three more ... further away this time."

"Engineering, I see a green status. Where were we hit?"

"Checking now."

Marina pitched against her straps.

"I'm still not seeing the source," Howard reported.

"Six more." There was a note of panic in her voice. "Doppler is negative; they're outbound."

"Outbound? — The Patrol is firing back."

"I'm detecting an engine flare."

Marina's restraining belt bit into her right side as she watched the flow of sensor data. "How did they hit us from that distance?"

The hull rang like a bell, dull and distant.

"One hit, two misses ... six more from the Patrol."

"Bridge, engineering, damage is limited to the hull. What are we being hit with?"

"Best guess is a rail gun, three rail guns."

"Roger that. The shells appear to be liquefying on contact. Thermal sensors show large splash zones on the structure but no damage."

"The Ka Kek ship, a single ship, is maneuvering … approaching at seven gees … they're using their chemical boosters."

Marina paused, taking a deep breath, as deep as she could under four gees. "Based on intel, they'll be in range to launch missiles in about 15 minutes. We're free to launch at any time. Sooner will be better." She paused again, briefly, hoping for confirmation.

"Helm, Increase thrust to 4.5 gees."

As Batfish bounced from one heading to another, Marina deployed ten of its eighteen missiles, two at a time, from the amidship launchers. Each quickly maneuvered to point at the Ka Kek ship and reduce its signature. Together, they formed an elongating trail, falling behind Batfish. Inert and difficult to detect, they waited.

The hull rang again. Mascord glanced at Marina, but she did not alter her orders to him. The status board remained green. It was impossible to tell if the shells from the Patrol ships were finding their mark, but the twisting maneuvers of the Ka Kek ship told Marina that they were having a desired effect. Each turn by their enemy gave Batfish a few more seconds to reach safety.

"XO, the Patrol reports that the fourth ship has been found," Brown said. "They're accelerating but far away. No threat."

"Very well, Comm."

Another shell struck, sounding different from the previous. The statuses remained green.

"Bridge, engineering, the auxiliary space has been breached — A pinpoint leak. Egebe is searching for it."

"Very well … Cancel that, Matthews. Bring Egebe forward to main engineering. We'll take care of the leak after this is over."

"Roger that, bridge."

Shells struck Batfish five more times despite the abrupt turns they made every few seconds. In each case, only the hull suffered damage. As the Ka Kek ship closed upon the first pair of missiles, Marina initiated the pre-programmed attacks of all ten. The first two accelerated directly toward their target. The other eight spread into an elusive pattern that brought them into the path of the accelerating ship. One from the lead pair flashed briefly and then shut down, a victim of counterfire from an unseen defensive beam. The second missile exploded a moment later, but a third strike by the enemy's beams was recorded as ineffective by the targeted missile. Two by two, the remaining eight missiles hammered the Ka Kek ship. Only a shattered, tumbling wreck remained after the final pair struck.

Marina stared intently at the display, fearful that the imaged ship would return to life. The crew on the bridge remained silent, eyes fixed on the same display. The first thing she noticed or acknowledged was the pain she was feeling. "Helm, reduce thrust to one gee."

The relief was instant. She released her safety belt and stood.

"XO, I have a message from the Patrol ships — They're complimenting us on the murder of 16 Ka Kek — I'm not sure what they're trying to say."

"I'm hoping it's just that. Respond with a thank you for the compliment and their assistance. Engineering, send Egebe and Miller to the auxiliary space. Make sure they're suited up."

"Roger that, bridge."

Marina returned her attention to the Ka Kek ship, concerned about the response that was certain to follow. That single ship had attacked without regard for the two Patrol ships. With the space around Seemak filling with ships, the chance of another attack seemed high.

"Quinn, are you free to talk?"

"Emma, I am, but not much else. Are you in orbit?"

"Yes, I'm aboard Fredericksburg with a close escort and over a hundred other Seemak combat ships. We'll be directly over Raygao in five minutes. Your signal is weak but improving."

"Do you have your instructions?"

"The pilot has the landing instructions, but we are to wait for Captain Juun. He'll let us know when we're cleared to depart. He's boarding now."

"Be warned. He's friendly but compromised. You should be able to trust what he tells you, but don't expect him to remain true once he's out of sight. Who's coming down with you?"

"Just Juun, the pilot, and a single fire team."

"Not Adashi or Tormond?"

"No, Admiral Walsh didn't want to risk them. They're two systems away."

"Probably for the best. They would not be welcome."

"I gathered that from the message you sent to Lieutenant Zhào."

"You read that? I'd like to hear an explanation at some point, but for now, I don't think the fire team will be welcome."

"They'll remain with the shuttle. I'll go alone to meet the council."

"Emma, you're be landing at the government center. They plan to meet you on the pad. The team will not be allowed that close to the council."

It was a change to the itinerary sent to Fredericksburg a day earlier, but not necessarily a complication. Emma considered the implications before responding neutrally.

"That's interesting. Will you be there?"

"I will, with Me Ka Tak, the full council, a contingent of guards, and I'm not sure who else."

"That's good. Can you give me a formal introduction to the council?"

"That should be possible, although I may have trouble finding a trumpeter in time to blow fanfare."

"Cute. Short and formal is all I need. For this, I will be Emma Stewart, Ambassador for the Talmahk of Earth — Juun has arrived. I'll see you down there."

Emma had choreographed the meeting in her head using a limited data set, assuming she would have little control over events. A meeting on the landing pad greatly simplified the plan, eliminating some unknown variables and handing her control, at least for a moment. It also made the intentions of the council obvious.

The Patrol had been generous with the information that they provided during the week-long journey: descriptions of the competing families, biographies of the council members, the history of the Seemak, and the goals for which they aspired, goals of the four races, goals of the families, and the intended goals of the Seemak Union. She had analyzed that data, keeping in mind Quinn's conversations with Me Ka Tak and the Sal that had helped him evade capture. Those conversations gave her a less filtered view of Seemak society. The actions taken by the Patrol on Quinn's behalf had been curiously misaligned with the council's goals. It was a welcome but unpredictable point of data.

Juun came through the open door, drifting slowly with one hand poised above a guy wire. His eyes went wide.

"Captain Juun, welcome aboard Fredericksburg, and thank you for your assistance," Emma said soberly, hiding her satisfaction at his response.

"Ambassador — That's a perfect choice." He gestured at her dress. "I know at least one Ki Ti Tor Mahk that will find it … beautiful, although a little impractical up here." Fasteners held the skirt fixed to her knees, an inconvenient necessity in zero-gee.

The dressmaker back on Earth had initially refused the request, stating that he did not cater to oversized children. His position quickly reversed after the Navy had passed on Emma's name and hinted at the importance of the request. One or both pieces of information had been enough for him to have a design transmitted within 12 hours. A fabricator aboard the Kellen had turned it into a dress shortly before Fredericksburg had left the fleet. If nothing else, it was colorful, a floral design predominantly red and yellow with dark green winding through. It followed the themes she had seen in images of the clothing, art, and wall coverings of the Ki Ti Tor Mahk.

"I don't think it will change any minds, but it's a nice gesture."

"The gesture is the purpose," Emma said wearily.

She left her explanation vague. Goodwill was not her intention, only distraction.

"Batfish is en route," Juun said. "It's still two days away."

"That should not be a problem."

"They were attacked by a Ka Kek ship as they joined two ships of the Patrol."

Emma nodded slowly as she considered the implications.

Juun gave her a questioning look, wondering if Emma had understood his statement.

"Did you want to know of any casualties?"

She returned his questioning stare and then realized a response was expected. "Sorry — From your tone, I don't believe they suffered any?"

Juun nodded and smiled. "They did not, although the Ka Kek ship was destroyed — You're very different from your former captain."

"Thank you," Emma said without emotion. "We'll be taking this shuttle down. You may perform your inspection now if you wish."

"Thank you, ambassador. To start, your soldiers cannot bring their weapons to the planet." He gestured toward the SEAL fire team.

Emma gave him a nervous, pleading look, but his stance remained firm. "Very well."

Juun nodded. "And please keep them on the shuttle, out of sight. The council will be meeting us on the launch pad."

"Why is that?" Emma asked with a look of worry.

"I wasn't told," Juun answered straightforwardly. He gestured toward the shuttle. "I'll take a quick look and report that we're ready."

Emma led him around, under, and over the shuttle as he looked for any obvious external weapons or suspicious ports. She then brought him inside, where he inspected the passenger area, cabin, storage lockers, and void spaces for anything else that could harm the council.

"You can make your report from the cabin," Emma said as she closed the last access panel. "Will this be to your ship?"

Juun nodded, following her as she pushed from a seat toward the front. "Yes, they'll pass my evaluation to command."

Emma activated the connection at the co-pilot's station and stepped out of the cabin.

A moment later, Juun exited. "We're cleared to go … Whenever you're ready."

Emma led him back to a seat ahead of the fire team along the shuttle's right side. "We'll be leaving in a moment," she said.

Juun nodded as he pulled himself down. Across from him, along the left side, he noticed a pair of oversized seats.

"What …" The features on his face froze, and his eyes widened as they lifted upward, looking past Emma. With his mouth half open and disbelief spreading over his face, he watched Adashi and Tormond enter the shuttle. He stood quickly and lost his grip on the armrest of the seat. A member of the fire team caught his shoulder as he started to cart-wheel. What followed was a string of words that Emma didn't recognize but suspected all to be profanities. She saved them for later use.

"I'm sorry, Captain Juun. We were given no choice."

He turned his head toward her, eyes still wide. He opened his mouth but remained speechless.

Emma frowned helplessly. "The decision was made after the destruction of the Ka Kek fleet — They want their presence known to all … No one will be harmed. You are safe and will be free to remain on the planet after we finish our discussion with the council."

She performed a short introduction, unacknowledged by either party.

"Quinn wasn't lying," Juun finally said, looking between Emma and the Odishi.

"No, he wasn't. We need to be seated." Emma pulled herself into the seat ahead of him.

Once secured, Juun found the courage to address Adashi. "You will not be welcomed on Seemak, and your presence will not benefit the Talmahk."

"We have not come to your world for the benefit of the Talmahk." Adashi's terse reply stopped him from making any additional comments.

He turned to Emma, but her eyes were upon Adashi. A pained expression played across her face. "The council will meet us upon landing," she said with the demeanor of an obedient servant. "I will perform your introduction as you exit the shuttle and then state your desires."

Adashi considered her words briefly and then looked away.

The shuttle separated from Fredericksburg and broke orbit toward the planet. The passengers remained silent for the half-hour descent.

Quinn waited in a large bunker behind thick glass with Me Ka Tak, the five members of the Seemak Council, a host of functionaries, and a squad of armed guards. He held one small bag, anticipating, hoping this would be his final day on the planet. Unlike the Seemak shuttles, which came in tail down, the shuttle from Fredericksburg settled upon a set of wheels straddling the plenum used to reroute the tail exhaust typically seen.

As the electro-props spun down, guards led the way toward the landing pad. They were followed by the council, the functionaries, Quinn and Me Ka Tak, and finally, a last contingent of guards. Quinn followed Me Ka Tak to a position on the side, apart from all others and closer to the shuttle. He glanced down the line of five council members, seeing neutral faces on all. They waited patiently for Emma to emerge so they could lay claim to the planet Earth.

Emma exited after a short pause and immediately captured the attention of all present. Quinn cringed as Me Ka Tak grabbed his elbow and smiled at him; the smile of a fellow conspirator, he thought. The council, with the exception of Freeholder Jardin, was harder to read. He shared Me Ka Tak's look of amusement. Emma maintained a patient, almost regal pose, as regal as she could while standing in the most garish dress Quinn had ever seen. He walked to the end of the ramp and turned to address the council.

"Council of the Seemak; Freeholder Jardin, Freeholder Rasaan, Freeholder Ta Tok, Freeholder Ka Di Fa Tak, and Freeholder Jasmine … I present Emma Stewart, Ambassador for the Talmahk of Earth."

With her acknowledgment, Quinn returned to stand with Me Ka Tak. Emma descended the ramp, stopping at the bottom to face the council. Their patient gazes followed her down, but as she reached solid ground, all eyes snapped upward. Quinn turned quickly to see Adashi and Tormond standing just outside the entrance for the shuttle. They were familiar, like old friends, but not once had he been in their presence before this moment. Emma did not give him, or any other person, a chance to react to what they saw.

"Council of the Seemak, I present Adashi and Tormond of Iburak." Emma's regal pose had dropped away. "It is their wish that the Talmahk maintain a peaceful and harmonious relationship with the Seemak. They have ordered that our fleets come no closer to Seemak, and upon conclusion of our negotiations, they are to withdraw entirely from this region of space."

Emma's words were bitter and highlighted a persona unlike any Quinn had seen on her. Anger, hatred, and helplessness as one. He looked toward the council and saw that displeasure mirrored in each of the five faces. Emma turned to face the Odishi and performed a short diplomatic bow. Adashi gave her a curt, unreadable glance, and then she and Tormond returned through the shuttle entrance.

Emma returned her attention to the council. Her anger had softened. "It is the desire of the Talmahk of Earth that we form a strong and prosperous relationship with the Seemak. To achieve this end … we request membership within the Seemak Union. We will return to orbit and wait for your answer."

Emma gave Quinn a quick nod and then climbed the ramp. Taking his cue, he followed, glancing once at the council and then turning up the ramp. In passing, he exchanged a quick, nervous nod with Juun. Once inside, the ramp was raised, and the door was sealed. The pilot waited until the passengers were secure and the landing pad was clear of people, and then he started the electro-props. The shuttle lifted gently from the pad and turned toward the ocean.

Confused and fearful, Quinn was not sure what to say first. "Emma, they were not happy."

"No, they were not."

"You never gave them a chance to speak."

"No, I did not, but it was necessary … and not really my decision, was it?" As she finished her statement, her anger turned into a weary smile.

"Emma," Adashi said, speaking softly. "That worked perfectly."

"Thank you, Adashi."

Emma kept her eyes on Quinn as her smile gave way to tears.

March 28th 2128

Epilogue

Ophiuchi-C Two was a marbled jewel of blue, brown, and white against a backdrop of speckled black, permanently fixed at eye level, turning steadily. Juun glanced left and right, marveling at the scale of the platform over his head. The Beagle Island Elevator, named for the speck of land near the elevator's planned base, was growing right before his eyes, reaching downward as he knew it was outward. The name of that speck of land had been mildly contested, but the voice of one very insistent ambassador had won the day.

He shifted to the left, glancing toward the cafeteria's entrance as more people approached the window. Most were humans, but he had seen a couple of Sal and one Ki Ti Tor Mahk earlier. It was the only windowed room in the single pressurized section of the ring, so the crowd made sense. The reason for the gathering could be seen passing in front of the planet's southern pole—a shining point of light, growing in intensity.

There was a hushed excitement that allowed him to pick out individual conversations, although he had no idea what was being said; the humans used so many languages. Common was known to many, almost all that he had encountered, but was not a preference.

He returned his attention to the approaching ship. "Do you make anything small on Earth?" he asked.

Quinn matched his smile as he gave the question a moment of thought. "Politicians? Vacations? — What amazes me is that we had that ship designed, built, and on its way before the leaders on Earth could agree upon a permanent representative to your council."

"That sounds familiar," Juun said as he turned his head toward the entrance. "Speaking of the devil."

Quinn turned to see Tormond straightening out after passing through the doorway and Emma behind him, scanning the mass of people.

"Did I say that right?"

"Close enough," Quinn said as Emma and Tormond spotted them.

"Back to khakis?" he called out as they drew closer.

"Finally," Emma said. "A career in diplomacy was never a choice of mine."

"It was never his either." Juun tilted his head toward Quinn. "And you can see where that has brought us."

"I wasn't even on the planet," Quinn said. "All credit goes to Emma and Me Ka Tak."

Emma looked past both as the approaching point of light took shape; a long spine lined with pods at regular intervals, five at each, distributed symmetrically around the hull.

"Thank you for guiding me down here, Tormond; this is a labyrinth."

Tormond bowed, slight and solemn.

"Is Me too busy to join us?" Juun asked.

"In fact, she is. Someone needs to coordinate with the volunteers from Seemak." Emma narrowed her eyes at Juun.

"Adashi's on the surface with Niko," he said, ignoring Emma's pointed stare. "She's ensuring that Alpha Town will be ready for the settlers."

"Still no name?"

"That will be a decision for the residents," Tormond said. "One that they'll make once the town is established."

"Tormond and I are heading down soon. Are the two of you joining us?"

"Packed and ready," Quinn said, holding up his empty hands.

Juun nodded enthusiastically and then motioned toward the ship. "Here they are."

The crowd drew closer to the window, showing Emma a row of backs. Unperturbed, she wedged a shoulder between an oversized maintenance chief and a lieutenant. The chief broke from a conversation within a small group and looked down at her. "I'm sorry, ma'am." He shifted slightly and returned his attention to the group.

"No worries, chief." Emma pressed against the window as the carrier slid past. "No worries at all."

Dramatis Personae

The Stewart Family
    Alexander Stewart - Grandfather - CEO of Stewart Life Sciences
        Elizabeth Stewart (Husband: Ronny Clarke - deceased)
            Emma Stewart (Beanstalk)
            Ian Stewart
        Johnathan Stewart (Wife: Katelin Tremont) Professor of Finance, University of Montana
            Mary Stewart
            Ruby Stewart
            Ronny Stewart
        Robert Stewart (Wife: Lucy Taylor) CEO of Kuiper Mining Inc
            Chloe Stewart (Cthulhu) Heir apparent to Alexander Stewart
            Christopher Stewart
            Raymond Stewart

Crew and passengers of the Royal Fleet Auxiliary (RFA) Fort Rosalie
    Chief Coxswain Reggie Walker - RFA/Royal Navy
    Petty Officer Second Class James Davies - RFA
    Ensign Emma Stewart - US Navy
    Ensign Abby Webb - US Navy
        Lieutenant JG Niko Sasaki - US Navy
        Ensign Naomi Medina - US Navy
        Ensign Lucas Anderson - US Navy

Seaman First Class Garcia - US Navy

Crew and Riders of the USS Galileo
  Commander Ryan Hanson (Captain)
  Commander Rudy Klein (Ship's Medical Officer)
  Lieutenant Commander Irene Fedorov (Head of Engineering)
  Lieutenant Shaw (Engineering)
  Lieutenant Quinn Martinez (Navigation and Weapons)
  Lieutenant JG Emma Stewart (Sensors, Pilot)
  Lieutenant Ronald Smith (Rider - Team Lead)
  Chief Warrant Officer Rashidi (Senior Pilot)
  Chief Petty Officer Warren Blackrock (Coxswain)
  Petty Officer First Class Joseph Calvin (Rider-Operator)
  Petty Officer Second Class Craig (Corpsman)
  Petty Officer Third Class Carol Harris (Sensors)
  Seaman (Spaceman) Jones (Helmsman)
  Emile Sanders (Paleontologist)
  Mike Crane (Astrophysicist)

Crew USS Batfish
  Lieutenant Commander Quinn Martinez (Captain)
  Lieutenant Emma Stewart (XO)
  Ensign, Lieutenant JG, Lieutenant Marina Zhào (Engineering, XO, Acting CO)
  Ensign Matthews (Junior Officer)
  Chief Ezra Andersen (Chief of the Boat)
  Petty Officer First Class John Mascord (Helm)
  Petty Officer First Class Janice Howard (Sensors, Communications)

    Petty Officer Second Class Angela Brown (Communications)
    Petty Officer Second Class Femi Egebe (Engineering)
    Petty Officer Third Class Jason Ramirez (Sensors)
    Spaceman Hal Miller (Helm)

Crew USS Sturgeon
    Commander Samuel Strauss (CO)
    Lieutenant JG Duncan (Junior Officer)
    Petty Officer First Class Nguyễn (Helm)
    Petty Officer Second Class Nelson (Communications)

Crew USS Copernicus
    Captain James White (CO)
    Ensign Anay Mason (Junior Officer)

Crew and Riders USS Fredericksburg
    Captain Hoffman (CO)
    Commander Irene Fedorov (XO)
    Lieutenant JG, Lieutenant Abby Web (Science Team)
    Lieutenant Emma Stewart (Liaison to the Odishi)
        Adashi (Odishi representative)
        Tormond (Odishi representative)

SEAL Team Four
    Petty Officer First Class Jackson (SO)
    Petty Officer Third Class Gray (SO)

Personnel Atacama Station
    Commander Lily Davis (Station CO)

Captain Renard Garnier (Station CO)
Lieutenant, Lieutenant Commander Niko Sasaki (Station XO)
Sam Nowak (Programmer)
James Thompson (Biology Team Lead)
Spaceman Apprentice Kane (Cook)
Petty Officer Third Class Watkins (Engineering)
Rachael and Rana Zhōu (Mother and daughter)
Johnny (Producer and server of questionable beverages)

Earthside
- Admiral Grace Richie (Commanding Officer Naval Space Command)
- Senator Raymond Park
- Senator Skip Chelsea
- Senator Eglin Shaw
- Mr. Granger (Angry Neighbor)

The Odishi
- Adashi (Representative to the Talmahk, schoolmaster)
- Tormond (Assistant to Adashi)
- Rork Akane (Assistant to Adashi)
- Siljay/Red on Gray (Observatory Maintenance)
- Minister Aren Token (Administrator of Imaotak)

The Seemak
Me Ka Tak (Ki Ti Tor Mahk: Patrol Pilot)
Captain Juun (Sal: CO Patrol Corvette)
- Jouh Nee (ex-Patrol)
- Jair (Patrol Intelligence Service)
- Greer (Patrol Intelligence Service)

Vice Commander Joba (Patrol Intelligence Service)

The Seemak Family Tree
   Jass: Head - Freeholder Rono Jass,
        Council representative Freeholder Jardin
            Ka Tak: Jass Client family, family of Me Ka Tak
            Jardin: Jass Client family, family of Freeholder Jardin
   Rasaan: Council representative - Freeholder Rasaan
   Ta Tok: Head - Freeholder Ta Tok,
        Council representative - Freeholder Ta Tok
        Ka Kek: Ta Tok Client family
            Ti Mak: Ka Kek Client family
   Ka Di Fa Tak:
        Council representative - Freeholder Ka Di Fa Tak
   Jasmine:
        Council representative - Freeholder Jasmine
   The Mahkee-Porta Ree Confederation: Client of the Jasmine family, special representatives to the council - Ray Moold Jan and Toregan Teen
        Talmahk of Earth (Non-voting membership): Interim council representative - Emma Stewart

Local Routes

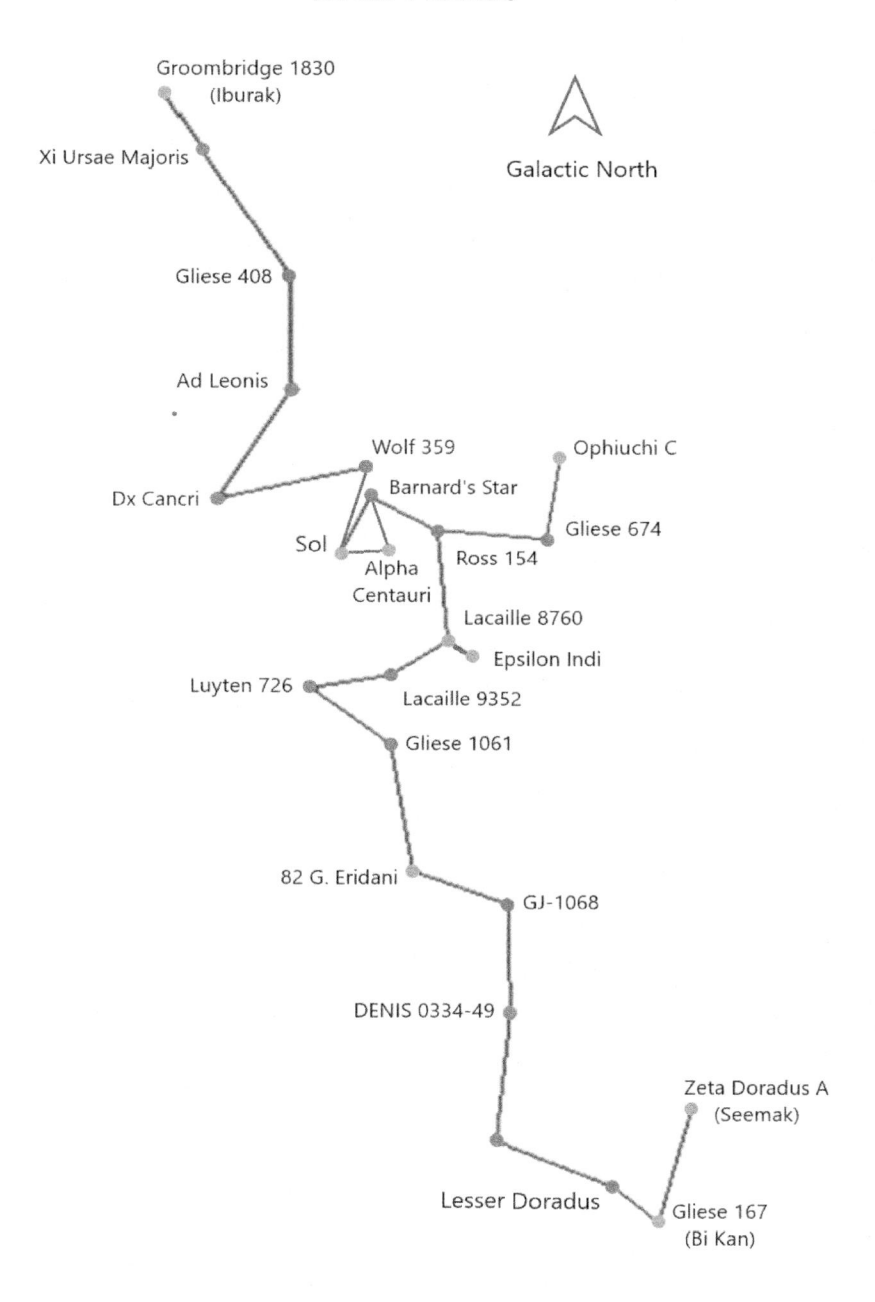

- Groombridge 1830 (Iburak)
- Xi Ursae Majoris
- Gliese 408
- Ad Leonis
- Dx Cancri
- Wolf 359
- Barnard's Star
- Ophiuchi C
- Sol
- Ross 154
- Gliese 674
- Alpha Centauri
- Lacaille 8760
- Epsilon Indi
- Luyten 726
- Lacaille 9352
- Gliese 1061
- 82 G. Eridani
- GJ-1068
- DENIS 0334-49
- Zeta Doradus A (Seemak)
- Lesser Doradus
- Gliese 167 (Bi Kan)

Galactic North

Printed in Great Britain
by Amazon